I0699664

FADING LIGHT

Fading Light

Published by Red Cabin Publishing

Spokane, WA

10 Years Anniversary Edition: April 2024

4 6 8 10 9 7 5 3 2

Fading Light edited by Amber Beuschel

Cover Art and Typography by Evelyne Paniez at www.secretdartiste.be(Resources listed on Acknowledgement Page)

LCCN: 2018932771

CIP data for this book is available from the Library of Congress

Paperback: ISBN: 1984204033, ISBN-13: 978-1984204035

Hardback: ISBN: 979-8-9877165-3-3

Also by Morgan Wylie

YA FANTASY:
The Age of Alandria Series:
Silent Orchids (Book 1)
Veiled Shadows (Book 2)
Daegan (Novella 2.5)
Fractured Darkness (Book 3)
Fading Light (Book 4)
Night Magic (Novella 4.5)
The Sol-Lumieth (Book 5)
The Rise of the Paladin (An Alandria Short Story Prequel)

YA PARANORMAL/SUPERNATURAL:
HAILEY: The Necromancer (A Shadow Realm Novella 1)
JAX: The Doppelgänger (A Shadow Realm Novella 2)
(A Shadow Realm Novella 3 forthcoming)
(A Shadow Realm Novella 4 forthcoming)

MISCELLANEOUS COLLECTIONS:
Dawn of The Witch Hunters (A Havenwood Falls Legends Novella)
Rise of The Witch Hunters (A Havenwood Falls Legends Novella)
Reawakened (A Havenwood Falls High Novella)
Rekindled (A Havenwood Falls Holiday Short Story Anthology 2019)
Redefined (A Havenwood Falls Novella)
Rediscovered (A Havenwood Falls High Novella)
Reunited (A Havenwood Falls Holiday Short Story Anthology 2020)
Reborn (A Havenwood Falls Holiday Short Story Anthology 2021)
Magic by Moonlight with Kallie Ross (A Havenwood Falls Spring Short Story Anthology 2022)
Remembrance (A Havenwood Falls Sunset Short Story Anthology 2022)

Thank You...

It has been almost 15 years since I began envisioning and sharing the journey of Kaeleigh, Daegan, and the crew's adventures in Alandria. This special edition is to celebrate 10 years of being published!!

Writing can be a very solitary experience, and yet there are so many people I want to thank who have been a part of my journey, bringing this story to life from beginning to present. From author friends offering support, advice, encouragement, etc. along the way to the technical support of editors and graphic designers to beta, ARC, and proof readers... my book wouldn't be what it is today without you. You know who you all are, I love and appreciate you! This edition is what I have always imagined this story could be and it finally is!!

To my husband, Steven, you inspire me, challenge me, and encourage me to be the best version of me I can be even when I wasn't sure who that was, thank you. And to my beautiful daughters, I continue pursuing my dreams so that you know you can pursue yours. I love you. Also to the rest of my family, you have been an incredible support and encouragement. Thank you for believing in me and cheering for me. Especially my momma: I can't tell you how much it has meant over the years that you liked my story, believed in it, and invested in it...me.

As in life, we grow, evolve, and take on new iterations of ourselves to become the best version of ourselves, so has this project...

From the foundations of this book, I want to thank the creative team: Claudia at for her creative genius with the cover art and Ashley at The Bookish Brunette for her beautiful fonts and layout. Thank you both! Your art has been a part of this journey for over 10 years.

In this edition, I want to give credit and thank Evelyne Paniez at www.secretdartiste.be for her amazing cover design, all created by her human layering process (no AI used)!

All good fantasy stories need a map! (At least I think so). And Alandria has gone through several versions when it's come to the map. From my scratchy drawing to Donna Dull with Sharp Covers who brought it visually to life to then Bill Morgan's edition, giving it that extra push to

Gerralt at Dimension Door's (https://www.dimensiondoor.nl) current spectacular version... I thank all of you!!

Thank you to Amber Beuschel—the wordsmith!—who took my story and my characters and helped me discover their greater potential all whilst getting crazy with ALL "there was" to highlight ;) the 2nd time around. You have made me better and for that I will always be grateful. Christine LePorte, you took a novice writer and helped shape my story in the very beginning, thank you.

Also a special Thank You to Steven James Wylie and Blair Masters for your beautiful original soundtrack *Silent Orchids* inspired by this book.

I would most especially like to acknowledge you, the reader. For it is with you that my story has wings. Thank YOU for 10 enchanting years and here's to many more!!

<u>Cover Art Resources Used By Secretdartiste:</u>
FONTS: Lucy Rose (title) and Athelas (other text)
RESOURCES:
Texture: depositphotos 159688928
Tree: shutterstock 135289205
Effect light particles: depositphotos 157239980
Texture snakes: depositphotos 230230888
Black leaves: depositphotos 6938110
Orchids: depositphotos 545655796
Butterfly: depositphotos 20049089
Branches, crown, leaves: www.hwwostock.com
Glass ornaments: www.fantasybackgroundstore.com

MORTAL REALM
CAVES OF VULDÜN
ARY'THN
FOREST OF DUL-ÌSTEACH
BRIDGE OF REVEALMENT
HUNTERS COTTAGE
THE STONE FOREST
RIVER OF RANCIER
MANDÜ TRÉ LAN
SHADOW RIDGES

THE AGE OF
ALANDRIA
NALRINIA
ELNYE
Guardian Grove
GÁRALDRATH MOUNTAINS
FERAÁNMAR
Crossing at Lumei
FOREST OF LUMEI
EXHILE
ANISE (LORTUNA)
LUMARI
ADETTLYN
TYLÍNYTH
EHSMIA
KLAVAÍ
KANDRI
ANDRIAN MOUNTAINS
LENORIA

PROLOGUE

HISTORY OF SHE. THE MORTAL REALM. APPROXIMATELY 16 YEARS AGO.

A darkness roamed the mortal realm seeking its next victim, the next body it would inhabit as its own. For centuries, the darkness—the soul of a woman from long ago—traveled and used its victims for her own devices moving forward through the annals of time. Bound to the realm of Earth and that of mortals, she continuously changed from host to host as the body only lived out a human span or earlier when compromised by the magic in her own soul. As an immortal soul unable to hold her own form, she was condemned to the life of a parasite, leeching off others for eternity. The soul of darkness, female in each manifestation, had no power without a body through which to channel her powers. The dark soul had been without a host for quite some time, giving her plenty of time to contemplate all she had learned through several lifetimes of travel and experimenting. The challenge was finding the right body, one who was strong and had an innate magical ability—a witch or one familiar with the elements and energies of the Earth. These victims became her strongest hosts, allowing her to most easily work through; they would be who she needed to enact her next plan.

Time passed for her in the formless state as it does for those who dream, minutes filled with vivid moments—some swift, some silent. Those which she remembered—her memories—were hard to grasp. Some were stronger than others and sometimes she was content to simply drift in the nether of this or that dimension as she walked through an event. In any case, she was never quite sure of whether she was, in reflecting, in the present, past, or future. That is, until a beacon would catch her attention, first a flicker, and then brighter, brighter, brighter, until it was a stiff glare in her face, impossible to ignore.

It is the beacon that gives her the urgency to overtake a human body. It is the frailty of life, the last surge of the soul, which sparks like a lighthouse in the darkness. Unfortunately, for the human, the body had to be dying for her to fully take possession and then would cease to exist when she was through with it as it would begin to fade at the age of disintegration.

Flashes of her original mortal body would surge through her mind when she began to displace the current soul of the body she chose, remembering the day she chose to unite her own soul with darkness for the benefit of power beyond any powers she had known previously. The choice had made her indestructible and immortal, reigning over all her enemies and those who would seek to belittle her. While there were downsides to a choice of such magnitude, she had yet to regret her decision, managing to survive centuries thus far. There was no question she would be around until the end of time.

Such a beacon was lit for her even now, glinting at her through the haze, separating her from mortality. It was the beacon of a soul extinguishing, passing from this life. This particular beacon she had been watching for many years now, waiting for a slip up like the one the human was about to make. The woman, an elemental witch was in her mid-thirties and practiced spells and potions beyond her limits and capabilities. Long wavy white hair was held up high on her head in a messy bun with tendrils slipping out attempting to escape the confinement; her skin pale, and her pale green eyes wide with curiosity as she checked on the bubbling potion. Even now, the woman was in a small room off the end of her house out in the middle of a field. The room had been designated only for magic it would seem, as it was filled with spell books and charms, and beakers boiling and test tubes—almost like a scientist's lab but this was strictly for magic. Unaware of the mistake she was about to make, the woman sang out loud along with a song playing on an old record turntable, dancing with bare feet on the well-worn wood planked floor. The dark soul could smell it in the air, the acrid scent of a spell about to go wrong bubbled and scented the air. Three stories tall in places, the house was charming, a rounded turret near the top windows surrounding it.

The woman did not fit the profile of one living out on the edge of town in a field surrounded by more fields and small copse of trees in clumps as if plopped down wherever the gods saw fit, but it did allow her the ability to practice magic more openly. Not only did this woman the dark soul hoped to possess have just the right combination of skill and talent she couldn't wait to climb into, but she also lived in a place that appeared to be between or in the midst of overlapping realms. The ancient energies she felt were foreign to her, but the possibilities of realms she could not otherwise access brought endless opportunities. She would do anything to get to, to divest her interests away from Earth, to discover what other powers were out there in the universe—powers more ancient than anything that could be found on this planet.

Watching, the woman picked up a small black device and pushed a button then held it to her ear. "Hello Mother, I'm preparing the spell one more time, the one we spoke of." She paused and the dark soul could hear another female voice speak through the device.

"Be careful, Lydia. That spell is strong. I wish you would wait for me to assist you," the voice spoke.

"I'll be careful. I have two specific reasons to be, you should not doubt that." The woman added a pinch of something to the brew, causing it to sizzle. She frowned. "Gotta go, Mother. I'll call you when it's done."

The woman, Lydia, closed the device and set it on the workbench, going back to her dusty book, her brow furrowed in concentration.

The darkness swirled about the house in the country, content to simply be near until the time was right. After many failed experiments, she knew the importance of timing to ensure the human body—Lydia—welcomed her soul in place of the one fading from this world. Slowing down to peer inside the windows, the dark soul was surprised to see two very young souls sleeping peacefully each with a shock of white curly hair upon their heads.

"No, this would not do," the darkness hissed, *"I will not be taking care of young in my new body."*

As a soul with magic, though she could not possess a body for long, she could manipulate and inhabit one for a short time. She had to hurry if her calculations were correct. With Lydia not yet dying, the dark soul was able to take momentary possessions if the need arose. Soaring down to the woman, through the greenhouse windows, she absorbed herself into Lydia's body and took control with enough wherewithal to do what needed to be done. Taking a minute to reacquaint herself with the use of a human body and all its movements, the inhabited woman then walked quickly to the third floor circular room. Unable to figure out how to pick up both toddlers in her arms at once, unaccustomed to handling children, she picked up one sleeping child and embraced her awkwardly so not to drop her. The darkness within Lydia uttered a spell that flowed out of the woman's mouth. Something unexpected happened then, Lydia stopped and closed her mouth at the last few words of the spell that would displace her child and send her elsewhere. The dark soul felt Lydia's muscles tighten and her grip on the child held firm, unwilling and fighting for control once more—the woman was more aware and stronger than she had originally known, she would provide an excellent host body.

"*Say the words,*" the darkness forced in her mind with a push of Lydia's own magic. Tears streaming down her face, Lydia fought with everything she had but in the end said the final words completing the spell. Wide innocent eyes, the gray of a spring storm, suddenly opened staring directly at her mom and through her, seeing the darkness inside. The child's energies began to swirl and the child itself began to literally disappear being displaced in the world. The darkness felt the woman's emotional instability and did not have time to deal with it. Reminding her mind of the bubbling potion now close to the point of completion, the woman took one last look at the other sleeping child and the dark soul considered there would be time to deal with that one after full possession. She hurried the woman back down to the magic room to check on the spell concoction she had been working on. The soul was practically thrown from Lydia's body once they reached the epicenter of the woman's strength in magic.

"Who are you? What do you want?" the woman seethed, emotion close to eruption, her eyes looking for something they could not see. "What have you done to my daughter?" Lydia shrieked, her hands shaking uncontrollably. "I will find you and end you."

"*Not in this lifetime, my sweet,*" the dark soul said but the woman would not hear her. Pushing a force of magic into the bubbling beaker, forcing Lydia's gaze to the potion.

"Oh no!" Lydia breathed, "That's not right." Her fingers shook and she began fumbling around, knocking over another test tube with a red liquid in it and mixed with another spot of liquid spilled onto the table, it too began smoking and bubbling. "No, no, no." The woman frantically grabbed a rag attempting to mop up that mess while the potion bubbled up and sizzled, a stream of black smoke rose out of it.

Quickly the woman reached for her cell phone on the opposite table, opened it up and hit a number leaving the phone open on speaker. When another woman answered the other end of the line, Lydia spoke frantically.

"Mother, I've made a mistake..." she paused, breathing through the smoke filling the greenhouse room. "I'm so sorry. I mixed something wrong, but I don't know what," she said shakily.

"Can you stop it?" the older woman asked through the phone. "Lydia! You have to stop it!" she shouted panic rising in her tone.

"Take care of the girls if something happens," Lydia said right as an explosion erupted, glass shattering from the beaker. The force of the explosion knocking the woman to the floor, hitting her head on a cinder block used to prop the door open on days she opened it to the outside.

Unconscious and lying on the floor, the woman's body waited, a trickle of blood streaming down her forehead. Lydia's body now primed for the dark soul to inhabit. The darkness hovered over her, awaiting the perfect timing as the woman's soul began to drift upward and separate from the body. She was ready to slip into the woman and take up her new host, to claim yet another human body. This one excited her with the possibilities of what she could accomplish with the extra magic this woman possessed. *"Now!" the dark soul seemed to say.* Finally, the dark soul slipped inside Lydia's body like a second skin and adjusted herself within once more, this time more permanently. She had much to get comfortable with, but it wouldn't take her that much time. Already she was beginning to feel a kinship with this body, hers becoming one with the human host just in time to keep the body from physically dying.

Unsure how much time had passed, Lydia's body awoke from lying on the ground for who knew how long. Gently touching her head, she pulled her hand away now covered in a semi-dried state of blood that was more sticky than dried. Her hair was a matted mess, full of the sticky red goo. Running her hands over her face then down her body, she felt alive, rejuvenated, whole again in human form. The dark soul now inhabiting the woman's body sighed, at peace for the moment, ready to begin again. Getting to her feet, she surveyed the damage done by the explosion, grateful it had not done more. She had hoped to have access to the woman's collection of magic and journals of family histories with magic. Those with magic usually kept a family grimoire of sorts or a book of shadows depending what kind of witch they were. A little unsteady still, she reached out to grab the table, but instead shook it. The little bit of liquid left in the exploded beaker spilled mixing it with what was left from the puddle of other chemicals and potions on the table.

Like a rocket-fire boost, an explosion twice the size of the previous one, slammed into the woman, throwing her through the glass windows behind her and out into the field. It was there, out in the cold on the verge of the woman's body's final death, that a presence, unbeknownst to the dark soul, had been standing unseen at the edge between the mortal realm and a realm of another kind. This presence stood at a shimmering doorway, an entrance to a place no one of pure heart would want to be, awaiting their future prisoner.

Draped in a cloak of black, a man young in features but with aged eyes, gathered the woman easily within his arms. Her hair transitioned from white to black, from roots to tips, within seconds before his eyes. She had fully taken the human's form. Stepping within the shimmering veil, he disappeared taking with him an evil they had been tracking for quite some time, an evil that needed to be removed from the mortal realm before more damage was done. What neither he nor his council knew, however, was that more darkness was about to be delivered, only this time it would be beyond Earth. Little did they know their decision was going to set another realm called Alandria on a path for destruction. And all that needed to happen to start such a reaction had already been triggered with the seed of darkness which had just nearly killed itself—only she was still far from death.

CHAPTER ONE

THE REALM OF ALANDRIA

KANDRI. THE PLAINS NEXT TO
THE KANDRIAN MOUNTAIN OUTSIDE
ADETTLYN.

It hadn't taken long for Daegan, Kaeleigh, Finn, and Ella to flee the Forest of Lumei. Maleina Endíl, the paladin and leader of Feraánmar the territory of the Ferrishyn warriors and Earth Faeries, had thrown what amounted to a large tantrum in protest at Daegan's defiance: joining ranks with Kaeleigh and her Alandria supporters. Against the very principals of an Earth Faerie, Maleina had poisoned the trees with lethal bites from her poisonous snakes. Thanks to help from Andreinna, the Dryad priestess and guardian of the forest, Maleina failed to destroy the trees and their life-giving energy. A darkness not from Alandria inhabited Maleina right before the group's eyes. The dark and ancient entity—an unknown female presence—possessed and proved her power by destroying the only portal within Alandria to the Twined realm of Tylínyth through Maleina. Her actions rerouted Finn and Ella from their previous direct route to the pocket realm—a realm within a realm—causing them to join Daegan and Kaeleigh on their journey to find the mysterious portal to the mortal realm. Each pair with a separate mission now joined together to battle what intended to stop them.

For the first time since exiting the forest under the guidance and protection of Andreinna, the four-some were utterly alone. At first they traveled swiftly through the land just beyond the forest; land seemingly barren and bereft of Alandria's magical energy, leaving it simple to traverse. Though they were moving through quickly, it felt unnaturally depressing. Maybe it was their isolation, or the barren expanse they continued to walk. In fact, even the atmosphere weighed in on the group, silencing any conversations they attempted. The group, trapped in a void that sucked not only the life from the ground but tempted them at their core with despair, but they pressed on for the sake of the mission.

"What is this?" Finn finally stammered out. Even for someone usually brooding, Finn appeared worn and withdrawn even more so. The warmth of his hazel eyes muted, and the usual luster of his sandy brown hair dulled.

Ella turned her head toward him. Her short blonde spiky hair fell unnaturally limp. Bleak shadows passed across her usually sharp grey eyes, altering her overall flawlessly bright expression as a Faerie but also what simply made Ella... Ella. As the granddaughter of Arileas, the governing leader of the Ehsmia people, her confidence exuded every aspect, but in this moment her shoulders slumped.

The group hung their heads, each one feeling oppressed, yet unable to explain exactly why or how. Despite not being able to express themselves on the matter, clearly Alandria was dying.

"It has to be Maleina," Kaeleigh muttered, her hand at her heart and moisture within her eyes as she surveyed the land.

Daegan eyed Kaeleigh, speaking the silent *Why don't you elaborate?* Naturally, Kaeleigh shrugged, but then went ahead and put words to her thoughts. "I mean, she is growing in power exponentially from what you," eyes narrowing at Daegan, "have told me about the past. How else could one do that? It stands to reason that somehow Maleina has been syphoning power from the very earth, right?" Her words grew quicker. "I don't know *how* she could be doing it, but I know she is connected."

"I believe you are correct, Kaeleigh, though I am still figuring how she accomplished it." Daegan pinched the bridge of his nose and sighed. "I feel like it is in the forefront of my mind, but just far enough away to keep eluding me," he growled in frustration.

His comment plunged them all back into silence, each one lost in his and her thoughts, the crunch of the dry brittle ground mixed with dead grasses under their boot-clad feet the only sound among them.

Daegan stopped and surveyed the grounds to the north, toward Elnye. The horizon stretched out in the bleakest way possible until you simply could see the land no more. Squatting down to the ground, he picked up some dirt, sprinkled it into the air, and watched it scatter with the wind. Frowning, he placed his hand flat on the earth, and dug his fingers deeper into the dirt. He whispered a few words under his breath—similar to how he had done when they first set out from the forest and made a vow to discover the source of Alandria's ailment. After not even a second, he made an inhumanly frustrated sound as he shot up from the ground.

"Daegan, what is it?" Kaeleigh had asked, rushing to his side, concern all over her face.

"It flows that way." He pointed toward Elnye. "There is a distinct current of motion under the earth, pulling in that direction." Wide eyes, saddened with despair and the reality of what he finally was grasping, he looked to Kaeleigh's for reassurance. "You are right, what energy is left in this place is flowing toward Elnye... to Maleina. I am sure of it. I must find out how!" His fists clenched at either side of him, unsure how best to express himself without having something to strike down with his sword.

Kaeleigh, more subtle than Daegan, reached for his hand and pulled herself over to him, resting her head directly on his chest only inches from his rhythmic heartbeat. Her calmness spread to him, and Daegan allowed it to, placing his hand around the back of her head holding her still. Absorbing her assurances of love gave him the confidence and serenity he knew he lacked.

"We will discover the source and the way of it," she had reassured Daegan. Squeezing his hand, she pulled out from his embrace, yet kept her hand within his.

Ella and Finn not unaware of the tryst between Daegan and Kaeleigh had begun their own conversation while waiting for Daegan's unorthodox ways of understanding the land to end.

Ella stepped forward and interjected herself into the conversation between Kaeleigh and Daegan. "I feel we have tarried here too long. We must keep moving, though I am loathe to interrupt your sacred moments, Daegan."

Daegan nodded. "Of course."

Traveling by foot during the day, building a fire and camping at night in the shelter of the base of the mountain, they were companionable at best but the lengthy silences were beginning to stretch Kaeleigh thin.

"These plains just don't end! They are much more vast than I originally could see," Kaeleigh suddenly announced after two days of walking in the shadow of the Kandrian Mountain. She paused, placing her hands one on her hip and the other shielding her eyes as she gazed up for the millionth time staring at the top of the sleeping giant they had skirted for what felt like forever. Reaching for her water bottle, she then gazed at her companions each beginning to look a little worse for wear.

"It is so quiet here," Kaeleigh huffed, not for the first time since they left the shelter of the forest. Rubbing her hands up her arms, she fought off an unwelcome chill that had begun to surround her. Daegan reached over and placed his hand beneath one of her elbows, sending waves of calming energy into her.

"How much further?" she desperately tried not to ask more than once a day but couldn't stop herself. "Still a day's journey," Ella had snapped at her the last time she asked.

"Sorry, I've asked that a lot haven't I?" she said sheepishly, looking past Ella out at the desolation all around her. As daylight grew scarce and night approached, Kaeleigh felt she might be swallowed whole by the bleakness around them. Even with Daegan sleeping by her side, keeping any boogeymen of Alandria away, the chill of the night still seeped in both physically and mentally. Kaeleigh wondered how they would make it much further in their current condition: weak and haggled from the draining journey.

Ella nodded but smiled sweetly, suddenly filled with grace once more. "I think all this..." she gestured around them, "death and despair is getting to me too," she admitted.

"It's getting to all of us, Kae," Finn answered, his hands busy building a fire for their camp and getting their sleeping packs set out.

Kaeleigh smiled at Finn, grateful for his reassurance even if he didn't show it the same way as she did. Her lack of understanding of Alandria still separated her from the rest of them, but what she did know she loved and wanted to continue learning. She couldn't imagine that desire ever changing or waning. In moments like these, she felt Alandria alive in her heart and that very life warmed her from the inside out, giving her comfort through the dark nights and focus during the days.

Unwilling to discuss some of the more unsavory parts of their journey in the dark such as Maleina or any evil, Kaeleigh smiled at Daegan her heart full of love blooming more each day. Climbing out of her sleeping bag she snuggled close to him, leaning against his legs where he sat on a fallen tree. She found more warmth from him than the sleeping bag itself. Kaeleigh looked up to him, her gaze adoring.

Before they knew it, the group drifted off to sleep, Kaeleigh finding her way back into her sleeping bag.

"Daegan?" Kaeleigh whispered.

"Yes, Kaeleighnna." Her name, a loving caress meant only for her to hear.

"Mmm, I like that." Kaeleigh's eyes closed for a moment, indulging the brief respite as she savored the sound of his voice. "I was wondering how we will find the Book of Lenoria once we are out of Alandria?"

"Yes, I too have been thinking on that," his voice rugged and sleepy from the late hour. "Arileas had told me to trust my instincts and to listen for the voices of the Orchids. They once instructed me on how to find you, you know," he admitted.

"No," she said with a gasp, suddenly feeling more awake than sleepy, "I had no idea!"

Daegan chuckled then continued. "When I entered Montana, a Wisp showed me the way to you. The Orchids also spoke to me, revealing more. So, I believe that is how it will happen again. Although I am not sure if the Wisps will reside where we will exit Alandria as they had in the mountains of Glacier National Park. That park is truly a magical place for creatures of such mortal magic to reside," he explained.

"Wisps are real in the mortal realm?" Kaeleigh's voice grew even louder.

"Kae go to sleep. We can talk about it in the morning," Finn shushed her.

"How can I? I just found out Wisps are real where I grew up, and you expect me to just push it to the back of my mind?" She was shocked.

"Yes, they are in the mortal realm, though there are not many of their kind left, especially in your United States. They originated from the isles of Scotland and Ireland, steeped in Celtic magic. And they only reveal themselves when directed strongly from outside magic such as my Alandrian desire for my destination, that and the influence from the Orchids overseeing the journey." He explained it all quickly and quietly, well aware that each answer would stir another question. "We can discuss that further along with the Orchids part in our journey in the morning."

"You know me well by now, oh wise one," Kaeleigh teased. "All right, for now we can sleep on that bit of information and the rest will wait until tomorrow," she relented, snuggling back down in her sleeping bag. Head to head, she looked back at him one last time before closing her eyes, but he surprised her by leaning forward to capture her mouth for a quick, silent kiss. Until she fell asleep, she would ruminate on his kiss, now mixed with the new magical information.

Chapter Two

The next day brought Kaeleigh many forms of surprise, starting with the excitement of not only getting to further discuss Wisps, but also the discovery other non-Alandria, magical creatures were hiding *and* living among humans in the mortal realm. Kaeleigh learned that some of them were good and some of them not so good. Kaeleigh was baffled to learn other creatures—other magic—had existed right under her nose in the world she had called home for most her life.

"So you are telling me that there are multiple kinds of magic in the world... and not just that, but multiple worlds... err... realms?" Kaeleigh frowned, trying to digest the discordant information. Now too, that they were closing in on the end of the mountain ridge, she felt lighter than she had in days and felt the freedom to get lost in her thoughts.

Finn laughed. "Don't hurt yourself, Kae. He's right. Think of it like *Star Trek* and how they discover new life and ways of living through-out the galaxy from planet to planet. It's the same: Earth—just as with other planets in our own galaxy—houses many different beings and is surrounded by other realms interacting with it." Her pursed lips and scrunched brows prompted him to continue. "Is it that farfetched to believe each realm or planet has their own magic?"

"No, I guess not," Kaeleigh considered.

"That Earth has its own magic and some beings within it such as witches and other fae outside of Alandria have even found access to said magic? Is it that hard to imagine?"

"Okay, after everything I've seen I can imagine that."

"Magic is a type of language that different beings learn depending on where they come from. Some are able to learn from another, but the easiest is the kind you are born into." Finn watched her as understanding dawned on her. "Does that help?"

"Yes, Finn, thank you!" Kaeleigh's smile reached her eyes as she processed the overload of magical information. She was already seeing things in a new perspective and couldn't wait to apply it all back in the mortal realm. Would she be able to see the magic Finn spoke of when she did? Lost in her thoughts, she didn't pay attention to Daegan stopping in front of her and ran smack into his back.

"Oh sorry!" Kaeleigh mumbled scrunching her face and rubbing her nose. "Why did you stop?" When no one answered her, she peered around Daegan's muscled back and gasped. Coming fully around him to stand next to him, she couldn't take her eyes off the land before her.

"Wow!" she exclaimed. "How is it possible?"

Stopped at what appeared to be an invisible line drawn in the ground, separating death from life, each stood in awe. The mountain ridge cascaded majestically down, meeting the ground; a natural landmark signifying the division of land. The land they stood on remained desolate and barren—land void of magical energy or any energy for that matter. But the land one foot in front of them transitioned into a complete juxtaposition—plains alive with grasses of tans and light greens, rolling into hills of greener grasses dotted with a variety of greenery and boulders. The beginnings of tree copses accented with colored floral lined the skyline with height variations all moving and flowing with the natural order of the land.

"I've never seen this area before. It's horrific and beautiful all at the same time," Finn's voice ended on a high note. The group all stood transfixed.

"Nor have I," Ella added finally. "I did not realize such a tragedy was happening to the land here. I have not traveled out this far in a very long time," she added.

Kaeleigh fidgeted in the background, near bursting with curiosity at what they meant.

Daegan simply shook his head, astonished at the extremeness of what he saw. A footfall away lay a glorious Alandria, just the way history had described it, just the way it should be now.

"This is how Alandria used to be... everywhere. At least from how the stories are told," Daegan explained.

"Yes, it is," Finn and Ella both said wistfully, their eyes wide with amazement.

"This is how she should be once more then," Kaeleigh said decidedly. She took the first step. Life-invoking energy soaked through her feet. She sighed blissfully. "Step across! The magic is tangible, it's like life being breathed back into my bones." Kaeleigh practically cried with relief to be out of the desolation. Closing her eyes, she inhaled slowly and deeply. Daegan's hand slid around hers, warm and comforting; his touch hummed like home. That zing of electricity grew stronger when his touch accompanied the natural energy of the area. Where they had been, however, it had been dulled by comparison. "Alandrian magic is literally filling me, refreshing me, can you feel it?" she asked no one and all of them.

Gasps of delight and bliss were muttered in agreement. Standing transfixed each with either eyes to the sky or mouths open wide drinking in the air, absorbing the life energy into their very souls, it was exactly what they needed to continue the journey.

Moments later, rejuvenated and ready to move on, they rounded the mountain's edge with a new bounce in their step and hope in their souls.

Alandria in this part, was much more open with a large expanse of sky above them, plains surrounding them except for the sleeping giant next to them serving as their guide and constant companion all the way to Kandri. Fortunately, the pleasant weather held only a slight chill in the shadow of the mountain throughout the day. The lavender skies broke through the clouds, revealing a sun so much larger than what they'd been able to see in the mortal realm. Not only that but vast amounts of unknown grass and wild flowers gracefully swayed back and forth alive with the forces of the wind. Everywhere the group looked, they encountered a scene not seen in the mortal world.

"I miss Chel," Kaeleigh said again, thinking of her best friend away on her own mission to the Shifter territory of Mandü tré Lan with Hal also looking for allies. "Do you think there are creatures out here with us? Chel would know right away." As a Shifter, Chel's gift of being able to hear and communicate with the more animalistic types had developed more the longer they had been in Alandria and had become important—not too mention her optimistic outlook and shining personality had lightened many moments along their journey. "It makes me uneasy not knowing." Kaeleigh frowned.

"Yes," Daegan and Ella said in unison. Ella moved her head forward so as to begin speaking.

"If you listen carefully, not just to the silence but beyond it, Kaeleigh, there are sounds of creatures scampering through the grasses." Ella was teaching Kaeleigh a skill those raised in Alandria would have grown up learning. "Though I cannot tell what they are saying, they sound playful and chipper." Ella inclined her ear and closed her eyes briefly demonstrating to Kaeleigh.

Kaeleigh did the same and some moments later, smiled. "I do hear them! I also hear the whispering of the grasses, leaves moving on the trees, and the sounds of whistling as the breeze whips through nearby trees." She turned, wide eyed to Ella and threw herself at the woman, reaching out to hug her. Ella, unused to dramatic shows of excitement, stiffened. "Oh, sorry, Ella," Kaeleigh stammered, backing away from Ella embarrassed.

"It is all right, Kaeleigh. I'm just not used to others embracing me." Ella often saw Kaeleigh and Chel hugging—a demonstration of their closeness. "I'm not comfortable showing how I feel with casual touch," Ella explained, "but I know you must miss Chel and her affection for you." Both women looked away for a moment, searching for a way to get pasts the awkward moment.

"So now that we are in such a wonderful place, I've been wondering about something," Kaeleigh found her voice.

"What is that?" Daegan asked.

"Well, back in the forest when we faced Maleina this last time, well, someone else took over her body, right? Like Invasion of the Body Snatchers or something!"

Daegan and Ella both gave her strange looks. "Never mind, Chel would have laughed. Finn you got it right?"

"It's an old movie reference from the mortal realm," Finn explained and nodded at Kaeleigh.

"Thank you," Kaeleigh said with mock relief.

"I think that is exactly what happened, and it's not something commonly seen—even in Alandria," Finn replied.

"Yes, I observed the same," Ella said, her interest fully on Kaeleigh's words. "Such a strange sight to see Maleina used like a puppet under the control of another. The other said those in the realm of Exhile called her *She*. I am not familiar with one called that within Exhile."

Daegan stroked his chin thoughtfully, his fingers rubbed against the stubble having grown since arriving in Alandria. Kaeleigh just knew he was about to say something important and could scarcely wait to hear it. "I believe she is the one we seek in Exhile—the one holding the Orchids imprisoned—and perhaps still remains there. Her presence possessing Maleina back in the forest seemed for that moment; it did not appear she could hold her takeover the entire time but maybe in increments, at least for now."

"Makes sense with what we saw," Finn added, his face stretched into that familiar serious line.

"Does that mean Maleina is not at fault? Or that someone is controlling her? Or perhaps that the other woman is just not strong enough yet to control her?" Kaeleigh rapid fired her questions.

"I think it means all of those things but I don't believe she is being controlled completely. That is to say, I am fairly certain she did many things of her own volition." He paused with a frown. "I wish to understand the purpose of the other entity and what her end goal is... does she mean to possess a being of Alandria completely, is that even possible? Is she able to gain enough power to enter Alandria in her own form? And what kind of danger does she present to us or does she just intend to rule?" Daegan seemed to be asking his questions more to himself out loud for the benefit of the others.

"Oh! I saw her before."

"What do you mean, Kaeleigh?" Daegan asked.

"In the Great Hall, in Ehsmia. Remember when I got pulled mentally and magically into the mural on the back wall? I saw her, well, I saw Maleina but as I fought her the image wavered and another woman's face replaced hers—a woman with jet black hair and eyes darkened with evil yet lit with a flame of vengeance." Kaeleigh shook herself out of the memory.

"If you fought her in the vision, then I fear we will encounter her again in the near future," Daegan said, his tone full of morose.

Ella inhaled audibly and looked up at the sky thoughtfully, her short white-blonde hair barely ruffling in the breeze. "I agree. For now, we need to keep moving and find shelter."

"What is it? What do you see, Ella?" Finn asked suddenly at her side. As an Elf he had increased speed over a mortal as well as others from Alandria. Until recently, he had kept his speed and other traits hidden from Kaeleigh, but now she knew the truth of who he was—at least the parts he was willing to share.

"I feel something stirring on the wind," Ella replied, quickly on guard. She picked up her pace, encouraging the others to do the same.

"Daegan, what do you sense?" Kaeleigh asked quietly as she tugged on his shirt sleeve. Her face grew concerned, and her gaze darted to and fro though their surroundings offered nowhere for an enemy to hide.

Daegan strained his eyes searching for anything out of the ordinary. At first, he looked with his natural eyes and then also through the eyes of his magic. He shook his head slowly. "I also feel something stirring on the wind, but it is still too far for me to gauge what it is. I agree with Ella. It is time to find shelter and get out of these plains. We are not far from the villages outside Kandri. Let us stop there."

Finn, agitated with so much conversation and the slow pace, he couldn't help but let it slip into his tone. "Let's go then, already! Can't we keep going and discuss while we walk? Otherwise we will never get there."

Well let's go, Daegan's eyes said. He gestured gentlemanly to Kaeleigh to go ahead of him. Ella followed behind Finn. "Thank you," Kaeleigh almost whispered. Then sliding her hand along his forearm, she moved ahead.

The group moved on, chastened by Finn's urgency as well as by the idea of the unseen enemy waiting for them. Kaeleigh, not so keen on long periods of silence broke the quick though quiet pace. "So what's the territory we are headed into like?" Oddly, the already silent group fell into an even heavier silence. Kaeleigh couldn't figure out what might be wrong with the question she asked and just as she was about to ask, Finn spoke up. Surprised, thinking it would be Daegan, she felt for his presence at her back; he was there but their connection, normally strong and clear, had gone dark. In its place, the connection was thick and full of emotion, specifically anger.

Finn continued. "It's not a big area... well, it actually is large... but not too many live there... if I remember correctly. It's similar to Anise outside Adettlyn. It houses a combination of races." Finn recalled more. "Being further out as it is makes it easier for the inhabitants to not fall into the same pressures and outlandish perceptions as other territories have struggled with for so long. They are outside the judgement zone, so to speak." Finn stopped a moment, catching his breath. "It has been many years since I was last there, but even then..." Finn's face shut down all emotion, and his gaze went to the ground. "I did not tarry long," his voice drifted off thick and forced. Silence fell again as Finn said no more, knowledge or memories plaguing his mind.

"As for me," Daegan reluctantly began after searching Finn's face. Finn's strange reaction to Kandri stirred his own, "I have not been there since I was a young boy, and my memories of it are frail, barely holding together even with the ones recently restored." Not long before they had left Ehsmia, Daegan's memories of who he truly was—the rightful heir to the throne of Feraánmar—were restored after a visit with not only the ancient *NaNai* tree but his long-believed-to-be-deceased grandmother who had been hidden with the Ehsmia people. "I lived there for a time, but I do not remember much. My parents were protective and kept me sheltered. I now understand." He paused. "My parents and grandmother were in hiding, moving from place to place. The moment we would settle, or the whispers of pursuers surfacing we would move once more. It was not a life with roots and connections, but from what my grand-mother helped me to remember, it was necessary to preserve our line."

"So so sorry, Daegan." Kaeleigh turned and gave him her hand, tightening her hold when he placed his large, tough hand around hers.

"It was long ago, Kaeleigh," he recalled.

"Yes, but it shaped your existence and left you without parents. It still hurts, and that I understand," she said more quietly, reflective of her own life.

"Where did your family go from there?" she changed the subject to a lighter one.

"Nowhere. This is where they were killed."

Chapter Three

"Ugh! Way to put my foot in my mouth," Kaeleigh muttered under her breath.

"Finn! Are you all right?" Ella asked, shocked when Finn tripped and stumbled, almost hitting the ground.

Kaeleigh stopped, confused at what happened to Finn, his hands braced on the ground for his balance. "Did you trip?"

"I... I must have," Finn stammered, dusting off the dirt from his pants. His hands shook. "I need just a minute." Hands at his waist, head hung low, he took a moment to regain his composure.

"Okay," Kaeleigh capitulated while turning to Daegan. He stood stiff as a board, his hands clenching at his sides before he crossed them about his chest. He stood with a scowl etched on his face. Kaeleigh being herself, placed her hand on the arm of his closest to her and send peaceful feelings through their usual connection. No go. Instantly, she felt blocked. He had blocked himself off from her? Confused, she found herself whispering, "Daegan?" Not even a flicker of recognition met her eyes so she tried again, this time louder. "Daegan?"

His scowl turned to her, but quickly softened. "I am sorry, Kaeleighnna, what did you say? I was caught in memories of a dark past starting to resurface once again."

"It's all right. I can't imagine what it was like as a boy to face what you did. Please don't shut me out."

He nodded, relaxing his posture and expression. Daegan grabbed her hand and pulled her along after him.

"Daegan?" Kaeleigh offered him a change of subject. "Do you know what Exhile is like? Has anyone ever been there before alive and returned unchanged? I have been trying to come up with ways to free the Orchids, but I just don't have enough information."

Daegan looped his arm around her shoulder, smiling. "It is said to be a place of vast desolation, much like your deserts in the mortal realm: dry, arid, and void of much life. I can't think of anyone that has passed through those lands unscathed. In all honesty, I don't know why anyone would have purpose to go there other than to pay for their transgressions in life. As for the Orchids, I believe we will understand when it is time how to release them."

The thought of going into a place where Daegan had never been and had never heard of anyone else leaving unscathed scared Kaeleigh, chilling her very core. "So we are going in blind and probably won't come back out, but if we do we will be altered in some fashion?" she squeaked out. "Awesome." Then with not a little passive aggressiveness, she muttered, "Maybe I should have learned more about it before I committed to going."

"Perhaps," he smiled, unaffected by her tone, "but remember you committed with your heart, so your heart will lead us in and out with purpose."

"How can you be so sure?" Kaeleigh voiced a bit softer. "Maybe my heart made a grave error and I'm pulling you into trouble with me. I mean Alandria needs *you*, so maybe I should go alone," she said feeling more certain she didn't want to lead others into danger.

He turned her and kissed her fully on the mouth, effectively shutting her up, both hands holding her head steady. Her eyes widened, brightened with a spark of desire, and a warmth spread, blooming deep within her stomach provoking passion for life. Daegan chuckled, feeling her spirit once more; her mind no longer in a place of despair. His own darkness receded for the moment as well. The reaction his body had to her baffled even his own mind; a feeling he had never had with a girl before. Something Finn had said in his description of Kandri and the way he seemed haunted by his own memories, triggered Daegan's memories. Or perhaps it was simply the place and his emotions were displaced, revealing themselves on someone who could actually take his internal, and perhaps external, aggression. Daegan shook his head, knocking loose the cobwebs decorating the attic of his mind. He looked down at the girl—the woman—in his arms and his heart stirred. She was the only thing he was certain of anymore.

"Alandria needs us both. Only together are we the Sol-lumieth," he reminded her, "I believe in your heart. It will not steer us wrong." The pad of his thumb swiped across her cheek under her eye affectionately. "The Orchids must be set free. We are the ones to do it."

"Your faith in me is unfounded, but thank you," she said softly, holding his wrists.

Daegan winked. "Come, we must keep going. The others look ready to move forward as well." Finn and Ella had now caught up behind the couple.

As the group descended a grassy hillside, the first signs of a village came into view at the base of this side of the mountain. Only a few people could be seen, moving as dots from their vantage point, though they could clearly see the village was surrounded with a tall, stone wall. Near the back of the village stone buildings appeared so close they might have been built into the mountain itself. Guards stood inside a single gate appearing to be the only entrance. No other guards were stationed along the top of the wall, and none could be seen elsewhere. As they grew closer, it became clear the wall was, in fact, more of a fence than an actual defense, and Finn made a point to say just that.

"Seems they do not put much stock into guards out this far."

Daegan nodded and squinted curiously at the village. "Something is there, though just outside the boundary. I believe it is magic. Do not get too close to the stone barrier in case it is spelled somehow." Then he muttered to himself, "Hmmm. I wonder if it really is... though I have not heard of this being done in quite some time."

"What does it mean?" Kaeleigh asked.

"It means they want to trick any 'visitors' into thinking just what Finn observed—that they have no strong defenses, and by doing that you lower your defenses as you approach," Ella answered for her.

"But why?"

"So a false sense of security?" Finn shrugged. "Maybe they plan to ambush when it's least expected?"

"So do we enter?" Kaeleigh asked, looking from Daegan to Finn to Ella.

"We need to stop for the night. If they will have us, it would be safer to go in than what I feel is coming out here," Daegan answered. He moved forward but slowly, knowing the guards had to have spotted them already.

"All right, then stopping it is," Kaeleigh agreed, tossing her shoulders back decisively.

At the gate, the guards searched their persons but oddly did not take their weapons from them.

"Do we need to check in our weapons?"

"Everyone is entitled to defend themselves in Kandri," the guard replied to Daegan when asked.

"If they let us—strangers—in with weapons, why did they even bother checking us?" Kaeleigh asked.

"Good question," Finn muttered thoughtfully.

"Perhaps they were looking for something else?" supplied Ella.

"Like what?" Kaeleigh bit her bottom lip nervously.

"I do not know, but I wish I did," Ella said.

"Could they be looking for the same thing we are? The book?" she whispered.

"Perhaps, but let us hope not. I do not know who all knows of its existence, but I imagine they are not looking to help us."

Eyes alert and observing, they entered through the stone wall.

"These walls were not established when I was last here," Daegan mused, trailing a hand along a couple stones. "I wonder why they were built."

Silently they watched the people of Kandri going about their business. Where the entrance had opened up into a cobbled stone town center, vendors and small huts offering their wares of breads and fruits spread before them. The group's presence caused quite a stir. Businesses halted their transactions, and both the vendors and villagers looked on uneasily as Kaeleigh and Daegan moved slowly through. Finn and Ella trailed behind them, stopping so Finn could lace his boots more tightly—though he was really using the time to check his surroundings without drawing attention to himself.

"Why are they all staring at us?" Kaeleigh whispered barley even moving her mouth to Daegan.

"I am not sure. Stay at ease."

"Easy for you to say," she mumbled, slightly smiling at one of the vendors she passed. "Should we say hello? Wave? Anything?"

"Yes, perhaps that would settle people down." Daegan started for one of the booths, but the moment he did, the villagers instantly backed away. He frowned, which did not help reduce his intimidating appearance.

"Here let me try." Kaeleigh placed her hand at his back and moved ahead of him. Without a word, Daegan stepped back and let her go ahead. Kaeleigh moved forward but was careful not to move too close. Then cheerfully, she ventured, "Hello." At the blank stares or confused expressions she realized they might not understand her. Inhaling slowly, Kaeleigh focused on her magic using her words and tried again—speaking the language though she had never learned. "Hello, we have just arrived and are looking for shelter. Is there a place you recommend for travelers to spend the night?"

Met with silence, she looked from vendor to vendor. A chill crawled up her spine. "Something strange is going on in this place," she whispered over her shoulder to Daegan. Finally, off to her side, a little girl peered out from behind a woman's skirt and gasped.

"It is you," she said with awe, "it is you, is it not?" She slid out from behind the woman carefully, and although they expected otherwise, strangely the woman did not try and stop her.

Kaeleigh bent down to the girl's level, who appeared about seven or eight. "I am not sure who you mean. We are just four travelers looking for a place to rest for the night. Could you tell me why everyone is, well, scared of us?"

The little girl nodded, eyeing Daegan from the corner of her eye. "Is he the other one?" she whispered, unaware Daegan could still hear her.

"The other who?" Kaeleigh coaxed the little girl, needing more information. Ella had moved in closer and left Finn to stand by Daegan who kept watch from behind.

The little girl, with short curly dark hair and dark blue eyes, gasped again and reached her hand out to Ella. "It is you too!"

Kaeleigh looked to Ella who shrugged. Neither woman could understand what this girl with eyes-as-blue-as-a-storm meant.

"Let me try something." Ella knelt down and held the girl's hand. Ella had gifts that none of them understood fully and if anyone could learn what was happening it was probably her. She looked deep into the girl's eyes. Ella then tipped her head up and looked at all those standing around them, but the vendors and the patrons simply stood and looked on not saying anything.

"Have you seen us before?" Ella asked her gently.

The girl nodded and smiled. "Yes, I saw you coming. We did not know when you would come but the lady in the vision said you were coming and showed me what you looked like."

Ella and Kaeleigh both turned to look back at Daegan and Finn who frowned. Daegan's eyes widened and he cautiously moved forward eyeing the other adults then knelt down to their level as well. At once the group realized it wasn't that the villagers couldn't speak, but that they were held in a trance of some kind. "Can you tell us who the lady was?" he asked quietly.

The little girl shrugged. "The pretty lady with the hair like fire."

Kaeleigh and Daegan exchanged a quick glance. Maleina and Andreinna both had red hair, not to mention a host of others in this world.

"What did the pretty lady say?" Kaeleigh encouraged with a smile.

The girl looked at each of them hesitantly as if deciding whether she should share or not. She shrugged owing no one allegiance and leaned forward, "She told me you were coming and I should invite you to stay and play. She said she put magic on the town and everyone would protect it by acting like watchmen." The girl pointed to the people around her.

"They definitely look as if they are under an enchantment," Finn agreed, waving his hand in front of one man near him.

"What is your name, sweetie?" Kaeleigh asked.

"Letoni," she replied innocently standing between the girls her hands now placed on both Kaeleigh and Ella's shoulders.

"Letoni, my name is Kaeleigh and this is Ella. What do the watchmen do?"

"They watch things," she said simply as only a child could. Finn snickered behind Kaeleigh and she quickly turned and glared at him.

"They watch the town, they watch for strangers," Letoni expounded.

"Are there any people here not under this... this spell? Others like you, Letoni?" Ella asked.

"They are like this when someone comes through the entrance to the town, but then it wears off once the pretty lady sees who has come. Then they go back to normal again. It's only those in this front area who are magicked. The rest of the town behind us is fine," she stated proudly as if she let them in the secret of her fun.

"Why are you not *magicked* when you are up here then?" Kaeleigh observed, using Letoni's word.

"Because I am the hostess. I get to invite you inside the town to stay. Plus her magic does not work on me. I have immutie... iminty..." she frowned perplexed at the word she was trying to find.

"Immunity?" Kaeleigh suggested.

"Yes! That, I have that," Letoni beamed, jumping up and down that Kaeleigh had understood her.

"Do you know why you are immune?" Ella prodded.

Letoni shook her head no.

Ella pursed her lips in thought. "There are stories of some that are immune to either specific magic or all magic within Alandria, but it is very rare," she explained to the others. To the girl she said, "You are very special, Letoni."

"Very special indeed," Kaeleigh agreed. "Letoni, could you show us somewhere we can stay for the night?"

Letoni's eyes lit up, the task she had been awaiting finally came. "Yes! I know just the place. Follow me," she said and she skipped off a few paces away and turned beckoning them to follow her.

The foursome glanced at each other warily. "We follow her right?" Kaeleigh inquired.

"Yes," Daegan replied thoughtfully, "But be cautious and on alert. If she is in fact working for Maleina—however pure Letoni's motives—Maleina will know we are here."

"If she doesn't already," Kaeleigh confirmed dryly. "This sounds like a trap."

Daegan nodded. "Agreed." They followed slowly behind Letoni.

"Maybe we should leave the village and keep going," Finn interjected, grabbing Kaeleigh's arm gently. "If Maleina knows we are here, she will be here soon. We won't have time to get to the portal."

Daegan sidled up next to her, glaring at Kaeleigh's arm and then Finn for gripping her. Finn dropped Kaeleigh's arm and muttered an apology.

"Oh stop it, Finn you were fine." Turning to Daegan as they continued walking she said, "He wasn't hurting me."

Daegan moved in close to her so no one else could hear. He whispered with a growl in her ear, "Nothing is harmless right now, not even me. I cannot protect you if you allow others to get too close to you." Kaeleigh frowned. To the others, Daegan quietly added, "At this point, I am not sure we have another choice. Eat, rest, and find shelter to protect ourselves for even a short time or face what she might be sending for us out there." Daegan pointed to the lands beyond the border. "I have mixed feelings here. I sense the spell now the little one pointed it out, but I also feel a sense of hope and I feel Alandria stirring here. I wonder if our being here is more for the second than the first," his voice full of both concern and thought.

"Are you coming? They will have food prepared for you!" Letoni cried, panting coming back from around the corner she had just turned.

"Yes, we are coming," Kaeleigh hollered back.

"We—the Ehsmia—will need to watch her as she grows," Ella directed toward Kaeleigh but nodded toward Letoni, "She will be a mark if her magic does what I think it might."

"I thought her being immune meant she didn't have magic like everyone else," Kaeleigh mused through a frown.

"It means, she has magic to deflect others' magic and possibly more. I will send word to Grandfather. I'm able to telepathically connect with him for brief messages," Ella explained then drifted off in thought as they all followed the little girl along the cobblestone path to hopefully food and shelter for however long it might last.

Chapter Four

Outside Elnye. Near the Gáraldrath Mountains.

Screams echoed throughout the cavern buried within the mountain, bouncing off the stone walls, ricocheting back to Maleina. The sound of her own voice surprised and shocked her ears. Maleina's head shot up, her eyes wide and—for the first time in a very long time—fearful. Rising from all fours to squatting on the hard and roughened ground, her head whipped around and surveyed the space all around her cautiously. She didn't know how she had arrived there. She couldn't remember anything except for being in the forest near Adettlyn, facing off with Daegan and trying to persuade him away from that little witch's clutches. Then the nerve of that forest nymph who believed herself to be the guardian of Alandria had shown up and interrupted her plans for the trees—her and that little witch who is supposed to be some kind of savior coming in with all her big power still yet to be seen. Kaeleigh. She had the audacity to join forces with the Dryad against Maleina, the rightful queen of not only Feraánmar, but of the whole of Alandria—at least in her own mind.

Maleina touched her head, and her eyes squinted in the darkness of the cavern she was currently trapped in, searching for an exit she could not find. The last thing she remembered was being surrounded by Daegan and those others, before roots erupted from the ground and wrapped around her ankles, securing her firmly to the ground. They would all pay. But then...

Then *She* was there—the mistress of darkness—inside her, fighting for control. Maleina had lost and that was what she was left with, a black hole for a memory, not knowing what *She* had done while possessing her body. Maleina had underestimated that woman; she did not think the other woman had enough power to accomplish much outside her realm let alone possession. That was a mistake she would never make again, nor would she ever admit to anyone.

"Get out of your head, Maleina. We have work to do," the mistress of the dark's voice reverberated inside the same space where Maleina stewed.

Maleina slowly pushed magic to her eyes, willing her to be seen in the darkness, but no one else was with her in the cavern. She pushed her magic further and ignited a flame in her hand, sending it to the far wall where a stick hung awaiting its purpose to be fulfilled as a torch to light someone's path. The space was small, not even enough room for ten men. No one occupied it other than Maleina and a mirror hung askew on the cave wall.

The mirror before her eyes filled with motion. A gray smoke swirled inside the glass, revealing her mistress' face. The smoke thinned before it clouded over the mirror once more. The eyes she saw were cold and harsh, with no hints of mercy.

"What did you do? In the forest? I can't remember what happened," Maleina's words were pushed through clenched teeth, her hands balls of fists at her sides as she slowly rose from her crouch.

"You don't remember? It must be a little side effect, no matter," *She* responded cooly.

"It matters to me," Maleina's voice grew with indignation.

The mistress of darkness pierced Maleina with her fierce stare; even through a mirror, Maleina could feel the power the woman possessed threatening to enclose around her throat from inside the mirror. After her possession experience it did not surprise her. Maleina dropped her gaze to the ground and took a step back.

"My apologies, Mistress," she murmured under her breath.

"You underestimated me, Maleina," she continued, dismissing Maleina's garbled apology. "You see, I have plans for Alandria, big plans. And you, my pet, are simply a tool." The woman in the mirror stared into Maleina's soul belittling her to exactly that, a tool. "A dispensable tool. It would benefit you to remember that, Maleina."

Maleina's jaw ticked as her teeth clenched within her cheeks. It was all she could do to restrain the fury rising within her. "I won't ever forget," she responded cooly.

"Good, then let us move on. Is the next phase of my plan in place with Adettlyn?"

"Yes, Syén is ready, though I must warn you, he is a bit skittish at times and needs... delicate reinforcement of his importance," Maleina explained, ready to relinquish the part she'd played with the ruler of Adettlyn. He was too needy and she didn't want to hold his hand any longer. She was going to get rid of him at the end of his usefulness anyway, perhaps this would speed things along.

"Very well. If he is unable to accomplish what I desire, he shall be removed. Permanently." *She* raised the side of her mouth in a sneer of utter madness. Maleina actually had wondered at the woman's complete sanity being held up in Exhile for however long she had been there. That would have to wear down a person at some point no matter how strong one was. "See to it, Maleina."

That she was not expecting. "Couldn't one of your other minions serve you in this manner while I further our... your plans? There is still much to be done," she added quickly.

"No. I trust only you with the discretionary needs of this duty."

Maleina's shoulders went back of their own volition. She hadn't expected to be praised either. Her head held high and her chin jutted out, after which she then bowed her head. "As you wish it be done."

Maleina turned as if to leave, but then halted. "Is there any more your servant can do for you? Or shall I take my leave?"

The mistress in the mirror, preened with a haughty sense of pride at seeing one of her peons taking her place fully before her. "No, Daughter of Mine, for that is what you now are—we have shared much in recent events. The more you come to fully realize your place with me, the more power I will bestow upon you and the greater position with me you shall hold when I have come fully into Alandria."

Something shimmered in Maleina's eyes, a twinkle of respect, a glimmer of emotion, and a hint of suspicion. She bowed her head lower and added a curtsy.

"You may leave, child. The exit is through that wall." She inclined her to the wall just beyond the place Maleina had been standing the entire time.

She wasted no time in her departure. Maleina turned and walked straight at the stone wall without a moment of hesitation. Right as anyone else would have expected to crash into the rock, she felt herself stepping through it and into a tunnel. The tunnel led her through the mountains, and opened through a slim crevice in the rock into the Guardian Grove forest. Many did not frequent the ancient, malevolent Guardian Grove forest due to its close proximity to the Gáraldrath Mountain and the darkness it emanated. Maleina used the forest to hide her secret passage way not only into the basement of the castle in Elnye but also to her private cabin hidden deep within the grove. Even now, held prisoner in the cabin and bound to Maleina's every whim, was the Soul Stealer to whom she needed to pay a visit.

<center>~~~~~</center>

"The time is growing close, I can feel it," *She* said aloud in her little dominion within the mountain. Her raven-black hair, trailing down her back and pulled half back out of her face, glistened in the darkened cavern. Her pale and porcelain complexion appeared warmer from the illusion the myriad of candles lit throughout her domain left upon her face. Flickering flames of candlelight reflected within her eyes, illuminating the menace residing there. Her one-piece black suit, which appeared one with her skin, revealed each of her sultry curves, though none were ever admired. She remained alone in her cave constantly though she could conjure clothing of whatever ilk and era she chose. Intently, she listened to the dark presence conveying its message to her. The Droch-Shúil's message came through loud and clear. The Sol-lumieth was on her way to find a means to get into Exhile. The girl and her companions would leave Alandria, the realm *She* intended to infiltrate fully and take dominion—finally having her own realm to rule after centuries of seeking to find her place.

"She is getting too close. The Sol-lumieth... I need her held back," *She* decided, reaching out her hand for the darkness to come to her. The smoky essence of the Droch-Shúil flowed to her, wrapping itself around her arm as it moved up to her neck. The ancient creature traveled around her long slender throat then back down her front and then around her waist until it reared its head, looking directly into her eyes. Red eyes blazed as the Droch-Shúil awaited the commands of its mistress.

"What is your wish, Mistress?" the darkness hissed with voices of ten thousand in unison.

She closed her eyes, luxuriating in the feeling of the darkness against her body. When her eyes opened again, hunger for chaos burned hot. "I know where they are. For now, make routine passes throughout Alandria. Check in with those Maleina and I have set up to serve our purposes. As for the others, I will await until they are precisely where I want them. I foresee them being detained in Kandri for a time," she said with a sneer. "Little Letoni will be hard for the human girl to say no to, she will keep them there long enough… and if not, well then that is when you will come in, my pet."

The Droch-Shúil moved over her once more, a symbiotic relationship of the sharing of darkness. *She* stretched her magic and reached for what it offered her, reenergizing the darkness within her, but it alone was not enough. *She* was not yet strong enough for her plan to be enacted. The timing had to be precise and the entry into Alandria was not ready. For that, she needed more power… more energy. And for that to happen in Exhile, she needed to pay a visit to The Orchids.

"Go now, pet. I have things to do." The Droch-Shúil swept away like smoke fleeing the only air shaft available. The Droch-Shúil, able to go anywhere it pleased, could traverse Alandria through even the tiniest of cracks in the realm, unrestricted as *She* was. All the Droch-Shúil needed was an opening made by darkness in a heart. And as long as people—human or otherwise—had intentional thought, wickedness would arise. On its own, the Droch-Shúil would be content to roam and dwell in other darkness, even alone. But with added guidance from outside influences, it made the most helpful companion.

The Mistress of Darkness, *She* who dwelt in the mountain of Exhile, crossed her arms and moved through the cave tunnels toward her prison. Her hips swayed with confidence and seduction; her plan was coming forth. Soon she would be the new ruler of an entire realm. Soon she would be the ruler of Alandria.

Chapter Five

"**S**amuel! What in the holy name of somebody are you... How did you..." Chel stammered lost for words, which didn't happen often. Eyes wide she still couldn't believe what they were telling her: her mortal realm boyfriend was there in Alandria, not the mortal realm where he belonged. But how did he get there? What was happening? Her brain was on overload, and she was about to have a breakdown.

"How *am* I here?" he asked smugly taking in her rare reaction, arms crossed with a satisfied air about him. In almost every way he was different than Halister Endíl. Samuel was a stocky, muscular fellow, covered with tattoos. He had a short yet thick and shaggy hairline of dark hair. His dark eyes matched it perfectly, complimented his tan skin and wide set nose and mouth. "Didn't you ever suspect anything, Chel? We did live together. Or did you forget me so quickly once you found new *friends*." Samuel flicked his eyes toward Hal just in time to see his eyes narrow the tiniest bit.

"Should I have suspected you of something? No, I trusted you!" Chel's head spun, as did the words that continued to spew forth. "You had to have lied to me is the only thing I can think of. I mean, you're here so... yeah... you wouldn't be here unless you were from here." The revelation tumbled out. "You knew about me the entire time we were together, didn't you?"

Samuel remained where he stood, arms crossed. He saw hurt in her glare. She too easily trusted. He nodded the admission.

"You're right, I did. You have a heritage here, and I was sent to keep an eye on you, to see when you were ready to come back... the idea was that hopefully I could help you transition." He then glared at Halister as if her showing up in Alandria was his fault. "But you left before I had the chance to slowly ease you into it. You just took off!" His voice rose, and he began to pace before her. "And a bang up job your parents did preparing you," he added the anger impossible to miss. "See, I had a plan. I was just about to bring you into it all, in fact, when you left. I could see the change starting to show itself even when you were unaware of what was happening with your body."

Hal had been leaning against a large boulder watching the show unfold before him. He tried as hard as he could to remain objective and not let anyone read him, keeping what his mortal colleagues would call a poker face. Things were about to get ugly if Chel's posture-change indicated anything. He pushed himself off the rock he'd been leaning on and stood taller, closer to Chel but still just behind her. She could handle herself with this guy. This Samuel, was the type who gave the Shifters a bad name; he was haughty, controlling, and possessive—all the things that would make a girl like Chel rise up against every time. If Samuel's expression of hatred toward Hal was anything to go by, he was not excited about the possibility of uniting Alandria with the other races, or at least not with a Faerie.

"I don't know what to say right now, I'm so mad I could spit!" Chel's fists clenched and unclenched at her sides over and over. Inhaling sharply, she held her arms out in front of her. Her skin visibly rippled right before her eyes. As quick as the anger consumed her expression, it was replaced with panic. She looked frantically from Samuel to Hal and back again, ending at Halister. "What's happening?" she whispered.

"It's the change. Haven't you prepared her at all, Faerie?" Samuel spit out.

Halister ignored him and stepped closer to Chel. "Remember what you learned about relaxing. Don't be afraid of it Chel, it's a part of you."

She nodded and closed her eyes, focusing, visualizing, seeking for the peace she needed. Breathing in through her nose and out slowly through her mouth, she found an element of control and the tremors slowed.

"Don't listen to this guy, Chel. Grab hold of your inner animal and command it forth. Take charge of her and wrestle her into submission. You're a wolf like your dad, right? Don't fight it, embrace it, let it become you, it's the most exhilarating feeling in the world to get lost in your animal." Samuel said with exuberant animation.

"That sounds kinda barbaric, Sam." Chel broke her concentration, opening one squinty eye. He shrugged and she turned to Hal. With one more breath in through her nose, she held it then released the air and asked, "Is that what I have to do, beat my animal into submission so I don't get lost and consumed by the shift?" Fear shone in her eyes, Chel didn't like the sound of that at all, it didn't sound natural to who she was or the way Halister had explained it to her before back in his home in Elnye.

"That hasn't been my experience with other Shifters I know, but I'm sure it's different for each person." Hal inclined his head to Samuel, trying to keep the peace for Chel at the moment. He was sure another moment would spring up where he could confront Samuel and the way he treated someone he was supposed to care about. "Your animal is an extension of you. She might have more will or her personality may differ a little from your own, but for the most part she will be just a different version of yourself. You are a team and will become one to channel your greatest strengths regardless of which form you are in." Hal's explanation calmed Chel visibly and her shoulders relaxed. Chel breathed out and closed her eyes once more, calming her animal and mentally telling her wolf she wasn't ready yet. Chel didn't want to change for the first time in the middle of nowhere where they had barely escaped the notice of the Droch-Shúil. She wanted to be somewhere safe and comfortable and preferably wanted to make the shift when she was back with Kaeleigh. How she missed her friend!

"Listen to him if you want, Chel, but he's not a Shifter and will never be one. He's not what you need," Samuel spoke with vehemence and started to walk away. He turned back to her, "If you're ready, I can escort you back home, to the land of the Shifters, where you're from, where you belong, where your family is."

There was so much underlying the words Samuel spoke and the tone he used, it took Chel a few seconds to digest what he had actually said. "My family? You mean my parents? They're here, in Alandria?" Chel bounced her way up to where Samuel was, unable to contain her excitement on her face; her earlier trial with her wolf subsided for the moment.

"That's what I was trying to tell you. I was bringing you home to your parents. They're worried sick about you." His eyes held a hint of satisfaction at being the cause of her joy and leaving Halister behind them.

"I miss them so much. Did they come back with you? Did they know about you from the beginning? Is that why they didn't want you to be my boyfriend?" At the sudden hurt she saw in his eyes, she quickly clarified. "You know, because they were afraid you might tell me something about who I was before they had the chance to tell me themselves."

"Right. No, they were already here when I got back. I didn't know they had left yet. And I don't know if they figured me out. Probably." He shrugged unconcerned, taking in the surrounding boulders and desert appearance to the entrance into the territory of the Shifters.

"Come on Hal! I want you to meet my parents," Chel looked back at him with a smile which he returned, but Hal didn't miss the scowl Samuel expressed behind her back.

"It would be my honor to meet them, Chel, thank you," he said pleasantly, but smirked at Samuel's back as Samuel reached for Chel's hand. Looking down, she hesitated—which Samuel didn't miss—but she went ahead and let him take it. Hal frowned, obviously conflicted as to how he felt about seeing them hand-in-hand. He knew that Chel and Samuel had had a relationship before she'd come to Alandria. Samuel had said they'd even lived together. Of course she had a life before Alandria! So did he, he reminded himself. In fact, he wasn't even looking for anything serious. *What was he looking for*, he thought to himself. Hal had just thought Chel would be fun to hang around for a while. She owed him nothing, and if she did still have a relationship with Samuel—even against his better judgement of character—that was better for him. Chel was one of those types that could get under his skin and leave a mark. He wasn't looking for that at all. As far as he could tell, the only downside to it all was that he wasn't so sure she hadn't already done just that!

The sky near the Mandü tré Lan was the same as anywhere in Alandria, but the air was oddly different; it became arid and dry similar to the high deserts in the mortal realm. Pine trees dotted the rough landscape, scattered with boulders of all sizes. Some were piled high, creating caves for any who sought shelter. The ground was more sand and dirt than not, but still allowed for sparser shrubbery and ground plants. The terrain was harsher and the environment tougher than other areas of Alandria. Hal wasn't sure how much was actually left in Alandria that was its old self, full of thick forests and green, lively foliage. The fear of what his mother had been doing or what she'd been a part of in this land he loved choked him and brought a pain to his chest. How could he not have seen it sooner? Rheina had, this he was certain of, but why had she waited so long to clue him in? His sister was nothing but secretive and closed off until she needn't be. There was more to his sister than he had been aware. He realized she was carrying a burden he knew nothing about, and that he could do nothing to help her. One thing he did know, he would do whatever he could now to serve Alandria and help his realm survive no matter what the cost. That would be his burden to bear. Even in this area, a place he didn't know much about, he was able to find beauty.

The more he thought about it, the more he realized he'd always had a soft spot in his heart for the Shifters. He thought their gifts from Alandria were fascinating. He would give anything to be able to shift his appearance just once to know what it truly felt like. How could he help Chel? He wondered. As he ran through his thoughts, he considered he did have knowledge and firsthand information from those he knew who shared openly with him. In fact, he'd even assisted in several of the young Shifters' first changes. But Samuel was correct, Hal could never know what Chel was going through personally. He could never be there for her like one of her own kind could walk her through her changes. Did he even want to? Something in him was drawn to her and he wasn't sure what to make of that. Perhaps he simply found her charismatic personality and joy for life enchanting and a breath of fresh air to be around. Alandria needed more like that, like her. So he did hope she would stay... Then his thoughts turned darker. His face scrunched in a concerned frown. He hoped he could keep her alive. War was coming and they weren't nearly prepared as they should be. Hal could help with that. After all, he was the son of the Paladin and one of the elite Ferrishyn guards; he had been preparing for this all his life. He could feel it in his bones.

Chapter Six

After several hours of walking through and around narrow paths, piles, and hills, Chel, Samuel, and Hal reached a dead end. The path suddenly ended in a rise of boulders standing tall in front of them like a giant wall.

"Well, that was unexpected," Chel said, a frown marring her face. She stood and scrutinized the boulders, trying to make sense of the monotony of color and texture. "Did you take us the wrong way?" she asked Samuel, hands on her hips. *What was with this path?*

"Nope, stay close," was all he said before he jumped up on one boulder, expecting her to follow him with a playful smirk.

Chel looked to Hal who was also examining the boulders with curiosity. A wall of boulders several stories high loomed before them. Big rocks the size of mortal cars fit snuggly with smaller boulders of various sizes, creating jutted out ledges like a stairway for giants. He shrugged his shoulders and then jumped up behind Samuel, but he didn't miss a beat in reaching his hand down for Chel to assist her up. She gratefully took his hand, smiling sweetly as she regained her footing. "Thanks, but I could've done that myself. Shifter, remember?" she winked at him playfully.

"I know," Hal said with a smile.

They climbed several boulder rows high then Samuel ducked behind one and didn't come out the other side.

"Well that's clever," Chel mused as she continued to follow after him. "Watch your step, Hal, there are loose rocks on this part." She gestured to the ground she had just traversed across.

"Thanks, but I could have done that myself. Ferrishyn, remember?" he countered.

"Haha, point taken," Chel conceded.

"It is friendly to offer assistance and care for another is it not?" Hal asked genuinely.

"It is, you are right," Chel replied. She quirked her head with a slight frown, thinking over her words, "Gah, now I'm starting to lose my contractions. Is that part of Alandria's magic, to take away all contractions from our speech?"

"Yes! It is part of our nefarious plan to adopt you into our world further," Hal retorted.

"Seriously?" Chel's mouth gaped and her eyes widened.

Hal barked out a hearty laugh. "No, of course not. You just can't help yourself when you're surrounded by such handsome warriors to emulate everything about them you can." He winked at her. "In fact, most in Alandria speak more formally. So I am not surprised some of it rubs off on you. I recall Kaeleigh doing some of the same." Hal's expression suddenly tightened. "Shall we? I believe your... Samuel is waiting on the other side for us."

Chel peered around the boulder Samuel had just climbed over. She could see Samuel just a short ways ahead of them, climbing over another set of boulders. "Yes, I suppose you're right." Chel hesitated then sighed with resignation. Her face fell and Chel's gaze covered the ground beneath her feet.

Chel could feel the warmth of Hal's presence before she realized he had moved closer to her. He reached out and lifted her chin so her eyes were level—or somewhat more level—with his. His warm hazel eyes searched hers.

"What is it, Chel? Are you all right?"

"What if..." she turned her eyes away from his and looked back where they had just come from, taking a deep breath. "What if they don't accept me? You know, because I haven't shifted yet or because I lived in the mortal realm all these years or because... well, just because they don't!" she blurted, her eyes welling up. Chel tried to hide her embarrassment and wiped her eyes.

"You're kidding right?" Hal's eyebrows raised in surprise.

Chel shook her head. "No, of course I'm not!"

"Chel, hey, you are one of the toughest people *not* to like and, believe me, I've tried," Hal teased. "Honestly, you have a lot to bring to this race, to *your* people. You will expose them to different perspectives than many of them will be used to. Sure there may be an adjustment period, but they will love you—it would be insane for them not to." Then laughing, "You can always come vagabonding with me if they don't. I have an open door policy." He winked, but his joke made her chuckle.

"Thank you, Halister. That means a lot to me." She gave him a genuine smile. Chel raised her chin and straightened her shoulders. With a calming breath, she was ready to face whatever was behind the next boulder. For all she knew it was a maze of more boulders, but either way she was ready.

"Plus your parents are waiting for you, and I'm sure have told the entire tribe all about you," he added.

"My parents! Yes, let's go." Chel bounced back as if never down, energized by the thought of seeing her parents. She grabbed Hal's hand and pulled him after her as she rounded the boulder looking for Samuel.

On the other side of the boulder was a short and ill-lit tunnel. Thankfully the light on the other side was just enough to guide them out of the semi-darkness quickly. After the last "adventure" through all the dark tunnels and caves they had gone, Chel was glad for the change. Stretching her hands out, she could feel both sides of the tunnel with each hand; the stones a polished, smooth texture beneath each one. Closing her eyes, she inhaled fresh air rushing past her from the other side. The air was sweet, filled with the luscious fragrance of blooming flowers of some kind. Reaching out with her senses that continued to get stronger and more sensitive, she could hear the sound of water splashing, children playing in the distance, and some gruff voices that seemed to be arguing. Though they were still too far away to distinguish individual words, she was close enough to recognize one voice in particular.

"Dad! I can hear my dad's voice." Chel beamed, her eyes flew open and she started to take off only to be stopped by Samuel at the entrance—or exit depending which way you were headed through. Confused and annoyed, she stopped. Why would he stand in her way? She placed her hands on her hips, cocked an eyebrow, and waited for an explanation.

"Just wait. There are guards on either side of this entrance and wouldn't hesitate to stop you if you don't know the proper way to get inside." Samuel watched her process his words, meeting her at eye level with a command of seriousness she couldn't ignore.

"After you," Chel snarled impatiently, gesturing him with her hands to lead the way. Even though in her heart and mind she was offering him another hand gesture that meant something entirely different.

"Thank you," Samuel replied. "Wait here. I'm going to inform the guards we have guests and gain you entrance." He went through the tunnel, calling out to someone unseen.

"You behaved," Hal spoke, a hint of sarcasm in his tone to which Chel grunted. "You were thinking of a different gesture though were you not?" he chuckled at her as he walked up beside her and nudged her toward the opening.

"You caught me," she shrugged. "How do you read me so well?" Chel asked looking up at him, curiosity shining in her eyes, wondering how he read her so well.

"It's a gift," Hal said with a hint of snark.

"Like a real one? Because I never know with you guys. I haven't figured out all your abilities and what magic others can do yet here in Alandria."

"If you mean can I hear your thoughts, then no. That is not a gift I possess." He turned suddenly in towards her and leaned his head down inches away from her own. "But with you, I can read more than one might think was acceptable. Perhaps I am simply a good observer of people and beings, perhaps I see everything about you, notice all your moves, and see everything you don't want people to see because I *see* you." Hal backed away just as quickly as he had appeared. Chel began to breathe more heavily and more slowly. The tunnel felt too small; she needed air.

Just then Samuel returned. "Okay, come on, we've been cleared to enter."

"Right behind you," Hal said and followed Samuel, leaving Chel for a moment to herself.

"He did that on purpose, didn't he? Probably to distract me so I wasn't nervous about meeting the Shifters. There's no way a guy like him would really be attracted to me... nah. Plus there's Samuel. I'm not exactly sure where we stand, but I can't believe he lied to me. If I'm honest with myself, our relationship wasn't what I wanted it to be in the mortal realm before I left. Oh Chel you've created a bit of a mess with this one," Chel mumbled to herself, shaking her head and walking out the tunnel entrance into the territory of the Shifters.

CHAPTER SEVEN

"Welcome to Mandü tré Lan!" A loud voice boomed as they climbed down from the tunnel entrance. The climb down was a longer journey than the trek up they had just made prior to entering the tunnel. The three eager travelers saw rocks, boulders, and stone everywhere they looked. In the middle lay a small lake filled by a tall waterfall pouring from the adjacent mountain edge, a run off of the nearby vast Shadow Ridge Mountains. Hal and Chel had traveled the base of part of those mountains on their way before they met up with Samuel, and something was not quite right about those mountains, something dark. They had given Chel the heebie jeebies as they passed them, though no harm came to them.

"You must be Chel!" The voice boomed again. A large man, one of the tallest and widest Chel had ever seen, stepped confidently out from behind the waterfall. His dark hair was cut short to his head, his cheekbones and jaw were strong like a Viking, but his eyes were welcoming enough. Not a trace of unease came off him. "I am Landon Wasel. We have been waiting for you."

"You have?" Chel asked. He was a Paul Bunyan type, made of pure muscle and looked like he could take down anyone or anything. "How did you know we were coming?" She looked to Hal for a reaction, but saw none.

"We have eyes all along our borders. They saw you a day back and Samuel offered to go find you and lead you here," he explained.

"Oh, well, thank you," Chel fumbled with her words. She wasn't sure what to think.

"Chel!" came the cry of two voices she knew well. Her mother pushed passed the large man with her father just after her, and made their way to their daughter. Chel broke into a run before she could think straight into her mother's arms, resting in both her and her father's embrace as he joined in. Tears freely fell down her face and she buried her head in joy at being reunited with the people she loved best. Everything she had held in and everything that had happened to her since she left and even before then all came spewing forth in one great rupture of emotion. Chel couldn't help but think of their last encounter in Montana when she first discovered her family had been hiding information about who they were—about who she was—and she had been so angry with them. She hadn't seen them since.

"I'm so sorry, Mom... Dad. I didn't tell you I was leaving... then I was afraid I'd never see you again," she hiccuped a few times, and her words grew tight in her throat.

"No, Chel," her mother's soft voice soothed. Her mom took her chin in her gentle hands and guided her gaze upward. "Chel, we are the ones who are sorry. We didn't prepare you as we should have. We thought we were protecting you, and giving you what was normal in your world, but instead we failed you."

"And we were not honest with you when we should have been many years ago," her father added with a glimmer of tears in his own eyes. "I thought we might have lost you. You and Kaeleigh knew nothing of this world. If something would have happened to you... I don't know... I..." her father choked on his words and pulled her tighter in his embrace once again.

"It's all right, Dad. I'm all right. I missed you both." Chel squeezed back tight then pulled back. "But I can't breathe anymore, guys." Chel laughed and pulled away from the group hug, wiping her face with the same mannerisms her parents used. It was so good to be among her family. At that, her mother furrowed her brow, searching for something.

"Where is Kaeleigh? We owe her an apology as well."

"She's not with us. We have a lot to catch you up on." Chel noted her mother's horrified expression and expounded further. "I mean, she's still with us, just not *with* us. She's on a different mission with Finn and others. She's all right though." Chel smiled. Thinking about Kaeleigh hurt her chest, she missed her and hoped they were truly all right. Chel could tell her parents had more questions about Kaeleigh, but were willing to wait for answers. "Oh! But Mom and Dad, I want to introduce you to my friend who has traveled with me here and kept me safe," she pulled Halister forward who had sheepishly stayed a little distant. "This is Halister." She turned to Hal and spoke to him, "Hal, this is my father, Rayalt—but you can call him Ray—and my mother, Lilane." Chel smiled like she had just brought a unified force together, but the vibes coming from the strangers in the room were anything but that. She assumed there might be some initial hesitation, but not outright hostility toward Hal. He smiled unaffected and stuck out his hand.

Her father was quick to shake it and gave Hal a sharp nod. "Thank you for keeping my girl safe and bringing her back to us." He then turned to Samuel. "Samuel, thank you for guiding them here safely as well." His words were sincere, but his tone was guarded.

It was no secret to Chel that her parents hadn't loved her relationship with Sam. Now Chel wondered if they had known his secret all along as well. She would have to ask them about that sometime.

Next her mother inclined her head to Hal, and reached for his hand as well. "You can call me Lil," she said with a sweet smile.

Chel was proud that her parents either didn't ascribe to the same feelings the others had toward Hal or they had been gone long enough they didn't really know who he—or his family—was in Alandria.

"Well, come on then." Ray beckoned them to follow him. "Landon, is there a place we can speak with our daughter and her friend before briefing the entire tribe?"

"Of course, Rayalt, you may use the meeting hall. I will make sure it is cleared to ensure you some privacy. Please let me know what service I can provide for you and your family while you are here." Landon looked every bit put out—though his words were accommodating—as Chel was uncomfortable. Everyone watched her move to follow Landon and her parents. Her mom and dad were so cute holding hands but when they reached back to hold hers as well, she felt they truly were once again a unified front.

Landon led them into a large opening, which appeared to be an entrance to a cave with more large boulders stacked up high and purposely around it; a small system of caves within a small hillside.

Chel hesitated. "What is this place?"

"This is the main cave; the place where we hang out, the large dining hall and kitchens, meeting rooms, and bunk rooms," Samuel explained. "It's pretty cool right?"

"Sure." Chel wasn't so sure though. The idea of being under a hill of boulders didn't sound reassuring to her. But she followed the group down a short tunnel into what looked like a fairly normal room—except for the compacted dirt walls complete with rocks and stones of different sizes.

"Will this do?" Landon asked as he led them into a large meeting room complete with tables and chairs tucked snugly into them. The room was sparse as far as décor went, but its function as a meeting room was obvious.

"Yes, thank you," Rayalt replied nodding to Landon. He ushered his family to one of the tables and they sat. Hal stepped to the side as they did so.

"I will leave you. I have a matter to attend to. Samuel will accompany me and I will return to check on you." Landon walked out the room without further words and gestured to Samuel with his head to follow him.

Chel, anxious to dive straight in the moment the group was alone, leaned forward conspiratorially. "So you already know *who* Kaeleigh is then, right?" Chel asked her parents in whispered rush. "I don't need to rehash all that, right?"

Chel's mom studied her shoes and her dad averted his eyes but then looked at her straight on. "Yes, we do. We kept it from her and you for her own protection. Plus we made a promise to her mother."

Chel's mom's face fell in sadness. "Her mother was a good friend, I miss her very much. Is she... is Kaeleigh angry with us?"

"I think she was, but she understands why now. I think we are all pretty much ready to move past all the secrets kept about the past, though I'm sure Kae's going to ask you for an explanation. She hasn't met anyone that will tell her much about her mom actually. I know she'd love to hear firsthand what she was like from you." Chel paused. She wasn't sure where to go next in conversation with so many questions and so much information spinning in her head. Then it just came out. "She got to see her. Kaeleigh, I mean, she got to speak with her mother."

Lilane raised her eyebrows at Chel, confused by her statement. "What do you mean? That isn't—

"In the In Between. It's a long story, but Kaeleigh was there for a time while Hunter, her grandfather, performed some kind of unwarding ritual. Her mom intercepted the magic during the ritual for a chance to see Kaeleigh, I guess." Chel cocked her head, trying to recall as much of the memory as she could. "I'm a little fuzzy on the details of that one because it all happened fast and was quite intense."

"That is almost unbelievable," Chel's mom started, "But if anyone could do it, it would be Eva. She was an amazing person in life." Her eyes welled up and a smile worked its way across her face. Though clearly she still faced grief from the loss, knowing Kaeleigh had had some encounter with her wonderful friend brought her joy too.

"What else, Chel?" Her dad was back to business. "We need all the information and to know where you've been so we can know what's to come. Why did you come here? Obviously it wasn't because you were searching for us. But what is this 'mission' you mentioned earlier?"

Chel had so much on her mind to tell her parents she didn't know where to begin and had to think through what all she could tell them at this stage. Chel and Hal had promised not to mention the Ehsmia unless necessary since they were still in hiding, but probably not for much longer with all that could be transpiring in Alandria.

"Sir, if I may?" Hal began, stepping out from the shadows where he had tried to give them family space to catch up. "You know who I am I gather. I assume you also know who my parents are." He waited anxiously as they nodded their heads. "My mother is out of control. The fact is she's actually *under* the control of an evil mad woman, a woman who is holding the Orchids' souls hostage in Exhile. She must be stopped. They both must be stopped. Kaeleigh and my brother in arms, Daegan, are on a quest to find a way to free the Orchids." He paused at their surprised intake of breath. "Our other companions, Finn and Ella, are set to go to the secret realm of the Twined called Tylínyth. We have only separated to find allies that will stand with us and prepare for the battle that is coming to Alandria. We have come to intercede with the Shifters." Hal paced forward, stalking invisible prey as his voice rose in confidence. "Alandria is dying. Her life essence is being sucked dry, but we don't know how yet. My mother is behind it all... it is unforgivable what she has done." Hal's gaze shot up with a steeled fierceness Chel hadn't seen there before—this was part of the warrior everyone claimed him to be, but she hadn't seen it yet amidst all his playfulness. "It is my vow to free Alandria from Mother's dark intentions and stand against her if need be. My sister and I have already separated ourselves from the Paladin. We will be part of the solution to saving this land. We are looking for those who will fight with us. We journeyed to Mandü tré Lan to see if any would join us. After all, this world belongs to us all." Finished with his speech, Hal lowered his head and stepped back, awaiting words any would give him.

Landon, suddenly standing in the rough entry of the room, stepped forward. Chel had not heard his approach during Hal's speech. Landon's arms were crossed and his body stiff, his violet eyes harsh and impossible to read. "You need to understand—you are not wanted here. You will not be welcomed here by many because of your family position. They have opposed the Shifters for too long."

Hal's eyes flinched, hurt by one interpretation, surprised by another. He chose to keep himself as unreadable as possible. "Actually—" was all he managed to speak but was halted by Landon's hand, who gestured him to wait.

"I understand and have heard reports of the connections and assistance you have had to many Shifters despite the stance from Elnye that Shifters are less than other Alandrians. For that, I am grateful to you. However, it does not change the consensus among us. I am sorry." Landon held Hal's gaze, but did not back down in his determination that the Shifters would not welcome him.

"I understand," Hal spoke quietly, nodded his head, and stepped back into the shadows of the meeting room built into the stone of their surroundings.

"Well, I don't. That's bull… crap!" Chel jumped up from the table where she had been watching everything intently. "Hal has saved me and others many times. He doesn't deserve to be ostracized because of who is mother is. He should get a fair chance to prove himself just like anyone should be able to." Her fists were tight and her face looked like she was about to explode. The skin on her forearms rippled again like they did back when they first met up with Samuel. The change was fresh under her skin, not quite ready to surface just yet, but she could tell she was close.

"Chel," Hal started, "it is all right. We'll figure something out. Right now you need to focus on your breathing. Relax your wolf."

"No, it isn't, Hal." She closed her eyes and took in a deep breath, then slowly released it allowing the calm he had taught her to find to wash over her from her head to her toes.

"Chel," her mother quietly spoke under her breath. But Chel raised her hand asking her mother to give her a moment.

Opening her eyes once more as the ripples subsided across her arms, she took one more breath and then stared directly into the tribal leader's eyes. "If this is how the Shifters treat people here in Alandria, then they are just as bad as the rest of them. I don't want any part of it." Fists on her hips, she didn't dare a glance at her parents.

"She's right." Ray said coming to her rescue. He stood up and moved to her side, facing Landon, then joined by her mother on the other side. "That's not how the Shifters used to stand with each other and for the beings of Alandria. Last I remember, everyone was working hard to create a unified Alandria, to stand with each other for the good of one another and for the realm."

"And how did that turn out, Rayalt? Not so good for any of Alandria, but especially the Shifters," Landon growled under his breath. "We have been under such persecution, it is a wonder we have survived this long. The accords fell apart. Royalty was murdered. You left the Shifters," he accused. "You have no idea what has happened since then. You no longer have a say in the leadership of this tribe. You abandoned your people." Though Landon's voice barely rose, the underlying anger was palpable. The fact that his eyes began to blaze with a heated orange glow, only made his presence more fearful.

"You know why I left," Ray growled. "Hope for our future was protected. She is here now, and might be the only factor that helps save Alandria. That was my destiny to follow. What happened here with the Shifters is horrendously regrettable, but my leaving did not cause it. Anyway, now we have a chance to make it right. But we only have a very small window of time to do so. Isn't that what you and all the Shifters want? To make it right for the future of Alandria, for their families?" Ray waited, allowing Landon to simmer down before he went into full change mode. One degree angrier and Landon would erupt into whatever creature lay beneath his skin. "Landon," Ray beseeched, "Those accords are still our desire, the unification of Alandria and her people. If we don't, Alandria dies. And worse, so do we." Then in a softer tone, "It might not be right now, but it would come to pass eventually. You know it. Even if we all here were to escape to the mortal realm, our magic allowing us to be who we are, that is, to shift, would become increasingly limited and eventually we would die out. We would all die out."

Breathing in through his nose, his jaw clenched and his teeth ground as he held his temper barely in check. Once his breath released, some sense had come over Landon and his beast subsided for the moment. The tension in his face a visible indication he was not happy about what he was about to say.

"Fine. He can stay, but he is on his own. I cannot stand for him and will not protect him from the tribe. They must choose for themselves if they will hear him out." Finished with his piece, Landon stalked out of the meeting room.

"He's really special, isn't he?" Chel said baffled, as she watched him walk away.

"You, didn't need to do that," Hal whispered from behind them.

Chel whipped around. "Of course we did. It was the right thing to do." She examined his eyes, noting they were a deeper hazel, more brown then usual. Something else surfaced in his eyes, perhaps a heart-felt sincerity he had rarely felt, but Chel couldn't be sure. Had he rarely had anyone stand by him as they did? Could he be as lost as she felt?

"Landon was out of line," Lilane chimed in. "He may be the leader of the Shifters, but I'm concerned about the state they are all in as a result." She worried the neckline of her shirt, her brows pinched in concern.

"He is doing what he thinks is best for the tribe. Any leader would stand up for his people, but I fear he has become too narrow-sighted for the coming battle. I hope his stubbornness does not jeopardize their safety," Chel's dad wondered out loud.

"I appreciate your stance," Hal thanked Rayalt. "However, I am concerned I have caused problems for your family by being here. Therefore, I will leave at first light."

"The hell you will!" Chel exclaimed, outraged. "You are Hal-freaking-Endíl, warrior extraordinaire! *You* don't run away from challenges. You are supposed to be here. We have a plan. How can I accomplish it without you?"

Hal shuffled his feet and seemed much more like a lost child in that moment than the soldier-leader he was. But then he slowly raised his head. His eyes twinkled in unison as a boyish grin began to stretch across his face. "Warrior extraordinaire? I like that. Well, that and as you said it, I'm 'Hal-freaking-Endíl' because you're right, I am." Puffing his chest out, he raised his chin and stood tall. He was surprised how much her words and their stance had moved him.

Chel laughed which she supposed was the purpose in his great show, to help alleviate the tension left in the wake of Landon Wasel, head Shifter. She then turned on her father, her eyes squinted up tight as she tried to imagine him in a role other than father. "Landon said you had a say in the leadership of the tribe and that they were 'your people.' What were you to the Shifters, Dad?"

Ray looked at his daughter with love and pride. "I was their Chieftain, what's known in the mortal realm romance novels as the alpha—I think your mother described them to me once." He winked at Lilane.

Chel would have spit out her drink if she had one, but instead nearly choked on her own tongue. "What?! You were their leader? That I did not see coming." She looked to her mother and pretended to whisper though she knew her father could hear her, "Was he any good at it?"

Her mother laughed. There was nothing more beautiful to Chel than when her mom laughed. Her eyes sparkled and anyone whose spirit was down would instantly feel uplifted. Chel smiled. She had missed her mom more than she realized. "He was very good at it, Daughter."

"You're biased, my dear," Ray reached for her wrist and pulled her playfully against his chest, leaning in to kiss her neck. Chel loved the way her parents loved each other. It was so romantic, but more—it was a love built on friendship and commitment and as such was strong and true and would stand against all the tests. She knew she wanted that for herself. That's why she never truly committed to any of the guys she had dated, even with Samuel she knew there wasn't a strong future—so why did she stay with him? Perhaps she was simply looking for it, but hadn't found it yet, that special connection between two people that conquered everything else. Perhaps she was afraid of being alone.

"Ok you two, I bet you could use some food and rest after your journey to get here," Lilane said as she pushed out of Ray's hold. He pulled her back to him once more and planted a big kiss right on her lips, loud and playful for all to hear.

"You two get a room," Chel laughed as she headed toward the door they had entered. She glanced at Hal and caught a wistfulness in his eyes. Something pinched in her chest. He probably hadn't seen much of that growing up and yet he carried a great potential for it if he ever chose to settle down. Though Chel didn't know if he could. Hal was a wild spirit like her, but where she welcomed it, he used it to push others away.

"Your relationship is refreshing," Hal acknowledged out loud with a growing smile. "It is good to see."

Done with the deep thinking, Chel realized she was famished. "Come on, let's get some grub folks. You wouldn't believe the things I've been eating out here. I hope the Shifters have as good of food as the E... um faeries did." Chel stopped just in time. After all, they didn't know who was listening. Hal gave her a nod of understanding and approval at her catch. Although, most believed the *hidden people*—or the Ehsmia—to be legend and not true at all so they'd most likely think she was crazy. Still she changed the subject as quickly as she could. "Did you hear my stomach just growl? It sounded like a beast ready to devour some poor unsuspecting critter... wait, do Shifters do that?"

Hal barked out a laugh behind her. The sound and timber of his laugh sent delicious chills down her back. What she wouldn't do to be able to make him laugh like that all the time. It sent a rush through her to be able to accomplish such a feat. Not that he didn't laugh much on his own, but this was a genuine deep laugh straight from the gut that brought surprise and hope with it. She liked it. Frowning at her sudden train of thought, Chel ran smack into the edge of a wall opening into another room. She hadn't paid attention to her path.

"Ow!" She covered her face with her hand.

"Are you all right, Chel?" Hal gripped her elbow with one hand and brought his other around to her back.

"Yes," she said muffled through her fingers. "I think I just rearranged my face."

"Oh, Chel, you're not usually so clumsy. Let me get you some ice," her mother said as she shot off into another opening that looked to house aged kitchen supplies.

"Come sit down, pumpkin," her dad reached for her other elbow and directed her over to a chair, pulling her out of Hal's grip. Being parents they had been watching the interactions between their daughter and the Ferrishyn warrior accompanying her, not sure yet what to make of him in regards to their only child.

Chel let go of her face, making sure she wasn't bleeding anywhere. "That's going to leave a mark, isn't it?" She tilted her head toward her dad for him to see.

Ray smoothed his finger gently down the bridge of her nose, "Only a little one." He winked at her and brought her in for a hug as she nursed her wound. "You're a Shifter, Chel, you heal fairly quickly if you hadn't noticed already."

Chel smiled. "Oh you're right!" The thought had crossed her mind and it explained so much. "Remember that time I flew off the swing set in second grade and gashed up my leg on a stick? I thought for sure I would need stitches! But, no. You just put a Band-Aid on it, and it was fine the next day."

"Yes, exactly. Thankfully it was just the one neighbor who saw it, so no one ever asked questions," her mother added, bringing over a glass of water for both her and Halister.

"Thank you," Halister politely acknowledged.

Her mother then moved over to Chel and caressed the side of her daughter's face and then kissed her on the head. "Food is coming. I'm not sure what they have to offer, but the woman in the kitchen said she'd have something brought out for you."

As if on cue, Chel's stomach grumbled again, sending everyone into another bout of laughter.

Chapter Eight

Outside Adettlyn. The Territory of Lumari.

Having left Ehsmia by himself, Aidón took great precautions sneaking soundlessly through the forest on his way back to Adettlyn. Everyone thought he was dead—everyone, and this would be his primary advantage. "Challenging" had been an understatement when he had to leave Kaeleigh and her friends. After traveling with them for some time and getting to know them, he had developed a fond affection for them, especially his great-niece, Kaeleigh. The fact that they had been able to release him from his wards and restore him to his former self had been a triumph in love and an eye-opening experience into Kaeleigh's power as she continued to grow into them. Aidón hoped Kaeleigh and the others were safe and well on their own missions. He knew this next part of his journey he would have to begin on his own as he sought out his own connections and allies within Adettlyn.

Aidón had been placed as the king-in-fact of the territory of Lumari in his brother Ryek's stead when Ryek went into hiding under the alias "Hunter." Unfortunately, Aidón's reign lasted a short time when his son, Syén rose up against him; his son attempted but did not succeed in killing Aidón, whereas he did with Syén's mother. Aidón fled for a period of time. He was aided by his brother Ryek/Hunter with his exceptional skills in magic to glamour and began to live again. Until he was caught by Maleina's men and imprisoned for stirring up "trouble" in one of their towns—all the while they were none the wiser to who they had captured. Everyone believing he was dead might enable him to sneak through Adettlyn unrecognized, though he could don a glamour much like the one he carried for many years, he preferred not to change his appearance too much having just found himself once more after all those years.

Memories occupied his mind as he continued to venture unseen through a rarely traveled part of the forest. He did not have far to travel from the place he exited Ehsmia—the magic let those leaving exit at various places to confuse any onlookers but also to aid them in their journey.

Aidón had slept the night in a tree to remain hidden and above ground, but his legs and back cramped from that choice. As he rubbed the back of his neck, trying to work out the soreness there, he heard a rustling. He paused and listened carefully. Again, he heard the noise. Surprised anyone would be so noisy in such a secluded place, he remained cautious yet curious and drew closer. Aidón stopped, the thought passing through his head that whatever was making the noise could be in order to lure him into a trap. Tall and thin aiding his ability to hide, Aidón stepped behind a tree hoping to stay out of the line of sight as he slowly moved closer.

More rustling. The branches of a tree ahead clearly bowed and leaves fell to the ground. Aidón furrowed his brow and squinted. *What could this be?* He wondered silently. The man stepped forward from one tree to the next until he was directly across from the noisy, leaf-shedding tree. He spotted a flash of white between the leaves. Then a moment later, the white moved in front of a larger opening and he gasped in disbelief.

"Hello?" Aidón whispered cautiously. "I mean you no harm," he added. He waited, but the creature did not stir.

Stepping out from behind the tree boldly, Aidón bowed low in the full sight of the creature he knew he'd seen. He knew the creature had no reason to trust him, but he hoped that he would.

"I am honored by your presence. I truly mean you no harm," he tried again.

Aidón was looking at a creature who appeared only on the rarest occasions—a mystic owl. The mystic owls were a race of Shifters which were said to have been wiped out many years ago, yet one perched proudly right before his eyes. The bird was unnaturally large, set with a pair of knowing, watchful eyes. Most were light in color. This one was no exception, covered with white, tan, and lighter brown feathers. The owl tilted his head to the side, sizing up Aidón—unafraid and nonplussed.

"I thought your kind were no more, gone from this realm," Aidón whispered half in awe, half astonished he would see one of the noble creatures. "What are you doing here?" Aidón was curious, the owls hadn't been seen in decades—at least not to his knowledge since he had been in prison for many of them. It was even rare that the owl shifted into human form, being much more owl than not. Myths and legends had been created about them as mysterious and rare as they were, especially since it had been discovered their race was wiped out... but perhaps not all, Aidón wondered if there were more of them, if the story was indeed a ruse to protect them.

"Please, your grace" Aidón addressed the owl, "if you could not mention my presence to anyone. I am searching for information and seeking allies to aid in Alandria's plight for freedom from the growing darkness." Aidón looked to the ground, his heart heavy with sadness. Every time he shared the truth about Alandria, his heart sunk a little more.

The owl tilted its head the other direction and resettled on the branch. Its big round eyes, responded to Aidón's words with intelligent sadness. Aidón wondered if this one would speak to him.

"You are one of the mystic owls. I have not encountered one of your kind in quite some time. I am full of hope that enough of you have survived and will grow in order to one day return to Alandria in full force." The thought occurred to him that the owl and even others might be hiding as well. "I hope we all can live to see an Alandria where the darkness has been eliminated." Aidón paused and watched the owl absorb his words. "I am honored to be in your presence. I am Aidón Sayaelíth, once of the proud lineage of rulers within Adettlyn—though my son has made a mockery of our name. It is my desire if more of your kind are here, that you would fight on behalf of Alandria and her survival. Join us as we face Maleina and the darkness she is raising in Alandria."

The owl ruffled its feathers and cocked its head back and forth, seeming to understand but certainly not speaking. In fact, the owl made no noises at all. Aidón waited for the mystic owl for a moment longer, but realized now was not the time he would communicate if he would at all. Aidón took his leave.

"Thank you for allowing me to be in your presence. Now I will be on my way. I must see what is left of my kingdom." Aidón turned around in order to slip away into hiding once again and head onto his beloved Adettlyn.

"Wait," came a creaky voice, one that clearly had not been used in some time.

Aidón, incredulous, spun around and faced the place the owl had been, the place that now rustled even more loudly behind a canopy of thick leaves. Where there had been a creature, a man now crouched on the branch. A fully grown adult male, pale-complected with light brown-red hair flopping in his face. The man watched every move Aidón made. His clothes were tattered remnants of what had once been a nice linen shirt and pants. His bare feet clung to the branch, all ten toes curled around to help him keep his balance. In no way did he represent the once regal race of creatures, Aidón realized, yet he possessed depth and insight he was sure. Aidón inclined his head as was appropriate to bid the creature to speak.

The Shifter opened his mouth again, then closed it, frowning. He cleared his throat and tried again.

"It has been many cycles of the sun—too many to count—since I have spoken, forgive me," the man-owl said, his voice still gravelly though gaining clarity and strength with each word uttered. "Not many of us are left." He paused, a great weight settling upon his shoulders as he contemplated what that truly meant. Emotion filled his eyes, but he swallowed and shook his head. His eyes met Aidón's and he steeled his spine, flattening his back into a complete upright posture. "You are the king of this territory?"

"I was for a short time and I will be once more," Aidón declared confidently, unconsciously straightening his own shoulders, back, and chin.

The owl observed him for who he was, easily able to see through the man's glamour. "Indeed you are." The owl acknowledged and inclined his head in response. "Those who are left, those who can, we will aid Alandria in her fight for freedom. She sheltered and saved us from complete annihilation when all seemed lost." Again the owl became choked up but he did not break eye contact with Aidón. "We will come to your aid. You need only to send a signal and we will find you."

Aidón fell to his knees humbly grateful. "Thank you. It is my vow to you, I will do what it is in my power to aid your people and see them restored to their former glory."

"We ask nothing in return," the owl said as stood up from his crouched position on the branch.

"It is my desire. What are you called? What is your name?" Aidón asked. He sensed his time was coming to an end with the Shifter.

"I am called Chetenôrth but you, Sire, may call me Chet." With that Chet transformed from man back into the owl right before Aidón's eyes, and took flight. Aidón watched in awe, unable to stop a single tear from escaping. Alandria still held beauty and mystery, despite the darkness that sought to repress it. The great owl rose higher in the sky and instead of growing smaller on the horizon, he simply vanished leaving a faint shimmer of transformation magic lingering in the air.

"I look forward to seeing you and your friends in action, Chet. Thank you," Aidón spoke quietly into the forest. He was now alone to continue his journey.

Chapter Nine

A idón reached the edge of the forest, which had kept him concealed on his journey. He checked his glamour, ensuring no one would recognize him. He had been gone so many years that he wasn't sure he would even need it, but knew it was better to err on the side of mystery.

The trees thinned out as he drew close to the other side of the Kandrian Mountain which rose behind the castle. The castle at Adettlyn was situated with the mountain at its back, Lake Ary'th at its front, and the southern tributary from the River of Rancier at its side. The trees in this part of the forest thinned then thickened again, on and off, creating challenges for sneaking in unseen. His best way to enter unseen would be to the south, sneaking in from the back of the castle; still guarded though not as heavily as the front—at least at last visit. For this reason, he would wait and assess his options from a distance. Once the cover of darkness fell and it looked safe, he would make his move. Luckily for Aidón he was aware of the secret entrance in the stone wall the servants used for quick exits or to get to the river via a shorter route than all the way around the front side.

Aidón admired the castle he had once called home from his waiting position. The castle was much larger than the one in Elnye, complete with turrets and spires. Large stones gave structure to it, as most castles did, but this one was fused together with branches and vines snaking throughout the walls—it was quite impressive. It hadn't changed much since he had left... or had it? He noticed something strange as he looked out the corner of his eye. A shimmering edge caught his gaze. His mind now focused on this strange glimmer, he looked at the castle from different directions, trying to decipher just what he was looking at. The thought dawned on him at once—his castle was under a glamour. But why? Aidón trained his eye on the castle, looking at it, beyond it, and through it simultaneously. Calling on his magic, he funneled it through his eyes and pushed it out toward the castle. No one else would be the wiser.

Aidón already on his knees, sunk further, his chest collapsed, shoulders following suit. His mouth agape in horrified awe at what he saw before him; it could not be truth, yet his soul within him confirmed it was.

The castle at Adettlyn was practically in ruin. The land surrounding it had taken on a brownish, sickly hue. Dried grasses and withering climbs of ivy had overgrown iron gates now rusted and falling from their hinges. Stones had crumbled to the ground, leaving gaping holes in sections of wall. The overall appearance was inflicted with devastation and despair; it was sad and bleeding energy. His home had been destroyed, its former glory and life crumbling and covered in an inky darkness that molded and decayed the very essence of life that flowed through the walls of Adettlyn. His heart broke at the sight. He never would have imagined his son would allow such a thing to happen to his home, the place Syén grew up and loved. As the leader and protector, Syén was charged with the upkeep of the castle. Aidón had been gone too long.

He had to stop it. He had to stop his son.

At twilight, his magic grew less powerful. As an Elf, Aidón drew his energy from the sun and from the moons, which is why his power waned in that period during which the sun was setting and the moons had not yet risen. The same applied in the early hours of the morning. He sat and got comfortable in his spot in the bushes until he felt ready. He knew he would need all the magical energy he could draw upon. Since Kaeleigh had freed him from his prison both externally and internally, he had grown stronger moving closer to his full potential, but he knew waiting for the extra boost from the moons would be the wise thing to do. He just had to be patient, then he would be at full strength once more because before meeting Syén he wanted to make sure he was strong—it would most likely be the fight of his life... again.

Once the two moons had risen high in the Alandrian night sky, Aidón felt rejuvenated and ready to take on the world, or at least his small part of it. He needed to get inside his castle and discover the source of the tragedy that had befallen Adettlyn castle. His gut told him Syén had something to do with it.

Sneaking parallel to the wall through the forest's edge, he got as close as he could to the secret entrance. It was invisible to the naked eye, though if one knew which stones to press, they would be granted entrance through a veiled doorway, glamoured to look like the stone used in the wall. On the other hand, if the stones were pressed in the wrong sequence, the doorway would remain solid and an alarm would sound to alert the guards above. One guard—wearing a long green cloak barely concealing his spear—stood positioned right above the entrance Aidón sought. All the guards were armed but hid either bows or spears. And all the guards were Elves, each different but similar with pointed ears, fair skin, and sharp facial features accentuated by hair in various subdued colors of blonde, white, black, or silver-ish blue. Looking to the right, he saw what he had been waiting for—a distraction.

Summoning his magic from deep within, Aidón sent it toward the cart being pushed by an Elf servant just outside the wall near the front of the castle. Instantly, the cart caught fire and the Elf screamed in terror. The guards ran to the front and left just one guard behind. Aidón grumbled under his breath at his failure to make a large enough explosion to get all three guards out of the way. However, the one left behind was distracted too, watching those of his guardian brothers as they put out the fire, leaving the entrance Aidón desired left unwatched. The opportune moment had arrived, and he would not let it pass him by.

At the wall, Aidón searched for the precise stone he needed to begin the code sequence. He hoped the new guard under his son's rule hadn't changed the alarm code in all the years he had been gone—that would've been most unfortunate.

Aidón had no time to think—acting was his only option now. He pressed each stone by memory just as if no time had passed at all. Aidón waited with bated breath for triumph or demise. Then the stone shifted. Fortune! The solid wall fell away beneath his hand. Smiling, Aidón stepped right in through to the passageway that led him directly into the castle.

The smell hit him first, a mix of must and rodent, but from the looks of the worn path, it was a well-traveled pathway still. Hopefully at this hour the staff would be occupied in the dining hall for the evening meal. His glamour made him appear as one of the staff, or so he hoped. It wouldn't be hard to adjust this or that, but he'd have to see a uniform to be sure. That said, he knew he did not want to face anyone until he knew for certain what to expect in this new order his son had created.

Closing in on the main entrance from the passageway into the castle, he could hear voices. If he remembered right, the passageway exited into a holding area for cleaning supplies and gardening tools. He recalled it opened up into the staff entry just outside the kitchens. He realized his exit could be problematic at this time of night. He'd figure it out.

Moving silently into the supply area, he waited and listened. He listened for familiar voices, for any information that might help him. To Aidón's surprise several of the voices did sound familiar. Gaining courage, he leaned around the corner as far as he dared to confirm who he thought he could hear. It would be good to know who all was present. He saw an assortment of new faces and familiar faces. Aidón discovered pleasantly he was not far off with his glamour; a few alterations here and there.

Fully confident now in the perfect uniform, he boldly moved into plain view.

"Where do you think you're going?" a matronly voice, stern and experienced, came from behind him.

Aidón froze. He knew that voice. He'd hand-picked the woman to run his kitchens many years ago. She both impressed and—truth be told—frightened him with her militant way of operations. Slowly he turned around to face her.

"I am not scheduled for kitchen duty tonight, ma'am," Aidón replied, his head inclined and his eyes shielded lest she see something in them revealed.

"You are now!" she rebutted. "I am short-staffed and we are behind. King Syén changed the menu at the last minute and I need all hands available... that means you," she added throwing a rolling pin up to her shoulders as if it were her sword.

Aidón sighed at his lost attempt to flee the kitchen. He had wanted to avoid this exact scenario, but he knew he could make it work. He would put in his time and learn what he could; perhaps she would keep him in the kitchen and not out in the dining room—one could only hope. The last thing he needed was his son to sense his presence right through his glamour as those with the same blood at close proximity could do that very thing. Unfortunately, glamour couldn't hide everything.

CHAPTER TEN

Aidón only had one close call, where head chef Carlona—a faerie well-gifted in meal preparation—had sent him into the dining room to clear plates between courses. Aidón stiffened, unable to prevent his body's reaction to Syén. Well within feet of his son, he did everything he could to keep his head down and not attract any attention. A serving spoon dropped to the ground and Aidón slowly bent to retrieve it. Out of the corner of his eye Syén noticed him, tilted his head and watched him carefully as he continued his eating and entertaining his guests. By his reaction, Aidón didn't think Syén had recognized him though.

Aidón had recognized the various leaders from the surrounding towns and villages near Adettlyn as well some of their own heads of shops and local businesses gathered around the table. Their conversation was perfunctory and Aidón wondered at their presence. He knew his son had no care for them and would normally not entertain their 'mediocre existence'—his son's previous words—but must have a purpose for their appearance. As soon as he could leave without making any more of an impression, Aidón did so, dropping off his dishes, and sneaking out of the kitchen before Carlona could call for him. He knew she would only remember a worthless servant if she remembered him at all, as glamour could work that way, confusing those in close contact.

Aidón needed to explore the castle while his son was indisposed with dinner and guests. For this reason, he quickly and quietly rounded a corner that led him to the main foyer at the front of the castle. He knew this structure like the back of his hand, yet he felt an unwelcoming presence pushing him from his path, leading him to the exit. Aidón stood tall and refused to continue moving where his feet began to lead him astray. His eyes wandered the front entry from bottom to top. The foyer boasted a grand entry several stories tall. Solid stones piled one on top of another which were fused together with what were once green vines snaking throughout the castle were now brown and almost lifeless. A darkness had taken up residence, siphoning the very life that used to thrive there, a darkness that could only be allowed in by the ruler of the castle. Aidón dropped his head in dismay, shaking it slowly. Then anger rose from his very depths, the place where the life and love for his home and the hope for his people resided. Aidón reached out to the stone wall, comforting the castle he loved.

"My heart is broken over your condition." Aidón closed his eyes and leaned his forehead against the cool gray stone and sighed. "I will have you restored before this is all over. I have returned." As he whispered, he pushed a pulse of his magic out through his hands and into the stone. Aidón eyes grew wide with excitement as a stream of golden magic appeared, glowing beneath his palm, then spread out from stone to stone. Pride swelled within his chest as the vines released a shoot of green through the existing brown, infusing life back into the living mortar of the castle. The small green shoot was much too small to return the castle fully to life but was nonetheless there, growing and emerging in the midst of death and darkness threatening its demise. Aidón smiled gently stroking the tiny green shoot while coaxing it to grow.

"Hold on to life, little one," he whispered, his heart filling with hope for his once beautiful home. Placing his other hand on the stone he added, "I will not abandon you to the darkness. You will live again." With that Aidón pushed away, removing his hands from the walls, and moved on. It saddened him that he was not able to restore the entire entry at this time, but it was more important to take into account the full extent of the destruction and ascertain how much magic it would take to restore life back to his castle.

As he sneaked down the hallway, he unconsciously let his hand glide along one wall leaving a tiny trail of greenery popping up as he moved. He paused and felt a slight tickle under his hand from a tiny shoot and realized what he was doing—that was a sure way to get discovered before it was time. As it was, someone would eventually notice the difference in the entry. He would have to move fast. As much as it pained him to not attempt to touch everything he could, he refrained in order to stay anonymous for the time being.

The halls were darkened, lit only with a burning sconce every twenty steps leaving sections of the hallway dark until the next sconce and circle of light. The pattern got disturbed when broken up by an open doorway with natural light flooding the space. He stopped in front of one large, wooden door. Leaning his ear against the door to what he knew was the library, he listened for any occupants inside though he didn't expect to hear anyone there.

As expected, he heard nothing, and he pushed on the iron latch to open the door. He did so painstakingly slowly, ensuring he couldn't be caught in case someone was on the other side of the door. However, the door did not cooperate. It creaked and groaned at the slow slide open. Aidón winced. Had anyone heard? Every little sound was so much louder in the silent hallway. He turned around quickly but finding no-one about, he ducked inside the door. Thankfully it was in fact, empty. Soundlessly, he lowered the latch to lock from the inside. He did not need to be disturbed.

The library was just as he remembered it, though lacking in the vast amounts of light and life he knew it had had under his rule. He saw the same shelves and the same ancient books, tomes, and scrolls keeping record of the histories of Elves as well as many other races in Alandria, not to mention Alandria herself. His brother, Ryek, had kept quite the collection when he was king. Aidón had always admired the tomes and loved spending time in the library.

Ryek had been one of the oldest kings, and one of the Originators of Alandria; for this reason, their library held more collections than any of the other territories held. Plus, Ryek had also been much more diligent about keeping the records themselves in comparison to the younger generations of Alandrians ruling then and since. Aidón was grateful to have such a trove at his fingertips as he sought information he knew would help him in this time. Aidón inhaled, taking in the smell of the old books and smiled. "It is just as I remember it." He padded quietly across the wooden floor of the library, stopping at the center of the tall room. Three tall windows spread evenly on the opposite wall of the bookshelves, dressed lavishly with red velvet curtains. To ensure no one from beyond the castle might see his movements through any windows, Aidón closed the curtains and then lit a candle left on a side table. He saw the room to be furnished with several single stuffed chairs opposite a long dais also covered in red velvet; the set completed by a large, round cream-colored ottoman.

"Now to the books," Aidón whispered. He passed ladder after ladder along dozens of floor-to-ceiling bookshelves. Then something caught his attention out of the corner of his eye. A large stone fireplace stood erect at the far end of the room. It was tall enough for a man to stand inside it and wide enough for ten to stand side by side. He longed to light the fire and bring warmth to this forgotten space, but he dared not attract unwanted attention. The gilded mirror hanging above the mantel had tarnished with time and neglect, barely reflecting the image of the great tree within its opposite wall.

Gasping, Aidón stepped down from the first wrung of the ladder and turned back toward that wall. He'd neglected to notice when he first entered. The castle was built amongst the trees originally formed on the land beneath it, and they had continued to grow tall and strong entangling themselves as part of the structure. As they'd grown over the centuries, they'd strengthened the foundation contrary to what would typically happen should a structure be built over ancient trees. In fact, not only did the castle grow stronger with time as the trees aged, but the vines worked as a kind of magical glue holding the very stones that made up the walls together.

What Aidón saw was one side of the great tree before him. The other portion of the tree would be visible on the other side of the wall in the adjoining room. Aidón placed his hand on the tree to feel its life beneath his fingertips. Though the tree was still strong, Aidón felt its energy waning as it attempted to flow throughout the structure of the castle. He did not need to be one of the Faeries in order to cultivate magic to grow and renew the strength of that which came from the land. As the rightful patriarch of this territory, he had some of his own magic. Each territory's governing rulers were entrusted to tend their land, their people, and their establishments and given the magic and power to do so. Aidón realized the state of his castle and his land had nothing to do with a lack of his magic from Syén the unfit ruler. Rather, the castle was being torn apart by darkness that had been permitted to reign untethered and roam unchecked under said ruler.

Aidón sighed, pulling his hand from the tree and returned to the shelves lined with books. He was running out of time. He needed to find what he'd come for, and his motivation had just sky-rocketed. His mission must not fail.

CHAPTER ELEVEN

OUTSIDE ELNYE. NEAR THE GÁRALDRATH MOUNTAINS.

Maleina emerged from the secret underground passageway through a doorway disguised as a large mound of dirt, coming out a distance from the Gáraldrath Mountains but still inside Guardian Grove forest. The passageway under the grove was not the only one in Feraánmar; someone long ago believed that multiple escape routes were needed both to and from the castle and the surrounding areas. Maleina carried a torch through the tunnels enabling her to see through the dark and dank passage. Roots from trees above had grown through the ceiling in some places and trailed down through the walls in others, creating a mesh root system that kept the walls strong. Maleina ducked and twisted to avoid such roots until she was freed of them. Night descended and the bright moons rose, creating a halo of innocence and light behind her in the sky—a dichotomy she found laughable as if light and dark could be enjoyed together in nature. Just an illusion! Maleina's fiery red hair trailed behind her. Light from the moon shone upon her so bright her hair almost glowed in the dark. The breeze fluttered the edges of her hair as she swiftly moved through the forest. Though she moved toward her castle, her home, she strode at an angle that took her to an outer edge behind the castle walls.

Muttering words under her breath, she walked around the outside edge of the clearing, disarming the wards she had set to keep anyone out. Invisible to the naked eye, a small cottage was glamoured with a sheer layer of invisibility. An onlooker would only see the clearing in the forest. If anyone stepped too close, they would become confused and move around it at a wide berth. Traps were set and triggered wards had been placed strategically in case anyone did get too close. What's more these wards also informed Maleina of any breaches. Once within the glamour, the cottage lifted off the ground and rotated on an invisible axis, the front door never in the same place for long.

Now that she was within the protection of the invisible shield, Maleina chanted the words to unlock the entrance. The cottage soundlessly stopped rotating and its door settled down directly in front of her. Her impromptu meeting with *She* of Exhile had left her feeling anxious and suspicious of what else the mistress of darkness was planning without her. Maleina felt it was a good thing she had plans of her own. One thing she had learned was that *She* was growing in her power. Though she didn't yet understand where in Exhile *She* was getting her power from or if she would truly be able to leave the extension realm. Maleina had her doubts but in the case *She* was able to move through Alandria on her own, Maleina knew that her power, too, was growing and she would ultimately be the one to put a stop to the other woman trying to rule Alandria.

Something whizzed by her head as she stepped into the small cottage, Maleina waved her hand to block it—whatever it was had been on a direct path to her head. Instantly, a shot of magic sent it crashing into the wall. Maleina sighed and continued to move further into the cottage, the flying object the least of her concerns.

"Jinthíya, could you please cease from throwing items?" Maleina droned in a bored tone. It happened every time she visited. And every time it was the same excuse.

"Sorry my lady," Jin's equally monotone voice said. "A habit. You know I did that just in case someone else was sneaky enough to elude your wards and come to pay me a visit."

"Has anyone else ever paid you a visit?" Maleina asked, clearly mocking with a raised eyebrow.

"No," Jin answered, almost sad that no one had tried.

"Then stop your foolishness!" Maleina walked slowly around the small cottage.

Not much more than a large square with a bed in one corner, a stove top fireplace and small kitchen set up in another, and a door to an enclosed bathroom in yet another. The room was sparse, but had all the essentials for one to live there comfortably for a time. Since Jinthíya had been staying there, she had gone to creating decorations of sorts out of paper or leaf chains… anything she could find to bring color into the space. When she was on assignment for Maleina, she had the freedom to do her job, but then she was compelled back to the cottage when she finished. Jinthíya had found ways to create diversions and take some time for herself while 'on' a mission. Sometimes a girl just needed some freedom. The girl had a convoluted past and a more confusing parentage. She was unaware where she had inherited her special abilities from, which further enslaved her to Maleina. With long dark hair usually tied back with a tight braid, she had just the right combination of curves and height. She was tall, slender and athletic, all of which fitted her perfectly to accomplish her job, though she thought little of these advantages.

Lying on her stomach on top of the bed, Jin kicked her legs up while she looked at what was likely one of Maleina's books. It was certainly roughed up enough to be from her library. Jin could sneak in and out of places without being seen quite easily—most likely a necessary trick for her particular talents. Her dark eyes set amidst her pale face found Maleina's eyes and studied her as Maleina sashayed across the little room, though Jin did not get up as Maleina would expect of others.

"I let you get away with too much insolence, young one," Maleina noted.

"But I provide too much of a good service for you to care about it," Jin tacked on, smirking all the while.

Maleina sneered though she nodded.

"What brings you to my humble cottage, this fine day?" Jin asked.

"You know why I am here." Maleina paused, letting an awkward silence fill the room.

Jin nodded and sat up.

"Did you deposit the blood in the drop funnel within the tree?" Maleina asked, turning back from admiring a particular trinket in the room. Most the things in the room had been hers at one time, instead of throwing them away she deposited them there in her private little cottage.

"I did," Jin placed her hands on her waist, her expression suddenly weary and aged. "How many more do you need? It is not as inconspicuous as it once was in these parts." Her eyes shifted about the room, not landing on Maleina's. It pained her, what she did, and she was sure it showed through her eyes.

"I agree. We will need to look elsewhere. Maybe even see about crossing souls into and out of the mortal realm?" Maleina paused, waiting to see Jin's reaction.

"It might be possible," Jin said, rolling her shoulders, "but I do not know for certain. If it is required of me, you know it will be done. Bodies, on the other hand, might be more of a challenge to get across." Jin wiped a hand down her face and stalked off to the shelf next to the door. She reached for a glass jar with wispy white smoke swirling about inside it.

"You kept it by the door? What if someone took it? All they would have to do is reach inside and grab it!" Maleina sounded outraged.

"You just reminded me no one comes here, who would take it and who would know to look for it?" Jin replied sarcastically. Flippantly handing over the jar to Maleina she said, "Here are your souls. I only have one more mission on my contract then I am done. I can't do anymore, Maleina.

"No, you are finished when I say you are finished," Maleina reached for the jar, but Jin pulled it back to her.

"But I have done everything on it you have asked me to!" Jin's volume rose in the tiny space.

"Yes, but the fine print states that I get to determine when the date of servitude is completed," Maleina explained.

Jin's mouth hit the floor. "That wasn't there! You made that up and added it in," she came back at Maleina.

"Did I? Or was it there all along and you never noticed it. It is not my fault if you do not possess the wherewithal to read over a binding contract signed in blood," she taunted.

Jin's eyes lit with anger, but then dissipated as quickly as it'd come. Defeated, her shoulders dropped, and resigned to her current fate she handed over the jar of souls.

"Do you really want the people of Alandria to see the destruction of your deeds?" Maleina's eyes narrowed as she took the jar. She then turned and moved toward the door, looked back at Jin with false innocence. "But... if you break your contract because you are suffering some kind of moral compunction, they will not allow you to stay after what you have done, child. However, if they are not wiser for it and they continue to see the Alandria they believe is there I would see no reason for you be on the run... again." Maleina sneered and opened the door.

Jin sighed. "There is nowhere else for me to go."

"I did not think so. Take the day off, roam Alandria if you feel it necessary, Jinthíya, but tomorrow is another day for harvesting souls," Maleina practically sang to her, taunting her as she held the jar of souls in her face. "When I am the uncontested ruler of this great land, you will sit at my right hand and live like royalty, my dear. It is only a matter of time."

Maleina left the cottage, sealing it back up, reinsuring the glamour still upon it. Jin could leave the cottage at will—Maleina could always find her if she did not return. She was not a prisoner unless Maleina felt her a risk, but the poor child had nowhere else to go. Maleina had no more time to dwell on Jinthíya. She had somewhere to be and her mistress would be waiting for the very deposit of souls Maleina carried in her hands. Only time would tell if these souls, poured into the Alandria side of the veil they were attempting to create would work.

~~~~~

"Soul Stealer," an enticing feminine voice echoed through the forest. Jinthíya stopped in her tracks. Did she really just hear a voice in the forest, or was it in her head? Looking around she waited for someone to make their presence known. Gripping her hands on her hips, she ground her teeth together; she hated her "gift" and could not understand why she was given it to begin with—no good could come from an ability to take another's soul straight from their being. No amount of cleansing could erase the things she had done, the lives she had removed from existence, the souls she had prevented from their afterlives. Jin was not a Ferrier—one of the beings created to guide a soul into their afterlife—but she often wondered if perhaps it was in her blood. In fact, the woman had no idea how she came to be in this life, not who her parents were, nor which dimension she hailed.

After Maleina's visit, Jin had to get out of the little cottage and breathe some fresh air. The forest always seemed to soothe her, and a short walk would do her good.
~~~~~

"Soul Stealer..." again the woman's voice whispered through her thoughts.

That voice again!

"Jinthíya or Jin. That is my name, not *Soul Stealer,*" she growled into the air. Frustrated her peaceful moment had been interrupted, she stalked back toward the cottage.

"Come to the mountain, Jin. I would like to renegotiate your deal with Maleina," came the voice.

Jin stopped, intrigued but wary. Her gaze sought the voice. "Where are you? Come speak with me face to face."

"I am not yet able."

"Who are you?" Jin asked cautiously.

"I am the one you are currently providing souls for in Exhile. My plan is almost complete: I will be in Alandria very shortly and will be the new ruler, Queen of Alandria..."

"And you want me to rule by your side if I continue to bring you souls?" Jin ventured a guess.

A laugh echoed throughout the forest in such a manner she could not tell where it started and where it ended. *"Let me guess, that is what Maleina has offered you?"* Again, her haughty laugh sent tingles down Jin's spine.

"What do you want from me then?" She threw open the door to the cottage and stepped inside.

"I was going to offer you your freedom, child." A pause. *"If you chose to stay and live amongst the people of Alandria, that would be your freedom to do so. But no, I do not need anyone by my side. I have more than enough power and will restore Alandria how I see fit—no longer needing souls and the blood of their hosts to sustain it."*

"What would you ask of me now, in return for that freedom?" Jin asked hesitantly, afraid to hope. It was as if the mistress in the mountain had read her mind.

"Look into your mirror. There is a particular soul I want... just one. One who will be in my way. One you are already quite familiar with as you already had a piece of it put into this crystal amulet," the mistress of darkness intoned, lifting the crystal up so the girl could see it through the glass mirror.

Jin watched as her mirror clouded with something like smoke. She inhaled sharply held it for a moment then slowly released her breath. Yes, she knew his soul, it haunted her in her sleep; the remainder calling to the piece she had stolen when he had been much younger. Time moved slowly for Jin; she did not age as others did and had remained as she appeared now for quite some time. Yes, she knew and could find his soul especially with the amulet. The mistress then passed it through the mirror, holding out for Jin to grasp.

Nodding slowly, she agreed to the terms, signing her name in blood to the overriding contract that suddenly appeared in front of her. For freedom, she was willing to do just about anything.

Chapter Twelve

Kandri. The Small Town Next to the Kandrian Mountains.

Settled into a lovely inn, Daegan, Kaeleigh, Ella, and Finn awaited the waitress who promised them a home-cooked meal. After the random things they had eaten over the campfire while they traveled, the group was eternally grateful.

Letoni had been correct, after they passed through the first layer of town there seemed to be an invisibly drawn line where something shifted. At least some of the people they passed were friendly even though wary of the visitors. The townspeople acknowledged them, however, with actual expressions, not like the shells of people milling in the front of the town. Letoni had led them down a narrow road boasting a variety of eateries—bakeries, cafes, pubs, anything a person could want to visit. She then had stopped in front of the tallest of the buildings, covered in stone similar to the cobblestone on the ground but these stones were smaller and varied in color patched together with thick gray mortar. A curved turret gave the front a unique and castle-esque feel that Kaeleigh found endearing. Kaeleigh smiled as she looked up, taking in the building and noting the swinging wood sign. The Inn at Kandri.

Dusk had been approaching for quite some time and was now fully upon them. Torches and candlelight bloomed throughout the village surrounding them, signifying life and activity was still bustling for the night.

"Why can you only see the blue moon here in Kandri?" Kaeleigh asked, peering up into the darkening sky as it grew brighter with the rising of the blue moon.

Finn looked up at the sky beside her, squinting his eyes to see past the torch right in front of him. "The white moon will rise just behind it. Some nights it is slower than the other and takes longer to rise, but you will see it," Finn explained.

"That's... odd," Kaeleigh had mulled. "I did not notice the moons rising at different tempos the other nights. Fascinating."

"It has to do with the cycles of the seasons and coincides with the equinoxes and solstices within the mortal realm," Finn added. "But truthfully, the magic of Alandria works in its own ways so it is not absolute with that theory, but tends to lean that way. Just as time functions differently in Alandria compared to the mortal realm, so also is it hard to understand the passing of time."

"That gives me a brain cramp, Finn," Kaeleigh chuckled rubbing her forehead. He too laughed and then entered the inn after the others had already gone inside.

Inside, they were seated at a large round table placed in the corner of a large room with tall ceilings braced with thick blackened wood beams. The waitress had brought them a round of beverages and told them to relax. Food would be brought out shortly. The restaurant was sparse of furnishings, other than tables, and people. Only a few dined, but sat at tables closer to the bar-top or front entrance.

"The owner of the inn will show you rooms to sleep in," Letoni had informed them with a big toothy grin. Then she skipped off but not without hugs for the girls and promises to show them many things when the sun rose.

"We will need to leave before dawn in the morning," Daegan said quietly.

"Letoni will come looking for us," Kaeleigh said with a hint of panic. "Will Maleina hurt her if we are gone?"

The table sat thoughtfully silent for mere seconds. "No," both Finn and Daegan said in unison, garnering a look of confusion from Daegan. However, Finn kept his glance straight ahead.

"O-okay," Kaeleigh responded looking between the two. "How can you be sure?"

"For one, her magic will not affect the girl," Ella chimed in. "And for another, she would rather capture her than hurt her, I am afraid."

Kaeleigh opened and closed her mouth several times before Ella finished what she had started.

"Of course we do not want her to get captured," Ella clarified. "I have sent word to my grandfather about her. He is sending word to a trusted source he has here to bring her and her family, if she has one, to Ehsmia. If they do not make it in time, the worst-case scenario is she gets taken... for now. We will find a way to get her later if not right away," Ella promised to herself.

Kaeleigh's eyes shot around the table. "I'm not sure why this hasn't been said, but why don't we take her with us?"

Daegan's eyes softened as he thought to answer her. "Our journeys are not suitable for the traveling or care of a child, or a child and her family. There are too many variables and uncertainties," Daegan explained gently. "I do not wish any harm to come to the child, but I believe Arileas will make plans to ensure her safety."

Kaeleigh frowned but nodded in concession. He was right, of course they couldn't take her with them. But perhaps they could warn her family? Only she had no idea how to find the little girl. She continued to drift off in her own thoughts without anyone picking up on her trail of worries.

Kaeleigh tuned back in when she realized everyone else had continued forming the plan to leave in the morning. Spoken in hushed tones, uncertain who might be listening or watching, they finished the plan just in time as food was brought to the table. A lovely waitress with short curly white hair covering her slightly pointed ears stopped in front of Kaeleigh. The woman looked to be in her fifties but in Alandria you could never be sure of ages. She bent down to prepare a plate for Kaeleigh, and whispered for the ears of those at the table alone.

"We need your help, Dearie," the waitress spoke quickly and quietly, but Kaeleigh and Daegan were able to hear her if no one else did. "Do not react to my words, some are watching." She gathered a portion and heaped it onto Kaeleigh's plate then turned and did the same to Ella's plate but continued speaking. "We are watched all the time. The curse on the front of our village keeps us from leaving to get help. We want freedom for Kandri once more. This is not living and many are tired of it, growing thin and hoping to expire sooner than they are called to," she said sadly. "If you can do nothing more than get help on the outside, we would be grateful."

Then the woman left. She didn't even wait for Kaeleigh to say anything. "Did you all get that?" Kaeleigh mumbled as she shoveled in a bite of food. She looked around the room innocently, noting who was present.

"Yes," Daegan replied. Finn nodded his head and Ella tapped her fork, digging in for more with a mumbled confirmation.

They spoke of little else while they finished their meal; they were all famished from the journey but also cautious not to say too much where they might be overheard. Not much later, a large wide man entered the dining room. His attire and physique were both burly and gruff. He wore his sleeves rolled up to the elbows, and immediately the group could see by the clothing he wore that he'd come in from working elsewhere. His apron was filled with tools for working with metal, indicating he was likely a blacksmith or something similar. Wild chestnut colored hair complimented by an unruly mustache and overgrown beard gave the man a crazed look. However, his eyes were warm brown and held kindness and a keen awareness. Kaeleigh wanted to trust him instantly. As if he could read her thoughts, the man sauntered over to their table.

"I apologize I was not here at your arrival. I am Dunstand and the owner of this inn," he introduced himself and gave them a short bow, still holding a segment of iron in his hand.

"Dunstand, I am Daegan. This is Kaeleigh, Ella, and Finn, my traveling companions," he introduced in return.

"We were shown the way here and told you might perchance have room available for us to stay the night," Finn spoke up, eyeing the Shifter, assuming his animal form might be a large bear based on the man's size.

"Indeed," Dunstand replied. He looked at the iron in his hand as if noticing he still had it for the first time and frowned. "Blasted thing," he set it down on a nearby table. "Apologies, sometimes my work goes with me, and I do not even realize it." He laughed a deep belly laugh then continued, speaking to Finn. "Yes, we have room for you. How many would you be having?" He eyed the group, curious how they would break up their rooms.

"Two," they all replied together. Kaeleigh and Ella reached for each other's arms, indicating they would be sharing a room.

"Indeed," the inn keeper/blacksmith laughed again, the jolly sound pleasing and contagious, making Kaeleigh giggle. "If you are finished now, I will have ye follow me up and I'll show you to the rooms myself."

They followed him up a short flight of stairs behind the wall encasing the giant fireplace that centered the dining room. Sconces placed periodically along the stone halls gave off enough light for them to see clearly as they went.

"Dunstand? Kandri seems... different than last I saw it many years ago," Daegan broached the topic carefully.

The man in front of them stiffened and stopped in the hallway. Without turning to face them or even uttering a word, he signaled for them to follow him. They followed. He stepped into an open doorway and indicated to Ella with a point and swirled his hand in the air over his head. She nodded understanding.

"Is it done?" he asked quietly.

Again she nodded. "But how did you know I was able to enact a dome of silence?"

He tapped his nose. But she lifted an eyebrow in disbelief. "You cannot scent my kind like the others," she rebutted.

"That is exactly why I knew. I have had encounters with your kind before and I recognized it—or the lack of it, you might say. It was a guess. There is much to say and little time to say it I am afraid before we are found out and someone comes to check." His expression was tight and his eyes hinted at a panic as wild as his hair.

"Clever," Ella acknowledged with an appreciative nod.

"What is happening here, sir?" Kaeleigh asked, leaning forward, anticipating his answer.

"I keep an eye out for little Letoni," he started, "she is very special and caught up in this in a way no one should, but the misses and I worry about her. Her family is affected just as the rest of us are if we go to the front of the village, but alas she is not." His eyes held sadness and his hands worried one of the pockets on the apron still tied around his waist. "For now she is safe, but I fear for her future. The wicked one will come for her at some point, possibly sooner than later. For now she serves a purpose."

"I have informed my grandfather of her existence and her need of protection," Ella informed him.

"Good, very good, yes she would be safe away from here I would think," he said thoughtfully. "The rest of it is, as I am sure Letoni told you—she is not well versed in deceit or hiding information if you did not notice." The large Shifter gave another belly laugh. "I pray her honesty keeps her safe. Villagers who venture up to the front of the town become sluggish if they get too close to the exit. Then they turn around and go back about their business forgetting why they wanted to leave in the first place. They serve as eyes and ears for the darkness without even realizing it is happening." He shook his head and clenched his fists in pure frustration. "We no longer go to the front. Supplies are delivered to the gates and they are brought back to us. My mate—Rinnia, the waitress you met in the dining hall—and I have not traveled to see others of our families in other territories in many seasons."

"How long?" Daegan pressed.

"The curse was struck about sixteen years ago. Of course, Letoni was not yet born, and only the last three or four did little Letoni's gifts surface as she is only now seven or eight."

"That long ago? You've been stuck here for that long?" Kaeleigh asked with an inhale of shock.

"Yes, I am afraid we have," he said wearily.

"Why so long? What happened here sixteen years ago that could have caused the reason for this?" she asked again.

"Our town is on the edge of an active—or once active portal to the mortal realm—and when the darkness destroyed Klavaí long ago our people have felt a presence of darkness ever since. Sixteen years ago, the kingdom of Feraánmar was overthrown. Rumors have it royalty had either gone missing or they were killed as well as future heirs to the throne," Dunstand supplied, "I would guess the witch wanted to ensure we did not leave as well. Though we do not exactly know why."

The room grew uneasily silent. Dunstand looked from one to the next, aware of the sudden tension and the somberness of their expressions, but unaware what he had said to cause it.

Daegan uttered a word in another language that could only be interpreted as a curse and raked his hands roughly through his hair. Kaeleigh's eyes were wide, rimmed with wetness at the implications. She looked to Daegan desperately seeking an alternative to what she believed was the truth.

"This is our fault?" she asked incredulously, grabbing onto his arm causing him to turn toward her, to see her, to defy her question.

"Of course it is not your fault," Dunstand said, the very thought incredulous.

"Not directly, no sir," Daegan began with humility. "You see we, Kaeleigh and I, were both displaced sixteen years ago. She to the mortal realm sent by her grandfather... the king of Adettlyn, and I to the wilds of Alandria when my parents—the original heirs to Feraánmar, who had been in hiding for quite some time—were murdered just outside your very territory." Daegan's hands shook. Kaeleigh reached out and took them in her own. He had never shared that information with anyone, let alone a stranger, but perhaps now it was time for the truth to come out.

Dunstand's mouth fell open. He looked back and forth between his guests, filled with awe as it dawned on him just who he was talking to. His wits quickly returned to him and he dropped to his knee humbly and full of loyalty in response to their story. As a man of simple faith, he was desperate for hope out of his current situation. Here was the hope he needed.

"Please Duntsand, sir, that is not necessary," Kaeleigh turned toward him. "All we need is a chance to make this right, can you help us? We need to get to the portal to the mortal realm and I fear that we are not going to be able to leave this town easily."

Dunstand held his hands together, hope shone in his eyes. "Of course. There is a way, but none use it for very long for fear of the magic wielder catching us. You must not let Letoni know or she might tell the witch."

They nodded in agreement. Kaeleigh looked around, suddenly noticing Finn was absent. When he had slipped out she didn't know. He had been distracted and distant more so since they had arrived in Kandri. Frowning, she mouthed to Ella asking where he went. Ella tilted her head towards the door, indicating he had gone out. *Obviously,* Kaeleigh thought.

"Where is this other way out?" Daegan asked, back to strategy mode. "When is the best time to reach it without too many eyes? How do the tunnels work? Is it possible to get lost in the mountain tunnel systems?"

Daegan's focus was on things of much importance, but Kaeleigh worried about Finn and had trouble paying attention. Noting the distracted look in Ella's eyes Kaeleigh would venture to say she was not the only one concerned. When all the questions seemed to have been sorted, Dunstand had a couple of his own.

"We were under the impression all the portals and the areas surrounding them were in the same situations we are, is that true?"

"No, it seems to be just your area that we have encountered so far," Finn answered popping back inside the dome of silence. Kaeleigh shot him a curious glance.

"Where did you go?" she asked him.

"Sorry I, I uh needed to use the bathroom," he admitted sheepishly.

But something in his eyes caught Kaeleigh's and couldn't let go, he was hiding something. Of all the times and places to be hiding something, this was not it. She thought they were past all that. She bit her lip, bringing her attention back to the inn keeper and his plan.

"We are a far way out from the main populace of Alandria, many have even forgotten we still exist, especially since we have not been able to travel from territory to territory," Dunstand said, his voice weighted with sadness. Then his shoulders struck back and he stood to his full height, a large formidable man in his own right. A fierceness lit his eyes. Kaeleigh saw that he was once a proud, strong warrior in that simple change in stature. "Alandria is still our home and she has been good to us even in our trapped state. We will fight. We will rise up against this curse if we can, and we will get free and we will stand up to the darkness plaguing our land. Indeed, we will fight!" The man stood with one fist clenched at his side, and the other fingers flexing, itching for a weapon to wrap around. He seemed to not even realize that he was so filled with emotion as he pledged himself and his wife to their cause. "There are others. I know they will fight, if they can get clear enough of mind to remember what they are doing and who they once were."

His words stirred something in Kaeleigh yet she didn't know what it meant. A thought struck her, "Dunstand, why do you refer to the one who cursed you as the magic wielder or the witch? Is it not Maleina, Paladin of Elnye?"

He frowned, considering her question. "No I think not, though we have not seen her face except for little Letoni who says she has red hair. We have had encounters with the darkness she wields called the Droch-Shúil—

"Yes, we've had encounters with that as well," Kaeleigh interrupted sullenly.

"—And we have heard her magic whispered on the wind, but I could not tell you for certain who she was. I would not think Paladin of the Faeries would have enough magic to entrap an entire village for so many years, simply waiting for strangers to come along in search of the portal to the mortal realm. In fact, that portal is not even well-known, many in this town alone do not know of it," Dunstand explained. Then as quickly as the conversation had started, it was ending. "We must go, someone might come looking for me, and if not me, then my mate and then they may raise an alarm. Be ready just before dawn, I will come for you," Dunstand warned. He then nodded to Ella who disabled the dome of silence. He motioned for them to follow him once more, and he showed them to their rooms at the end of the hall.

"Thank you Dunstand," Kaeleigh said to his retreating back as he headed toward the dining hall. He turned slightly and gave her a slight bow.

"Thank you," he whispered back to her.

"I like him," Ella stated. "He cares about his people a great deal."

Kaeleigh smiled. "He does."

"So does his wife, I could feel it coming off her in waves." Daegan nodded his agreement. "For tonight, ladies take this room to the left and Finn and I will take this one across the hall," Daegan directed. He shot a quick glance to Finn who nodded his approval of the assignments.

Sometime later in the girls' room, the foursome looked at each other in question. "Do we think it is Maleina? Or perhaps the *other* that has entrapped her?" Daegan asked their opinion with a lowered voice. They each shook their heads uncertain.

"It could be either of them," Kaeleigh ventured. Finn and Ella agreed.

"What does your gut say, Kaeleighnna?" Daegan asked again using her formal name when he tried to remind her to use her *other* senses.

"My gut... my gut says..." She closed her eyes and felt for her magic, the essence that created her to be all that she is and could be, and listened with her heart. With startled clarity, her eyes flew open. "The other one, not Maleina I mean. I wish we had a name for her, seems ridiculous to call her *the other one.*"

"You are sure?" Ella asked.

Kaeleigh nodded. "I don't know why, but yes I am sure. Whatever vision Letoni is receiving, it is to put Maleina at blame."

Daegan nodded, his eyes twinkling with pride at Kaeleigh. "You confirmed my suspicion. Well done, Kaeleighnna, your magic is strong. You must remember to consult it first, it is a part of you."

"Ok so now we know who we are dealing with and we have a plan... can we go to bed?" Finn asked, irritable once more.

Kaeleigh had noticed his hands twitching and his foot bouncing, eager to be out of the room.

"Good idea, Finn," Daegan said gruffly, his eyes narrowed. "We rise early tomorrow. Goodnight Ella," Daegan said with a short bow to them both, but his eyes remained on Kaeleigh, a glint of desire that made her blush. "Goodnight Kaeleigh."

Chapter Thirteen

Kaeleigh tossed and turned all night, or what was left of it. Her magic stirred deep in her core, agitating her skin where it poked and prodded her from the inside. Finally she sat up, admitting sleep had eluded her and didn't want to continue disturbing Ella, sleeping soundlessly in the bed next to hers.

Compelled to follow her instinct as Daegan had urged her to, she slipped silently out of her room and crept down the hallway, down the stairs to the dining room. In the pre-dawn hours, Kaeleigh was surprised to hear noises coming from the kitchen in the back room. The castle staff got an early jumpstart preparing breakfast. Not wanting to get caught slipping out of the inn, she moved quickly before anyone noticed her. Had she thought clearly about it, she probably should have woken Ella or maybe even one of the guys to go with her, but she wanted them to sleep a little longer knowing they would need their strength for the day's adventure. Something was strongly beckoning her to move. Try as she might, she could not repress the driving force within her, guiding her to the center of the village. In the back of her mind she thought it could be a trap, but the energy stirring her felt good and alive.

The village was quiet, only few were up as early as she, preparing to head to their quietly secluded existence within the town, or their mindless magically entrapped one at the front of town. If they had known what awaited them daily at the front, would they have still gone? Kaeleigh could not imagine a life like one these people were leading, where their minds were daily wiped of all memories they had—it wasn't living at all, it was prison, and a prison they weren't even aware of! Outrage for the people of the town grew deep within her as she walked down the center of the dirt path, the dawn approaching. The chill of the night's air kissed her skin and sent a chill over its surface. She thought of Letoni and of other small children like her. She thought of Dunstand and his mate Rinnia living with the knowledge of the curse of the village yet unable to do anything but wait. Her magic stirred deeper and deeper inside her flooding her system, flowing throughout her body, touching every nerve ending, and igniting her skin. She felt alive with the energy surging within her. Kaeleigh watched her own skin on her hands, holding the magic in but only just barely. A green shimmer emanated from within her, and she wondered, *Could the others see it.* Yet she did not know nor care. Kaeleigh had a mission and it was finally clear to her what it was, why her magic had been stirring within her, what her purpose in this place was.

Several curtains moved inside windows she passed, apparently her presence had been noted. Pausing where the dirt road turned to cobblestone, she began to realize that once she crossed it, her presence would be known exponentially. Breathing in through her nose, she gauged her magic once more but there was nothing more to know, she knew what she had to do. And she didn't have a lot of time in which to do it. About to step over the line of demarcation, she heard her name whispered on the wind.

"Kaeleigh," Daegan called to her quietly. "Wait."

She did. Turning to him, she saw he was not alone. Ella was also with him.

"You were not in the room when I awoke so I got Daegan," Ella explained as if she had read Kaeleigh's mind.

"And Finn?" Kaeleigh inquired almost absently, her focus intense and unwavering.

Daegan shook his head and shrugged. "He was not in the room when I got up, but left a note saying he would meet us at the designated spot." His gaze searched Kaeleigh's. "What are you doing, Kaeleighnna?"

"Alandria called me here, my magic stirred and showed me what to do. It is time to free these people," she said matter of factly. "Come, your added magic will help."

"Once we cross this line, what we do will become *her* knowledge I fear," Ella informed them.

Kaeleigh held out her hand to both Daegan and to Ella, each taking one. "We move fast. Then continue our plan, but first I have to get to the center of the town where the curse was enacted." She pointed straight ahead toward a dried up fountain; plants surrounded it that had expired from life long ago, frozen in time.

"It is there we shall go then," Ella agreed, her face a mask of focus and determination.

"My magic is your magic as always, Kaeleighnna," Daegan said his head inclined in her direction.

She nodded her thanks, then together they stepped from the dirt part of the road onto the cobblestone part.

"I don't feel anything different," Kaeleigh whispered. Daegan and Ella both shook their heads. "It's silly, I thought maybe I'd feel a shock or something." Kaeleigh let out a nervous laugh. Then shook it off. "Ok, let's go."

They moved quickly toward the fountain. Unexpectedly, Kaeleigh's heart rate accelerated, her palms grew sweaty but refused to let go of Daegan and Ella until they reached the fountain. Hearing Ella's breathing next to her, she figured she wasn't the only one being affected by outside forces to which they could not see nor feel. Daegan squeezed her hand and she shot him a quick smile, appreciating his support and his presence. After all who wouldn't appreciate such a handsome man at their side giving of his magic without question to her? Thinking of him made her heart warm and calm the rest of her body without even trying. Love bubbled up in her chest causing her to giggle under her breath. It was most inappropriate timing, but she couldn't help it.

Reaching the circular fountain, she noted the condition of it was actually quite good underneath overgrown, rotting vines and dead plants. Empty of water, the only sign of destruction was a long narrow fissure in the base of the lower pool. The crack began at the edge and ran to the center of the fountain stopping at the base of a three-tier tower of smaller bases and fountain shoots, shrinking in size as it ascended. Out of the crack rose a thin plant grown from under the fountain, twining itself around the tier until it reached the top, branching out with several off shoots from there. Not one blossom bloomed from the growth, not an inch of green lived within it, not an ounce of living energy flowed from it. Kaeleigh couldn't take her eyes off of the dead growth that had risen from the fountain floor; something was very wrong with it. Tilting her head, she study it for a second before looking at it with magical senses, seeing beyond what was visible to the naked eye. Gasping she took a step back.

"It's coming from that branch. It is dead of life, but it holds a poisonous magic that flows from it, inundating the entire front area up here," Kaeleigh gestured animatedly still using hushed tones trying not to attract attention. She could see the issue so clearly.

"Can we pull it out?" Ella inquired studying it as well, her lips pursed in concentration.

Daegan stepped up and looked for a weak spot in the branch. Testing his theory, he broke a piece of it off from the top. It snapped with an audible crack as dried wood should. Instantly the branch grew back its lost limb. "Well, if she had not yet known what we were up to, I would wager she does now," Daegan grumbled. "It cannot be broken or pulled out, I am afraid. It will simply continue to regenerate. The curse must be broken with magic, Kaeleigh."

"I know." Kaeleigh's eyes were hazy, seeing something they were not all seeing. Moving in closer, she lifted her hand gently, feeling the air around the plant. "It feels thick and dirty," she informed them with a scrunched up nose. "Ella, Daegan place your hands on the edge of the fountain and funnel your magic through it once I begin. It needs to feel freedom, it needs to feel clean, it needs to be rid of the poison and protected for the future. Does that make sense?"

"Yes," they both replied in unison, placing their hands on the edge.

"Ready when you are, Kaeleighnna," Daegan added, his eyes found hers when she looked at him with a moment of clarity. His gaze was warm with life and love and pride for her. "I am with you," his whisper reached her ears.

Kaeleigh beamed at his mental and verbal praise, feeling his strength and confidence, she nodded and bent down in front of the fountain. Emotion and magic welled up within her. Her thoughts and desire were already with the people of this town and the town itself. Visually, she saw in her mind's eye the freedom this village would enjoy, the prosperity and the growth, the comings and goings, the life and the love the people had for one another and for Alandria. Her magic wove through her being, twisting and turning its way out of her system when she allowed it to go forth. Not yet, not quite enough, she allowed it to build even further pushing her body to its limits as the container for the magic Alandria had given her to use for its very people and lands. Her hands found the edge of the fountain. With eyes closed she stepped over the edge and into the dry fountain. Kneeling down, her hands reached for the fissure the poisonous weed grew from and dug her fingers deep inside touching the earth beneath. Reaching for the root with her fingertips, she felt where it lodged but knew it would not relent with a simple tug. Inhaling deeply, Kaeleigh reached for a calm within herself as she held her magic at bay for one more beat, building it beyond her known limits. For the people of Kandri, for little Letoni, for Dunstand and Rinnia, for Alandria...

She released her magic in a violent push from her core. It burst forth, shooting down her arms and through her fingertips straight and true into the very earth of the land. She felt the resistance from the poison push back at her, attempting to dislodge her hold. Kaeleigh pushed back, immediately feeling the familiar surge of Daegan's strong masculine magic. Then the feminine, powerful, and sweet magic from Ella mixed with his then joined with her own. A sudden snap came from the growth of branches at the top of the tiers. Pieces of the branch broke off all on their own, falling end over end until they landed at the base of the fountain where they shattered into tiny pieces until dust was all that remained. Piece after piece continued to fall as Kaeleigh flushed the ground of Kandri with her magic, calling its life forth as it once was and restoring it. Weaving her own magic into the dirt, she sowed the promises of its future, sealing it with the love she, Daegan, and Ella shared for Alandria back into it.

"It is broken," Ella panted quietly, moving away from the fountain.

"Release your hold, Kaeleigh," Daegan whispered suddenly behind Kaeleigh, catching her at the same time as she fell back into his arms. He lifted her out of the fountain and held her as she regained her strength.

Kaeleigh's breath came in fast, short gasps. Her body shook with small tremors of exhaustion as the remnants of her magic siphoned off and crept back into her soul.

"Well done, Kaeleighnna," Ella acknowledged formally, her eyes took in the sight before them. "I have seen and experienced the magic of Faeries to grow, but I have not felt your particular magic before, at least not like that. It is fascinating and powerful... very powerful," Ella said excitedly with a hint of awe in her tone.

"Open your eyes, Kaeleigh," Daegan spoke into her ear with a slight chuckle.

His rough cheek brushed against her own from behind her, the action sent chills down the flesh of her neck all the way down to her toes. He was warm and comforting, he was home. Open her eyes she must, though she wanted nothing more than to stay in his arms.

Kaeleigh's sharp inhale held shock and excitement as she looked around her. The fountain was a stark contrast from what they had seen before. Overgrown brittle, dead weeds and vines slunk back into the ground from where they had come. Kaeleigh witnessed the fissure within the base of the fountain sealing itself back up, creating a solid foundation once again. Surprisingly, water filled the base then circulated through the tiers of the fountain, washing away the dust and debris left from the branches as well as refreshing the sheen having withered from time and age. Beautiful large blooms of yellow, pink, and lavender blossomed straight from the ground as their stalks of green raced to catch up. The overall drab and dreary effect across the front of the village and the shops was once more full of life, reflecting the golden light from the emerging dawn. One more surprise caught Kaeleigh's attention. She leaned forward to gently caress a beautiful white orchid. Kaeleigh gasped as many more shot up from the ground, surrounding the fountain. The sight brought joyful tears to her eyes as she leaned back into Daegan.

Daegan placed his hands on either side of her arms and tenderly kissed the back of her head. "We cannot tarry any longer, I fear retribution to follow."

"I agree," spoke Ella.

"Will she retaliate against the people?" Kaeleigh asked, suddenly aware many of the people had come out of their homes and shelters and had made their way as close as they dared. Eyes were wide with surprise and shock at what they witnessed. Some wore smiles, others wore expressions of amazement as they looked around with awe and even confusion as to what had happened. But all of them had clear eyes and signs of life etched into their faces.

Letoni ran through the crowd of people with a huge smile on her face as she spun into the center and right up to the fountain. She dipped her hand into the fresh, sparkling water. Her smile would have reached the skies if it could have. Her eyes were bright as she turned to the people.

"It is cool and refreshing," she said with awe. "You are finally all free from the curse. I can feel it. You can play with me now!"

Letoni turned toward Kaeleigh, her eyes suddenly serious. "Something is coming. It is time for you to go," her voice uttered in a strange tone not a young girl's but someone much older, a voice Kaeleigh instantly recognized as her mother's. Her heart ached but the words sent chills over her skin. Then quickly in contrast, the little girl's voice said, "I want you to stay and play with me, Princess, but I do not think you can, can you?" Her eyes grew sad as she held out her hand.

Kaeleigh's gaze shot to Daegan's to make sure he heard what she had. His imperceptible nod indicated he had, then he proceeded to look for their way out.

Kaeleigh reached for the little girl's hand and leaned down to Letoni's level so their eyes met. "No, I'm sorry I can't. I will meet you again though, I know it. Follow your heart always and wait for Arileas and the Ehsmia if you can. They will take you and your family to safety. Dunstand and Rinnia will help you, okay? You must stay free, Letoni. I wish I could take you with me. Do not let the pretty lady take you, promise me!" Kaeleigh's eyes bore into the little girl's hoping her intent would be understood. The little girl nodded. That was all the time Kaeleigh had before darkness broke out in Kandri.

Chapter Fourteen

Just as quickly as the dustiness of Kandri had receded, darkness much darker than the pre-dawn sky approached and covered the village, rumbling with an unnatural thunder. Daegan grabbed Kaeleigh's hand and shouted at Ella, "It is time to go!"

"The Droch-Shúil!" Kaeleigh shouted back. Hints of red eyes were already fading in and out through the darkness.

"It is not coming closer," Ella replied, looking back over her shoulder as they weaved and bobbed their way through the growing crowd intent on watching the sky. "I think our magic is keeping it out. "I have never seen that happen before!" she shouted in excitement.

Kaeleigh and Daegan both shot quick glances over their shoulders, watching with amazement and terror all at once. They finally stopped near the inn at the back of the town looking for Dunstand or Rinnia.

"It does seem to be what is happening," Daegan mused with curiosity. "But we do not know for how much longer it will last."

"This way!" Dunstand shouted from behind them. He had emerged from the inn with the shorter, round waitress they had met last night—his wife, Rinnia. Obviously a Faerie with her slightly pointed ears and her *srontas* marking—the marking every Alandrian is born with indicating what type of being they are—in the shape of a curling leaf indicating so just inside her elbow; she was a lovely woman. Her smile quickly turned to terror as she caught sight of the darkness rolling in.

"Hurry, we have not much time to get you out!" Rinnia called. The sound of the rumbling thunder grew louder and more constant... more like the roaring of an angry beast.

"Finn! We can't leave without Finn, where is he?" Kaeleigh shouted, panic rose in her chest. Just then she saw him coming up behind the large inn-keeper.

"I'm here, Kae. We have to go now!" Finn said, yet the look in his eyes was tortured and strained.

They all turned to follow Dunstand and his mate behind the inn and through an alley of stone blending in with the buildings; an alley so narrow they had to turn sideways to get through it. Kaeleigh wondered how Dunstand made it through the tight fit. After several minutes of single file movements through the alleyway, the group stopped.

"Are we there?" Kaeleigh whispered low.

"Almost. It is just up here," Rinnia answered her quietly just in front of her. Daegan behind Kaeleigh, leaned forward to see beyond her.

Hearing an audible click, then a sound of stone sliding on stone, the fleeing group watched as a shaft of warm light flickered and sent the darkness away from their space. Dunstand stepped through and each one followed one by one.

"Close it, Finn," Dunstand called quietly behind them. Finn stood at the back of the group. The sliding stone sound broke the silence once more.

"I hope no one heard that," Kaeleigh muttered, "though I don't know if anything could be heard over the growing din of that monster out there."

Daegan's hand slid over her shoulder and she reached up and laced her hand with his, relishing in the comfort he provided her. Dunstand moved ahead and lit a couple more torches mounted on the wall. They were inside an entry space, nothing more than a dark cave made of tightly positioned stones, narrowing into a tunnel of smooth rock then pitch black where the torches stopped. Dunstand looked even larger as his shadow grew and flickered in tune with the torchlight against the cave wall. He faced them, his features drawn and weary, though the spark of hope and life Kaeleigh had seen before had noticeably grown.

"You did it. I do not know how, but you freed us. And one day soon, I know we will be able to leave once that monster out there leaves. Though I think for now it is more here for you than to guard us. I am sorry for that, but I am so grateful for what you have done," he whispered happily, emotion shining in his eyes. Rinnia came next to him and looped her arm inside his, a feat considering how much shorter she was than he and patted his arm. She too beamed with happiness.

"Thank you," she added. "Now you must flee while you can. Others out front will try to distract the beast to give you time, but do not count on much. Be very careful when you come out. To your advantage, the exit of the tunnel is not known by many especially those on opposing sides."

"How far to the other side?" Ella inquired, leaning down to straighten the tall leather boots she wore.

"It is about a half a day's walk," Dunstand replied.

Rinnia pulled out a cloth sack. "It is not much but hopefully it will help you make it through until you reach the portal." She smiled, handing it to Kaeleigh.

Kaeleigh took the sack and immediately smelled something delicious.

"Food for the journey," Rinnia shrugged.

"Thank you," Kaeleigh smiled and lunged at Rinnia with a full embrace.

"It is the least we can do, Dearie," she replied, happy tears running down her cheeks as she let Kaeleigh go. "You must be on your way now."

"When you come out on the other side, the rock formations should hide you, ensuring the safety of your passage. You will have to skirt through the ruins of Klavaí to the back wall of rock where there is a trail leading into the mountains on the other side. I do not know what forces might be guarding or watching that portal, so be wary," Dunstand explained leaning forward so not to speak too loudly.

Daegan extended his hand to the man, gripped his forearm instead of his hand, and gave a warrior's shake. "Thank you for your service to Alandria. We will send word when the gathering for the fight has come, we would welcome any who would stand up for the freedom of Alandria."

Dunstand gripped Daegan's forearm in return, a glimmer of pride in his eyes as he nodded and stood tall. "We will come to Alandria's aid when the time comes. Be safe." He handed each of them their own torches, and each one expressed thanks to the large man and his mate. Kaeleigh stopped before Dunstand and gave him a big hug before she followed Daegan into the tunnel followed by Ella who had given the inn-keepers and their rescuers a regal bow. Finn followed behind her, but Dunstand reached out, grabbing his arm holding him behind a mere fraction.

"You need to tell him what is eating you up inside, Finn," Dunstand encouraged the man with warm and understanding eyes. "We will see you in battle," he added before letting Finn go.

With a hesitant step and a shimmer in his eyes, Finn nodded though he was unable to say anything. He nodded to Rinnia, took the last offered torch, and followed to catch up with Ella who paused waiting for him.

"I do not know what he spoke, but whatever is weighing so heavily upon you must be dealt with soon or it will come to your ruin, Finnlan." Ella searched his hazel gaze, unable to pierce beyond his tightly erected walls, guarding his heart and his mind. Not that she could read minds as some would think, but she was gifted at reading people.

"I fear it will either way," he sighed, his tone resigned and bitter. He looked in her eyes and wanted to crumble. The truth he held would turn her away from him faster than she could blink, but he knew in that moment he would do what was right when the time came.

Chapter Fifteen

Elnye. Territory of the Ferrishyn.

Arriving at the top of the staircase in the old wing of the castle in Elnye, her home and position of power, Maleina practically glowed; her hair the illusion of flames dancing upon her head as she sauntered down the hall. A fresh surge of power seeped from her pores and escaped, evaporating wastefully as her body could not contain all the energy flowing through her. Downstairs, below the castle ruins of the eastern wing, in an unused part of the dungeon, was the tree—her tree of life. The spindly, leafless tree flourished from the nourishment of blood, magical blood that contained the life energies of Alandria, brought to it from the Soul Stealer, Jin. The tree not only survived on the blood of Alandria, but also a magical mix infused with the very essence of Alandria herself. The extra power gave Maleina abilities beyond her own, mixing the magic of whomever it came from within her. The first several times, it took her days, months even, to gain a grasp on what the magic of the different races could do and how it interacted with her own. With the revelation she had to absorb the blood intravenously, came immense energy and power. It had become her addiction, siphoning the life from Alandrians she wished to conquer. Inhaling deeply through her nose, Maleina felt invincible, powerful.

The clicking of her heels on the stone floor echoed through the corridor so loudly she almost missed the coaxing sound of her mistress' voice calling her through the mirror as she passed. *She* had called to her once before in the same manner, but then it was used to intimidate Maleina and make the point she was not unreachable in her castle of stone. *She* could always find Maleina, or so the mistress thought.

"Maleina, it is imperative we speak," her voice whispered once more.

"I need to reach my private chamber, Mistress," Maleina whispered harshly back, "please allow me a moment to get there."

The air around her had gone silent—filled, however, with the weightiness of an expectant pull allowing her no room for deviating from her current path to her chamber. Maleina arrived a few moments later at her chamber only to be detained by her faithful yet suspicious husband, Wren.

"Maleina, my dear, might I have a word?" Wren's voice called from the far end of the throne room opposite the entrance to her private chamber.

She turned, something about his expression caused her to pause. He had aged some in the last couple months as if time had suddenly caught up to him or advanced him beyond his years. Maleina thought she could find a way to help him, possibly by slipping him some of the blood from the tree without him knowing, that might do him some good. No time for it now.

"I am in the middle of something, it will have to wait," she replied impatiently.

"You mean, *I* will have to wait." Wren sighed wearily. "Maleina, I am worried about the children. I have not heard word from them since you sent them on separate tasks—your silly little missions you had to involve our children on, and may I remind you the heirs to this throne," his voice raised but only slightly, though she knew he was frustrated with her.

"Wren, I do not have time to expound on any of it just now. But I received missives from both of them just the day before last. They are well and will be home soon," she lied straight to his face. She knew where Hal was and had an idea to bring him home. Rheina, the traitor, had gone off-grid, she had no idea where her darling daughter was or what she was up to; her spies were apparently blind to Rheina's whereabouts.

"Of course, dear," Wren said quietly, humbled by his wife's ambition to rule. He was beginning to believe taking the position of Paladin was the worst mistake of their lives. He turned and left the throne room without a backwards glance.

Maleina watched him leave, her heart beat rapidly knowing *She* could be listening and did not want to give her anything to hold against her. Slipping inside her chamber, she quickly closed the door and locked it. One quick perusal of the room to ensure she was alone and the wards were still set to anyone other than herself. Pulling out a flower-shaped item, she set it on her elaborately detailed wooden desk and watched as the pulsating warm light glowed from within, an indicator that *She* was waiting to speak with her. The contraption served as a communication device powered by magic which allowed them to speak between the realms; an item of power or a mirror or some object was needed to funnel the magic through in order for a full conversation. Maleina chanted a spelled word, the pulsing light increased as the flower orb opened to a full bloom in order to open the lines of communication as well as the two-way mirror encased within.

"Mistress, I am here," Maleina opened with, inclining her head.

"Maleina," *She* spoke with barely a detectable hint of panic in her tone. "The Sol-lumieth is about to leave Alandria. Are you not aware of this?"

"I am," Maleina said though her eyes widened slightly at the news. She had not known they were that close. "Do you not have a trap set in Kandri?" she asked pointedly.

"Do not forget your place, Maleina," *She* scolded quickly. "Yes, the curse is laid in Kandri, but my servant the Droch-Shúil has informed me they—she—broke it and found a way to protect the city barring my monster entrance!" *She* shrieked and slammed her hand on something unseen on the other side. "Send in those that serve you there and stop them before they get to the portal into the mortal realm!" she demanded. "I need more time. That girl must not get to the entrance into Exhile yet. Everything must happen according to the timeline!"

Maleina had not seen her mistress out of sorts before, it gave her pause and an idea. "Yes, mistress. I will alert the Ónarach immediately. They are already in position nearby," Maleina explained. "Is there any-thing else, your servant may do for you?" Her head bowed, she was able to conceal her small mischievous smile.

"Just get it done, Maleina. I will be in touch," *She* said then shut down her side of the communication, leaving Maleina smirking in si-lence.

"Of course, I will inform the clones," Maleina muttered to herself as she closed her side down as well and prepared her message to be delivered.

<p style="text-align:center">~~~~~</p>

"Valus?" Rheina stopped, grabbing his arm. They had been traveling mostly by night for days. For the first time in those days, Rheina felt the stirring of the *other* soul—the Orchid—residing within her. Valus had been warned of her presence and how she liked to appear out of nowhere but usually always with cause, but he had yet to witness the occurrence—now was his chance.

"Rheina? What is it?" Tall, muscular yet lean, the handsome Valus with his blonde hair, intelligent gray eyes, and dark long lashes stopped before her. He grasped each of her arms with his large hands, his eyes full of concern. He had been watching her on and off for the past few days as she pulled into herself, remaining quiet except to ask or answer questions.

"She's coming." Rheina's eyes appeared slightly panicked and her gaze shot to his, concerned for his reaction.

Valus' eyes widened, but nodded. He pulled Rheina closer within the shelter of some trees and a large boulder offering her a sense of privacy if she needed it. "Let her come, Rheina-lee. I want to speak with her."

Rheina nodded nervously, her throat working overtime swallowing. She inhaled deeply and closed her eyes. A ritual to bring the other soul forward was not necessary but at times it made the transition easier on Rheina.

When Rheina opened her eyes, no longer were her green ones shining but now stormy gray ones reflected back, at him. Valus fought back the gasp threatening to choke his throat. Instead he swallowed and inclined his head to the stranger now before him within the body of the girl he was growing comfortable with.

"Young man," the aged voice spoke through Rheina as she inclined her head in return. "Your service is appreciated and your companionship as well." She smiled slowly then offered, "Rheina is a dear one, but I am afraid I have kept her from forming attachments. Be careful with this one, I am fond of her and will avenge her however necessary."

The sneer on Rheina's face matched what the woman said, but did not match the face it came from. Valus took a step back, his brows pinched, but nodded. "I understand. She is very special." He paused thoughtfully. "Does she remember or is she aware of the conversation you and I have?"

"Yes, she is still here, but I have taken over the reins so to speak," she responded.

"And who are you? I am Valus Montrinno at your service." He swept his hand behind him and one at his waist as he bowed formally.

"I am Kanessa Lithvytís and I am of the Orchids, but I am also a Reafían traveler with harbinger traits," she said quietly.

Valus gulped loudly. "I am also a Reafían traveler," he said in awe. "I have not met another of our kind, only my brother and I remain that we know of." The Reafíans were a rare race of people who could break away from their realm and freely enter others without cost to themselves; often used as hunters to seek out great evils.

"There are a few more, but not many," Kanessa said sadly. "I am currently supposed to be held in Exhile with the other Orchids, but I felt I could be used better elsewhere. That witch's wards could not keep me, especially in soul form." She smirked as if her little secret gave her pleasure. "I can return as needed. Rheina has allowed me an open invitation so I have a means to help the others and do what I can for Alandria. Though I travel, Alandria has always been my home," she explained.

"Can you tell us of our mission? What are we to do for the Orchids?" Valus asked, his eyes held caution thinking of the dangers of Exhile.

"Yes, but things have changed slightly since last I spoke with Rheina. The time frames have altered slightly, and you have a bit more time until you are required in Exhile. The Orchids would like you to take Rheina to the outer edges of Alandria, beyond the known boundaries to this generation and seek more allies to aid in the coming war." Kanessa went on to explain their first destination and how to get there, mentioning she would be remaining with them for a time but would let Rheina come forth once more.

"We will do our best to find these allies," Valus said nobly and bowed his head in parting. When he lifted his head, beautiful green eyes that took his breath away once more stared back at him instead of the stormy gray ones.

"Hi," he said quietly with a small reassuring smile.

"Hi to you too," Rheina said with a slight blush, her eyes ducked away from his. "Well, you have now met my constant companion. Are you afraid of me?" she asked quietly.

"Afraid? Why would I be afraid?" he asked with a slight chuckle. "Because you have the soul of an old..." he coughed and cleared his throat correcting himself, "older woman inside you? It makes you twice as intriguing." He reached for her hand unabashedly without her offering it. She gave it, but looked down at their now joined hands as if she had never seen such a thing. He chuckled again. "Rheina-lee we are going to have quite the adventure!"

"Thank you," she said, "for being with me and for understanding even as little as you can with my... situation."

"There is nowhere else I would rather be." Valus winked at her and they continued on their altered path to their first destination beyond what they knew as Alandria's borders, the first to do so in a very long time.

Chapter Sixteen

Mandu tré Lan. Territory of the
Shifters.

Not long after food had been devoured, Hal and Chel sat talking and discussing all events leading up to now with her parents. Chel conveniently skimmed over the part where she was kidnapped by the servants of the Droch-Shúil, not wanting to have "that conversation" with them yet. She was still sorting out things in her own head and wasn't ready to talk about it out loud; however, the sly look Hal had given her suggested he knew what she was doing but gratefully hadn't pointed it out. Inwardly she groaned, assuming he would try and bring it up sometime. She just wasn't ready.

"So what is the plan? I'm assuming you have one, coming all this way to the territory of Shifters," her dad eyed them with both optimism and skepticism.

"Well," Chel's eyes shifted from her dad to her mom then back to her dad, "of course, we have a plan."

"And don't say to gather all the Shifters together in a meeting, announce what you're doing, and then expect them to just sign up willing to fight," declared her dad.

"Yep, that pretty much sums up what was in my head. Hal? Anything different from you?" Chel's shoulders slumped in defeat.

Hal looked taken aback as Chel drew the conversation to her at first, then straightened his shoulders. "Of what I know of the Shifters, I had expected to take some extra time getting to know them and feeling out where their desires for Alandria were at. Then when I felt we had similar agreements, I planned to entice them to our cause and draw them into an allegiance. Or at the very least get them to save their own skins by fighting with us until we got control of Alandria once more." Hal shrugged on that last bit, part sarcastic part truthful.

Her dad laughed, patted Hal on the back and walked over to a map on the wall that neither Chel nor Hal had noticed before. "I think he might be on to something," Ray announced to her mother, Lil, with a playful smile. She rolled her eyes much the same as Chel would have which caused Hal to nudge Chel's arm and point it out.

"Is that where you get the eye rolling? Or does she get it from you?" he mock whispered out loud.

Again Ray laughed and pointed back to Hal like he was on to something. "See! I told you it was a bad habit that would come back to bite you someday."

"Why do you think I've been doing it for so long?" Mom batted her eyes flirtatiously at her dad. "I keep waiting for someone to bite me." A growl came from Ray's chest as the heat in his eyes rose.

"Ew, come on you guys. We have company." Chel covered her eyes pretending to hide, but the smile underneath it all suggested she liked watching her parents tease each other. "Can I look yet? Plus we still need to come up with a plan."

"Yes, what is the plan?" a male voice came from the entry into the common room. Samuel leaned against the stone wall with a smirk on his face but his eyes followed only Chel. Atmospheric pressure suddenly shifted in the room, causing everyone to drop the playfulness a notch. "I was beginning to wonder if you had forgotten about me, Chel," he said stalking forward toward the table. "I was coming to see if you got fed, but it looks like you have. Good." Samuel stopped his motion and looked around the room and casually smiled at her parents.

"Hello Samuel," her mother broke the awkward silence, "you are welcome to join us. Perhaps you could even catch us up a bit more on what has happened with the Shifters since we've been gone." She paused. "You've been gone for some time too haven't you?"

"Yes, though not as long as any of you. I would be happy to catch you up on what I can. But first, I was wondering," he looked back to Chel. His expression had softened speaking to her mother, "Chel, if you would go for a short walk with me, I'd like to show you around the area a bit and catch up ourselves." He smiled hopeful, revealing a glimpse of a little boy wanting to be accepted.

Chel quickly glanced to her father and mother who nodded. "Sure, Samuel. I'd like to see around the land a bit more and get some fresh air."

"Fantastic." Samuel smiled.

"What should Halister and my parents do while we are out?"

"Why should I... I mean to say that someone is on their way to show Hal to quarters he can use while here," replied Samuel.

"Thank you, Samuel," Halister nodded. "Could I ask if you have a library or some kind of archive room where I could look for resources to help Chel and even possibly the future of Alandria?" he asked with a straight face, not ashamed stooping to use Chel's name for cooperation.

"When you put it that way, of course we do. Ask your guide and she will show you where it is located. We have no secrets here from the prince of the Paladin," Samuel sneered. "But Chel doesn't need help. I can guide her, she'll be just fine."

Chel and her parents watched Samuel and Hal, heads bobbing back and forth between the two men as the tension mounted. Samuel held his reactions and his animal better than even Landon had. He reached for Chel's hand and placed his inside it and pulled her along. "Come Chel, I have much to show you."

Chel furrowed her brows, annoyed by the testosterone match. However, she needed to learn the area and get the most information she could while she had a willing participant. Plus a part of her did care about Samuel. They had been friends and much more before Alandria. She wanted to hear how things back home in the mortal realm, back in Montana, were since she had left. Chel sighed and let him lead, holding her shoulders back and her chin high.

Chel looked at the surroundings as he led her through tunnels of stone. "Do these tunnels ever make you feel closed in? Or like the stones are going to topple onto you?" Chel eyed the ceiling and wall structures of boulders and stone with distrust.

"No. They are built well," Samuel answered, though he watched Chel curiously. "It is a natural habitat for the animals that are our other halves. The caves and tunnels protect us from outside enemies and weather."

"Maybe my animal doesn't like them for some reason because I'm finding it hard to breathe." Chel grumbled and rubbed her chest, grabbing at her neckline collar.

"We're almost to the outside exit. Down this hall are many of the meeting rooms and some of the bunk rooms. Most of the Shifters who have families live in their own caves disconnected from this main cave, but some do connect to the main tunnels. Many of the single Shifters, or young getting ready to live on their own, move into either the bunk rooms or into single rooms with a roommate," Samuel explained.

Chel looked down the hall, taking it all in. Similar to a dorm building, it was a long hallway separated consistently by arched doorways rounded decoratively with smaller rocks and stones. But unlike the drab and dull construction of a typical dorm, this hall was smooth, flat stone colored with nature's grays and browns held together with some kind of clay-colored mortar. Chel's eyes lit with remembrance and perked her head up and turned to Samuel. "Something you said reminded me of something I wanted to ask someone."

"Ok, shoot," Samuel encouraged.

"The weather. Since I've been here the weather seems to be pretty much the same daily. Well except when it's overwrought by something magic-related," she reflected. "Is it always the same or do they get other weather here like rain or snow or tornados or anything else like we do back home?"

At first Sam's eyes narrowed. "Chel, this is home. You have to stop thinking of Montana or anywhere in the mortal realm as home." He shook his head but continued, "Alandria is mostly consistent with comfortable weather comparable to Montana's mid-seventies I think. But I've seen it storm over the Shadow Mountains. I'll show you those, and you can see the snow caps way up high. We get wind storms here in this territory, but to be honest I haven't traveled much outside of Mandü, other than to get to the mortal realm portal and back." He paused thoughtfully. "I've heard of it raining in parts, but like I said it's mostly the same everyday... that I know of."

Chel nodded satisfied but found Samuel's tone strange. "Okay. Just curious." Down another long hall tunnel and more of the same stone, Chel could finally smell fresh air. Up ahead must be an exit to the outside. She breathed deeply, ready to see the sky once more. "I had no idea these caves could be so elaborate with all the attached tunnels," she mused. "When we came in, it didn't look big enough to house all these different rooms and halls from the outside."

Samuel's eyes lit up with genuine excitement at her observations, "It's pretty cool isn't it? It's so amazing being a Shifter."

"Is it?" Chel mumbled quietly forgetting everyone in the space there likely had excellent hearing.

He turned and stopped her in her tracks. Samuel was much closer than she was prepared for, their faces only inches apart. He put a hand on her shoulder and stared deep into her eyes. Very seriously he noted, "Yes, it is. And I'm going to show you how amazing it can be, how much you'll love it when you finally shift. I'm surprised that you haven't yet." Samuel stopped for a moment and looked wonderingly at Chel. "You must just be one of those slower-to-develop-Shifters, you know like back in the mortal realm when people 'bloom' a little later along than usual."

Chel raised an eyebrow and crossed her arms, her silence sending Samuel a clear message of disapproval.

"What? It might be true," and with that, the man turned around and walked off.

Chel rolled her eyes and let out a huff of air before following him. She was more curious than annoyed at the moment to see how the rest of the Shifters lived in this land so different from where she came from.

Finally reaching the exit from the mass tunnel system, Chel took a deep breath of cool air. "What is that smell? It's lovely," she acknowledged while looking for the source.

"It's from a specific flower to this area that's in bloom right now. Similar to Jasmine, I think," Samuel answered without missing a beat. "It grows all around here." He then pointed to a bush crawling up the side of a planter beside them. A leafy brown vine crept up the side of a planter blooming with small bright flowers, each section a variety of colors from bright green, purple, pinks, and blues.

"It's beautiful," Chel gasped. "I love that smell." She inhaled another chestful of its fragrance before she looked expectantly back to Samuel to see what he had planned next. Around her, she noticed quite a few people scattered across a common area. Children played some kind of a game, running freely. A group of women sat at a wooden table, watching the children and chatting, not unlike a scene Chel had seen many times in a park in Montana.

The women eyed Chel cautiously as she and Samuel made their way closer. One of them whispered not too quietly about how Chel was the girl who had brought in an outsider and another made the rebuttal that Chel was just as much of an outsider even though her dad used to be from there. Another one of the women prattled on about how she heard Chel hadn't even shifted yet—that she didn't belong there.

"You'd think they would at least try to gossip a little more quietly," Chel complained under her breath. "Do they not think I can hear them because I haven't shifted yet?" Chel eyed Samuel from the side.

"Just ignore them," he responded.

"Easier said than done," Chel mumbled. Her first response was to appear inconsequential and ignore them, but then she remembered who she was. "Forget that advice. I'm made of tougher stuff and those women will realize who I am in the end. I don't care if they like me or not," Chel said with more gumption than she truly felt. But of course, she actually did care if they liked her. She held her shoulders back, lifted her chin, and didn't bother to give the women the courtesy of not noticing them. Instead, Chel looked right at them, smiled as they drew close, and watched the women squirm. Samuel reached for her hand and gave it a squeeze.

"Hi Samuel," one woman flirtatiously waved despite the fact he and Chel walked hand-in-hand. Chel noticed the barest blush on Samuel's face.

"That's bold," Chel mumbled though she realized she wasn't even the slightest bit jealous—other than she couldn't believe the woman's brazenness. But that wasn't even all, after the first one, another one of the women eyed him like he was a piece of Shifter man-meat.

"Lovely day for a stroll, isn't it, Samuel?" the woman asked with feigned innocence.

"Wow, are you Shifter of the Month or something, Sam?" Chel teased but did wonder what the story here was. She realized that Sam must have had a life here before she had met him only a year or so ago in Montana, but still. Samuel barked out a laugh that caused Chel to jump. She was happy at least she hadn't lost her touch with making people laugh, but Samuel's deep timber didn't effect her the same as the thrill she received when she made a certain Faerie warrior laugh, still it was a nice accomplishment.

Samuel looked at her and winked. "Ladies, I'd like to introduce you to Chelnáh Marzén. I'm giving her the grand tour." He looked back to

Chel. "Chel, this is Serena, Jolie, and Matiss. Those little ones belong to Matiss." He pointed to the three children.

Luckily for the woman, she wasn't the one who had addressed Samuel flirtatiously or Matiss's Shifter hubby would probably have a thing or two to say about it.

"Nice to meet you," Chel stated in a friendly tone, no sense in stirring up real trouble.

"And you," Matiss acknowledged apparently on behalf of the group since the other two smiled tightly and nodded their heads as if that completed the pleasantries for the moment and they would go no further.

"Carry on. We will see you up in the hall later," Samuel announced and kept walking.

Chel followed at his side pondering the interaction among the women. She hoped the rest of her interactions wouldn't be as stiff. Examining her feelings, she glanced up at Samuel. He was a handsome guy with dark floppy hair, a little on the long side, with dark eyes and tanned skin. He wasn't as tall as Daegan or Halister and he was stockier in build, a man of bulkier muscles she'd always noted. This was something she had learned was more a physical feature for Shifters. In her brief survey, she realized she didn't have those butterflies that used to stir in her stomach when she first met him. In fact, she didn't feel much of anything internally other than slight annoyance she needed a guide to look around and couldn't look around either by herself or with Hal. The thought she wanted to look around with Hal struck her more profoundly than any so far.

"Sam, where are you taking me?" Chel inquired as they began to head toward a dirt trail that lead away from the main area.

"Down this path you will find where the majority of the Shifters live, the ones who live off-campus so to speak. They have their own little village. Where we were is more the meeting area, public kitchen, library, and bunk house." He looked at her with a wide smile. "I think you'll like this, we're almost there."

"Sounds great," Chel said as she followed him on a walking path wide enough to hold three to four people walking abreast. Trees lined each side of the path with a denser area on one side that led to a forested area, and a lighter spattering on the opposite side leading down to a source of water. "Is that a lake down there?"

"No, it's actually run off from the mountains that have made a small river. It's big enough for us to play around in though," he waggled his eyebrows with suggestion. Chel laughed off his comment with a playful shove against his shoulder, but felt uncomfortable with the idea, uncharacteristic for her.

Every once and awhile Chel could see through the sparse trees and beyond where the sound of the water was coming from. More so, she was drawn to it. She wanted to discover every crook and cranny and learn what everything this new world that could have been hers had she grown up there held. Chel would have to sneak off and explore on her own for a bit while she came up with a plan on how she was going to convince Shifters to fight for Alandria. Spacing off, she realized Samuel had gotten ahead of her. Chel jogged to catch up so not to miss anything.

The path widened and opened into a quaint village hidden within the valley between two cliff walls nestled against the edge of the Shadow Mountains. The main path was lined with a number of small stone homes, but higher up other openings meant to be doors and windows to more homes were built right into the boulders. They reminded Chel of some kind of apartments. *How snug!* Chel thought, yet something in her caused her to eye them with caution.

"How sturdy are those homes up there?" she asked Samuel quietly.

"Oh they're totally solid. Remember many of these have been here centuries," replied Samuel, gesturing to the different buildings.

The village seemed happy, flowers growing in pots and small gardens lining the sides where there was empty space enough between boulders and dwellings full of what appeared to be all kinds of vegetables some known to Chel and some unknown specific to Alandria.

"I wish I had my drawing stuff," Chel whispered in awe as she looked from one side to the other not willing to miss any of it.

"Oh you haven't seen half of it yet," Samuel said. At the end of the village road, there was a narrow path leading off the main one and up.

"Do you live in one of these?"

"No, I have a room in the bunk house. I've come and gone a lot in the last few years, but maybe now that I'm back for a while, I might see about settling in one." Samuel shifted, suddenly looking uncomfortable as he eyed one of the openings higher up. Chel couldn't help but notice.

"Who is up there, Sam?" Chel and Samuel both watched as a shadow of someone else watching them disappeared through the window. The hairs on the back of Chel's neck stood up.

"Nobody." Samuel was quick to calm. "Don't worry about it, Chel. She hardly ever comes out of her dwelling anyway."

"What? Why? Who is she?" If anything, knowing that a woman who hardly ever left her home and was now watching them, a woman whose home Samuel had nervously yet clearly noticed, drove her curiosity higher.

"Her name is Callie. She's blind," Samuel replied. At the confused look on Chel's face, he explained further. "It's highly unusual for a Shifter to be born blind. She doesn't participate in any Shifter obligations. Truth is, she basically just takes up space."

"Samuel!" Chel scolded. "That is no way to talk about someone just because they are blind. Has anyone ever helped her attend anything? Does she have family? Aren't you all supposed to be like a family?" The more Chel was learning about how this tribe functioned the less she wanted anything to do with it, though her passion to defend the woman surprised her.

"Some have tried, but she's not very receptive," he grumbled, a hint of anger at the edge of his voice.

"Well, maybe she just hasn't met anyone willing to try very hard," Chel replied with her own indignation, crossing her arms and giving one last look up at the girl's opening. "And why is she up high? Maybe she should be on the ground so she doesn't accidentally fall."

"Nah, she's a Shifter. She can handle herself just fine." One minute Samuel sounded like he was condemning her and the next he sounded like he had the tiniest bit of pride in this blind girl. Chel would get to the bottom of it she was sure. "Come on," Samuel tugged at her arm, "maybe you can meet some of the tribe."

They continued walking and Chel took note of each of the dwellings. Some villagers came out of their homes and offered a tentative wave, but others simply looked through their windows or doorways and kept to themselves. Samuel and Chel climbed up and up away from the village until the path became rocky, and they had to maneuver over fallen rocks. The air grew thinner the higher they climbed as did the trees and foliage. After about an hour, they finally reached the top of the giant wall of boulders. Samuel reached back and pulled Chel up the last few yards, right up onto the top plateau of stone. She let go and gained her balance.

"Whoa," Chel breathed, "it's breathtaking." The view before her was of the entire village they had just gone through beneath them and the meeting hall beyond that. The forest spread out beside the village, and the mountain range rose up along the other side.

"That over there," he pointed to the forest, "is the Stone Forest. It's got trees of course, but it is named as such because of the stone monuments and boulder positioning that it looks like it was placed purposely." He swung his arm out in front of them. "And that is the Shadow Mountain Range. It's one of the biggest in Alandria, perhaps even the biggest of all. I'm not sure on that." He inhaled deeply, adjusting his breathing for the thinner air. "Those are the main borders on either side of our territory."

"It's amazing," Chel admired as she looked all around her in a full circle. "I wish Kaeleigh could see this with me."

"She probably wouldn't be able to though," Samuel was quick to say. "It's highly unusual we let outsiders in—ones that aren't Shifters, I mean."

Chel cocked her head and frowned. "But she's my friend."

"She's not a Shifter," he rebutted.

"What's your point?" Chel came back with her hand on her hip and an *I-dare-you-to-continue-this* look on her face.

"My point is that the Shifters have been ostracized and cast out from most of Alandria for a very long time, and so we do the same to outsiders. We protect our own even at the expense of *friends*," he said, employing air quotes.

"That's not right, and not how I do things." Chel was filled with anger. "My friends are important! I don't care if they are frogs or aliens!" Chel's mood turned sour and the beauty of the view ruined by the asinine thug next to her. "You are no different than those who have done wrong to you. I'm not condoning what they have done, but it doesn't give you or anyone else here the right to do the same in return." Chel stalked back to the path that had brought them to this point, intent on making her descent back to the main path in the village and walking straight out. She noted on the way down there were actually many more dwellings in the rocks than she had first seen from the ground level.

"Chel, wait," Samuel sighed in frustration. "You're right." He followed her, begging her in his familiar patronizing tone. Not everyone might notice it, but she did. "Come on, there's more I was going to show you. You need to meet some of the members of the tribe too, Landon wanted me to introduce you."

Chel stopped. She pouted for a moment longer then took in a deep breath. How was she going to leave on her own? Maybe it did make sense for her to meet some people and see if she could find any that might be endeared to their cause. That's right, their cause. She couldn't lose sight of that. What about Samuel kept getting her off track? Chel sighed, trying to brush off her frustration with him. At that same moment, Samuel's feet hit the ground behind her, and he reached out to grab her arm. Chel pulled away from him.

"Fine, let's continue. But know that I'm not happy with you right now. I do need to meet the people and understand this territory if I'm to be a part of it, so go ahead," she gestured for him to take the lead with her hand.

"Thank you," Samuel said, a sly smile stretching over his face. "I knew you'd stick around. You need me, let's face it." Chel rolled her eyes at his wink and scowled.

"Don't count on it, buddy. I haven't needed anyone in a long time," she huffed but even as she said it an image of her handsome and playful traveling companion, Hal, flashed through her mind.

Chapter Seventeen

"Over to the left is the school house/training ground where the youth learn the basics of being a young Shifter," Samuel explained as they walked back through the village.

Chel frowned. "I wish I had known and had the opportunity to learn that when I was young."

They took a narrow path at the end where the cliffs opened up, leading to more dwellings with even more space in-between dwellings. The path even opened up at the end to the other side of the park-like setting they had walked by in the beginning. Though this time, the park was empty of visitors other than the occasional person walking on their way to another place.

Chel's shoulders dropped as she examined the entrance to the training area. "Can we stick our heads in?"

"I can bring you back later, they are in session right now and those are usually kept private for focus. If we talk to the instructors, I bet they would make arrangements for you to observe if you want," he offered.

"Sure, maybe," Chel responded with a grin. She didn't want to disrupt their lessons, though what she wouldn't give to have had those lessons earlier in her own life.

"What all do they train for, and how long do they train before the lessons aren't needed?" Chel asked.

"They are trained to fight for battle or simply for their own protection. Not just that, they are trained to shift, the ins and outs of what to expect when they do, and how to control it. The young ones attend lessons until they are twelve usually and sometimes beyond if they are interested in more, then they train until sixteen even if they've shifted before that. If they shift early, then their training becomes more focused on fight training and survival skills." Samuel kept walking while Chel absorbed all that he explained. "You know, like surviving in the wild, but also against magic—though that is harder to prepare against."

Chel scrunched up her face as she continued to walk then flopped down on the same bench that the women had been sitting on earlier.

"What are you doing, Chel? I still need to show you the strategy room with all the maps. It's connected to the library," Samuel attempted to coax her to keep moving. Though despite his words to move on, he stood next to her and put his foot up on the bench and leaned over to peer at her. "Or we could take a quick break." He shrugged though his words didn't seem as relaxed as he appeared.

"As a Shifter, why do *you* think I haven't shifted yet?" Chel mused out loud unconcerned with his desire to keep moving.

"It probably has to do with being raised in the, err... mortal realm," he said those last two words as if it was a disgusting place to be even though he lived there himself for a time. "There's really no other reason I can think of, it's not like you're slow in any other developmental area of life." His gaze dropped then quickly came back to her face to meet her solid frown.

Chel felt it useless to push more. He was clearly not open to any other reason for it, so she changed the subject. Samuel was not who she needed or wanted to discuss matters with anymore.

"Did you say a library?" Her eyes lit up with false excitement. She enjoyed libraries as much as the next person, but right now she just wanted some quiet time. Maybe she could get some time alone after that.

"Yes, it's not much, but it holds all the records and histories we have of our area and some of the greater area of Alandria as well," Samuel said dropping his foot and stretching his arms above his head.

Chel rolled her eyes. His displays of "manliness" were getting on her nerves. He was like a peacock strutting around in front of her saying "look at me, look at me, aren't I pretty?" She got up and half-heartedly sucker-punched him in the stomach. Unfortunately, he reacted completely opposite of what she wanted. Instead, his chest rumbled and he gripped her arm, pulling her in towards him. Apparently his need for her attention overrode his senses.

"Did you want to play with a real man, Chel?" Samuel growled, his eyes glowing and his animal close to the surface. Not in anger, but in excitement.

Perhaps some would have been pulled in by his magnetism, perhaps even she would have back in Montana... but not anymore.

"When I find one, I'll let you know," Chel winked playfully, but pulled out of his hold and stepped away nonetheless. He couldn't miss the rejection.

He sighed. "What happened to you, Chel? Don't you want to be with me anymore?" Samuel asked, his eyes steady staring straight into her, anger on the cusp of his emotions now. Hot then cold.

"A lot happened to me, Samuel." Chel sighed sadly. "Honestly, right now I don't know what I want, other than some time to figure that out. Can you give me that?"

Samuel was quiet. His eyes lost focus for a moment then came back. "Of course, I can give you time. I still want you, and I want you to take whatever time you need. I'm not a barbarian, Chel. I can wait for you."

Though he said the words, Chel got the feeling there was more, something lying just under the surface she couldn't quite pick out. Maybe Kaeleigh's and her parent's hesitations about Samuel were finally ringing through her own. Now she thought about it, Shifters could sense other Shifters, or any animal for that matter, so why didn't her parents—experienced Shifters—know Samuel had been one? But then a new thought hit her. Or they did know and just hadn't said anything to her because their own secret would've been out in the open... her mind began racing.

"Thank you." Chel said giving him a smile. "Now let's see this library of yours," she announced.

"Ours," Samuel corrected.

"Right," Chel paused, "ours." She would have to adapt to the Shifter life here pretty quickly if she was to fit in and make any alliances; she only hoped it could be done quickly. Chel had no idea how Kaeleigh and the others fared out in other parts of Alandria, or how much time they actually had. Now she was in the Shifter territory, she felt removed from the outside world of Alandria. In fact, it was like time moved differently from one section of Alandria to the next, although she knew it wasn't. Chel felt separated from Kaeleigh and the rest of her team and the rest of Alandria; the only one who could tie her to anything else in this realm was Hal. Hopefully he was having more luck than she was at making friends—though she hoped he didn't come across the women from earlier she and Samuel had encountered. The very idea forced her hackles up.

"Samuel?" she started, "I never asked you—or I guess you've never said—what is your animal? What can you shift into, I mean?" Chel asked with uncertainty. "I'm sure it's impolite to ask such a question, but I think that's probably something I should know right, since you know, we lived together for a time and all," she felt the need to clarify her statement.

"A fox... a black fox to be specific, Chel. They are pretty rare," puffing out his chest, Samuel replied with pride. "It's similar to a red fox but it's black and bit bigger."

"That's pretty cool!" exclaimed Chel. "So are there other types of foxes too? As there are in the mortal realm? Or are they different because they are Alandrian?" She scrunched her brows in thought. "What about other animals? How many different types of animals are there to shift into?" One question came after another.

"Many of the animal types are similar or even the same as in the mortal realm. Animals as well as humans can cross the divides of our parallel realms. So we do have both. For example, we have the wolf just as we do in the mortal realm, but then in Alandria we have a Lielmär—a type of horned rabbit—obviously native to Alandria." Samuel thought of another example. "Or we have a bear, but we also have a creature that is smaller but resembles a bear with tusks. It can get a little confusing, but you'll figure it out. We also have animals like cheetahs, polar bears, and many bird types, including owls that you would find familiar. And as far as how many, I have no idea but it's a lot." Samuel peered at Chel from the side of his eyes, "So do you know which animal you will be? I mean, I know you haven't shifted yet, but do you have an idea?"

"Oh, yes I do actually. I was able to see my animal when we crossed the Bridge of Revealment on our way in. I believe I'll be a wolf like my parents." She smiled, feeling more comfortable saying her animal out loud. Chel was about to turn around and reveal her newly acquired marking on her back by pulling at her neckline, but seeing something strange on her arm she stopped suddenly. One of the tattoos she had designed within the sleeve she was most proud of on her left upper arm caught her attention. It was different... it had changed positions, like it had moved and she got a strange sensation she should keep her srontas marking—that marking that designated her as a Shifter—to herself for some reason. She couldn't understand what difference it would make, but she listened to her intuition whenever she could. Putting her arm down, she awkwardly put it behind her back, but noticed Samuel watching her.

"Chel, I have to tell you something," he broke the awkward silence. He finally felt they'd established some trust and could come out with it.

"All right, what is it?" She ducked around a boulder and followed him through a dark tunnel, only to realize it was not actually dark inside but the sun outside gave a different illusion.

"Halister is going to cause problems here for himself, and I'm afraid for you," he spoke carefully but bluntly.

"What are you talking about? He doesn't want to stir up trouble. He's here to be my guide and to help me seek allies to save Alandria." Chel couldn't imagine how any ulterior motive from Hal, although as soon as she mentioned the part about their mission, she closed her mouth. Did Samuel already know? She couldn't remember. Was she supposed to share that bit of information with him or keep it to herself? Why couldn't she remember? Grrr. Well, it would have come out sooner or later as they needed to actively seek those who would fight alongside them for Alandria.

"Nonetheless, he will stir up trouble, it's just a matter of time. I think you know that already, though. Plus how can you associate with him when so many Shifters were persecuted and imprisoned by his mother and her followers?" Samuel spit. They had paused just outside a room with a closed door. "Shifters have always been looked down on as lesser and demeaned by other Alandrians. Some more than others. Some have even lost their lives for standing up to the Paladin if they refused servanthood."

Chel looked up and down the hall hoping no one was overhearing him, his voice had not lowered since coming indoors. "It is all wrong! And I know for a fact, that Maleina has her hand in a lot of the territories, spreading her deceit and hate for not only Shifters. But *he* didn't persecute them. In fact, Hal did what he could to help and even befriended the Shifters in Elnye. I think you need to give him a chance and not label him based on what his mother has done," Chel shout-whispered angrily.

Samuel raised his hands in surrender. "I don't want to fight with you, Chel, even if you are cute when you fight back." He smiled looking for hers in return, but when she remained closed off with her hands at her hips, he backed down and his voice grew serious once again "I just felt as a friend, that I should warn you to try and keep your distance from him for your own good in this tribe, or you might find yourself ostracized as well."

Chel was not happy about Samuel's threat-warning; however, she realized now wasn't the time to make a decision about what he was saying. What was more important now was to figure out what was going on in the Shifter territory and to stick to her mission. He opened the door to reveal a small, musty room with a large round table in the middle. Bookshelves of various sizes lined the walls. Various books and scrolls of parchment were scattered haphazardly on the shelves. She walked in and trailed her fingers along one of the shelves. Dust everywhere. Had anyone been here? In the last decade? Crinkling her nose, she sneezed several times before adjusting to the dust.

"Bless you," a feminine voice came from beyond the stacks. "I believe that is the customary acknowledgement when someone sneezes in the mortal realm, is it not?"

Chel looked to Samuel. He however, was grimacing. Clearly, he was unhappy at the person whose voice floated toward them.

"Callie, *what* are you doing in here?" Samuel asked. Chel tapped him on the arm to get his attention. *The blind girl?* She mouthed. He nodded, but it was Callie who responded.

"Yes, I may be blind, but I still like the smell of books and there happens to be a few in here that I can read... well, kinda." Chel could hear the frown in her voice, yet she wasted no time jumping into the conversation.

"Hi! I'm Chel," she introduced herself to a bookshelf as she stepped forward trying to catch a glimpse of Callie. She simply couldn't be satisfied talking to someone at the other side of the room.

"I am over here, Chel. Use your ears," Callie chuckled.

"Smart-ass Shifter," Chel mumbled.

Callie laughed. "I like her, brother."

"Brother?" Chel asked, confused.

"Yes, she's easy to like," Samuel agreed but also didn't refute her 'brother' statement. Something in his voice was disturbed. Chel may not have been one hundred percent in sync with him right now, but she could still read between the lines.

"You didn't mention she was your sister when we passed her home in the village," said Chel.

"No, he would probably not claim me to anyone who he did not have to explain me," she didn't sound sad, but instead had a level a snark that Chel could relate to. Humor over hurt—it was a common coping defense Chel herself used. Chel found Callie on the floor surrounded by a pile of books. Callie sensed her presence, cocked her head, and smiled. "You smell good, I like your wolf," Callie bluntly said. The sound of books slamming onto tables and muttering under Samuel's breath alerted them to his displeasure.

Chel laughed. "Well, thank you." Chel looked at the titles of books she could see. "What are you... searching for?"

"There are some magical books that when I touch them the content actually pops visually into my mind so I can see what it is sharing with me. I was looking for a story I remembered as a child, just for fun." Callie shrugged.

"For fun, huh?" Chel frowned. The titles of most the books Callie had displayed were anything but a fictional stories for a child. The books appeared to be more on research topics. "You know I can read right?" Chel whispered conspiratorially.

"Busted," Callie acknowledged quietly. She held her finger up to her lips, asking Chel to keep her secret.

"For now," Chel replied. She would have to hunt Callie down on her own time to have a further discussion about the titles she was looking at. Callie nodded, a smile in her vacant eyes.

"Brother, what are you looking for?" Callie asked Samuel. His feet scuffed against the hard ground as he moved about.

"I am not sure to be honest, Callie." Samuel sighed with frustration. "I thought Chel might enjoy learning some history of the Shifters. She did not have the opportunity to learn as a youth. Do you think perhaps she could find something in this old dump to help her figure out how to shift into the wolf you think smells so good?" Samuel chuckled exasperated, amused by the things his sister said but still annoyed she outed his avoidance of who Callie was to him.

"That sounds like a good idea," Callie said thoughtfully. "She might find the books you used to read to me as a young girl to be helpful. I did."

Chel observed Callie silently as she spoke to her brother. It was a strange sensation to watch someone when you can look directly at them without the person knowing that you were looking. Callie appeared to be about sixteen, but Chel knew age could be deceptive in Alandria. Callie was slight, but had well-defined muscles. Perhaps being a Shifter kept one more toned than an average human? Chel's own body could answer her question as she never worked out but remained muscular though a bit curvy. Shifters held muscle differently than the more athletic build of the Elves. The questions abounded. Callie's light auburn hair spilled past her shoulders in slight waves, framing an angelic face set with pale brown eyes and an upturned nose. She was paler than the average person, likely from spending most of her time indoors or in the shadows, Chel surmised.

"I will look for those, good suggestion, Callie." Samuel walked over to the shelf with the histories on it to look for the one she talked about. "Callie, you should go home. I will walk you," Samuel stated as a final thought.

Callie made a noise of protest, getting up with practiced ease. Her frown marred her beautiful face and something inside Chel felt frustrated for the girl.

"She can stay with us Samuel. Perhaps she can help."

"No, she needs to be at home. She's been out too long as it is." His voice held no room for argument, his decision would not be swayed.

"Thank you, Chel, but he is always right," Callie grumbled, but Chel heard the hint of sarcasm in her tone. "Good luck with your search."

"Perhaps we will meet again," Chel said, hoping the girl would hear her desire to talk with her. Callie's countenance lit up briefly, though not enough to catch Samuel's attention.

"Perhaps," Callie's reply was a mix of sadness, truth and secrecy at once. What a mysterious girl! Chel would hate having an overprotective brother boss her around when she was more than capable. In fact, she wouldn't stand for it. Why should Callie? Chel stopped herself with the promise she would have to discuss these restrictions she felt Samuel had placed on her. Callie was strong, not some frail or weak girl that should be sheltered and kept hidden from the world. If her first impression of the situation was right, Chel had an earful for Samuel too. The time would come she was sure.

Callie felt her way to the entrance of the stacks but moved with ease through the rest of the room, barely touching a wall for help. She must have visited there often to be so familiar with it. Chel did notice that under her breath she was whispering something. Was it numbers? She must be counting her steps, Chel reasoned as she went from one "landmark" to the next. Chel watched as Callie felt for the table by the entrance, then not again until she felt the doorway and counted again.

"She's amazing," Chel said, words filled with genuine awe watching her leave.

"She is, but she shouldn't be out," he grumbled as he flipped open one book then tossed it aside apparently not the one he sought.

"Why? Why shouldn't she be out? I can't imagine being cooped up in a cave the rest of my life. That's not living, Samuel. And why didn't you tell me about her?"

"For her it is. You don't understand. There are those who would hurt her. It's for her protection," Samuel growled and threw another book across the room, a much stronger reaction than called for, Chel observed. "And I have my reasons," he replied to her last question.

"Sam? You coming?" Callie's voice echoed from outside the entrance.

Samuel turned to Chel with an odd expression. "Look through that pile there." He pointed to a different stack than the ones he had been tossing around. "I'll be right back. At least she waited for me this time." He let out a pained chuckle, revealing more affection than exasperation for his little sister.

Chel frowned as the man she felt was becoming more and more obscure to her stormed out of the room. So he wanted to protect his sister, but from whom? Other Shifters? Chel felt something amiss could explain the odd situation, and the strangeness of it drove her desire to figure it out.

Once the brother and sister duo had left, Chel began looking around the library. She moved from bookcase to bookcase examining the different types, titles, and scrolls collected there. It was nearly impossible to make sense of the stacks as they weren't in any kind of order resembling libraries back in the mortal realm. There were no categories listed on signs. No Dewey Decimal numbers on the spines. Nothing to indicate what she was looking at. However, most of what she could read was in English.

After a few minutes she picked up one off the pile Samuel had indicated she go through so politely. She huffed out loud to herself. The book was covered in dust. Blowing it off only seemed to agitate her nose, causing her to sneeze several times once again. Chel placed the book back on the pile and sighed in exasperation. Why couldn't there be anything on a topic of interest to her here such as art or the history of these Shifter markings? An idea sprung to mind. What was it that Callie had been reading? She recalled on one of the books Callie'd been holding she'd seen a picture of a marking similar in coloring to hers and Kaeleigh's. What else could she find out about her marking?

Finding the book she had been looking for, Chel sat on the same floor Callie had been just minutes ago. Comfortable, with her legs outstretched and her back against the wall, Chel observed the book she held in her hands.

"Another dust bag," she mused. "Incredibly, this thing has more dust on it than the others." Instead of blowing the bulk of it off, she tried wiping it off on her clothes, then blew off what little was left. Fortunately for her, it only made her sneeze once. "What an interesting design," Chel murmured, brushing her fingers along the smooth and shiny *srontas* etched on the front cover of the book. The cover texture was rough; a hardback covered with a kind of cloth instead of smooth like most hardbacks found in the mortal realm. The book's edges were frayed, and the writing on the front scratched and tattered, practically unreadable. In fact, even if it had been more or less readable, Chel wasn't able to read the language that was written. Perhaps the Shifters did have their own language?

The lettering was vaguely familiar—why was that? Chel closed her eyes and thought hard. She remembered a book and some art that her parents had hidden in their home. The memories that had come flooding back to her since being in Alandria continued to surprise her.

Gliding her thumb across the lettering she tried to recall if she had any thoughts about what it could mean, but she didn't. Opening the book, she gasped as symbols and markings the likes of which she had never seen floated up off the page swirling right before her eyes. Greens and blues swirled together faster and faster, causing her to sit back as far as she could without it touching her face. "What is happening?!" Chel whispered, partly in fear, but also in amazement of what she saw.

One of the symbols stopped abruptly in front of her face then flew into her eyes. "What the…" Chel dropped the book onto her lap and swiped at her face. She rubbed her eyes, afraid of what had just got in them, hoping she wouldn't be blinded as Callie was. Had the symbol done something to her?

When she opened her eyes, her vision was slightly blurry. The symbols and markings had stopped spinning. "Maybe it was my imagination," Chel rushed out with both relief and disappointment. Picking up the book once again, though her grip slightly shaky, she glanced down at the page she had opened up to. She could read it, all of it. "Whoa!" With amazement, Chel read that page and then the next and the next until before she knew it, she had gone through the entire book. Unfortunately, she hadn't found anything about her specific marking or Kaeleigh's for that matter. She had really wanted to find something helpful she could share with Kaeleigh and the others. Chel went back to the first page, but the writing there was different than the first time she had read it. "Well, that's interesting. Are all your pages different?" Chel flipped a few more pages and each of them were different as well. "Do you understand me?" Chel rolled her eyes and looked to the ceiling, noting more of the smooth boulders that miraculously—in her opinion—held up this room and all the other tunnels and rooms. The back of her neck broke out in a cold-sweat, feeling like those boulders might fall on top of her at any moment. She then decided it would be wise not to look up again.

"I'm talking to a book. Maybe you really have lost it this time, Chel Marzén." She let out a huge breath, gazing around the library just to make sure no one else was nearby or listening. Samuel hadn't come back yet. How much longer would he be, she wondered.

Chel resolved to make the most of her time by herself so she went for it.

"Book, can you tell me about my marking or about my family?" She waited for half a beat and sucked in her breath when the book's pages flipped all on their own, landing on a blank page. Chel's nose scrunched up in confused frustration. "Well, that's not exactly helpful... unless, oh should I draw it?" The book remained unmoving.

"I guess that's a yes?" Chel gently placed the book on the ground next to her while she got up and scrounged around for some kind of writing utensil. Realizing she hadn't seen a pen of any kind since they arrived, she wasn't sure where to look. However, the Shifters had hand-drawn maps and written histories they had to have some kind of tool. The eager Shifter spotted a charcoal pencil over on a dusty table and took hold of it.

"All right Book, if you want me to draw in you, keep the page open. If you do not want me to draw on your open page, please close the book or turn the page." Hesitantly she waited, her pencil poised for action, and her hands removed from the book so as to be sure she wasn't forcing the book to stay open or any pages to close. Nothing happened. The book remained open. "Okay, well, here goes nothing." Chel shook her head and inhaled deeply.

Cringing as she began drawing on history's old pages of parchment, Chel hoped she wouldn't be implicated or worse, hung, from disrespecting Alandrian history or property. She had no idea how they punished people in Mandü tré Lan, but she was pretty sure it wasn't pretty. Chel drew swiftly, not even needing to think about what her marking looked like. She knew as it was as much a part of her as any other art she created to decorate her body. The charcoal applied smoothly and allowed her hand to flow fluidly from one stroke to the next. Brittle crinkling sounds came from where she touched the ancient paper, but it held together without cracking or tearing. As her last stroke brought the image to completion, the book filled in the coloring just as it was on her back as if it knew it as well as she did. Maybe it did. Chel's surprised intake of breath sounded loud in the quiet space. She couldn't take her eyes off the drawing. It was an exact replica of the one on her back, now etched in time and a history she was becoming a part of—perhaps she always had been, but now she recognized it.

"What does it mean?" she quietly asked the book.

Writing began to flow across the top and bottom of the page and all around the picture, all written in what seemed at first in an unreadable language. The letters and symbols unscrambled themselves before her eyes yet again, and she could read it. Chel's eyes were wide with surprise as she read the history of not only her family, but of their families before them. Long descriptions of Shifters who served as chieftains and leaders of the tribes one after another filled her mind. She didn't think her dad had been a chieftain, but his name was listed in the lines of successors in the book before her. Chieftain Rayalt Marzén. She was sure the book didn't lie. One name not listed, however, was their current leader, Landon. "If he had succeeded my father, why isn't he named?" she wondered aloud. "Unless he hadn't officially been named..." Chel took a few deep breaths and thought on the information continuing to unveil before her very eyes.

"What does this mean for me specifically, Book?" She could get use to speaking with books as if they were just another person.

It means you are the rightful Chieftain—Chieftess—of the Mandü tré Lan Shifters, next in line after Rayalt Marzén. The book's responses were not audible but written within its pages. After a pause the book continued. *The srontas is a symbol of that status but also your shifting abilities. Wolf is your main animal.*

"What do you mean, *main* animal?" confused she asked.

Wolf is your primary animal, but you as Chieftain have the capacity to shift into any animal necessary to you at the time or desire, just as your ancestors before you, the book expounded. *Others have the gifting to change into a secondary or even tertiary animal, but only designated ones. Chieftains and ritually designated chieftains in the event there is no heir, have the ability. It is rare. It is special.*

Chel sat dumbfounded. "I haven't even been able to shift into Wolf. How could I... How can I change into another animal?" Sadness filled every word she spoke. Already a failure.

You will find your way, young one, the book addressed her. *Your time is approaching. Wolf is taking her time with you for reasons only she knows. Trust her and trust yourself. Many Chieftains have come and gone, fulfilling their paths; their stories documented in these pages.*

"Thank you," Chel breathed in and released a sigh of relief, the book being the only one so far able to put her mind further at ease. "Do you document the *srontas* and stories of the other races in Alandria?"

No, young one, only the srontas and histories of those born Shifter.

Chel heard someone coming down the hall and figured her time was up. "Thank you, Book. You have been most helpful. I will return when I can to read more histories."

It is my honor to serve the Chieftain, please return at your leisure. The Shifters are awaiting you.

Chel gently closed the book, guilt flooded her that such a book should not be closed up and stored on a shelf with other ordinary books, but she had to go. Chel promised herself she would return and give the book a place of honor and respect when she had a place to do so.

Chapter Eighteen

"So Faerie boy, what makes you think you are welcome here?" A Shifter stood with his arms crossed, making every attempt to intimidate Halister. Shifters acted in packs, and three others stood with identical scowls behind the vocal one.

"I do not think that, actually," Hal replied, leaning against a boulder taller than he. His casual stance and carefree expression put the Shifters on edge, the ones in back emitted low growls from their chests. "I am here only as a friend and to guide a friend, one of your own," he explained. Hal had simply been trying to enjoy a moment of solitude in a quiet part of the boulders in between the main cave and the village when these others had rudely interrupted him.

"She might be a Shifter—though that is still to be seen," some of the goons laughed out loud. "But she is not one of us. She has been raised mortal and she does not know enough about what it takes to be a Shifter in Alandria, nothing of the guts it takes to survive here," the lead Shifter glared at Hal, daring him to make a move and itching to fight.

Not moving, Hal glared right back at the Shifter. "And you are?"

"Danik is my name," said Danik confidently as if Hal should have heard of him.

"Danik, let me tell you something." Hal slowly uncrossed his ankles and stood up. He put his hands behind his back. "I will fight you and I will win. Not here and not now, but someday." He took a step forward and then another one. The Shifters raised their brows mockingly, not nearly afraid as they should be but warily watching Hal take step by step forward. "Chel, the Shifter you so rudely mentioned, knows enough about hardship and standing strong and being more loyal than you could ever be." He eyed Danik steadily, not raising his voice nor his fist. "Did you know she faced the Droch-Shúil not once but twice and survived? Did you know she was held captive in the Caves of Vuldün alone in the darkness and survived? No of course not, because you don't even know her, nor have you given her the chance to prove herself as 'one of you,' a Shifter. She is and she will rule over you one these days, just wait and see." Hal now stood practically nose to nose with the Shifter called Danik, but showed no fear nor any sign of backing down. He knew how the game was played.

Danik stepped back out of Hal's space, right into the brainless pack behind him. A growl erupted from Danik's chest on the verge of a shift. He started to take a step forward, but this would have been one of an act of aggression—a sign he was ready to fight, but the tightness of his face showed perhaps he wasn't as ready to face off with Hal in an actual battle as he showed himself to be.

"This is not over between us," Danik grumbled as one of his guys pulled at his arm from behind.

"Yes, it is," Chel's voice unexpectedly boomed steadily from somewhere beyond the boulders. The emboldened young woman rounded the corner; Chel instantly cataloged each person's face and scent. She glared at Hal, who quickly backed away from her, raising his hands in surrender, though he couldn't hide the twinkle in his eye and smirk on his face. "That was not your story to share," her voice lowered. She watched understanding dawn on his features, he lowered his eyes and nodded his head slowly.

"We go," Danik said as he spit on Hal before turning to storm away.

"I think that is a wise decision, Danik," came Landon's voice from a different direction. Another unexpected visit, but still Landon noted those involved slowly roving his eyes over each one of them, not necessarily disapproving, but making a necessary stand nonetheless. "Move along."

Landon eyed both Chel then Halister warily then he himself turned without further word.

"He must have important places to be," Chel mused with a slight smirk.

Halister nodded conspiratorially. "He must." Hal sobered and looked to Chel. "I apologize for disclosing experiences that belonged only to you, that was not my place."

"Thank you, Hal. It's all right, I just hadn't figured out how to tell my parents about spending time with the Droch-Shúil yet. But now the cat's out of the bag, so to speak, so I'll have to talk with them about it soon." Chel bit her lip with disconcertion.

"You say very strange things sometimes." He smiled. "Would you like to speak of it first with me? For practice?" Hal inquired on the sly.

She touched his arm gently with her hand. "Not yet, but thank you. Perhaps soon though." Chel looked out around the village. "It's peaceful right here. You can see the Stone Forest but also the village." She quieted for a moment. "Have you seen or discovered anything of value to our mission?" she asked, changing the subject.

"After you and Samuel left, I was shown to my temporary quarters then I explored a little but hadn't gotten too far. I met a few Shifters," Hal's eyes shifted away, suddenly taking an interest in a nearby tree. "But they were not as welcoming as one would hope." He looked back at her. "Then I stumbled upon the fine gentlemen you saw moments ago. So far I am not inspiring faith in our mission for Alandria."

"Ha!" Chel declared, "I'm not sure 'gentlemen' is the term I would have used, but whatever."

Halister bowed his head and took Chel's hand in his own. "I vow to keep the things you share with me to myself, Chelnáh of the Shifters." He said it so formally, Chel's eyes widened yet she spoke nothing. Instead, she watched him as he kissed the top of her hand to seal the deal.

"Um, thank you, Hal but that was unnecessary." A slight tinge of pink crawled up her cheeks as she withdrew her hand.

"Where did you leave your brute of a Shifter?" Hal changed the subject.

"He showed me around the village a bit. I met a few Shifters but not many. Then he showed me the library, or archival room I guess it was called. They have some interesting history documents and ledgers they keep. Most of it seemed boring, but I did find one interesting piece of reading, but I'll share that another time." Chel paused for breath. "I was actually coming to look for you to see if you'd like to look at the histories with me as I have no idea what I should be looking for."

"I would gratefully accept your invitation to do menial and boring tasks for the sake of Alandria," Hal vocalized officially but gave her a boyish grin while saying it.

"Fantastic." Chel rolled her eyes but smiled in return and looped her arm in his, guiding him where he needed to go.

Chapter Nineteen

After hours of continued searching in the library, Chel and Hal still had not finished going through the annals of Shifter history when Samuel finally returned to join them.

"I didn't expect Faerie boy here to join you for the menial book work while I was gone," Samuel directed to Chel, but his eyes watched Hal.

Hal kept his head down, but his lip raised in a smirk while he reached for the next book in his pile. "I did not expect you to return as I was unsure of your literacy," Hal rebutted. A growl reverberated through Sam's chest across the room.

"Oh, seriously? Can we not work in peace?" Chel fumed. For the next few minutes no one said anything. The simple sounds of pages turning and books dropping onto piles. The competitive spirits of both men rose to the surface, each in their own way but palpable nonetheless. Hal began folding blank pieces of parchment into airplanes, shooting them across the library toward Samuel. The tension between the two young men became explosive. It took all of Samuel's strength to remain calm and keep himself from shifting into his animal.

"I think we may have exhausted our resources for today," Chel sighed placing her last book from her pile on the "gone through" pile. "Plus I don't know how much more of the two of you in the same small room I can take." She looked around and saw similar piles near Samuel and near Hal as well. "We went through most of the stacks and haven't found anything." But something caught her eye on one of the shelves. One particular map of Alandria called to Chel. Clearly it was an older map. It showed a great expanse of land outside the known borders of "Alandria." Chel couldn't stop looking at it.

"Do you think this is accurate?" She showed it to both of them. Slowly each made their way over to get a better look at the map. Samuel examined it for a moment then shrugged.

"It's possible, though I've never heard of any of these areas." Samuel pointed to the surrounding areas outside Mandü tré Lan and even further south.

Hal took his turn, his brow pinched and his head cocked. His finger traced a point north and then east outside the mountains bordering Elnye.

"I've never been over this mountain and have heard no stories of any other doing it. It is hard to believe it is accurate, but perhaps we should hold onto it and speak with someone who is older, wiser than us." Hal stared into Chel's eyes. Chel got the message.

He meant Arileas or someone like him. Chel understood and remembered their agreement to keep not only the Ehsmia but also their relationship with Arileas a secret. Samuel grunted unaware of the secret. "Go for it, it's probably just someone's drawing of wishful thinking."

"Ok, I'll keep it safe," Chel said as she rolled it up gently and held on to it for the moment, not sure where she would store anything of value on her. Her heart pulled her back toward the book she communicated with earlier but she wouldn't risk taking it out with the guys there. Chel had yet to visit her room and didn't know how far it would be to go with hidden articles. She had been told it was near her parents' cavern and she hoped it was alone so she could have some quiet time after all the book searching and tension she had to wade through to get even a normal conversation going. Chel caught Hal watching her as his gaze slid toward the stack where the chieftain book was located, wishing she could grab it as well. The thought of the swift kiss he had placed on her hand earlier warmed her chest. For goodness' sake it was only her hand, but she wished it was her mouth. Her eyes quickly darted away when a knowing lit his eyes. Hoping she hadn't blushed, she distracted herself with a readiness to see her parents. This alone changed her train of thought.

"Actually, the more I think of it, that might be a good idea," Samuel conceded. "Chel, would you like me to take that for you and keep it safe?" he asked suddenly interested.

"Or I could hold it for you?" Hal offered, his arms crossed over his chest as he now leaned near the door.

"Actually," Chel paused, her gaze traveling from Samuel to Hal with confusion on her face, "I'd like to look at it a little longer so I can familiarize myself with this area, being a new Shifter and all." Chel batted her eyes in a terribly over exaggerated way, fed up with whatever was going on between those two.

"Sure that would probably be fine. Perhaps I can get it from you later," Samuel answered easily. Chel's gut told her if she gave him the map she might not see it again any time soon. She knew she should trust her intuition even though she was uncertain the reason behind it. Changing the subject he added, "I have a couple things to do before the evening meal. Are you all right, if I meet up with you later, Chel?" Samuel asked. He stole a glance at Hal whose shifty eyes spoke volumes. That creature might try something right under his nose!

"I will be fine. Actually, I was hoping to find my room and take some time to myself for a little bit if you two don't mind?" She looked from Hal to Samuel, an eyebrow raised in question.

"Good. I'll see you later," Samuel said and strode to the doorway, exiting beyond it.

Hal waited a beat then looked at Chel with a gleam in his eyes. "That was quite the show you just put on there, Chel."

"I don't know what you are talking about, Halister." She grinned conspiratorially then waggled her eyebrows as she waved the rolled map in front of his face. "Do you think this could be true? Could there be more beyond the borders of Alandria that have been explored previously?" Her eyes lit up with the possibility of something new out there, something more to be explored.

Hal sobered and chewed the inside of his lip. "Honestly, I do not know. It is possible. Though why no one has never mentioned it before I do not know." He thought. "I do think it was wise of you to hold on to it. We need to somehow either copy it or get it to Arileas before it is gone forever."

"How can we do that from here?" she whispered.

Hal sighed. "Before we left, Arileas gave Daegan and myself a way to contact him should we need to get a message to him in a dire situation. It can be risky so it would need to be worth it." He looked at her then at the map. "I think this could be worth it. Maybe he already knows but maybe the knowledge that knowledge is being hidden might be reason enough. Would you allow me to take it, Chel? I can sneak out of these borders easily on my own and get to a high place for connection. Will you trust me with this?"

Chel turned her head and looked to the ceiling, deeply considering his words or so she led him to believe. "Yes, I will trust you on this matter. Go quickly. You need to be back before evening meal so they don't suspect you were outside the borders."

"Yes, you are correct. I will be back before nightfall. Thank you." He received the map from her and quickly leaned forward and kissed her cheek before either of them thought too much about it. "Stay safe," he whispered into her ear and quickly ducked out the doorway and left Chel standing where she stood.

Chel stood there, her feet rooted to the ground, her mouth ajar with words she wished she could've said, and her heart fluttered with the anticipation of more. Relaxing her body and allowing herself to breathe normally, she waited until her heartbeat came down and headed to find her room. "Well at least it wasn't my hand." As soon as Hal had turned the corner, Chel realized her chance and ducked back into the library to retrieve her desired prize.

Minutes later, in her room, Chel picked up a note folded on her bed. It was from her mom...

Welcome to your room. I hope it's comfortable for you. Dad and I are in the room at the end of this hall. Come visit when you have the chance. We want to catch up more. Love you, Mom.

Chel guessed her room was a simple, standard room in this section of the tunnels with sparse walls made of the same stone throughout and a few pieces of furniture. In her room, she had a bed and small table for a nightstand, a simple wood chair in one corner. A chest sat on the ground at the end of the bed. When Chel opened it, a plume of dust wafted out of it right into her face choking her for a good couple minutes. She had hid the magic book from the library in her backpack she had kept with her and only now brought it out.

"I could hide it here," she murmured. Chel couldn't bring herself to put it in that dusty place, though. And in truth, if someone were looking for it, wouldn't they look there first? She hunted around the little room for any hiding places but didn't find any.

"Well, as much fun as that was, I will go crazy sitting in this room," she mused considering her options. She flopped on her bed, bored. Just as quickly, she shot up and put her shoes back on. Chel was so grateful for the traveling clothes that Arileas had provided them with instead of the matching linens that had adorned them from the Twined camp. Decision made she stood up and the floor squeaked. Moving her feet back forth between the boards she found a loose one and pried it open with her fingernails. Proving to be quite hard, she found an item used to snuff candles and used the end of the handle to pry the board the rest of the way up. There! A hollow cubby under the wood floor beneath her bed.

"Perfect!" She grabbed the book and wrapped it with a loose piece of material and placed the book into the hole. "I'm sorry I have to hide you in a dirt hole when you deserve a place of honor where you could be appreciated. It's just for now," she vowed, covering the hole and sealing it back up. No one would be the wiser.

Satisfied, Chel left her bedroom, closing her door carefully so as not to draw attention. She took herself out for a stroll and began to explore some of the areas of the village she had wanted to see while there was still some daylight. Breathing in the fresh air, she felt more alive, freer than she had in quite some time. Missing home was a given, but there was a part of her that felt connected to this place, she wished she could remember it—she needed to ask her parents for more information about what it was like when she was a toddler here and if there was anything that might trigger a memory. On her way back before darkness of night fell, she was about to come upon the cavern entrance where her parents were staying. Unexpectedly, she had that feeling—the one where it felt like someone watched her. The little hairs on the back of her neck stood up, but she didn't feel danger. She was impressing herself with her growing awareness of her body's physical response to her environment. Pausing in the middle of the path, she turned full circle, unafraid of showing whoever it was they were caught. Using her nose and her ears, she focused her senses like she had been learning more and more to do; it was becoming more natural for her. She recognized the scent.

Smiling, she turned and ducked into a crevice shadowed from the fading light of the sky. Glancing up, she zeroed in on her path and jumped onto the first boulder she could reach, then quietly climbed boulder after boulder until she reached a perch she could jump from. It would land her in front of the opening she was after, the same opening she had caught a slight younger girl with auburn hair peering out from once before. Chel jumped.

"Hello, Chel," Callie's perky voice giggled from inside the doorway. "So nice of you drop in, literally. I rarely get visitors."

Panting, Chel smiled. "I wonder why. Maybe if you had an easier entrance you might get more of them," she replied sarcastically.

But Callie's face fell and she sighed. "Yeah, but if it were too easy then I would probably be dead."

Chapter Twenty

Adettlyn. Territory of the Elves.

M oving the ladder in the library, Aidón searched for the directional sign etched into the column of one of the bookshelves. He knew approximately where it was but had not visited this section in quite some time. He climbed the ladder, seeking the small indicator—the sign of the Elves: a circular shape of a crescent moon and a sun merged together. It was small, smaller than the size of a coin, dirtied and worn with time keeping it from eyes untrained to find it... along with the spell placed on it that only a rightful king or queen given the knowledge from the previous one could find.

"Aha!" Aidón whispered in exaltation. "I found you." His fingers traced the symbol etched into the wood that for all intents and purposes should have faded with time but had not. He spoke the ancient words that would permit the continuation of his search.

Tysn'âth

"Now to find the next clue," Aidón murmured to himself. His eyes sought its twin, though opposite in direction from where he had started. Climbing down the ladder, he moved back to the beginning of the shelves and found the next symbol low on the shelves. Almost anyone could find if they had the mind and the vision to see it, but no one ever had. Once more, tracing the image with his finger and uttering the next word in the sequence, Aidón's eyes widened as the symbol lit up but only for a mere second.

"And now for the final one," he whispered tilting his head back, gazing high near the top of the shelves. Muttering under his breath about why Ryek had to have placed a clue quite so high, he moved to the middle ladder and placed it accordingly for accurate position. Aidón did not fear heights, but his stomach did tend to quiver unexpectedly when unnecessarily high. "It is for the mission," he persuaded himself then sighed, resigned, as he climbed higher then higher again. He climbed until he reached the top of the third stacked bookshelf, looked down foolishly, then dropped his head on the wrung above him. With legs shaking, heart pounding, and breath labored he continued to climb one more bookshelf higher, keeping his head high and his eyes on the end goal, never to look down again. Paying attention to the titles of the spines of the ancient tomes in front of him, he distracted himself with thoughts of books he would read when time and freedom permitted him to sit in front of the large fireplace and relax, enjoying the leisure of his home and his people once more in the future. His time as king the first time was gone in a flash, not long enough to thoroughly integrate himself into the people of Adettlyn and the surrounding area of Lumari. Aidón planned on being king for as long as he was allowed. In truth, Kaeleigh was the rightful heir to this throne and he welcomed her to it, hoping she would allow him to serve as her advisor and as the castle curator.

Abruptly, he realized he was at his destination. Running his hands across the various books, stopping at a shelf stacked with ancient scrolls, Aidón lifted a few gently. Underneath the scrolls etched into the wood of the shelf itself rested the third and final depiction he sought. This symbol however was different than the first two; this was a symbol of a flower, an orchid to be exact. Aidón knew all about the Orchids, had even been a part of the secret organization. He uttered a third word in the ancient tongue and watched with awe as the Orchid illuminated. He waited for something to happen, but nothing did. Aidón frowned and turned his head to look at the books surrounding the area he was in expecting something to stand out, to show him the way to his prize. He waited a beat then decided to climb down to get a better view and review his steps.

"I did everything right or the symbols would not have lit up, leading me to the next one. What could be the problem?" Aidón chastised quietly as he descended the ladder one wrung at a time. He found talking out loud, even as quietly as he was, helped to distract him from the feeling of falling into utter doom. Finally leaping from the ladder to the solid ground where he regained his gravity and stabilized the wobbly feeling in his legs, Aidón breathed deeply in through his nose calming his body's reaction. He had been king. He should not have weak feelings when it came to the heights of this room, but in fact he did and he would have to find ways to conquer those at another time.

"Now, what went awry?" Placing his hands on his waist, he surveyed the entire wall of books and literature, seeking something he missed in his earlier perusal. There at the end of the last bookshelf, in the middle shelf, one spine stuck out a fraction further than the others otherwise perfectly lined up. "You clever library." Aidón chuckled and rushed toward that particular book. The library still had enough reserve magic in it the symbols and clues would reset and not be in the same place once he retrieved the item he sought. He loved that about this room and the castle itself; it was alive with its own magic, cooperating with or fighting against the current ruler.

Lining himself up with the book in front of him, he read the spine: *the Kings and Queens of Alandria, A History*. "Appropriate choice," he said under his breath. Gently tugging the book out from its home in the shelf, Aidón cradled it closely in his arms. Looking inside where the book had just been, he saw nothing and frowned. Holding the book away from his chest, he gazed at the cover and saw the symbol of a key etched on the front and thought it an odd depiction for the kings and queens of Alandria... but perhaps not. He opened the cover to discover only one page; behind it the center of the book hollowed out, a tiny locked chest buried within it. Aidón smiled as he touched the delicate little box. After attempting to open it on his own, he tried the ancient word for "open": *Cyílint* but nothing happened. He read the title on the page still in the book though most the page was missing. It read:

For each of the kings and queens of Alandria, your essence will guide your way.

Aidón pondered that statement for a moment, his brows pinched thoughtfully and his head tilted back. Suddenly his eyes illuminated with understanding.

Touching the little interior box, he said the ancient word again, but this time fused it with his power as not only an Elf but his special magic as the named king of Adettlyn. A slight click echoed in the silent room. Though no one else was present, Aidón still chanced a look behind him to double check. The lid to the little box unlatched and Aidón pried it open the rest of the way. Inside a small cushion was covered in royal blue silk; and lying upon it was an aged key, long handled with only a couple thick teeth that would fit a very specific old lock. Aidón held the key reverently in his hand then tucked it away within his cloak. Not wasting any time, he closed both the lid of the chest and the book, and placed it back into the bookshelf where he had found it, finally pushing it back in line with those next to it. He needed to ensure anyone who might come upon it would not find it easily. He uttered a few words quietly, re-kindling the spell upon it, cloaking it amidst the other books so only those deemed worthy could find it. Moving the ladders around to an alternate order, he quietly made his way back to the door with one last look back into the library. He sighed and vowed to return as soon as he could, should he be given the opportunity.

"I shall return. Thank you for your service," he whispered then turned and quietly lifted the lock on the heavy wooden door, slipping out into the darkened hall once more.

~~~~~

Aidón needed to make it to a room on the top level of the castle. Sneaking down the hall further to the end of that wing, he hurried to get to the staff stairway where he could hopefully climb relatively unseen. Coming to an abrupt halt at the end of the hall, he stood with his mouth ajar in utter shock. Parts of the castle wall at this end of the far wing crumbled onto the floor, so much so he could see some of the outdoors beyond the castle walls through the broken bits. *How can the castle staff tolerate this?* He wondered. "The vines remain stable for the most part, holding the majority of the stones together... here they are wilted and weakened... simply too much devastation to understand or repair." Aidón shook his head sadly. He reached out to touch the wall where the defected parts began, sending a rush of magic through his hands into the wall hoping to stabilize the stones surrounding the holes. His magic did more than he had intended, as if the castle was pulling what it needed from him. The openings closed once more, broken stones and vines knitted themselves back to their original solid state. Aidón smiled at what he had done, though he felt weakened by the effort. He wanted nothing more than to push his magic, no matter how much effort or energy it required of him to bring the rest of his home to life.
~~~~~

Yet he knew now was not the time. He would have to wait until the time when Alandria was free.

Compelled to move on, Aidón made his way up the steps made of a different type of stone than the walls, these were much smaller and easier to adhere together with a natural substance. At the top, he reached a door already slightly ajar. *My advantage,* the older man thought. A few staff lingered near the doorway going about their business. Aidón breathed in through his nose as quietly as possible, steeling his spine, and pushed open the door. He then walked through purposely without sparing a glance at any of the workers, intent on his purpose hoping no one stopped him.

Unfortunately, his plan was thwarted. Someone had seen the dash down the hall.

"You there," one of the women called, her arms full of freshly laundered and folded linens.

Aidón stopped in his tracks and slowly turned toward the woman. She was an older Elf, one he recognized as serving in the castle when he was last there. His glamour intact, she would not recognize him right away if he could make their encounter short.

"Yes, madam?" he inquired softly.

She tilted her head and squinted her eyes. "Are you new? I have not seen the likes of you here before. I know everyone in this castle."

"Yes, I... I just recently arrived," he said truthfully in case she could detect falsehoods.

"There is something familiar about you, but I cannot say what," she stared at him once more, then shook her head dismissing him. "Take these linens to the guest room at the beginning of this wing for me as you seem to be headed that direction. The king requires it and several other rooms for his guest arriving tomorrow and we are short staffed." Her tone left no room for argument. Aidón was glad to do it for her if it would prevent more questioning. Piling the linens high in his arms, Aidón shifted under the heavy burden on the nearest wall.

"Steady there?" she asked him, shifting the linens in his arms to better stabilize him.

"Yes, I'm all right now," Aidón responded gratefully. Straightened and secured, he turned to place the linens in the room she directed him to.

As he walked down the hall, lit more brightly than the hallway below, the woman gasped quietly. Aidón refused to stop, though he couldn't help but look back. A trail of greenery sprouted from the wall and trailed behind him from the point where he'd steadied himself like a homesick puppy following devoutly after its master.

CHAPTER TWENTY-ONE

Inside the room at the end of the hall, candles were lit and oil lamps blazed around the room, illuminating it in more light than Adión had seen thus far since the sun had gone down. A suite at its finest for guests and dignitaries, Aidón wondered who would be staying there now. As per his instructions, he set the linens down on top of the bed, stripped and awaiting the beauty of its new dressings. Realizing he should not tarry, his glance was quick and purposeful, taking in all he could from the thick wooden shelves, the night table, and the bed frame complete with four posters draped in the sheerest fabrics and smoothest silks. Aidón spun to head out the doorway, but was halted by the same woman from the hallway. With arms folded across her chest, her stance strong, and a frown scolded on her face, she was not going to allow him easy passage. Her head tilted and she pursed her lips whether in determination or confusion, it was not clear.

"I placed the linens where you directed, did I not?" Aidón asked hesitantly, gauging the woman's expression, hoping to place her face in his memory with a name.

"You did indeed," she responded, her gaze flicked toward the linens on the bed. "I cannot help but find you familiar though your face is not recognizable to me." Narrowing her eyes, she peered at him as if the longer she stared the better the chance she would see something different in him. "How is it possible greenery sprung from where you touched the walls? Who are you?" she drilled.

"I mentioned before I am new and would not have had a chance to meet you before unless you get out of the castle much, perhaps you have seen me in the village?" Aidón offered to misdirect her.

"Yes, perhaps." She shrugged, moving aside for him to pass her though she did not seem convinced.

Before he left, he asked, "Who is the guest that will be attending this room?"

The woman frowned as if he should know already. "The Lady Maleina, of course. Aren't you paying *any* attention? You'd better get with it. She of all people will certainly not tolerate forgetfulness, age, or familiarity. She will be in attendance as of tomorrow early morning."

Chills ran down his spine. Aidón stiffened then relaxed immediately, hoping she would not notice the change in his stance. "Like I mentioned, recently arrived. I did not realize who would be arriving," Aidón admitted hoping she would let it slip as a side effect of his aging appearance.

"Do not be letting any of the other staff hear you. There are no excuses in this castle. They would not let you off as easily as I," she warned.

"Thank you," Aidón inclined his head in gratitude then continued on his way.

As Aidón passed her, she reached out and grabbed his arm. "Oh! I think I must have seen you at the bazaar in Anise the other day. Could that have been you?" she asked excited to have solved her puzzle.

"I do believe it could have been," Aidón replied quickly. He wanted out of there. Every minute he stayed near her was a chance for her to change her mind and keep at this guessing game.

"Carry on," she directed, "you seem to be in quite the hurry." Releasing his arm, she allowed him to go on his way. Aidón nodded his appreciation and slipped by her quickly before she could stop him for anything else.

The thought of Maleina here in his castle kept tingles of fear running down his back. His son was in league with that wicked woman; he had assumed so, but to know for sure and to know she would be in his home leaving a trail of her darkness with her stirred the anger within him. If Aidón thought even the slightest chance to save his son from his fate existed, he would attempt it. Of course, Syén would not be allowed his freedom, but rather have to pay for his sins sitting in the dark dungeon below the castle just as his conspirator, Maleina, had done to Aidón for all those years. Through Syén's plot to over-throw Aidón's future seat at the throne of Adettlyn, he was the reason for Aidon's retreat into hiding and ultimate cause for ending up in Maleina's dungeon. Nor would Syén be allowed any chance at freedom since he had robbed his own mother—Aidón's wife—of her own freedom by having her life taken from this world. In fact, Syén was fated to pay with his own life one way or another. Aidón's heart sank, though his son was no more a son to him than a stranger now.

"What is he doing with Maleina?" Aidón wondered quietly to himself as he continued to sneak down the stone catwalk stretching from the wing of the castle he was in, across the back of the entry foyer, and into the opposite wing... exactly where he needed to get to before Syén finished dinner. Head bowed, Aidón did not want to attract any attention in this wing of the castle, as it was the wing of the king's bedroom... or in this case his son's current suite. He remembered the room fondly. It was spacious and grand with a fireplace at each end of the room and tall windows on the wall in between with a view of the forest and mountain on one side and on the other a view of Lake Ary'th. Aidón loved the lake, loved spending time on it in the quiet of the early morning. One of the staff along with a few select guards would go with him, quietly leaving the castle before the majority of the staff bustled about; they would fish from the deep section of the lake. The light breeze sweeping across the lake would ruffle his cloak and his hair tickling his neck as it brought the sweet smells the flowers opposite shore along. The memory stirred hope that one day again he might partake in such joys.

Very few staff were present down the hall he traveled. The sconces lit low, preserving the oil until the king had need of the light—this worked in Aidón's favor, blending in with the shadows where he could. A chill in the air swept in from some crumbling stone in the outside wall. He rubbed his arms. "I can't. I can't," he forced himself to walk and to not restore. Now was not the time. He put his energy into picking up his pace until he reached the last door of the hall. A large double wood door loomed in front of him. When it had been his room, it had been kept locked with a simple lock. He was surprised to feel a magic boundary emanating from the entrance. Clearly his son did not trust his own staff or guards, feeling the need to keep them out at their own peril according to the type of magic used. Leaning close, but not yet touching the door, Aidón closed his eyes. He felt the magic surrounding the door using his own magic to sense whether or not the magic powering the lock was an

Elvish type or from another source. If it was their own magic, it would be easier for him to tear it down, but if it came from an outside source it would cause more trouble and probably a bit of noise.

"Aha, so it is magic from your own making Syén. Very good." Aidón whispered as he felt around the air with his magic. He whispered a few words and immediately felt the magic respond to him and release the spell. Realizing it was not a very strong spell to anyone familiar with their ancient magic, he found himself disappointed in the magic his son used—or the lack of magic he used. In this case, however, it would serve Aidón better that his son seemed to still be inept at their family magic. Sadly, it had not been passed on like it once had been long, long ago. He did hope to be able to share it with Kaeleigh if she so desired to learn in the future.

Placing his hand on the door handle, he felt an audible click when he whispered the word for "open" once again under his breath. He listened at the door momentarily then quickly moved inside the dark room. Aidón paused to allow his eyes to adjust to the darkness of the room. Unwilling to light a candle and alert the guards outside the windows, he waited for the light of the moons to filter into the room. He could tell the bed and furnishings were still where he had left them and assumed the same colors and textures were also the same. He had loved picking out the colors with his wife. She had so much fun making the suite their own after it had belonged to King Ryek/Hunter for so long before that. Adding a feminine touch here and there, had made her smile; neither had it been overly done in either masculine nor feminine, but a wonderful blend of colors that their race gravitated toward with light blues, greens, and silvers, with the addition of black to add an edge. The crest of the Elves hung on the wall in a large tapestry above the bed enclosed with sheer fabrics in light green and silver. Thinking of his wife pinched his chest. Though it had been years, her absence was still missed.

The combined light from the two moons streamed in through two separate windows creating a lovely beam of both blue and white light through the large room. Cold stone floor seeped through his boots, wishing not for the first time he could light the magnificent fireplaces and allow the heat to warm his bones from the inside out. Quickly, Aidón took advantage of the lit floor lining his path to the opposite corner of the room. A screen of fabric set up a dressing area in a windowless corner. He ducked behind it, kicking pieces of fabric and clothing to the side so not to step on them, and re-arranging them in order to not draw attention to any subtle differences. A long mirror, clearer than others he had spotted around the castle, hung on the stone just behind the changing area. Practically from floor to just above his head, it was a large mirror. What only the kings knew—except he wagered Syén did not yet know of it as he had never had the chance to pass the information on—was the mirror enclosed a secret entrance way to a hidden room above the king's chamber.

Placing his hand on the side of the mirror, he whispered the words under his breath and inhaled sharply when it had worked. Illuminated in a soft blue light right next to the mirror, otherwise unseen, was the same image of the symbol for the Elves. He looked around for something with a sharp tip. Finding a pin for fabric, he pricked his thumb then squeezed a drop of the red liquid that would serve as his password to the hidden room above. Placing his thumb over the symbol, the blood seeped into the stone. Magically, the blood would not be seen once the ritual was complete—all part of the magic.

The mirror moved out from the stone wall, subtly swinging toward him. Looking around, ensuring no one was at his back, he opened the mirror fully, stepped up and into what was an extremely narrow dark stairway. The mirror swung shut behind him, locking him in until he could find the time to sneak out.

Chapter Twenty-Two

Exhile. The Land of the Unforgiven Dead.

The Orchids remained imprisoned in the heart of the charcoal cragged mountain that stood a lone soldier in the desolate and barren landscape of Exhile. Once fifteen, now only ten remained, and even several of those left were mere shells of what they were as souls. *She* had been showing up to the gates of their prison, siphoning off more and more of their essences as the days went by. Something was stirring and they all knew it; something was coming and they were afraid. They were running out of options and time.

Several Orchids paced, seeking relief from their agitation and confinement, hoping for answers they believed would not come in time. Others sat in mediation searching for answers in the archives of their minds and ancient histories, something they could have overlooked when examining all their options. Alandria was in trouble and so were they. They were doing all they could for Alandria from their current and very inconvenient location and lack of means. For some their hopes lay completely with the prophecy of the Sol-lumieth, whom they understood to be both Daegan and Kaeleigh together.

"She is amazing," Eva whispered in awe, having just come out of a trance where she could *see* Kaeleigh and the others based off of Cley-una's ability to make contact with them.

"She is," Cley agreed, "Together they will bring a united Alandria back from death. I just know it." She beamed with pride. Having seen her son Daegan with Kaeleigh and having watched how the people interacted with them made her giddy with hope for the future. The Orchids just had to get out of the current situation so they could get on with the freedom and healing for Alandria.

"What if they do not make it in time to free us before we are all wiped from existence?" another Orchid—a Shifter—asked quietly voicing what many had thought.

"They will. They have to," Eva said strongly, her belief in them and the prophecy unwavering.

Daegan's father and a mighty Ferrishyn, Dy'lánd, strode up behind Cley-una and placed his hand on her shoulder. A strong steady presence was his in the midst of their uncertainty. "I agree, they will." He then paused and gazed into his wife's eyes.

Cley-una turned to him and gave him a small sad smile. "He is strong and he is good, but I worry when the truth comes out he will be blinded by his need for vengeance. The time is approaching quickly, he will know soon enough," she spoke softly, her words only for her husband.

He pulled her close and placed his chin on the top of her head. "Yes, he is all those things you spoke and more, but he will also be able to see the bigger picture when needed, that is why he will make a great ruler," Dy'lánd said confidently. "He will find forgiveness. My concern is more for the other—the Elf—if he will be able to find forgiveness for himself."

She looked up at him, her eyes full of emotion. "I forgave him."

"As did I, that very day," the large Ferrishyn warrior agreed, wetness rimming his eyes.

"Perhaps we will get the chance to tell him ourselves if we are released when he is present," Cley offered, sniffing as she pulled away but still held onto her man's hand.

"The time frame is changing," another of the Orchids said, truth ringing eerily, from behind a boulder.

"It is necessary the allies gather soon, or Alandria—us included—will not exist as we created her to be," said one of the older Faeries sitting next to Tylna.

"Yes, and many of them still need to wake up and remember who they are and that they *can* indeed fight," Tylna, grumbled, playing with the edge of her shirt hem. She sat on the ground, her back against the dirt wall and her legs outstretched in front of her. Her blue hair stood out against the drab background of the cave. Tylna was the first queen of Feraánmar and also Daegan's great grandmother on his father's side. "Very important indeed," she muttered to herself, hoping.

Chapter Twenty-Three

Hal made his way towards the exit to the borders of Mandü tré Lan. He found what he hoped was the easiest and fastest passageway to get his message sent and get back in time for the evening meal. He caught a glimpse of a cloak flash a short distance ahead of him then get lost behind a set of large boulders. Hal could have ignored it, but something in his gut told him to follow whomever it might be despite the bad feeling churning in his core.

Silently, as the warrior he had trained to be, he moved closer to the mysterious boulder ahead of him. Someone was definitely hiding behind it. He readied his knife. He didn't want to hurt anyone if he had merely surprised a random Shifter sneaking about, but he would be prepared. Whispers were caught in the wind and carried to his ears. Hal flinched with recognition. Samuel. Samuel was behind that boulder. What was he doing out beyond the borders, sneaking around the boulders?

But then he heard another voice, a voice that sent chills down his back, a voice he had heard since he was a small child. Maleina—his mother's—voice also came from behind that boulder. Was she there in person? How had this happened, had she followed him? Had they seen or heard him? Certainly not.

Hal wasn't certain how he would react the next time he and his mother came face to face. He wasn't yet ready. A cold sweat broke out on the back of his neck, slowly dripping down his back causing as much discomfort as the possibility of an encounter with her. She had disowned him as her son in the woods of Lumei, though he had planned to do the same except she beat him to it. Through it all, however, she still held a soft spot in his heart and he was afraid she always would. Not that what she had gotten away with was all right, by no means was it, and he planned to bring her to justice... he just hoped it didn't come to her demise before he did so.

Samuel mentioned something that called Hal back to attention. Chel. They were speaking of Chel, though his mother refused to use her name and only called her that mutt brought in with that witch, Kaeleigh, who thought she had enough power to take control of Alandria. His mother's words dripped with bitterness but then she laughed. He recognized her cackle as something new she had been doing, he couldn't remember a time in their past where she ever laughed like that. It was beyond disturbing and halted his steps as he continued to creep forward, getting as close to the boulder as he could without being noticed.

Peering slightly behind the boulder, Hal could see it opened into a small chamber but could only see Samuel's back. His mother was not present. Hal frowned, trying to see how she was communicating with Samuel. Was there something inside the chamber? Or something Samuel held?

"Chel and your son are trying to stir up the Shifters."

Hal jerked back in surprise but let loose a sly grin, placing his hand to his chest. Stirring up the Shifters? The Shifters were a bunch needing to be stirred if any did. Hal almost chuckled out loud, but would never jeopardize his excellent position to collect information.

"They are making them uncomfortable and attempting to make allies," Samuel warned Maleina. "And they are preparing for a fight, but that is all I know so far. They have been quite secretive about how much information they give, or perhaps they do not even have an end game, just seeing how many they could rally." Samuel shrugged unconcerned with what he was sharing with her.

"Will the *Shifters*," Maleina said Shifters as if it was a dirty word, "join their cause whatever it may be?"

"Some might, but too many have too much at stake. They would rather leave Alandria than to go against you, My Lady," Samuel said bowing his head. "They may have reasons they think are valid, but they do not want to fight."

"Good. That is good. Perhaps you can stir up some of your own trouble." Maleina's tone suggested she had a plan. Hal had a feeling he would not like it. Unfortunately, something happened to the voices and suddenly his ears popped as if he was magically flung out of the hearing space. He couldn't hear anything. What was his mother's plan?

A couple minutes later, his ears popped again. With his fingers he pulled on each ear and rotated his neck attempting to normalize his hearing. His mother must have been able to create a dome of silence even through her communication device, unless Samuel did it, but Shifters usually didn't have active magic like that.

"How did you do that through the glass?" Samuel asked slightly in awe.

So his mother had created the silence—it took powerful magic to do it in another's physical presence let alone through a mirror or other reflective surfaces. Hal mused further while he listened for any clues to what he missed while kept out.

"Never you mind, my pet," she purred, "it was just in case prying ears were anywhere nearby."

Could she know Hal was there? He didn't think it was possible.

"You just can never be too careful these days, you do not know who is listening and who is on which side," she continued.

"True."

A pregnant pause weighed heavily before either of them spoke again. Hal had to check his ears to see if he had missed another dome of silence being created.

"Will you be able to carry out the plan?" Maleina questioned with a harshness she hadn't yet used though Hal had begun to realize it as her voice of power. "Remember, I can always find someone else; lines of others await for their turn to please me with their service. It does seem I have an insurance policy with you I have not tried to cash in on... yet." The crystal-clear threat was left hanging in the air; Hal felt the weight of it though he did not even know what it was regarding. What could she have on Samuel?

"No... I mean, yes, My Lady, I am fully capable of carrying out your order. No need for further action, I will start right away," Samuel assured.

"Very well," Maleina conceded, now with pleasant undertones, "you have three days. I will see you then."

"At the designated meet up?" Samuel asked for clarity.

"Of course," she purred, "where else? I would not dare enter the Shifter territory honoring our deal."

Hal could hear the lie in her voice even from his hiding place. He didn't need to see the way her eyes shifted or the seemingly innocent purse of her lips. Trouble was coming for the Shifters and he needed to warn them. And Chel.

"Thank you Maleina," Samuel said, his words slightly muffled as if his head was lowered most likely in a bow. "Your servant will do as you wish."

Hal jumped expertly behind a pile of boulders a safe distance away to hide while Samuel passed by. He still had to send his message to Arileas. Now he had even more information to add.

Samuel crept out of his mostly enclosed meeting place between several boulders slanted together at the top. He looked each direction for signs of anyone nearby. His hiding spot was half-way up a hill between the main caves of their territory and one of the higher hills surrounding their valley. He moved quickly away from the boulders and began to head back down the hill but then stopped in his tracks, lifted his nose in the air smelling something, and looked around him once more. His lip lifted in a snarl, but it didn't appear he knew who or where the spy was. "Who's there?" he demanded.

Hal stiffened, held his breath, and thought invisible thoughts. It must have worked as he heard Samuel move down the hill again. Before Hal moved to make sure he was safe, he waited a minute or two. When he peered around the corner, he could see Samuel's back moving quickly away from him back to the Shifters. Hal had to be even quicker, he couldn't risk letting Samuel out of his sight for too long not knowing when he would strike with whatever his and Maleina's plan was. He had up to three days and he was sure he'd need every bit of that time to try to round up help.

Scurrying over the boulders, he climbed up and over the meeting place Samuel had just been. It was a strenuous and rocky climb, but the higher he could get the better to send his message to Arileas—something about the height and easy access for his whispers to travel on the winds and reach the aged Ehsmian guardian. Oddly, the sun felt warmer in this part of Alandria. He knew it was the same sun all over Alandria, but the fact that it was so much hotter feeling than he knew it should be had him wondering if there was, in fact, magic within the borders of each territory allowing for variants in the weather. Approaching the top, a slight breeze ruffled through his hair and brought relief to the sweat beading on his brow. He stood tall for a few minutes and took in the view before him. He could see much of one side of Mandü tré Lan from this vantage point. Right in front of him was the peaks of the Shadow Ridges still towering above him. The top of those mountains might have been more ideal for him to communicate with Arileas, but there was no way he could get up there and back in time, let alone survive such a trip. Danger lurked in those ridges.

Breathing deeply, Halister closed his eyes and lowered himself slowly to the ground into a position of meditation, his intent to visualize the Ehsmian entrance they had walked through not that long ago. He pictured knocking on their cavern wall, waiting for Arileas to answer and allow him in. Mentally he heard a click, then visualized traveling through the dark tunnel right into the opening of white light threatening to blind him. He knew better than to fear the light—it was actually a warm and inviting beam, one that sheltered him. A less informed person would have certainly turned away. A pulling sensation kept him moving forward as if in fast motion through the center of Ehsmia straight into the chambers of Arileas. Hal could see him as if he was speaking with him face to face.

"Hello Master Halister," Arileas spoke with a smile. "Did you and our Chel find the Shifters with ease?"

"Yes, and hello, Arileas. Sir, we have some potential information and news we thought you should be aware of," Hal began.

"I see." The elder nodded his head and folded his hands in front of his mouth waiting for what Hal would tell him.

"Chel found a map that looks quite ancient in the Shifter library archives. It has lands beyond the known borders of Alandria. Is it accurate? Do you know of such expansions?"

Arileas nodded his head slowly in thought or in memory, it was hard to say. His eyes squinted and turned his head looking at something Hal could not see. He was a man of few words, yet many mannerisms. "It is accurate. I am surprised they have one of the origin maps. I wonder if they know what they have," he mused more to himself it seemed.

"What is an origin map?"

"When Alandria was created, so much magic was involved the borders continued to expand as the land formed even after the original maps were drawn. We had thought the borders had solidified, only to learn that they continued to expand and grow beyond our known boundaries.

"Rather than explore these or move beyond them, we remained happy to live and thrive within the origin areas. We had been partitioned off within our borders by Alandria herself, alive with her own reasoning and growth. Perhaps she was not ready to show it to us. Perhaps the land was not yet ready." Arileas put a finger to his head in thought, then his eyes grew wide. "The maps, though, also continued to grow and expand and seemed to have some of the life magic of Alandria herself." Arileas sat back in his chair and stared at a symbol on his desk Hal couldn't make out as the edges of his sight was foggy like looking through a frosted window. "The elders asked Alandria to stop growing so we could care for her properly as we felt there were not enough of us at the time to be spread that thin. Then we separated the maps and asked the elders of each territory to keep them safe and hidden until Alandria brought them back into the light; a choice that may not have been our finest at the time. We did not want unprepared citizens to find the maps and go out exploring or exploiting the land before we had been able to share it with them properly. Alandria must be getting ready to open her borders, maybe to Chel alone, maybe to others. Time will tell." Arileas shrugged his shoulders, though not without letting a sparkle shine in his eye. A secret was now out in the open to Hal.

"What do we do with it? I have it here with me, if you can keep it safe, I can find a way to get it to you," Hal offered.

"Indeed, what to do with it?" Arileas tilted his head perhaps in thought perhaps listening to some unheard voice, one could never be quite sure with him. Hal waited him out. With quick motions, his head straightened, and his eyes blazed with insight. Arileas stared straight into Hal. "Keep it there for now, find a safe location for it and tell no one about it, but the one to guard it, she is trustworthy." Just as quickly as he shifted from serious and straight-forward he was back to light-hearted and inquisitive.

"What else do you have for me, young one?"

Hal nodded succinctly, forcing himself to shift gears to keep up with the older man. "I overheard one of the Shifters who had known

Chel in the mortal realm—in fact the more I think on it, I think he was there to keep an eye on her instead of protect her—anyway, I caught him communicating with Maleina. They have a secret plan he is to carry out within three day's time. I was kept out of the actual plan by a dome of silence and could not hear it," Hal growled frustrated. "But my moth—Maleina—made a promise to him to stay away from the Shifter territory if he complied with her request—".

"Which means she has no intention of keeping that promise," Arileas interrupted, "and in fact, means to attack the Shifters in one way or another."

"Yes, I am afraid so. I could hear the lie in her words whether the Shifter could or not—though if he were as trained as he says he has been he should have been able to hear it also... which means," Hal once more started to elaborate his thoughts but was cut off by Arileas.

"You need to get back there and watch him. He will strike fast on the plan in order to then try and prepare the Shifters if he has any actual care for them," Arileas finished, nodding at the confirmation he felt in his own words.

Hal chuckled, baffled by the elder's swift perceptions. "Thank you, sir, you are once again correct."

"Master Halister, I merely voiced the thoughts you had first come to. Believe in your instincts and forgive yourself for things you have not done to become who you are fully meant to be." He paused, letting his words sink in as Halister listened. "They will all need you before this is over," Arileas added mysteriously.

With that, Arileas pushed Hal out of his mind, back into the reality of where he sat on top of a hill of boulders.

The light of day had faded behind Hal and a lavender sky faintly bloomed around him illuminated with oranges and pinks; the beauty of the sun setting against the Shadow Ridges. He might have tarried too long, but it was needed. He ruminated over what Arileas had said.

"The old man knows more than he says and says more with fewer words than any others I know," he mused as he began the rocky climb down. He wasn't sure what it was, but he was certain something would be awaiting him back inside Mandü tré Lan. He couldn't shake the feeling, but Hal would be ready to face it.

Chapter Twenty-Four

"I mean I know we just met so you don't have to tell me anything, but why would anyone want *you* dead?" Chel burst out in shock at what Callie had just told her.

"Because I am blind. Because I am useless to this tribe. Because I take up space. Take your pick," Callie replied with a shrug.

The hurt in her voice, even underneath the flippant attitude, was apparent to Chel. It broke her heart.

"Well that is a load of bul-loney," Chel finished awkwardly to which Callie cocked her head with pinched eyebrows then laughed.

"I do not know what that word is, maybe something you learn in your mortal realm, but it made me laugh," she admitted.

"Yes, it's an expression that is lacking at the moment, but one to express disbelief. I cannot fathom this tribe—which is supposed to be about family I thought—would want you dead. Why?"

"That is why Samuel wants me to stay in the shadows, to stay in my home and keep to myself. If I am out of the way, then they don't remember me, and if I do not attract attention to myself, then I will be safe—that is what he tells me anyway." Callie's eyes blinked multiple times, clearing away the emotion trying to rise up.

"That doesn't make any sense to me. Why though? You aren't hurting anyone and just because you can't see doesn't make you useless; in fact, it makes you even more useful. I bet your other senses are much more sensitive than the other Shifters here," Chel stated.

Callie's eyes lit up and she let a small smile come through. "From what I understand, it is because I cannot fully function as a member of the tribe. You see, any tribe member who cannot do this... well, that is a weakness and something they need to take care of with precious resources instead."

"Are those Samuel's words?" Chel was mortified. Who was this guy? Her anger at the whole situation was coming to the surface. "If Samuel told you that, I'm going to bust his you know whats! That's the biggest load of crap I've ever heard," Chel fumed, her hands at her hips as she paced in front of the small entry. "What is the point of having a tribe if not to take care of their own, not saying you need taking care of, especially now, you are more than capable, living up here on your own and sneaking about the village all on your own. Ugh!" Chel began to forget who she was talking to in her furor. "He and I are definitely through. Definitely. I think I have some hopes to dash. I mean, if he's even holding them out any longer." Chel threw her hands to the sides. "I don't know what I ever saw in him to begin with," she continued forgetting her audience.

"You and Samuel are mates?!" Callie gasped. "He never told me."

"WHOA! Whoa!" Chel stopped pacing and faced Callie. "You didn't know we were together?" Chel's head began to spin, but she regained her composure. "No, no we aren't mates. Um, how to explain... so, in the mortal realm we dated. Yes, we lived together even for a short time, just before coming here. I don't really know what to think now because the whole time we dated, I had no idea he was a Shifter." Tears began welling up in Chel's eyes. "I mean he lied to me the entire time we were together. I'm not sure why he was really even with me. I'm guessing there's more to that story than I know," Chel thought out loud, allowing herself to truly think through her situation and past for the first time. "How could I be so naive, how could I be so bli—" Chel caught herself before she finished her statement and quickly recovered it. "How could I not have seen there were other motivations for him being there? I just don't know what they were."

"Samuel gave up the possibility of having a mate to treat you as one without being one officially?" Callie was shocked at Chel's revelation.

"Well, if our time together counts as *being mated,* I'm not sure I want to be mated. Truth is, we got along in the beginning. It was physical but also more than that, at least at first. He was so supportive of my art and going to college, but then things started to change. He would get irritated when I kept trying to include Kaeleigh and Finn and then after that we didn't really get along that well."

"Here, we mate with another for life," Callie explained, "but if one takes another Shifter and um," Callie blushed, "you know *mates* and that one isn't their official mate then they risk forfeit of their true mate."

"That's... confusing," Chel scrunched her eyebrows.

"Yes, and no, I guess unless you grew up here the customs would make more sense I think. So your parents did not teach these customs to you even on the outside?" Callie questioned.

"Not really, I suppose they wanted me to blend in and dating is a part of the culture in the mortal realm. Though for the record, I didn't date that much, it just never felt right," answered Chel. "Samuel was the only one who ever felt *right*... and even he wasn't completely right," Chel mused.

"Because your animal knows our ways," Callie said matter of fact.

"Perhaps," Chel said with a smile. She liked the idea of only having one mate, but not everyone in Alandria functioned that way, one in particular sprung to mind... Hal was just an example who spontaneously popped in her thoughts.

"So what can I do for you, Chel? I am sure you did not come all this way just to check in on a helpless blind girl," Callie teased, her countenance and humor back to what appeared natural to her.

"You seem like the only one who would tell me things straight," Chel paused, looked back out the entry remaining open to the outside air, and sighed. "To be honest, I miss having a girlfriend I can talk with."

"I have never really had many friends I could talk with so I am not sure how good I will be at it, but I would love to try." Callie beamed. "There was one boy when we were younger. He would visit me and bring me anything I needed but Samuel scared him off several years back. He has not come back since. It can be lonely when Samuel does not come either."

Callie noticed her infrequent use of contractions and how she would revert back to Alandrian non-use of them—except for those who had studied or experienced the mortal realm. Samuel's speech must have rubbed off on her some.

"I'm sure it can be." Chel paused, her face contorted with frustration. "I don't understand what's going on here, but something seems...

off," Chel struggled to find the right word. "I do not believe such treatment is the way Shifters are supposed to function." Finally Chel stopped moving and sat on the floor, leaning against the cool wall of stone.

"I guess you might be correct, I think I have talked myself into believing it because I could not remember anything different. Plus why would Samuel lie to me?"

"Indeed, that is the question, why would he?" Chel ran the question over in her mind searching for reasons, but found no explanation. Pulling up her knees and hugging them close, her countenance brightened and changed subjects.

"So why *I'm* here is to create alliances with Shifters who are willing to fight for Alandria," Chel began, "I want you to be my first candidate." She paused and reconsidered her last words. "Hmm, that didn't sound right. I'm new to this recruiting thing. Not candidate, how about volunteer?"

"Volunteer for what? And what do you mean by fight? You remember I do not see, right?" Callie reminded Chel unnecessarily. The slender wood chair Callie sat on teetered as she gently rocked on it.

"Like I said, I bet your senses are stronger than anyone's here... even that old grumpy Landon's. You are more than capable and would be a great asset to have in a fight." Chel took a deep breath and continued. "Alandria is dying, the magic is being sucked out of her. Maleina has gone too far and has moved against the natural order of Alandria—granted I haven't been here that long so what I'm telling you is coming from several others, though I trust them and you can too. And I do have experience with this darkness." Pausing she gathered strength and steadied her heart. "Darkness has been let in, the Droch-Shúil," at the mention of its name Callie gasped loudly. "So you have heard of them?" Chel was relieved Callie seemed to understand the danger, at least her tone indicated as much. "That's good. I mean good that you know, not that they are good of course." Chel was eager to open up completely to Callie, whom she was quickly learning to like and trust. "See, I was captured by creatures serving the Droch-Shúil for a short time." Chel inhaled a steadying breath. She held her hands together to keep from revealing the shakes, which occurred when she thought of her time with the Droch-Shúil which happened almost every night in her dreams—her nightmares. Coming back to her point, Chel continued confidently, "I'm loving

Alandria more and more and I do not want those creatures doing more damage and killing off this place anymore than one who has lived here all their life." Chel's fists had clenched and her gaze was fierce. Tiny hairs erupted all over her arms, shocking her out of her angered and fearful state. Her heart rate sped faster than she thought possible, her breathing grew shallow and more staccato. The shift was upon her once more. Her timing really sucked. Chel gasped almost inaudibly but Callie's head whipped toward her and her nostrils flared.

"Chel," Callie said in low soothing tones. "Chel, have you shifted before?"

"N... not yet." Chel breathed slowly out of her nose, at least she tried but it proved challenging. "This is faster than the other times it started. It just hasn't gone any further yet." Chel's eyes were wide in panic, frantically looking about the small cavern for something, anything, though she had no idea what.

"Okay, Chel." Again Callie's tone was low and calm. "I am going to tell you a story and I want you to listen best you can. Focus on my words or on the sounds of my words, all right?"

Chel bobbed her head in understanding.

"A long time ago, there lived in Alandria a beautiful young woman. She was fair with dark hair," Callie hadn't gotten far before Chel's gaze found hers in question.

"How do you know she had dark hair?" Chel asked her teeth chattering from initial shock of the change.

Callie laughed softly. "Good question, you are listening. This story was told to me by my mother before she died. Now, focus on slowing your breathing—I can hear your heart all the way over here—and I will continue the story."

"Sorry," Chel mumbled, her head falling back against the stone allowing the coolness to seep into her head and cool her heated state. Beads of sweat popped out from her forehead and upper lip, dripping down her neck to be absorbed by her clothing.

"So this woman was loved by all in the tribe, for you see she was a Shifter. She was kind and loyal, but also fierce and ready to take on anything. Eventually she found her mate and they were happy. The tribe rejoiced for you see he was next in line to become the Chieftain."

At that, Chel's head lifted and she looked from blurred eyes at Callie. She was glad for the briefest moment that Callie couldn't see her mouth agape. Could she be telling a story of one of her relatives? She hadn't wanted to tell anyone yet the revelation she had come to from her time with the magic book until she had spoken to her parents. Callie continued, none the wiser to Chel's thoughts.

"The couple was adored by the village. The woman's mate was strong and capable and had been trained by the best in our territory. He had even traveled to train with the Ferrishyn warriors in Elnye for a time, and learned much from time spent in Adettlyn with the Elves as well. You see, long ago we used to have more open borders and sent apprentices to spend time in each territory to make alliances and learn each other's ways." Callie paused to take a sip of water.

Chel knew she was evaluating her heart rate as she cocked her head, listening. She had mostly gotten it under control. The story and Callie's method was proving quite helpful. She would remember in the future to mentally use stories to distract and calm herself and others if necessary.

"Good, you are under much more control," Callie observed with a nod. "I thought I was going to have to bring you through your first shift, not sure how well that would have gone over." Callie chuckled.

A thought struck Chel. "Do you shift?"

Callie nodded. "I do. I learned when I was a pretty small child, actually younger than many of the youth do. I think my animal was trying to protect and take care of me. You want to know a secret?"

Chel nodded enthusiastically. "Of course!"

"My animal is not blind!"

"So when you're in animal form, you can see?" Chel was baffled.

Callie nodded enthusiastically. "So why do I not stay in animal form? That is your next question correct?"

Chel smiled then remembered Callie couldn't see it. "Yes, why don't you?"

"I did for a long while when I was younger, but I couldn't communicate the same to my parents when I was little, and I wanted to make my weakness stronger. My animal ensured I could do it and has helped me even when I am in this form, but she has not been able to give me her sight. I still shift often, but I am now comfortable in each skin."

"Wow," Chel mustered. She couldn't imagine herself in that position. "That is truly amazing." She was glad she had gotten her animal under control and grateful for Callie's help through storytelling.

"Please do not share that information. Most here know that information, though we guarded it tightly when I was young from any outside the tribe unsure what would be done with that knowledge. Especially now that the territories are not as friendly to Shifters as they used to be." Callie looked sad. "I had always wanted to go to the other territories so I could see them to even my limited degree in my animal form."

"That's how you get around so well even in human form... because you learned the paths and places when you were animal." Callie nodded to Chel's conclusion. "See that's what doesn't make sense about Samuel's claim that the tribe sees you as a weakness and would try to harm you..."

Callie tilted her head, listening closely.

"They guard your secret, they have not tried anything even when you were young and at your weakest or even since when you're parents have gone." She thought carefully and then asked the question. "How did your parents die?"

"They were killed many years ago. They ventured out to one of the other territories to send a message from Landon to L'nalrinia—one of the Faerie cities—and were attacked along their route. Three other Shifters were killed along with them. The only one to return was Samuel; somehow he had escaped. He thought since he was young and uninteresting he was able to sneak passed whoever killed them." Callie sighed with a shimmer of wet in her eyes. "It was long ago, but I still miss them everyday."

"I imagine you do," Chel agreed sadly, thinking of her own parents.

"So I need to know how the story ends," Chel changed the subject.

Callie's eyes perked up and her smile returned. "Oh right! I nearly forgot. You like the story then?"

"I do, I want to learn as much as I can assuming it is true, right?"

"Yes, it is true." Callie smiled knowingly.

"Ok, where was I?" she asked thoughtfully more to herself than Chel. "Right. So the leaders used to send worthy candidates to learn and explore the other territories. This kept Alandria more united and strengthened—granted they did not share *all* their secrets but each territory was quite generous with the knowledge they offered." Callie smiled and tilted her head toward Chel conspiratorially. "Side note: I like to gain knowledge and histories whenever I can, and there used to be something long, long ago in the realm before Alandria called the Council of the Kings. It was more a governing body rather than individual kings I think. Anyway, they would pool their resources and knowledge and were much stronger because of it—from my limited understanding of what it was. Either no one will talk of it anymore, or no one remembers the history of it."

"I bet I know someone who would, when the time is appropriate I will introduce you and he can tell you all about it. I have a feeling there are not as many left who remain with that knowledge," Chel added.

"Thank you!" Callie beamed. "I would love that!"

"Ok, back to the story. Then what happened?" Chel asked, like a child sitting on the edge of her seat waiting for the finale.

"Anyway, the beautiful young Shifter and her mate had become secretive, traveling much to the outside lands. No one knew exactly where they went or who they met. Things in Alandria were growing dark—you mentioned the darkness growing, this was the first it had been seen in a long many years—people were dying and disappearing. The peace that had reigned in Alandria for so long was no longer. Territories grew suspicious of one another, Elves and Faeries became distrustful and standoffish. Shifters became ostracized and outcast because the magic they possessed was so much different than those of the Faeries and Elves—we were too different and different was suddenly bad almost overnight, though it had been growing for quite some time." Callie stood and shook out her legs, then remained standing while she finished.

"What happened to the couple?" asked Chel.

"I am getting to them," Callie smiled. "Things were bad. The Chieftain at the time—the young man's father—was growing old but not too old to rule, when he was killed. It was time for the young man to fulfill his role and become the new Chieftain of the tribe. He accepted it proudly, though saddened at his father's death—his mother had passed on several years before that time. The tribe grew restless with he and his mate's continued wandering away from the tribe when they were needed to remain here. But then to the tribe's joy, the woman became with child. She was so in love with that baby before it was even born.

They stayed close to home for most of the pregnancy and even after for a couple years—except once when a small private envoy of Ferrishyn came to Mandü tré Lan to speak to our new Chieftain and his mate did they go out beyond our borders to meet them. You see, the woman had become close friends with Princess Eva of Feraánmar. She had often gone to visit Elnye before things had taken a dark turn. The Elves and the Faeries had called a unifying assembly; they had created an agreement between them with the Elders oversight to become unified and work together again, putting all the past behind them. The Shifters were included too, but only to a point. We didn't attend the Agreement signing. We didn't even hear about the battle until it was too late." Callie paused for another drink. "Elves had then come to our territory and called a meeting with our Chieftain and his mate privately. They left shortly after that, the Chieftain, his mate and their young daughter, that is, very rushed and emotional was their departure. The nature of the meeting with the Elves was not known until later: Princess Eva along with her mother and father, the king and queen of Feraánmar had been killed in an uprising. It was still not known where the family had gone, but when they returned they returned in the night with a young child not their own, barely even walking. They kept the child with them at all times until they were called upon once more by the Elves. The Chieftain and his mate were secreted away in the middle of the night and when they returned, they did so without the other young girl. Streaks of blue trailed down her face as she held her own child, cradling her close. They remained with the tribe for only a short time when the tribe called for a vote. They elected another Chieftain in his place to care for the tribe, demeaning the current Chieftain's position with his care for another race over his own. The couple and their young daughter left never to be heard from again..."

"Until now?" Chel asked, chills erupting over her flesh this time not from a looming shift, certain she knew the story from this point.

"Yes, until now. Your parents have been gone a long time, Chel." Callie gave her a small sad smile.

"Why is Landon the Chieftain if that is not who was elected?"

"The elected Chieftain was mysteriously killed one night, no one knows by who or how it happened. Magic was definitely involved based on the stories I have overheard. Landon is not considered an official Chieftain since he was not made successor by official channels. He is more an advisor or elder until Alandria deems another to become Chieftain."

They both sat quietly, while Chel processed all the information.

"Maybe since your parents are back, your dad can be the Chieftain again, technically he is the rightful heir," Callie stated.

"I have much to speak with them about, I don't even know if they would want to. I mean we had a life and a home back in Montana—in the mortal realm—I don't know what happens to all that. I do hope my parents have a plan." Chel sighed.

"Your parents are Chieftains whether they hold the position or not, of course they have a plan," Callie said confidently with a smile.

"You are not only amazing, Callie, but also a wealth of information. I appreciate your faith and confidence in my parents. I'm sad to say I haven't had that much in them myself mainly because I was in the dark on all this for so long. I wish I had grown up knowing who I was and how all this worked." Chel slumped back against the wall.

"If you did, what would have been different? What would you have done?" Callie asked.

"Well, I would have wanted to come here and see it for myself, I would have wanted them to train me so I would know all about shifting when it came up, I would..."

"Exactly my point," Callie interrupted Chel's rant. "You would have wanted to come here. There was obviously a reason they stayed away for so long, keeping you from this."

"To watch over Kaeleigh and allow us to grow up together without the worry of what was happening here while we were out there. We wouldn't have been ready to come back into whatever was happening here. I get it," Chel conceded her point. "I understand the reasoning. I just wish I had known or that they could have told us both, but everything happens 'in the right time,' right?" Chel used air quotes that Callie couldn't see, thinking of when Arileas and others told them everything happens in the right time so often. She almost chuckled but it would have been lost on Callie.

"I can't tell you how much I have loved having some girl time and getting to know you, Callie. I need to see my parents before the evening meal, and I see it is getting dark out." Chel moved over to Callie and placed her hand on her forearm and gave her a little squeeze.

"I was all right as a friend?" Callie asked suddenly a shy young girl.

"You were fantastic, I think you have a real future in friendship," Chel said as she went ahead and assaulted Callie with a big hug not caring anymore if she should or shouldn't.

"Oh, thank you, Chel!" Callie beamed as a single tear slid out of the corner of one eye.

"I have something I want to trust you with. I think you could keep it safe for me, could you?"

"Absolutely, no one usually comes up here, and I have several hiding places," Callie clapped her hands, excited to be in on the secret.

"After I speak with my parents, I will bring it back to you under the cover of night," Chel said.

"I will be here. Someone drops dinner off at my door, so I will not be at the evening meal," Callie stated.

Chel's face fell, her heart hurt for the treatment of her new friend.

"Do not be sad for me Chel, I am not for myself. It is the way of it for now, and I trust you to find the truth in the matter," Callie winked at her.

"You read me pretty good for a blind girl," Chel responded at the door, looking back at Callie. "Talk to you later!"

Chel slipped out the doorway, climbed carefully down the boulders realizing it wasn't actually as hard as it first appeared, and out into the budding evening. The moons were rising in Alandria and darkness was falling—hopefully in only the most natural way.

Chapter Twenty-Five

After the evening meal, Chel was relieved to get a few minutes to check with Hal about his time with Arileas. Hal continued eyeing her strangely. His eyes darted about though. He was obviously—to her anyway—disturbed by something. The meal was abuzz with Shifters, conversation, and meeting new and old friends of her parents. The experience was both exhilarating and exhausting.

Before Chel had taken the magic book to Callie, she showed her parents the book and explained their heritage the same way the book had first shown Chel. Ray was surprised the book had communicated with Chel in such a manner befitting a Chieftain, apparently that was unusual. Hal had caught up to her as she left her parents' room, heading back to Callie's. He gently gripped her elbow and steered her back down the hall toward her room. "Can I speak with you privately?" Hal said in hushed tones.

"Of course," Chel replied. She looked up and down the hall to ensure they were alone before she slipped them into her room. In light of all the "mate" talk earlier, Chel didn't know if there were rules about having boys in her room. She almost giggled at the thought. Not to worry, though, Hal had disappeared shortly after he slipped the map back into her hands once inside her room, but not without a warning before he did.

"Chel, I overheard Samuel planning something with my mother. I don't know what they are up to, but it's going to happen soon and I want you to be careful." Hal scrunched up his nose hesitating, but said it anyway, "I know you two are close, but I'm asking you to stay away from him until we learn what he's up to."

"Are you sure it was your mother?" Chel had asked Hal after he first came back all animated, explaining where he had been.

"Absolutely. You do not have to believe me, Chel, just promise you will be careful and watchful around him until I know what their plan could be," Hal made her promise.

Hal's sincerity and concern for her safety had made her promise not because he asked her to but because she believed him. Chel trusted him along with the backing of her own gut.

"I believe you, Hal. Samuel's got some issues, but I wouldn't have thought him to be a bad guy," Chel expounded, "I'll keep my distance, and if I can't, I'll make sure others are around so I'm not alone with him."

Hal nodded seriously. "Good. Please be careful." He reached up and moved a piece of hair out of her face, tucking it softly behind her ear. His warm, gentle gaze roamed over her face longer than casually acceptable. "Remember if you call for me, I will hear you." He mysteriously slipped out of the room, leaving Chel standing in her sparse room clutching the map and her magic book.

Snapping out of whatever spell Hal had woven over Chel, she headed back to Callie's place to bring her the book. Callie had lit up when Chel handed her the book, apparently Callie had an affinity for books and didn't need to see to be able to listen to what the book would share with her.

"This is a very special book, Chel!" Callie had whispered, her eyes wide with anticipation. "I cannot believe I missed it all these years in the library. It must have not been ready to be found until you came. It will only share with me the general histories of the chieftains, but not their secrets in case you wondered."

Callie hid it in a secret floorboard she had under her own bed, but Callie's was tucked away quite out of sight. Chel was confident in Callie's ability to keep it, and the map Hal had returned to her, safe.

The next morning both Hal and Chel went to Landon and her parents. They had agreed earlier to not mention Samuel until they knew more of his plot; Hal and Chel realized they weren't sure they could trust Landon, but he was the tribe's current, if not rightful, leader.

"Mom, Dad, Landon, thank you for granting us an audience," Chel began reverently unsure of basic protocol for addressing the tribe's leader.

"We have news that could impact the entire tribe," Hal finished for her.

Landon crossed his arms and frowned. "Out with it then."

Hal nodded succinctly. "I have reason to believe Maleina will strike out of Mandü tré Lan very soon."

"How could you possibly know this unless it was you who communicated with her? And if she knows you are here, then even more reason for her to seek us out." Landon's voice grew. "We were under her radar for so long. You have brought this upon us as we suffered your presence these past days? You are no friend of the Shifters!" Landon shouted, pointing a thick crooked finger at Hal right in the face.

To Hal's credit, he barely flinched. Somehow he managed to remain calm and even unfazed by the brute of a man accusing him of such falsehoods.

"I simply wanted to warn you so you could prepare the Shifters if she should launch an attack." He paused and prepared to divulge a low blow to Landon's understanding. "It was not *I* who communicated with her, but I overheard one of *your* Shifters. So before you start pointing fingers, perhaps you should look among your own people and examine their state." Hal stood tall from where he had been leaning against a table with nonchalance until Landon had pointed in his face interfering his personal boundaries. "*Your* people as you call them, Landon, are not happy and shudder in fear at the thought of going against what you might say. That does not make you any different than Maleina from where I stand." Hal did not back down but the room had grown still, the silence so heavy it threatened to drop like a tidal wave when released. Chel showed her support for Hal by moving silently toward him.

Landon's face was so red he rivaled a beet on the brink of explosion. "You, *Faerie*, have gone too far and stuck your nose into affairs that do not concern you. Watch your back," Landon snarled.

"That is enough, Landon," Ray said with an eerie authoritative calm Chel had only heard him use a handful of time while growing up—his serious "dad" tone. "I believe him."

Chel realized now it was actually his dominate Shifter tone that made him Chieftain because Landon's reaction was similar to hers without the tears. And the fact he declared he believed her friend made her heart soar, they were not alone. Her parents would stand with them.

"And *you*, Rayalt Marzén, you no longer have any say here. Stay out of my way," Landon said through gritted teeth and stormed out.

"No longer," said Ray under his breath, practically outright declaring war with Landon without actually doing it.

Chel knew if he was willing to challenge Landon for his position back the people would most probably support him. She hoped the Shifter loyalty to her dad would still be intact and hoped he was up to that task. A secret part of her wanted to see her parents both in full Shifter mode to see what they were like. Chel knew nothing of how they lived while here, but she still knew her parents and was pretty sure they'd be great leaders.

<div align="center">~~~~~</div>

Over the next couple days, Chel spent time with her parents catching up and asking all the questions she had been waiting to ask. She was so relieved to have all she had learned and experienced out in the open. Her parents were shocked to hear Callie had told her their early story. They were unaware that anyone even cared.

Since their warning-turned-confrontation with Landon, Chel, Hal, and her parents had been reaching out to individual Shifters. They found a scattered handful loyal enough to Alandria and their cause to take a stand with them. However, too many were frightened, and many would simply rather hide in the mortal realm until the end of their days if they had to rather than fight. Chel knew the mortal realm to be nice, but if they had originally been from here and this was their home, she couldn't believe how easily they were willing to give it up.

Chel had spent time each day with Callie and truly loved her company; they were becoming fast friends. Chel couldn't wait for her to meet Kaeleigh.

On the third day, Chel was on her way to visit Callie. Hal stopped her as she exited the dorm building, waiting for her.

"You seem to be forgetting today is the third day and I have yet to find out what Samuel is doing or what he is waiting for—" he stopped her outside the door then casually leaned against a boulder, one foot propped on it, and his arms crossed at his chest. Hal's eyes roved over the entire compound, at least as much as he could see, but kept landing back on Chel's.

"Are you waiting for me?" Chel asked sweetly, batting her eyes knowing he was more likely guarding the building because she was in it.

Hal looked over at her and puffed out his chest. His eyes took on a playful glint that she had seen less and less of since they arrived. Chel realized she missed his carefree attitude and wanted to see the stress of this time over if for nothing else than to see him smile—she stopped and calmed herself down. She needed to focus on the important—their mission—not get carried away with infatuation.

"You seem to be in need of a handsome warrior to escort you on your way," he playfully chided her for leaving on her own. Clearly Hal was just as enamored, however, and that made it all the harder for Chel to keep her feelings in check.

"Ah, well yes, you see I had one—several in fact—but I seemingly drove them all away; apparently, they couldn't handle my sweet personality." She batted her eyes mockingly again.

"Ha!" he let out an uncontrolled laugh. "The truth finally comes out."

"I can't help it if I am just too good for them," Chel kept bantering.

Hal paused, his face sobered but his eyes did not leave hers. "You *are* too good for them, Chel, remember that. You deserve the best."

His words struck a chord in her heart, but she couldn't help notice his fallen expression. "Thank you, Hal, but why do you look so sad?" she dared to ask.

"Ah fair maiden, because alas I do not count myself among those who could be your best," he replied again with a playful tone, though the honesty in his eye almost floored Chel, rendering her speechless in their little game.

Instead she looped her arm in his and tugged him along with her. "You are right, there are too many big bad wolves in this neighborhood for little ole me and my red cape. I need a protector."

Hal chuckled but looked at her slightly confused. "You, my dear, will be one of those big bad wolves soon enough, and if I might point out, you are not wearing a red cape."

Chel laughed merrily, happy to have steered him back into good humor. "Point to you. The red cape was alluding to a mortal story of a girl who went into the forest with a red cape to visit her granny and there was a big bad wolf who ate her granny—at least in one version it did—anyway, forget about it. Not important."

"I like to learn your mortal realm stories and believe it or not, I have heard of Little Red Riding Hood, I was just giving you a hard time."

"Oh." Chel lightly punched him in the arm.

"Where are we going?" he asked.

"I want you to meet Callie, she's a friend and I think you'll really like her. She's where I hid the map and the book I was telling you about." Chel pointed up a bit further along the path. "She lives just up there."

"Can we trust her?"

Chel thought carefully. "Yes." She inhaled a short deep breath. "But you should know, she's Samuel's little sister."

Hal was quiet a moment, then nodded. "If you trust her, so do I."

Simple as that. His faith in her made her want to be the best version of herself, to be worthy of his confidence. Chel smiled and nodded.

"Chel, before we go in, I think you should know I believe Samuel was in the mortal realm...for you. I mean, I think he was sent to spy on you and your parents and keep tabs on your whereabouts by whatever means necessary." Hal hesitated, unlike him to beat around the bush. "I am afraid much of your relationship was false."

Chel gave Hal a small appreciative smile. "I had pretty much already figured that part out. Thank you for telling me though. I appreciate your honesty at the risk I wouldn't believe you." She reached up on her tiptoes and planted a quick peck on his cheek then pulled away and began to climb up the boulders.

"You are welcome. I will always be honest with you, Chel," Hal replied quietly but she heard him.

"Callie, we're here," Chel hollered when she stepped inside, "I brought Hal, the Faerie I was telling you about." Chel took a minute to look around, but no Callie.

"Maybe she stepped out and did not know you were coming?" Hal offered.

"No, she knew I was coming. Just a second," Chel asked as she closed her eyes and held out a hand asking Hal to stay where he was. Inhaling deeply, she categorized the scents she could smell and the stronger the scent, the more recent the person had been there.

"Get anything?" asked Hal understanding what she was doing as if it was the most normal thing she could've done right then.

"I smell me, Callie, Samuel and one other who is vaguely familiar," Chel said tilting her head in thought and memory. "I was here yesterday and Samuel's her brother so of course his would be here, but it is also as strong as Callie's scent right here," Chel stated.

"Which means what?" Halister lead her to the conclusion.

"Samuel was here recently along with the other scent. Oh, what is it? I almost have it..." scrunching up her face didn't seem to help jog her memory, however, and she sagged her shoulders in defeat.

"It will recall when you need it most, Chel, do not be so hard on yourself."

She nodded. "Perhaps she just went out with her brother and a friend. But that makes no sense because she said she didn't have any friends, and her brother didn't come to visit that often. There is no way he wanted her out of her house either, he said it wasn't safe for her."

Hal braced his chin between his thumb and forefinger in thought. "What if he knows my mother wasn't going to make good on her word and he moved her somewhere else?"

"Yes, that's possible," Chel mused as she walked through the small space to make sure she didn't miss anything. Plus she wanted to check on her book and map to ensure they were still where Callie had hid them. Spotting a folded piece of paper on top of the bed, Chel grabbed it and read it. Her name was on the front very small, but there. Callie had left her a note, knowing she was coming.

Chel, I am sorry I am not there to see you. Samuel is taking me somewhere. He said it is not safe and he would not be around to protect me if the worst should happen and the Shifters get attacked. I cannot imagine that happening but he was very angry. Spouting something about doing her bidding and getting her what she wants but she still will not honor her word. Does that make any sense to you? Your items are still safe if you want to leave them for now. Destroy this note. Get safe. I will look for you when it is all right for me to leave whatever hole Samuel is putting me in.
  Your friend,
  Callie

Chel looked up at Hal and handed him the note so he could read it for himself. He frowned. "Seems our timeline is about up then, does it not?"

"It does. I only wish we knew what he was after. It was serious enough he moved his sister in case Maleina does come through on her backwards threat to attack. Or he was just getting her out of the way so he could take care of whatever business he has with your mom."

Chel turned suddenly at the sound of a heavy thud on the ground. "Hal!" Chel screamed as she saw him on the ground. Standing behind him was Samuel and another Shifter holding a thick stick. Danik. Danik was one of the Shifters with the bad attitudes who had confronted Hal the first day they arrived. He had hit Hal over the head with it.

"Perhaps the answer is both, did you consider that option?" Samuel sneered. "Hello, Chel, lucky finding you here," Samuel's voice had never been darker. How had she never seen this side of him before? His eyes had grown darker and brighter than normal, charged with the adrenaline of a hunt and the closeness of his change. Danik stood by him, waiting for his command like a poor mutt desiring to please his master.

"Callie had better be all right!" Chel demanded, her voice full of authority. He would not gain a sense of her fear. Keeping her breathing low and her heartbeat slow, she kept her wolf under control.

"She's fine, Chel, thank you for your unwanted concern though."

"No need to be the bad guy, Samuel. I like your sister and care for her well-being. I know you care for her too, though you just show it in the strangest way," she finished.

Samuel blinked and caught his gaze glancing away from Chel for a brief second then brought it back with a frown like he wasn't sure what had just happened. He straightened his shoulders and glared at her, but answered more genuinely. "She is safe for now." He quickly glanced at Danik without his noticing and Chel caught the subtle hint to leave it alone for now.

"What do you want, Samuel?" she asked instead, leaving it for now.

Only someone looking with a keen eye would note his shoulders dropped the slightest in relief. "I am to take you to Maleina," he stated like it was no big deal.

"Oh is that all? Well, all right then, why didn't you say so in the beginning?" She rolled her eyes.

"You would come with us easily?" he asked confused.

"No." She replied which added to Danik's confused expression. "But thank you for asking. See, I can be polite." Chel needed to stall them and find a way out. How she would do so was another question she needed an answer for, and quick. Two bullish Shifters stood between her and freedom.

"I won't hurt you, Chel, as long as you don't make it harder on yourself. Come with us quietly and I'll allow you to walk out on your own," Samuel explained.

Not seeing any other option at the present and she did not want them carrying her out of there, she nodded. "All right. You win, I'll walk out of here with you."

"No screaming when you get out all the way until the exit of Mandü tre Lan, agreed?" Samuel added suspiciously.

"I will not scream." Chel crossed her heart, something she used to do in the mortal realm when she was younger.

"I will go down, Chel, you in the middle, and Danik, you take the rear. Do not let her out of your sight," Samuel growled as he turned to stalk out.

"Wait! What about Hal?" Chel gestured to Hal lying on the ground unconscious. She had felt his pulse to ensure that was all he was. She hated leaving him like that, but maybe he could track her.

"Leave him," Danik growled. He spit on the back of Hal's head as he walked away from him. "Dirty Faerie scum."

Chel stared Danik down until Danik turned his head, not nearly as dominant as he pretended to be. Chel almost laughed, but instead she settled for a smirk which threw him off. She realized he had no idea his own animal recognized hers as more dominant.

"He'll wake up with a big headache, but if we do more damage, Maleina will definitely come in after him. We just needed him out of the way to get you alone. Come on we need to hurry," Samuel shout whispered as he hurried out the door into the village.

Chapter Twenty-Six

They filed down the suddenly empty road through the village to the nearest turn that would lead them out beyond the roads of the village and out of eyeshot of anyone who looked out their window. In single-file just as Samuel had instructed they walked swiftly and quietly staying close to the boulder walls and sneaking behind any trees within the vicinity.

"You left him to follow me didn't you?"

"You are a smart girl, aren't you?" Samuel said sarcastically and pushed her further along now at her side instead of single file. "Yes, this way, he'll be able to come after you and straight to mommy dearest," Samuel let loose, not seeing any reason to hide it any longer.

"This is a trap not for me, but for Hal, isn't it?" The color drained from her face, leaving her pale and nauseated looking. She would have fought more had she realized she was being used as bait to trap Hal.

"Yes, dear Chel, you are bait and this is a trap, but I heard you are already familiar with those so you should be good with this one. No Droch-Shúil as far as I know."

"That was low, Sam, even for you," Chel said through gritted teeth barely breathing since he mentioned those fowl creatures of darkness that had held her captive early into their entrance into Alandria. Her heart rate accelerated, tiny hairs sprouted on her arms, she was fighting the change again. "Not now," she whispered. "Why always at the most inconvenient times do you try to come out and play," she whispered to her wolf, starting to bond with her more and more.

"Not now, Chel, get your wolf under control," Samuel practically spat at her.

Chel saw it. The spark of fear that flashed in Samuel's eyes. He was afraid of something. Of her wolf? Of her not getting to Maleina in time? That had to be it. Thinking helped, she could get her breathing under control for a little bit but she was so on edge, her time was coming soon. Her wolf wanted out.

"Focus. Focus on something," she told herself out loud, looking around for anything that could help her or give her a distraction. Thinking of Kaeleigh and Daegan and Halister, she wondered what they would tell her to do in this situation. As of right now, she was on her own. Doubt did not plague her to whether Hal would come after her, she knew he would and therein was the problem. How could she warn him? Until the path narrowed again which she knew it would up ahead, both of the guys flanked her, not allowing for much wiggle room. Her breathing slowed once more and she found it easier to think without her wolf clawing at her insides to get out before Chel was ready.

Listening to her surroundings which is what Daegan had told her before: *Chel, you are a Shifter—use your gifts unique to you.* She couldn't walk and close her eyes at the same time so she found a spot on the ground to watch and zoned into her surroundings. First she inhaled slowly, sensing anything and everything she could, searching for any possibilities. Chel listened with her sensitive ears for something helpful.

Hearing some animals further away than she would have thought possible, she zoned in on them. Unable to decipher what type of animals they were, she realized their communication was much more clear than other animals she had listened in on before. Shifters! That must be the difference between regular animals and Shifted animals, she could understand them more clearly. Remembering the time they dealt with that bearish creature, she had attempted to communicate back but it hadn't happened the way she thought she should be able to. Determined and stubborn as Chel was though, she would try again—she was stronger, more in tune with her Shifter side now.

Chel directed every ounce of mental power into the innate magic she had as a Shifter and focused it on those voices she heard in the distance. Samuel was too focused on where he was leading to notice or hear her communicating telepathically. Chel wasn't sure how it worked entirely, if all Shifters in the vicinity could hear her or just the ones she was directing it at. At this point she had to try something, she was being taken further and further away.

"Who is this?" a hesitant voice came back in her head.

"I am Chelnáh daughter of Rayalt Marzén. I am being captured. Please tell Halister Endíl not to follow. It is a trap. I repeat a trap for him," Chel replied in her head, rushing the words together as fast as she could in case they didn't get it all the further away she got.

"The Faerie?" the voice responded in question.

"Yes, the Faerie." Now angry at the utter disrespect she heard in his tone she ground her teeth not to lash out at the only helpline she could find. *"If you support Rayalt and the way Alandria should be, please warn Halister and my parents if you can."*

"I will do as you ask, little Chieftess," the voice said with a tone not disrespectful but almost awed and surprised, Chel thought. He said he would give the message to Hal and that was more than she could ask for at the moment. Relaxed a little at the possibility of warning Hal, she was able to think of her next move. Chel no longer recognized the part of the Stone Forest they had entered; it appeared they were heading North based on where the sun was setting. She would bide her time for a little longer, looking for the perfect opportunity then she had her part to play.

A slight breeze tickled her nose and Chel fought the sneeze she felt coming upon her, but she wasn't able to stop the onslaught of sneezing that suddenly overtook her. She recognized it for the opportunity it could be and stopped in her tracks to sneeze then duck away and behind Danik and Samuel, racing to get away from them, heading back the direction they came from.

"Chel, stop!" Samuel shouted, but it didn't sound like he was pursuing her as fast as she thought he might.

Chel turned to see both Danik and Samuel standing still, hands at waist simply waiting.

"That's odd," Chel mumbled. When she turned around victoriously, she ran smack into something hard and fell back hitting the dirt path with a thud. She groaned and peered through blurry eyes to see what she hit.

Landon standing there with a triumphant sneer on his stupid face, holding a stick just like the one Danik hit Hal over the head with. The last thing she saw was his eyes full of hatred, glaring straight into her while hearing Samuel's voice just behind her.

"I told you not to run," he mumbled with a sigh.

Then everything went dark.

~~~~~

Halister strode clumsily at first down the path from the village homes back to the dormitory. Rubbing the back of his head, and rolling his neck and shoulders he grumbled about getting bested by amateur fighters. Swords, knives, honor, combat, any of those things he was superior at, but sticks behind the back was a new low brought against him. Not to mention he'd lost Chel because of it. He blamed only himself—well, himself and the imbeciles who took her, not willing to face him. He had one guess one of the brutes was Samuel. Seemed fitting he would come back to Callie's place; Hal should have seen that coming.

It dawned on him all at once that it was Chel all along Samuel had been after, the plan with his mother all of it was about Chel... he was still working out why his mother would want Chel. If only he had seen the signs a little sooner, he could have protected her better, been there with her—although he had been with her just then and little help that did. The irony was not lost on him he had lost the only girl he had actually started to care for because he was trying to protect her.

Hal stopped in his tracks. His mother was using Chel as bait... bait to get him back to Elnye or at least in her service. The absurdity of his mother's plan struck him. She had never struck him as desperate, nor did she strike him as even caring if he was with her or not, but the sting of his dismissal and disowning her must have wounded her pride something fierce for her to spend her resources tracking him down and even attacking the Shifters. He was assured now she would, if only to send a further message that she could. It would be a bonus for his mother to take out the future of the Shifters at the same time as retrieving her ungrateful son.

Just then he heard two voices from the side of the path coming from a different direction. Two Shifters he had not seen before were calling to him by name.
~~~~~

"Are you Halister, the Faerie?" the taller one asked. His face was smudged with dirt as if he had just been rolling around in it.

Halister nodded and waited for them to approach. He would not admit to the wave of dizziness he felt just turning to face them. "I am. And who might you be?"

"We are inconsequential," the other Shifter, a female replied, her eyes darting back and forth through the village behind him. "We got a message from Chel."

Hal's eyebrows perked up, interested. "Go ahead, then."

They looked at each other uncertain.

"Really, I do not have all day, and I have the worst headache you can imagine. Please speak or be on your way," Hal bluffed feigning nonchalance unsure their motives.

"She spoke in our minds. Interrupted our own telepathic communication—it takes strength to do that," the female looked up to the male for reassurance, he nodded.

"What did she say?" Hal was growing impatient.

"Said it was a trap for you. To tell you to not follow her, but warn her parents of what is coming," the girl finished and fidgeted with her hands, nervous.

Hal nodded, had figured as much out for himself but hearing the lengths Chel had gone through to warn him meant more than he could verbalize. He needed to get to her, but if she was finding away to communicate then she was all right—at least at the time she sent the message.

"Thank you. Was there anything else?"

"No, that was all," the male added and dropped his head as they backed back into the slim forest behind them.

Hal now had a choice. Follow the path to find Chel or do as she said and warn her parents and prepare the rest of the Shifter territory for the onslaught that most definitely was on the way to their doorstep... and all because of him. Hal inhaled sharply, holding it for a count longer than he should have been able to. Oh how he wanted to be Chel's hero, to sweep in and fight the bad guys and rescue his damsel in distress, awaiting her kiss of gratitude. But his allegiance as of right now was to Alandria. He would trust Chel, trust she could take care of herself until he could get to her, trust she would be all right and even if delivered to his mother, trust she would be kept alive.

Hal wanted to follow his heart, but his loyalty tugged at him harder. Looking once more up the path the two Shifters had come from, he took note of where that path started. Turning to find Chel's parents, he jogged off in the opposite direction of where his heart wanted him to go, holding his head with one of his hands, the other on the hilt of his sword.

Chapter Twenty-Seven

The Kandrian Mountains. Seeking the Mortal Realm Portal.

After what felt like hours walking through darkened tunnels inside a mountain lit only a few feet in front of each from the light given by their torches, Daegan growled and stopped abruptly with a hand braced on his head.

"What's wrong Daegan?" Kaeleigh asked full of concern, reaching over to touch him but before she could, Daegan whipped around, his fierce gaze landing on Finn.

Heavy silence permeated the tunnel not wider than two people wide. Finn had stopped behind Ella and watched Daegan with surprise then understanding, remembering Daegan could pick up the strong emotions and feelings of others around him.

"If you have something to say, then say it, Finn! I can no longer take the intensity of your feelings hitting me like a battering ram." Daegan's fist clenched and unclenched.

"I... I need to tell you something, but do not know how or when—if there would ever be a better time to do so," Finn started, but uncharacteristically nervous he shuffled his feet and dared look at anyone or anything else other than at Daegan after seeing the blaze fury in his eyes.

"I do not know what we face outside these tunnels or if there will be another, this is the time, Finn," Daegan demanded.

"You do not understand," Finn mumbled with exasperation, his head hung low and hands on his hips.

"Now, Finn. For the sake of us all, but especially yours, be rid of it." Daegan lowered his eyes, awaiting Finn.

Kaeleigh and Ella looked to each other but shrugged, neither one understanding what the men were talking about but aware the need was great for Finn to share his burden.

Finn turned around and raked his hands through his hair, gripping it on the top pulling at his thick head of hair. Releasing a strangled cry of outrage, he kicked stupidly at the rock and dirt wall of the cave then leaned his palms against it, dragging in deep staggered breaths. He then let out a harsh laugh. "You already know."

Daegan sighed. "I had my suspicions. The timeline and events all pointed the same direction."

Kaeleigh's mouth opened then closed, looking from Daegan to Finn, confusion written on her face. About to say something, Daegan continued.

"Say it. You need to say it to release it," Daegan gritted his teeth bracing for the words.

Finn shook his head still up against the wall then pushed off. When he looked back at Daegan, his gaze shifted to Kaeleigh then over to Ella, each of the girls confused but waiting to find out. They would be crushed when he told them, when he admitted his mistakes long, long ago—the reason for his banishment from Alandria. He had nothing more to lose... and yet he had gained much more than he had thought he would ever gain again. But still...

Afraid to look, but needing to all the same, Finn looked straight into Daegan's eyes. Finn's voice came out shaky. "I was sent in as a double agent to Maleina's forces sixteen years ago, passing information on to King Ryek... to Hunter," he amended, his eyes glanced softly to Kaeleigh then back. "I was about to be weeded out, but King Ryek told me I needed to do what was necessary to stay within her ranks. Maleina had become suspicious of my presence. The darkness had been witnessed in Alandria, races were turning against each other, evil was stirring and it was only a matter of time before something much bigger occurred. We needed the information." Finn sighed sadly. "Only... I crossed lines against my own morals, against my better judgement, against the laws of Alandria. It was not far from here." He paused and his eyes took on a distant look. "We were seeking who we were told were traitors, but I knew better. I knew Maleina was hunting down anyone who would possibly stand in her way to the throne. I didn't recognize the man and the woman. The family had been hiding a long time, and I had never seen them…" Finn roared in agony again, fists clenched at his temple, emotion thick in his throat. "It is not an excuse. No matter who they were, they were innocent. It was my only chance to advance into Maleina's inner circle, to have all the information at my fingertips. It was a mistake, but I still did it."

Kaeleigh inhaled sharply, knowing how the story now ended, her eyes filled with tears overflowing silently down her cheeks.

"I was a bowman and a sure shot. Maleina watched to ensure it done. I have never shot my bow since." Tears slowly streamed down Finn's face, enhancing the pain reflected in his eyes. He didn't dare look to Daegan now, he would not be able to finish his confession. Inhaling a stuttered breath he said the words, "I killed them. I took the lives of your mother and your father, Daegan." Finn sank to his knees before Daegan, his arms outstretched before him. "My life has been forfeited since that day, it belongs to you to take."

"Oh no," Kaeleigh breathed, emotion choking her. A tear-streaked face turned as her gaze shot to Daegan. He remained stiff, one hand fisted at his side and the other holding the hilt of his sword. His eyes blazed with a mix of rage, sadness, and oddly… relief. Kaeleigh could not know what Daegan would do, his parents' lives taken right in front of him and the killer confessing right in front of him. He had every right to enact justice for his parents, but Finn was her friend. Ella moved close to Kaeleigh, not speaking but remaining close.

Daegan's head bowed, his breathing shallow and shaky. When his eyes opened and he raised his head, the moisture evidence of his emotion ran down his face in the form of a single tear as it fell to the dirt ground.

Ella had taken Daegan's torch while Finn's lie on the ground still blazing on the rocks and dirt, flickering the shadows of their event on the walls forever to be a part of the memories of that cave.

"Finn," Daegan's voice scratched from a raw place in his chest, "I cannot forget that day, forever etched into the mind of my youth."

Finn's head dropped, and his shoulders racked with silent sobs.

Daegan placed his hand on the top of Finn's head. His words were quiet and solemn, "But I forgive you. I have had a long time to think on it, and more so when I understood the truth. I have raged at you in my heart, but I also know what you were doing and the why of it. It does not change my past, but maybe it can change your future." Daegan stepped away and Kaeleigh rushed him with her embrace practically knocking him over with the force and intensity of her unguarded emotions; she let him feel from anger for him to sadness to relief. The tunnel suddenly felt much tighter than it had been at the start, Daegan needed to get out as soon as they could.

Finn shook his head, and looked back up at Daegan with startled awe and confusion. "No. No, no, no." He stood up and leaned a hand against the wall for support. "No, you do not get to forgive me and just let it go," Finn said between pained sobs. "I deserve death! I deserve more than that... Exhile," Finn broke off trying to understand what was happening.

"Perhaps even banishment from all you knew and loved? From your home and your family? To never know if you could go home again? Stuck in the mortal realm?" Daegan supplied gently. "You have paid your debt, Finnlan. You have given Alandria a fighting chance because you have guarded and protected Kaeleigh, enabling the prophecy to be fulfilled. She would not be who she is without you." He grabbed Kaeleigh's hand after she had released him to continue speaking. "I have found the meaning of love again." Daegan smiled at her. "Because of you. For that I am grateful and offer forgiveness."

"It's not supposed to be this easy!" Finn, though spent, tried to pace but the space was too tight. "I want to be punished! Are you not angry? Do you not hate me? Do you not want to kill me?" Finn roared at Daegan.

Faster than a blink, Daegan was on him, had him pinned to the tunnel walls by his forearm. In the shadowed light, Daegan looked much bigger, much darker, and much more dangerous; the jilted warrior had arisen.

Kaeleigh and Ella froze, barely breathing, not knowing what to do.

"Like this? Like this Finn?" Daegan seethed between gritted teeth, his eyes wild. "You want me to scream at you? Tell you how you destroyed my life and left me alone and family-less for years?" Tears now streamed down his face, Daegan unaware even of their presence. "Is that what you want to hear? Is it?" Daegan shouted and pushed into Finn one last time then shoved himself away so quickly he was at the opposite side before anyone knew what happened.

Finn nodded profusely, his Adam's apple swallowing with difficulty. "Yes, and I want you to kill me," he said softly.

"I will not," Daegan said catching his breath, wiping his face. "We are too few good fighters as it stands now. I will not take away one of Alandria's finest in her most greatest time of need. We need you Finnlan Talaín." Back to stoic and regal Daegan, he could see the greater picture and needed Finn to be a part of it. "It is time you forgive yourself, Finn, and become who you are meant to be just as the rest of us are."

"Take a moment. Ella help him recover his torch. I need a moment with Kaeleigh." Daegan grabbed her hand and pulled her along with him a little further down the tunnel. He dropped his torch and took hers throwing it to the ground, enough to see with but casting the light lower. Daegan pulled her close to him and leaned her against the tunnel wall. Breath heaving in and out of his chest, practically out of control, his hands found Kaeleigh's face. He threaded his hands through her hair and held her head in their grasp.

"Daegan?" she asked just as breathless, anticipating his movements.

"Kaeleigh, I need you, kiss me... please," he said quietly, his voice tight with emotion. His forehead rested against hers, hands trembling within her hair.

Not another word, Kaeleigh tipped her head up and found his lips, his masculine and sensual lips responded to her own. She lightly feathered her mouth across his, tentatively at first but quickly his need became her own and she kissed him like he was the air she needed to breathe. He kissed her back with the same fervor for several minutes until they felt the presence of the others coming toward them. Unwilling to break apart from each other, their chests heaved attempting to catch their breaths and leaned into each other as long as they could.

"You are my light," he whispered so quietly though she heard him. But much too short a time later, the light from Finn and Ella's torches preceded their arrival, and Daegan moved away from Kaeleigh, his hand tightly gripping hers. He kissed her forehead and picked up their torches.

As Finn and Ella hesitantly moved into their view, Daegan and Finn's eyes met. For the first time since Daegan had met Finn, the cloud of guilt and damnation had receded in his eyes, not yet gone, but time would find a way. They nodded, not needing words.

"Come we must continue. I feel we are almost at the end of the tunnel," Daegan said.

After another length of time walking Kaeleigh had a thought. "This is the Kandrian Mountain, right?"

"Yes," Ella answered her.

"And your home, Ella, was in the Kandrian Mountain wasn't it? My question is why is there not a tunnel that simply connects Ehsmia to Kandri or this other place we're going?" she asked thoughtfully.

"I see why you would think that," Ella replied, "the truth of it is, Ehsmia is like Tylínyth it is technically a pocket realm—a realm within a realm—within Alandria and not exactly a physical manifestation of Alandria. Does that make sense?"

"I think so. So if someone randomly drilled a tunnel into the middle of the mountain they wouldn't just end up in Ehsmia, is that what you're saying? That is why it appears taller and different inside it than the actual dimensions of the mountain range itself," Kaeleigh mused.

"Correct," Ella confirmed.

"Interesting... and pretty cool!" Kaeleigh beamed.

"Yes, it is." Ella smiled at Kaeleigh.

Not much further, the tunnel began to wind around corners and got narrower before it got wider again, opening into the back of a dark and small cave.

"I can smell fresh air," Finn noted with surprise. "This must be it!"

Everyone lifted their noses and inhaled deeply, relishing the pure air infiltrating the dry and dusty cave.

"Remember we do not know what awaits us outside the cave," Daegan warned, but still moved toward the lighter part of the cave. They no longer needed their torches and threw them to the ground, kicking dirt on them to extinguish the flames.

"Girls wait here while Finn and I stick our heads out to see what lies outside," Daegan instructed.

Both of the girls frowned. Why were the girls always doing the waiting and the men the checking? They agreed to wait, however. This time.

Daegan and Finn crept to the edge of the cave, grateful for the specifically placed boulder so they could peer around it and look outside.

It was full daylight by the time they reached this point, with medium cloud coverage. They had walked most the day inside the tunnel.

"I think it took us longer to get here than Dunstand had thought it would," Finn grumbled.

"Indeed," Daegan agreed. "I do not see nor sense anyone outside this immediate area, do you?"

Finn's eyes traveled over the entire scape, watching, listening but didn't see anything. He shook his head in response.

"Get the girls and we will sneak out," Daegan told Finn but Finn stopped him placing his hand against Daegan's arm.

"Thank you. You did not have to respond the way you did to me. Though I do not deserve any kindness from you, I am grateful for the chance to fight for Alandria. My life is still yours if you require it at a time of your choosing," Finn explained then went to fetch the girls before Daegan said anything else.

Chapter Twenty-Eight

Daegan, Kaeleigh, Finn, and Ella crept quietly down the craggy mountain from the cave they had emerged from. The cave opening being roughly two stories off the ground, they had a slight hike down. Crumbling rocks and rolling boulders slid from beneath their feet as they carefully trudged down, making a trail where there was none—or where the remnants of one had been but someone purposefully covered it so not to lead to the cave opening only to discover where it led. The light of full day and the warm sun was definitely a welcomed sight when they had come out of the dark and cool tunnels. Large boulders and rock formations had helped to hide them as they made their trek downward.

Close to the ground, they had come to a point where they could see the ruins of Klavaí—it was exactly as it sounded, the small village from long ago in ruins, ash and rubble.

"What happened here?" Kaeleigh asked between pants as she descended the last big rock, albeit a bit uneasily. Daegan reached up to help her down from the last large boulder, holding her waist, letting her jump down with his help. "It looks like a fire destroyed it with all those burn marks and ash."

"The story goes like this," Daegan began. "Long ago a band of magic users came through, cloaked in black, chanting something very old. The magic they wielded was unusual for Alandria but not unheard of; it was very old and very powerful. Used in the wrong hands it was destructive and that is exactly what it was," Daegan told, a hand gestured to the ruins. "Darkness had fallen upon the quiet little guardian town, but their night had only yet begun. The magic brought forth created such a forceful wind swirling about, uprooting everything in the ground, lifting anything not tied down and throwing it. Buildings were not unscathed as you can see. Fires erupted, thatching from roofs the perfect kindling. Stones and wood tumbled from tops of buildings to the ground. Some have since fallen into ruin with the weathering of time and the elements, but most were destroyed that day." Daegan paused as they got closer to the ruins and lowered his voice. "It was said they searched for something."

"Did they find it?" Kaeleigh asked, her gaze taking in the entire scene, enraptured with his story.

"No one knows for certain," he shrugged, "but it is believed they did."

"And the people?" she asked tentatively, her eyes sliding to see the tension building in the set of his jaw. She already knew the answer.

"None survived to tell of it, but it is rumored some escaped into the mortal realm through the portal they guarded. I hope they did."

"Why have none come back I wonder?" Kaeleigh inquired. They all stopped at the edge of the village. Smaller than Kandri, this village was set back further into the cleft of the mountain, blending in the stone and coloring—at least from what was left. A thick wall had bordered it, but now most had crumbled leaving wide openings for anyone to trespass just as they were. Even though long destroyed, the air of the village held a lingering empty sadness, with subtle undertones of the menacing evil that stole its life. The air was cooler and lifeless as it swept over their skin, sending chills up Kaeleigh's spine. "Well, not to here but to Alandria at all?"

"Perhaps they feel they have failed, or perhaps not many escaped and the ordeal too great that as time passed the memory of this place slipped through their fingers losing all knowledge of Alandria as well," Ella added, standing on top of a large flat rock to see over the bordering wall, or what was left of it.

The place itself was almost hidden in perpetual shadow, the sun unable to touch it in any natural way; magic disrupted the natural way of things in this place. The residue of darkness was so absorbed into the very fiber of the village, it gave off its own atmosphere—temperature, weather, energy signatures, everything—contrary to what was happening around this land. It was magical, but not in the good way.

"This place gives me the creeps," Kaeleigh acknowledged, rubbing the goosebumps on her arms.

"Me too, Kae," Finn agreed.

"I fear there is no other way through to the portal," Daegan's tone and frown put them all on alert. His stance locked and his gaze fixed he whispered, "Something still stirs here. Move silently as you can and be ready." He pulled out the sword from his hip holster and eyed them all, encouraging them to do the same.

"Ready for what?" Kaeleigh had to ask.

"For anything," Daegan said vaguely, his teeth showing through his smirking smile with a hint of an edge glinting in his eyes. After the tunnels he was ready for a fight and it showed.

Armed and ready, they followed Daegan into the small city of rubble. Eerie was the silence as it whispered in their ears, taunting oblivion and madness, beckoning them into its depths. Kaeleigh reached for Daegan's hand free of the sword and he gripped hers tightly in return. To their left a rock clattered with movement. They froze, all eyes snapping toward the noise. Nothing happened. With a sigh of unease, they moved forward toward the back of the city. Everything was in ruin, nothing spared, nothing living had flourished since. No grass, no weeds even. No miniature shoots of green weaved their way through the debris and rubble for no light shined directly on this area.

Kaeleigh looked around with stunned awe and sadness, her heart broke not only for the people who lost everything that fateful day, but also for Alandria's loss. This village was like a gangrenous extremity, hidden in shadow, festering underneath, unknown to the rest of the realm.

Another rock slipped from their right. They froze, sword and knives extended at the ready. Still nothing happened. Coiled tension mounted beneath their skin.

"What is it?" Kaeleigh whispered tightly beneath her breath. Daegan simply shook his head unsure.

Moving forward was a painfully slow process when everything in Kaeleigh just wanted to flat out sprint through to the end, but feared what might jump out in front of her, leaving her unprepared. But the slow tenuous movements bolstered by the unknown presences stirring drove her crazy.

Ella inhaled sharply, her head snapping the opposite direction. "I saw Ónarach," she whispered, "maybe three over there." Instead of pointing she nodded in the direction she was looking.

"And I saw one back there," Finn added, signaling a different direction.

"Oh, and there's one up there," Kaeleigh whispered, looking up on top of the tallest building left though half in ruin.

"We are being surrounded," Daegan informed them quietly. "Keep walking and stay close. We need to get as close as we can to the portal before they engage us. We do not know how many there are. Remember they have clones of themselves, but are dispatched easily."

The foursome moved tighter together as they moved, picking up speed only a little not wanting to draw the creatures too soon. Walking through the ruin was not easy with rubble and debris scattered about the ground in all directions, boulders and pieces of buildings thrown about, a history untouched. Kaeleigh especially had to maneuver around them with a little more attention, but noted how Ella seemed to flow with the ground as if she was one with the grid of the land, easily swaying and dodging; those she couldn't dodge she fluidly leapt onto or over what was in front of her. Kaeleigh watched with envy and intent study seeing if she could control her body in such a way. After several tries, and almost tripping herself up—which they didn't have time for her to rectify at present—Kaeleigh suddenly felt something inside her physically shift as if her body finally caught up with how her mind and her magic had been merging with Alandria. Her footing became confident and her moves sure, she was able to move around obstacles with greater ease and less attention, freeing her mind to be outward on the possible attack and her responses. Amazed, Kaeleigh smiled widely and caught Ella watching her with her head titled and eyes narrowed on her moves. Ella's eyes widened with understanding of what Kaeleigh had done and smiled in return, giving her a nod well done. More fully in sync, the group moved as one through the final section of the ruins. Noting the side streets barricaded with fallen building and areas of darker shadow, they kept to the middle though they were more of a target in the open until they reached a blockade of rubble and stone stacked almost as high as the highest standing structure.

"This did not fall this way," Ella pointed out, studying the blockade.

"No," agreed Daegan, looking for ways around it, but it stretched all the way across the access to the end of the city up against the mountainside. He felt the stones and jerked his hand back quickly. "There are evil intentions on the other side," he whispered, gritting his teeth.

Finn also paced the length of the piled stones, searching for an opening, looking for the weak spot but seeing none. "It is purposeful for us to go over if we want to cross the rest of the ruins," he informed them, hands on his waist gauging the condition of the girls and their weapons. "We will be outnumbered."

"We have defeated greater numbers than these before," Ella said with a confident smirk, her hand pulling out another knife from her boot.

"How many of those do you have?" Kaeleigh inquired her eyes wide with surprise.

"A few more," Ella said with more energy than she had been exhibiting thus far, even winking at Kaeleigh. She too was ready for a fight it would seem.

"All I have is this dagger you gave me, Daegan." Kaeleigh showed them hers.

"And your magic, Kae, remember your magic. We trained for this," Finn reminded her pulling out his other knife as well.

"Right. My magic," Kaeleigh informed herself, nodding with a decisive gesture.

"Stay near me," Daegan said directly to her. "We will fight close not allowing them to separate us or pick us apart," he instructed further. They all nodded and began to climb up the haphazardly heaped boulders and debris that created a blockade from where they stood to where they needed to be.

All stopped just before they reached the top and held on. They ducked their heads, listening and waiting. The enemy already knew they were in the ruins, knew they were coming and where they were headed. The element of surprise was hardly on their side. Instead they opted for stealth and uncertainty, allowing the Ónarach on the opposite side to wait them out a bit more. Finn slowly raised his head enough he could see some of what lie on the other side. Two rows of ten Ónarach in each, waited with knives and spears. Luckily no bows and arrows he could see; hand-to-hand it would be. He mimed to Daegan and the others what weapons their enemy had so they knew what to expect. They went in with at least some knowledge, which was better than none.

Daegan lifted his fingers in a show of countdown from three… two… one… then they sprung up to the top, crouching as one. Daegan stood when he confirmed there were no bows and arrows, at least in the group on the ground. From the top, looking down, he was large and commanding, standing with an authoritative stature of a true ruler.

"You will depart this land or be removed from it," Daegan demanded of the Ónarach.

Strange hissing and snickers came from the horde, mocking him. "You do not command us, princeling, only our lady does," they hissed in unison as one.

Kaeleigh shivered and mock whispered, "It is so creepy when they do that."

"Your lady is not the ruler of Alandria nor will she be," Daegan countered with strength and authority. "Step aside or we will forcefully remove you."

"Try us, princeling," they hissed, lowering their weapons.

"As you ask," Daegan said with sneer, lifting the corner of his mouth. Without looking at the others he jumped into the horde. As if tied together, united as one they all jumped after him, landing next to each other automatically backing up to each other forming an oddly shaped circle square moving into the horde fighting as they went.

Swords clashed, the clang of metal on metal a refreshing sound. Each were a warrior in their own right; the sounds were the sounds of home, of coming victory, and the exertion of pent up frustrations being released. Igniting a fire within each of them, they moved together and yet separate fighting the filthy Ónarach taking them down one by one. More from within the ruins joined the foray as if drawn by the sounds of battle or perhaps they could feel each other being dispatched back to where they had come from. One by one as they were struck, they went up in a poof of ash and smoke only to be replaced by another one.

"Yes!" Kaeleigh shouted in the middle of the sounds of fighting. "My sword showed up!" Kaeleigh's fighting took on a new vigor and strength as she became one with the energy of her ancient sword *Nithylrith*. It hummed with the energy flowing through it into her arms, one the extension of the other.

"Stay together!" Daegan shouted as they had begun to separate. The Ónarach's numbers had been decreasing as they took out more and more, but just then a new wave showed up out of nowhere it would seem. "Stay together!" he shouted once more, noting Kaeleigh out of the corner of his eye moving away from his back, drawn into the battle fervor.

Trying to move back into the circle, Kaeleigh noted briefly she was further away than she had meant to be. Suddenly the clones had surrounded her, fighting off three and four at a time was at first a simple task especially when her sword simply appeared in her hand opposite the dagger and she quickly switched.

"Kaeleigh!" Daegan shouted at her, but she was too far now to get back. She simply had to keep fighting.

"I'm trying! I'm ok!" she shouted back. Finn had separated from the form to try and get to her as Daegan was too heavily bombarded with the evil creatures. "Finn stay with them!"

"Not a chance!" he shouted, his knives flying faster than anything she had ever seen before as he got stopped by another group of the clones. Their numbers seemed to be multiplying exponentially.

"Where are they coming from?" Kaeleigh shouted exasperated with the energy she was exerting.

"The shadows. They just keep coming," Ella shouted back. Then she screeched with rage as an enemy sword sliced her arm. She kept fighting, renewed with rage to end the evil creatures.

Finn then roared, being overrun with his own set of clones but still handling himself well for the time being. Blood ran down his arms and nicks along his legs began to seep through his pants. Kaeleigh couldn't see Daegan, but she could feel him, his strength waning though determined to win the fight more and more seemingly impossible to do. Their bond was stronger than ever before. She pushed her magic toward him, offering him her strength, though he only took a little then pushed it back at her. The Ónarach had pulled her further away; she had begun to climb up piles of rubble behind her only to realize she was actually climbing part of the mountain. Kaeleigh had taken the high ground; that she could use to her advantage.

Kaeleigh's magic stirred inside her more quickly than it did earlier at Kandri; the outrage and urgency of the situation forcing it through her. Her sword illuminated with excess energy—whether its own or because her magic flowed through her and funneled into it she wasn't sure. From inside her rose a war cry Kaeleigh had only felt one other time before. Her energy erupted out of her as she swung her sword in a wide circle, taking out every Ónarach surrounding her. Her magic shot outward from her, traveling on the surge of her battle cry in a visible wave of color, knocking the remaining Ónarach out with a single blast of energy. Gone all at once, the Ónarach exploded in a cloud of dust and ash sprinkling down onto the ground. Kaeleigh fell to her knees the surge of energy taking its toll on her, though not nearly as much as it had in the past. She grew stronger. Panting from the loss of energy and adrenaline, Kaeleigh lifted her head and found Daegan's eyes blazing into her own, a mix of shock and pride. His eyes were not the only ones staring at her, but Finn's and Ella's as well; their gazes a mix of shock and disbelief. Everyone gained their breath and wiped ash off their heads and clothes, making their way to her stumbling some as they went. Daegan ran to her, climbed up to where she knelt on a large flat rock, bent down and kissed her fully on the mouth. The dust and grime mixed with his sweat and blood on his face mixed with her own, and she didn't even care. His kiss was swift but full of life and strength, filling her, renewing her energy with his love.

He pulled away panting, and wiped the hair tenderly away from her face. "You are amazing, Kaeleighnna iliathe'yll Sayaelíth. You saved us, thank you."

"We are not done yet, Daegan. I need you for this next part," she nodded outward behind him. From where they were, the entire city or ruin could be seen as if in a valley below them though not that far in actuality. She touched his face, pulled his gaze to her own and stared directly into his soul. "Feel me, see what I am showing you," she encouraged.

His eyes widened and he nodded. Without question he turned and poured his soul and magic into the land of Klavaí. With a great roar, he slammed his fist on the ground, shaking the foundation of the ruins with the reverberation of his power. Uttering, "*Thantül*," the ancient word not many had heard or even knew the meaning of even in Alandria; a word that brought release and freedom to something shackled and bound.

The land responded with a groan of its own, a protest against the darkness keeping it bound, shaking itself free from the bonds imprisoning it in a perpetual state of ruin and desolation. The ruins remained, but the empty lifeless void kept within shadow receded back into itself; a sucking back into the ground from whence it came like the reverse motion of smoke filling the sky from a single point of ignition. The air was fresh and sunlight permeated the ruins, casting a beauty none would have thought possible again. The ground itself seemed to sigh in relief, taking a deep breath brining life back into its foundation.

"My turn." Kaeleigh smiled, love shining through her eyes they passed over the city. Kaeleigh reached into the cracks between the boulders bringing handfuls of dirt up in each hand, holding them out before her. In her mind's eye she had seen and heard herself and Daegan doing that very thing, where the inspiration came from she couldn't say, but it welled up within her so strongly she could not refuse it. Gently she said the words she didn't even know how she knew, words of healing and restoration, of growth and change. Ancient words. *"Lyn ínyth."*

Releasing the dirt from her hands, she let it slip through her fingers. The granules of dirt were swept up and carried on a wind stirring from the words themselves to the village below. Almost instantly, where the scattered dirt passed over, shoots of green emerged through the rubble. Grasses protruded out from under rocks and debris. Surrounding trees, hollowed out and burnt to a crisp along the sidelines, grew whole and strong once more; branches clothing themselves with leaves. Buds bloomed and flowers erupted from below the earth. Other greenery and vines climbed with renewed life, shooting up and covering the mounds of rubble and the ruins of buildings in memory and honor of the life once occupying this place. Whether Alandrians would ever rebuild this place she did not know, but at least it would stand as a monument of life and light, no longer death and darkness. Last but not least...

"The orchids!" Kaeleigh breathed, in awe at the magic and amazement of Alandria. Looking up to the sky now bright and big over the city of ruins, Kaeleigh gasped and pointed. "Is that... Do you see that bird?" Above her, high in the sky, almost unrecognizable was a large white bird soaring over the city, crying out, calling to her below. Grandfather. A single golden tear fell from her eye, landed on the ground directly at her feet, and bloomed the largest white orchid she had ever seen. Kaeleigh bent down and gently stroked it, feeling the magic and energy within the beautiful bloom. Looking back in the sky, Kaeleigh saw nothing, the bird nowhere to be found, possibly a figment of her imagination. But she didn't believe it so.

Daegan pulled her to him once more, wrapping her in his strong arms, holding her tight and kissing her once more; this time his kiss was gentle and filled with awe. Remembering they had an audience, he pulled her back slowly with a chuckle, the relief of what they had done bubbling from within him. When he moved away enough for her to see beyond him, Finn and Ella were both on the ground taking a knee, inclining their heads in her direction.

"What are you both doing? Get off your knees," Kaeleigh asked with slight embarrassment.

"Princess, you demonstrated an incredible show of power when you wiped out the Ónarach," Ella began, "We have weapons to accomplish similar things, but the force of your energy was swift and strong, usually needing several magic users together to recreate a similar effect. If there was doubt before, there is none in my mind. You, together, are the freedom for Alandria and us all." She bowed her head further.

"And the power to free and heal is beyond what a single Elf or Faerie can do. That was amazing!" Finn stood up and shouted with exuberant joy like he had never shown her before, looking out at the city of ruin now covered with beauty and life. "Just look!" he said his arms wide, feeling the freedom of the moment.

They rested a moment, recovering and relishing in the peaceful existence of the newly freed ruins of Klavaí. Staring out and marveling at the magic of Alandria for longer then they realized, the sun began to fade and the evening began to rise bringing with it the two moons of the night sky.

"Where is the portal?" Finn asked, suddenly remembering why they were there.

"I sense it is just beyond the rocks up there," Daegan pointed up a narrow trail that disappeared between a cleft in the mountain where two ridges met.

"Shall we be on our way?" Kaeleigh asked almost tentative to leave the peace of Klavaí.

"Yes it is time," Daegan confirmed helping her up just as Finn helped Ella to her feet.

The four of them ventured up the path to a small valley filled with green grass and wild greenery just as below. "I wonder if this was always here protected from below or if this is new?" Kaeleigh asked, fingering a blossom on a shrub next to her.

"I do not know," Ella responded looking around at the magic of the little valley. Nothing else existed in this place, but for a small paradise and a large boulder with vines of flowering greenery covering it like a curtain. "It is beautiful. I have never used this portal before."

"Nor have I," Daegan responded at the same time Finn said, "I haven't either, only heard of it."

Kaeleigh lifted her hand, allowing a small creature to land on her extended finger. She laughed. "It tickles, but isn't she beautiful? She looks like the one you have in Ehsmia, Ella."

Ella came over to inspect her claim and gasped with surprise. "She is the very same butterfly, Kaeleigh."

"Oh!" Kaeleigh's eyes grew wide and smiled as the butterfly landed on her nose then fluttered to Daegan and did the same. The butterfly then repeated the action with Ella and again with Finn. "What is she doing?"

"She is honored at what has been done for Klavaí, she is giving her thanks. She had lived here many years ago and is happy the butterflies can return here once more, the true guardians of the portal," Ella explained then the queen of the butterflies flew away toward the portal. "She guides our way until we are through the portal."

"Thank you," Kaeleigh said as they went to the portal.

"Does this one work like the other one, Daegan? Do we need blood?" Kaeleigh asked him, staring at the flat boulder.

"No, we simply say the word to open it," explained Finn.

"Like this, Princess," Ella resorted to a formal address of Kaeleigh once again, "*Olínthinyl*". Then she simply walked through it and the others followed.

A new adventure awaited them in the mortal realm; their mission to the portal complete, yet their separate missions had only just begun.

Chapter Twenty-Nine

The Mortal Realm. Somewhere in Tennessee, USA.

Finn, Ella, Daegan, and Kaeleigh emerged out of the portal from Alandria in darkness. Daegan threw his arm in front of Kaeleigh, stopping her from moving forward.

"Hey," she said, obviously winded. "What was that for?"

"I am not familiar with where we are. It is dark, too, so please allow me to ensure it is safe before you step into possible dangers unawares," Daegan's cool tone replied. He gripped her wrist and moved his thumb in slow, enticing circles. Her skin shivered under his touch; knowing his touch affected her was oddly satisfying.

"Oh, that makes sense," Kaeleigh said, trying at once to equal Daegan's tone and suppress the desire to respond to his touch. "Ella, do you know where we are? Why is it so dark?"

"No, I have not used this portal before, although Grandfather mentioned it should emerge us somewhere in the state of Tennessee. Are you familiar with that one?" Ella asked. There were a handful of portals within Alandria, each connected to a different place geographically around the world like a doorway, but some were connected to other realms such as Exhile, and, of course, one had been connected to Tylínyth before it was destroyed.

"Not really. I mean I know of it and where it is on the map, but I've never been there," Kaeleigh looked at the others puzzled. "Finn?"

"Only once before, but not enough to be too familiar with it. It is part of the southern states within the mortal realm's United States of America, you know, where Kaeleigh and I lived? But our state was closer to the northwest corner of the country," Finn explained. Then he added, "Though I am not sure that is too helpful."

"I have also been there but only briefly. No matter, we will discover where we are very soon," Daegan said. "Move slowly and cautiously toward the sliver of light," Daegan motioned to a small slit of light coming out from what appeared to be a door.

"I see it," Kaeleigh acknowledged. Stepping forward, she realized Daegan's hand still encircled her wrist. "You can let go, Daegan, I can find it."

"Perhaps I simply like touching you, holding your hand whenever I have the chance." She could hear the smile in his voice. Yes, she did like his touch, but she knew she needed to focus on other things.

Finn, who was in front of the group, cleared his throat, "I found a handle," he said quietly. "It *is* a door. I'll slowly crack it open and peer out."

"Sounds like a plan," Kaeleigh said too quickly. "I don't like being in the dark, not to mention it smells like a dank cave: musty and moldy. I am tired of being in dark, dank, caves."

"I agree," Ella said quietly just as Finn cracked the door open.

Light flooded further into the room from a dangling light fixture just outside their door, illuminating stacks of crates and shelves of bottles that looked to be chemicals for cleaning scattered around where they stood.

"Great. We're in a cleaning closet. Can we learn to direct the portals to more interesting locations as exits?" Kaeleigh said examining the room they arrived in. Stretched before them was a small room constructed of large gray oval and oblong stones. Though not a cave, it made sense to Kaeleigh why it felt like one. The portal, invisible to the human eye, was the back flat wall.

"If we needed to, could we get back into Alandria through this wall?" Kaeleigh whispered pointing back at the wall.

"Yes, but we would need the same conditions and sacrifice we used when entering Alandria through the portal in Montana last time," Daegan explained quietly as they waited for Finn's assessment. "We would need a drop of blood from each requesting entrance to ensure they attain the blood of an Alandrian, to know exactly where the portal entrance was, and the ancient words to gain entrance," Daegan reminded her.

"Right." Kaeleigh nodded.

Finn slowly closed the door, careful to avoid the click of the latch, and flicked a switch igniting light in the cleaning closet. Each covered their eyes instinctively until they adjusted to the brightness of it. "Ok, so it looks like we are surrounded by a structure of some kind made completely of this stone." He patted the wall next to him. "It appears to be a medieval ruin of sorts for tourists based on the sign I noticed. Regardless, we should be able to blend in if we do come across any people." He paused, looking them over each individually. "Except I think we will need to glamour ourselves slightly, enough to blend in with humans: what they wear and how they look. Tone down points on ears, and any things else that stands out as *other*. Just in case."

Nervously Kaeleigh shifted her feet and sighed. "I have not done a glamour on my own yet. I don't know how," she admitted sheepishly.

"Perhaps I can help," Daegan offered. He slid his large hand up her forearm to her elbow and turned her toward him. "After all you have done, it will be simple. Close your eyes and inhale and exhale steadily through your nose, shutting out all distractions. Stir your magic, your energy, from within and focus on the image you want to look like; you do not want to change too many things though, keep it simple. Feel the image taking shape over your physical body." His voice was low, soothing, and hypnotic. Kaeleigh could listen to him talk to her for a very long time, but unfortunately they didn't have that right now.

"Ok, I'll try it," she whispered.

"You are not changing into someone else, think of it like wearing a costume, but magically," Finn added quietly and Ella nodded her agreement.

Kaeleigh nodded and focused her energy. Closing her eyes and shutting out everyone around her, she did exactly as he instructed her. A moment later she inhaled deeply and blew out that breath the next beat.

"Did it work?" she whispered in her bubbly way, as she opened her eyes. She couldn't see herself and was bursting with curiosity.

"Yep," Finn said. He smiled, proud and excited. "Good job!"

"I did it?" she asked excitedly. She looked from Ella to Daegan. Each nodded an affirmative, though Daegan looked her over a little more thoroughly than the others.

"Well done, Kaeleigh, you look quite human." Then more subdued, "and beautiful as well." Kaeleigh blushed.

Finn then motioned they move to exit the cleaning closet. After flicking off the light, he pushed open the heavy wood door wide enough from the group to move through single file. Finn took the first step out and moved quickly so the others could follow before anyone noticed their arrival. Entering what appeared to be a stone hallway, fresh air hit them as they each stepped out of the dark supply room.

The foursome were surrounded by stone—stones on the ground, stones on the walls, and stone on the ceiling above them—and they crept silently toward the sound of rushing water, cautiously keeping their eyes and ears open for anyone else. Their tunnel of a hallway opened up to the outside, each gasping with awe as they filed out from the tunnel. In front of them was a waist-high stone wall, but beyond that was a blue sky, a canvas filled with the fading light of the afternoon, and beautiful land as far as their eyes could see—which was pretty far from their vantage point. And below them—far below—was a valley of farms, trees, hills, towns, roads, and rivers stretching out before them as far as they could see.

"Look!" Kaeleigh hurried right up to the stone wall and spread her arms wide. "Wow," she breathed. The others joined her, looking at the magnificent view in front of them. Ella stood up on her tippy toes to look over the edge. Directly below them and a part of the ruins they stood on was a nine or ten story waterfall, the source of the rushing water sound.

"Careful!" Finn reached for her shirt to pull her back down. "That's quite a fall if you were to take it," he explained, nodding over the edge.

Ella looked at him strangely, cocking her head. "I would not fall, it is very human of you to think that I would, Finnlan," she said seriously. She then softened and added, "But thank you for your concern, it is touching." Finn nodded his head tersely.

Moving water had always contained a magic all on its own for the group, but one this size was simply awe-inducing. They stood silently watching, feeling, experiencing the falls.

"It's so beautiful!" Kaeleigh exclaimed unafraid others would hear her as there was no one else nearby. "We must be at some lookout point or something."

"It truly is a spectacular sight," Ella commented.

Finn agreed, but added, "I wonder where we are."

"Let's find out," Kaeleigh moved around them unafraid back in the mortal realm, somewhere she felt familiar and at ease with even if she didn't know where they were at present. She moved one direction, pointing to another hallway opening made of stone, leading them back into the ruins built into the side of a mountain. Daegan, Finn, and Ella followed Kaeleigh.

After traveling through several stone caverns and remarking on stone statues, rock formations, and a swinging bridge Daegan outright refused to cross, they made it to the top. Luckily a solid stone bridge was close by. It was stunning just how much stone and rock lay everywhere. It covered everything that wasn't a garden. The group emerged from the stone tunnels to finally reach the very top, finding among the ruins an area for tourists, complete with a gift shop and restaurant.

"We are in the south, I think we are not far from Chattanooga, Tennessee," Kaeleigh explained, pointing to the arrow on the placard that directed them to the left to Tennessee.

"Now that you say that, Kaeleigh, I believe I *have* heard of this place...or at least I have read about it in mortal histories." Daegan mused. "It is a unique city, its name having something to do with a rock or a stone..." he tilted his head and frowned thoughtfully, trying to tap into his memory.

"It doesn't matter what it is called, it's beautiful," Kaeleigh inserted to help him out. "Let's go over there." She pointed to the restaurant area.

The sun was beginning to set, tinting the sky with slivers of pinks and oranges. They found a table outside the restaurant and sat, soaking in and enjoying the beauty of the sunset. After all they had been through in the last few days, it was refreshing to simply be and sit and bask in nature's re-energizing process.

"So this is a place, humans—I mean people—just come to visit and walk around?" Ella asked, noting all the people around them either taking pictures or walking around admiring the beauty of nature. Learning so much at once about the culture of these mortals was overwhelming, but the discovery process in it was nonetheless refreshing.

"I would come here often if I lived nearby, I can feel the vibrations and the energy of nature just jumping off the plants and flowers; its different than in Alandria, but for the mortal realm the energy is richer up here," Kaeleigh noted, taking in the area all at once with her magical senses.

Ella nodded, "I can feel it too."

"It will be evening soon and I'm not sure how long we can stay here," Kaeleigh rubbed her arms with her hands to fend off the evening's chill. The air had grown chilly in the late fall air, giving hints at the coming winter.

"I would love to stay here and enjoy the view, but I feel it is time for us to leave, Finnlan," Ella urged.

"Agreed. We should be on our separate ways. We have missions to accomplish," Finn stated.

"Yes, it is time," Daegan concurred, rising from the seat he had taken to watch the view after ensuring they were indeed the only ones present.

"Right. Daegan and I need to find the Book of Lenoria, our key to finding the entrance to Exhile to hopefully free the Orchids," Kaeleigh agreed, gripping Daegan's hand as he stood beside her chair.

"And Ella and I need to get to the Twined headquarters and the mortal realm side portal into Tylínyth. We need to ensure no one was hurt from Maleina's outburst of magic that destroyed the portal from the Alandria side and gather what troops we can find to fight with us," Finn acknowledged hesitantly rising from his seat as well. He looked back out at the view and sighed. Confessing the truth to Daegan about his parents, had lifted a weight. The truth was known. By no means did Finn feel less guilt, but the secrecy of it was no longer eating him alive, activated stronger every time he was in proximity with Daegan. He looked to each of them and saw echoing agreement, but also hesitancy to let go of the peaceful moment.

Ella stood first and extended her hand toward Finn which he grabbed allowing her to pull him to his feet. All four of them found the exit to their brief yet refreshing sanctuary and moved to depart the ruins of rock and stone. As soon as they exited, Kaeleigh gasped, her eyes wide with joy and surprise.

"Look coffee!" she screeched, pointing across the street at the most unique looking Starbucks she had seen in a small building made of stone to match the surrounding area. Her eyes pleaded with Daegan. "Can I get some before we leave? Please?"

He chuckled. "How could I refuse you? Lead the way."

"Before you do that, we will say our goodbyes and take off from here," Finn explained with Ella nodding next to him. "We have to find our way to Locast Ridge, refuge for the Twined and portal entrance into Tylínyth as quickly possible."

"Of course," Kaeleigh said with a lump in her throat, sudden emotion rushing out at once. They had been a team, and now they would go their separate ways. She lunged toward Ella for a Chel-style hug. Ella braced herself against the incoming show of affection but relented. Kaeleigh whispered in her ear, "Take care of him." And then Kaeleigh gave Finn a hug as well. The group stood silent a moment as if waiting someone to pronounce a benediction of some kind.

Ella spoke first. "Kaeleigh and Daegan, it has been an honor traveling and serving Alandria with you. I wish you haste and safety on your journey." She formally bowed her body, bent at the waist, straightened and moved away. The actions were not lost on Kaeleigh.

"Be safe," Finn said looking Kaeleigh in the eyes, "Take care of each other, make sure you are in Alandria when the time comes. We will all need you." He turned to Daegan and added, "Protect her with all you are, Ferrishyn." He paused a moment, then reached his hand out for Daegan's. Daegan gripped Finn's hand in return, but instead of shaking it, he gave Finn the brothers-in-arms grasp of a warrior. His forearm grip was strong and ended in a mutual pat on the back, both a nod to formality and camaraderie.

"I give you my word, I will protect her," Daegan said with an inclined head.

"And Daegan?" Finn asked quietly, "Thank you. You are a better man than I."

"We will meet you in Alandria for battle," Daegan ended their goodbyes.

Finn and Ella strolled off down the street in the direction of trees and a road sloping downward. "I hope that they can find their way to where they are going... for that matter, I hope we can too." Kaeleigh frowned and looked to Daegan. "Any idea where we are headed yet?"

Daegan gave her a slightly boyish grin. "For now, we are headed that direction for refueling." He pointed to the big green letters that everyone knew meant coffee.

She smiled and reached for his hand. "Sounds like a plan to start with!"

Chapter Thirty

Exhile. The Land of the Unforgiven Dead.

Slamming her fist down on top of the blackened stone surrounding the scrying pool, the black waters within rippled from the force. *She* could not remove her eyes from the still waters. The scene most recently played out before her had left her disturbed. The Sol-lumieth—Kaeleigh as she was called—and those with her had just passed through the portal from Alandria into the mortal realm. It was not to be... and yet it had.

"Maleina's Ónarach proved to not be much of a match for the warriors traveling with that *human*, the one who keeps interrupting my plans!" *She* seethed between her teeth. "Kaeleigh is about as human as I am, and we would do well to remember it. Maleina thinks the Sol-lumieth's magic is immature and inconsequential... I am not so sure," the mistress of the dark conceded ruefully.

A remnant of her faithful companion and loyal servant, the Droch-Shúil, remained sheltered up in a corner crevice of the cavern waiting to be called. Its red eyes longingly followed her every move, desiring to be needed, needing to be used. The Droch-Shúil, a collective creature whose purpose for eons had been to dwell in darkness until called upon, was ready to be given direction. It had been called upon for such a purpose thousands of years ago for assistance with the destruction of the first realm, Lenoria. Only one with immense power could summon them and indenture them to servitude willingly. Others before her had tried to force the Droch-Shúil to do their bidding, but the true power of the creature had been released against them; the creature would not be forced, it waited for a master worthy of its faithfulness. The mistress of the mountain had earned the creatures loyalty over many years, wooing it to her side with many bloody sacrifices. *She* carried a piece of the Droch-Shúil within her, enough darkness to recognize the kinship. Through her magic and the darkness she allowed through her heinous acts she was able to internalize tendrils of the Droch-Shúil's smoky darkness; something not many had figured out or were willing to sacrifice for. But not many had been in her situation, and not many had her focus of purpose that had carried her for centuries.

It was almost time, time for the creature to act on behalf of its queen, she was almost ready to traverse the realms. The Droch-Shúil had been waiting patiently for her to be able to roam the lands at its side—a compatible partnership of darkness.

"Their journey is that much closer to us, my pet," she said, beckoning the darkness to her; a pale graceful limb stretched out toward the corner where the Droch-Shúil awaited her. Without hesitation, the darkness swept down and wrapped itself around her arm; its essence purred against her skin though tangible and thin as wisps of smoke.

"I must increase my power even more, the Sol-lumieth will be here soon enough." *She* looked back into the black waters of the scrying pool not seeing anything different than the first time. Her obsidian eyes reflected the water itself, but instead of the instant rage she had originally felt, the corner of her lip curled with disdain and evil intentions. Her eyes found those red orbs of the Droch-Shúil blazing only inches away from her own. "I must visit the Orchids once more."

Keeping the darkness attached to her body, she left the comfort of her dimmed cavern and strode through the rocky tunnels to where she held the Orchids prisoners. It amused her to be able to simply think of something to wear, conjure it mentally, and it simply fit itself to her body. Her outfit choice at present was her new favorite—unsure which era she conjured it from. Clad in a black, skin-tight leather one-piece, top to bottom, she felt invincible. *She* wore three inch black heels and her hair in a high ponytail at the top of her head, the black fall of it trailing down her back. This outfit held an air of attitude that gave her the extra edge she needed when doing the darkest deeds, such as the one she was about to do.

The dirt floors of the tunnels kept her heels from causing a commotion and alerting the prisoners to her arrival. She much preferred to sneak on them unawares, though with their extra senses as Orchids it proved harder than she thought it should be. Already, she could hear them whispering, preparing for her arrival. The scent of fear and anger deliciously assaulted her senses the closer she got. Rounding the corner, she could see the magical force field entrapping them in their own wing of the cavernous tunnels. They had no hope for escape from their prison, even if the one they call the Sol-lumieth was making her way to them—a delusional hope born from desperation.

"Hello my tasty morsels," *She* crooned darkly. Though there were not as many of the Orchids as there originally were, they kept volunteering to be the ones she chose. *She* wasn't stupid, she knew they were protecting the royalty, giving them as much time to try and work a way out of their current situation, but for now she didn't care. Let them have their delusions!

An older man stepped boldly forward, showing not a trace of fear though she could smell it lingering faintly on his skin. The older man stood as tall as a man of stocky build could stand, clearly a Shifter. His wiry white hair struck something within her... a memory? *She* shook her head slightly and blinked her eyes. Odd, she rarely had memories, but something about him pulled it from the recesses of her mind. Gasps came from several of the Orchids behind the man, to which he turned his head abruptly, his eyes chastised the drawing of her attention.

"What is it?" *She* demanded, her fists clenched at her sides.

Several of the male Orchids stepped forward in front of the women, Eva especially, shielding them from the Mistress of the Mountain's gaze.

Her ire growing, she sucked in a deep calming breath. *She* needed her wits and control for the task ahead of her. She forced the words, "Never mind do not tell me. We have business to attend to." Her lip curled up at one side as she surveyed the Shifter who had stepped up to sacrifice his energy to further her needs. Hunger stirred within her.

A piece of her hair fell in front of her eyes only to glimpse a strip of white receding from her head of black. White? An internal strike to the gut caught her off guard, causing her to suck in air. *She* quickly recovered and reined in her composure as if nothing had happened, but she caught the gazes of the Orchids watching her carefully.

"No matter," *She* attempted to sound aloof and unconcerned though the implications of it were quite concerning. "Back to your purposes here..."

She appraised the man still standing before her. Old or young, Faerie, Elf, or Shifter, it didn't matter; a soul was a soul and that was all she needed to complete the transition to enable to her to traverse into the realm of Alandria! She beckoned the woman who stood directly behind him, using him as a shield. Her lip lifted in a sneer, and her eyes ignited with a deep hunger. "Lucky you, you're going to be next!"

Chapter Thirty-One

The Mortal Realm. Somewhere in Tennessee, USA.

"Finn?" Ella asked yet again. Finn did not respond. Ella frowned, not sure if he chose not to respond to her or if he was so lost in his mind and memories of the past he was trapped, unaware of anything else.

Luckily, Ella had spent time in the mortal realm in the past as she searched for the Twined—those born half mortal and half Alandrian, those who either were unaware of their heritage or those who needed to learn how to properly use what they knew. She had begun her adventure several decades ago looking for those lost from Alandria with Finn back before he had begun running errands for the king of the Elves, before he had been unknowingly forced to leave.

He had not even said goodbye.

She understood why now, but still she felt the ache in her heart only Finn could have mended. She had loved him like no other. Their relationship was reckless—him being an Elf, her being a Faerie—but the Elf king's son had been involved with the Faerie princess to the degree they secretly wedded and bore their daughter, Kaeleigh. Ella believed love blossomed where it chose to plant the seeds. Their's had been a secret love affair, but that was many years ago, and she didn't know if he even cared.

"Finn!" Ella nearly shouted. There was no sense in daydreaming about what might have been. She placed her hands on her hips, refusing to move until he acknowledged her. It was time to deal with truth.

Finn stopped moving, his back remained to her as his shoulders rose and fell with his rigid breath. "Not here, Ella," Finn whispered, responding to her for the first time in hours.

The further they had walked and the longer they were on their own left to nothing but their silence, their thoughts, and the nature surrounding them, his past and the confession with Daegan caught up with him. Finn had grown sullen and moodier the longer he was left inside his own head, thinking thoughts best left where they lied in the past. Daegan had said he forgave him, but Finn wasn't sure he could forgive himself. He could momentarily get distracted, get focused on a task, but at night he could find no rest, let alone forget.

"We better find a place soon Finnlan Talaín. We need to talk," Ella stated. "Or I need to talk and you need to listen, but either way you will stop ignoring me. We have a task to do *together* and if you continue to push me out, then I will dump you somewhere and continue this on my own." Drawing in a deep breath, Ella reconsidered her words because as it would be he would probably insist she continue without him. "And you had dare not encourage me to do just that." She paused and her voice softened. "As I figure it, you owe Alandria... and you owe me." Her words held a hint of emotion, but she quickly followed it up with a prickly tone, "Pull it together, Finn, until we can talk about what really needs talking about."

Ella stormed passed him, not looking his way, expecting him to make a quick decision and follow her; she knew the way just as much as he did, even better. She did not need him for this task, but she truly wanted him at her side... she just hoped he wanted to stay there.

Finn sighed and went after Ella, following behind her, a puppy heeling its master. Beyond moody, Finn's entire stature crumbled with the revelation of how his actions had impacted Daegan and ultimately Kaeleigh.

One mistake.

He had paid for it over and over again. Finally back in Alandria, friendship restored and put to rights with Kaeleigh, even on decent terms with Daegan, re-united with Ella... only for it to implode on him. His life would never be what it once was, he only hoped he could make it up to Ella by helping with the Twined camp and fighting for Alandria. In all his life he could never make it up to Daegan, nor could he undo what had been done so many years ago, but he would fight with all his life for Alandria to be free so that Daegan and Kaeleigh could see the brightness of the realm as it once was before darkness and tragedy struck it down. He vowed he would see Alandria restored if not for anyone other than Daegan and Kaeleigh.

Resolved to share it all with Ella and hold nothing back, he caught up to her quickly and focused on the task at hand.

"Ella, wait!" Finn jogged up to meet her. He reached for the inside of her elbow and tugged her to look at him. "I am sorry, Ella. We will talk once we arrive at our destination for the night. But until then let us talk of our plans with the Twined. I want to hear how you have kept the program running all these years of my absence."

She smiled and acknowledged the olive branch he extended to her. "Yes, I have been wanting to update you for quite some time now since I was made aware of your return."

He grabbed her hand and squeezed. "Thank you," he whispered.

She nodded. "After you..." her eyes flicked up to his hoping she did not just burn the tenuous bridge they had been rebuilding but continued regardless. He was made of stronger stuff. Besides, she was straightforward and direct. Drawing in a breath, she simply continued. "After you left Alandria, it took some time to regroup and find others who wanted to be a part of our vision and believed in the Twined the way we did. But I did find them, and we began to build what it has become now." She paused and suddenly looked far away, the light coloring she did have to her skin, disappeared.

"Ella? What is it?" Finn asked.

She turned her gaze up to his, eyes clouded with worry. "Do you think they survived that blast from Maleina or whoever that other woman was back in the forest before we left Grandfather? Could they have made it to the caves designated for emergency shelter within Tylínyth in time? I could not forgive myself if..."

Finn cut her off, "It would not be your fault, but yes, I think they made it. You have raised a smart and well-trained group, and you left Elder Tillin in charge in your absence. He knew they needed to find shelter before we had even left." He hoped what he said was the truth, but the look on her face was not one he wanted to see again.

Ella steeled her shoulders, back to the present moment. They continued to walk. "Right. You are right, Elder Tillin is more than capable and we had multiple scenarios and back up plans and protocol. They should be all right." She smiled at Finn.

"How many are registered with you?" Finn asked to take her mind off the negative.

"Over a couple thousand, but they do not all live in the realm of Tylínyth, some rarely even return except for their required check-ins to ensure us they were still living and functioning according to mortal society. I cannot tell you how much we stress the survival of our races by not revealing what they are able to do with magic and or otherwise. The Shifters are taught strictly about not changing forms in front of humans and being careful to avoid heavily populated areas of humans while in animal form to stay out of wild animal protective custody. They are well trained and we have only had a handful of mishaps where we intervened with magic or had to erase memories," she admitted proudly.

"Well done, Ella. You have truly done a masterful job," he encouraged. "Is there a way to contact them all, or call them all in to enlist with those willing to fight for Alandria when the time comes? Or do we have whoever is at our disposal at the time?" Finn held his finger to his chin thoughtfully.

"There is a way," she told him, considering his thought process. "I do not know how many will put their lives on the line and fight for a place that either refused them or they have never been. Those who stayed at the camp and train daily know they may be called upon for such a reason, but those who chose to go out on their own have no such ties or thoughts to consider."

"They will consider it. If Alandria falls, it will impact their *human* way of life when all the races who survive suddenly flood into their world through portals and suck up the remaining life of the magic that does exist in the mortal realm. They do not want that to happen, it will lessen their abilities and their lifespan if the magic is extinguished too soon."

"True, but you cannot force them into battle, Finn, you know that," she chided.

"I do and I will not approach it that way, though it is the truth and they need to be aware of all consequences of the war whether they choose to fight or not," he stated assuredly.

Ella agreed. "Tell me about the mortal realm, Finn. Where did you live, what was it like to live as a human?" She had been waiting so long to ask him questions. Ella extended her hand to Finn and moved them as only Alandrians could—teleported from their current location in Tennessee to Locast Ridge, an area near one of the greatest of lakes—Lake Michigan, in a blink of an eye. She knew it had been some time for him since he had traveled that way, thus she took the lead. Finn had told her all about living in Montana, so she was somewhat familiar with what life in the mortal realm, specifically the States was like. He had filled her in on where he worked at the Montana Rail Link, how he had come to be in Kaeleigh's and Chel's life. He had never had anyone else to talk to about everything his life had become living as a human, and he found it enjoyable to share it with someone else—with Ella.

"You really care about them," Ella said, looking softly at Finn.

"Yes, I do. Chel drives me crazy, but in a little sister kind of way and though I doubt she knows it, I would protect her just the same," Finn admitted.

Ella squeezed his hand like he had done to her before, though she was unaccustomed to the practice. "It says a lot about you, Finn. You are a good Elf no matter what else you might feel or think." She watched his face flinch. She wanted nothing more than for him to believe her, and she knew he would in spite of past events.

"We're almost there," Ella stated, much to Finn's relief. "Before we get there, we need to talk about what you have been avoiding."

Finn nodded. It needed to be discussed and now might be their only chance.

"We can wait here then transport under the cover of darkness closer into the city," Ella offered, not allowing this opportunity to be missed. She sat, pulling him down to the ground with her, and made herself comfortable against the trunk of a tree.

After many minutes of silence, the weight of the moment they both dreaded settled upon them. Ella could hold out no longer.

"Finn, what happened?" she initiated.

"When?"

"With Daegan's parents... what went wrong?"

"How do you know something went wrong? Maybe I am a mindless machine and simply did what I was told," he spat back.

"You do not believe that," she sated matter of fact.

"Do you?" he asked, unaware how much her opinion mattered to him until that moment. Afraid of her expression and what her answer would be, he held his breath.

"Of course not, that is absurd. The Finn I know now and knew then would never be mindless in anything."

His shoulders slumped as he released the hold he had on his breath and allowed his heart to beat again though suddenly fast and erratic. He waited a second then sighed, reluctant but decisive to go into the darkness of his past, the moment that marred his future.

"King Ryek of Adettlyn had me sneaking information to him from within Elnye. It was a risky but very important mission and he had asked me if I would do it. Of course, I wanted the position, it was a great honor to have been asked by him." He looked to Ella. "Unfortunately, it took me away from what we had started with the Twined and for a time I thought I could still do both, but quickly learned my involvement with Maleina would not be good for you or the Twined if she were to find out about them." He took a breath. "I was undercover, fraternizing with potential enemies of Alandria—or whoever the king suspected were conspiring against Alandria—bringing him much needed intel to launch necessary protections. At one point, Maleina went underground and we did not hear from her for weeks. When I had gone to her before, I had kept a certain glamour disguising myself for my own protection and that of the Elves as well." Finn stared out into the fading light of day, a reflection of his current mood. Night would soon fall. A cool breeze picked up and crickets started chirping.

"What happened then?" Ella prompted.

"I had garnered a new glamour and sought her out, found her hide-out based on previous intel and pushed my way into her personal entourage. King Ryek felt something big was coming and wanted someone on the inside when it started to inform him as early as possible. I had an invitation to stand with her personal guard. It was my chance to get into the inner circle, to attend her planning meetings, and to go with her on outings—a desirable position within her growing ranks. Even then she was assembling power and followers, we assumed to take over the throne of Elnye or someone else's throne." His eyes glossed over, remembering the day. "The king had given me permission to do what was necessary to infiltrate her ranks. Maleina had met my trainers on a ride and given them a task for me. We followed the targets out of Kandri until we caught up with a carriage. She had called the travelers out—a man and a woman, though we thought there were more originally we did not see anyone else in the carriage." A tear fell shamelessly down the side of Finn's cheek, gathered under his chin, and awaited another to force it further. He turned his head but continued, his speech grew thick with emotion; regret threatened to crush him.

Ella reached over and gripped his hand tightly as he continued. Tears welled in her own eyes for what she knew was coming but also for Finn and the pain and guilt he had carried for so long.

"My orders were to kill them. I did not recognize who they were—they had been in hiding for such a long time—I understand now. I am not sure to this day how King Ryek expected me to recognize them, but nevertheless I did not—I'm not even sure how I would have gotten out of it had I known who they were, though things would be much different now if I had." Finn's shoulders slumped. "Back to the moment, I had a job to do, and I wanted it over as quickly as possible. Looking back, there were clues had I had the wherewithal to observe them; my mind was addled with the command to take innocent lives. That's not an excuse for what I did, just how I remember it." He breathed slowly, his hand shook as he lifted it to brush a stray hair out of his face. "I used my bow back then—never since have I—I knew my shot would strike. I aimed true and sure, hoping for a quick kill to not leave them in pain; the one mercy I could bestow. They had fallen side by side, their hands laced together with their last movements." More tears fell from his eyes, trickling from a single drop now to a steady drip of truth revealed. Shame gripped Finn as he covered his eyes with one hand while Ella still held his other.

"I stood motionless, but detached. I had to prove myself to Maleina. I had already committed the ultimate crime in my own mind, now I needed to make it count for something by getting the information the king wanted. She charged me with cleaning up. The others had left and I was alone with the lives I had taken. The man, he spoke to me and forgave me. I couldn't leave them there. I called for one of the messenger birds to retrieve the Ferriers to carry their souls to their afterlife. I had never seen such a thing up close. Right then I knew they had been special but still did not know how." Finn finished shaking his head.

"What happened to Daegan that day?" Ella asked quietly.

"I am not sure. Our intel said it was going to be a family, but there was no child. We searched the area for days but found none. Now I know he had found King Ryek also known as Hunter at some point after that, though I am not sure how long after."

"Then?"

"Shortly after that I was inducted into Maleina's ranks, and though she knew me by another name, I always suspected she could see through my glamour." He paused and furrowed his brow. "She recognized me when we were last in Elnye with Kaeleigh and everyone. I think she would have arrested me on the spot had it not been for her desire to acquire Kaeleigh or to cause me further grief by allowing me to wallow in guilt and fear of retribution. I'm actually surprised Alandria has allowed me to travel freely within her borders for so long. Part of my banishment came with a clause of further punishment by Alandria herself if I were to come back." He breathed in deeply and took his hand back from Ella, wiping his eyes.

"Several weeks had gone by before I was able to get back to Ryek with the information that Maleina was going to attack during the peace agreements. He had tried to warn the other territories which might be why several did not show in full force, but still the agreements were to go on as scheduled." Finn adjusted his position and stretched out his legs. He pinched the bridge of his nose as he continued his tale. "The agreements—or accords—were supposed to be a weaponless event where we were all unified siblings of Alandria. But King Ryek and King Ranan Eytht of the Faeries were able to encourage all to still come armed in case of attack—too many royalty would be in attendance." Finn crossed and re-crossed his ankles while Ella held incredibly still, listening to his story. "Ryek was able to have a hiding place prepared, but things went wrong. He wasn't able to escape with his son, Kaeleigh's father Prince Brandt, in tow. It all went wrong. It was all my fault."

"No it is not. You made a choice. It resulted in the safety for the greater good of Alandria, though it is sad and regretful innocents—especially royal innocents—of Alandria were caught in the crossfire. Maleina was going to attack either way. She must have had information on who would be in that carriage, I doubt it was all happenstance, but perhaps. You made a mistake that many would have in your position. As you said, they had been in hiding, unknown to most." Ella reached for his hand. "You saved lives and gave many a fighting chance or the least the ability to flee and fight another day. They were warned. What they did with that information was out of your hands." She paused. "You gave Kaeleigh the chance at seeing her grandfather, in fact you gave her the chance to live at all. If King Ryek had died in the agreements, his granddaughter would never have had a chance. You did that. Yes, it did not go how you desired or would have had it, but you did your job. Yes, there were consequences and it was tragic what befell Daegan. We have all made sacrifices."

"Ella, I killed innocent people. I was banished from Alandria because of it. King Ryek sent me away himself though it was his order I infiltrate Maleina's ranks. I do not blame him. I was a risk and he had to follow up with sentence."

"He bestowed mercy upon you when he did not kill you. He gave you the greatest responsibility—his granddaughter—when he would not be able to ensure her safety himself. The king knew the fault was his, and you were taking the fall for it," she reminded him. "You may never be able to forgive yourself, but I know this all played out for a reason. It is hard to see it when you are so deeply involved and others are hurt because of it." Ella took a breath and gave Finn a small smile. "Follow your heart, Finn, you will find absolution somewhere."

Finn sniffled and his head shot up, suddenly alert and changed subjects unexpectedly. "There, the area of industry we need to cross through is closed. We need to make our move soon."

Ella jumped to her knees and peered out from the hiding place they'd been sitting in. Before her chance was gone, she turned to Finn and studied his face. His eyes were so full of guilt, emotion, determination, and resolve to make amends for Alandria. Grabbing his chin, she pulled him toward her face and without notice, not giving him the chance to pull away, she kissed him fully on the mouth.

Trying unsuccessfully to pull away, Finn was flooded with feelings of unworthiness. Yet Ella held on and pulled him closer to her. He felt forgiveness, loneliness, desire, and love from her. For the first time he began to glimpse a future, one that was brighter not just for Alandria, but also for him. What began forceful and hopeful turned to a softer, gentler invitation for him to take in return. And in return he did.

~~~~~

Slipping out from the tree line, Finn and Ella crept quietly through the field of tall and dying fall grasses.

"We could transport closer into the city instead of walking out here in the open," Finn noted watching her from the corner of his eye, shocked at the vulnerable feeling he felt back in the mortal realm though no dangers knew where they were or would attack so blatantly in the mortal realm.

"We could, it is true," Ella stated obviously. Looking up at the night sky, observing the stars and the moon Ella seemed to relax allowing Finn to do the same if only a little. "The sky here when it is revealed like this is as beautiful as ours, even though they only have the one white moon," she said wistfully, reaching for Finn's hand. "I would simply like to walk for a time and enjoy this moment with you."

Finn blew out air, deflating his instinctual warrior actions and allowed her to grip his hand. Her small feminine hand felt comfortable within his. She was warm and soft, even with the few callouses on her hands—rewards for her hard work and consistent training as a warrior. She impressed him in every sense. Finn glanced her way several times. Ella's eyes glimmered with the moonlight reflected in them. Her skin shimmered beneath its glow, giving her an otherworldly aura. For the first time, in a long time, he felt relaxed enough to enjoy the moment with her. He wiped his free hand over his face and swept some of his floppy hair away from it. When he turned back to her, she too was studying him.

"What?" he asked his throat tightened at the look in her eyes.

"I've missed you, Finnlan. Can I simply spend time remembering and committing these subtle changes I see to new memory?"

Finn laughed. "I have forgotten how direct you are. It's refreshing to be around." His smile was genuine. He enjoyed being around Ella again, working with her, being close to her, and watching her. He very much liked that she took what she wanted.

"How is this for straight forward?" Ella turned fully toward him. "I want what we had again, Finn. I want to be with you, I want you. I have
~~~~~

always loved you and want to explore the possibility of that again, if you would have me. I know you were... are... close to Kaeleigh, but I also do not sense those specific feelings for her in you, they were muddled before so I did not interfere," she paused, watching for a reaction. "Now that your mind is clear, I cannot help but approach the subject." Her gaze slipped and her head bowed in uncertainty, something Finn was quick to see. Quickly, she regained courage and forced her rebellious body to return her gaze to Finn.

Finn stared at the beautiful Faerie who offered herself to him with open love and desire. The emotions she stirred in him, the desire and hope for a life at all—but one with her—seemed more than possible with her by his side. Maybe he could return to Alandria, find redemption by helping to save the realm. He could sequester himself away with her within the hidden mountains and their realm of Tylínyth and work with the Twined. He wanted to believe in the possibilities as the questions ran through his mind. Afraid to hope, but unwilling to let her slip out of his grasp again, Finn stepped forward and pulled her against his chest.

"I would have you for eternity if you would have me. You honor me with your absolution and offer for a future with you," Finn said humbly, wetness rimming his eyes. "My heart has truly always been with you, Ella Zolnís of the mountains. I did not think a happy future could be mine, but with you it feels possible. I am forever grateful for your love. I only hope to give you a fraction of what you deserve, but I would spend the rest of my existence trying. I love you, Ella."

Finn bent down and took her mouth gently, intimately, putting all his love and his emotion into his kiss, hoping she felt what he could not say with words.

Ella responded with her own kisses in return. She reached up and laced her hands around his neck, pulling him more to her level while he reached for her waist and lifted her closer to his, taking a blissful moment to themselves not knowing what the future held once they reached the entrance to Tylínyth.

Headlights in the distance suddenly interrupted their moment of passion, causing Finn to flinch out of Ella's embrace. She pulled away and shielded her eyes.

"Straight in the eyes those lights are almost as bad as a Quarian Sun," Ella said with a chuckle.

"A car is headed this way. Our time alone has come to an end, I'm afraid," Finn said as he pecked a kiss on her forehead before turning to move. He tugged her hand and pulled her down the street.

"Let us go."

But Finn paused and looked around. "I do not remember this area, much has changed. You will have to lead the way."

Ella was already tugging his hand the opposite direction right before they disappeared into the night and transported to their destination.

Chapter Thirty-Two

The small city was alive at night. This city, Finn noted, had a subtlety to it that would be missed in a larger one; large buildings were large but not so large to feel intimidating, and small buildings still held an element of charm. They chose well with this city to be the mortal realm entrance to their realm of Tylínyth—for the Twined could come and go and not stick out in this city. The night was unseasonably warm for a fall Michigan evening, but the perfect air and the perfect breeze off the lake made it enjoyable. Music came from inside a pub they passed as the door opened, the sounds of laughter and people enjoying themselves was prevalent. Others walked up and down the sidewalk even late this evening, as they talked amongst themselves. A peace lingered in the air, Finn breathed it in deeply desiring some of it for himself. One look at the beautiful Faerie next to him, and she too enjoyed the city activity if her pleasant smile and general wonderment at all the lights was anything to judge by.

"I like this place," she spontaneously said, feeling his introspection.

"It is nice," Finn agreed. "How much further?"

"Just a bit further." She pointed to a tall building three blocks ahead of them. The building was possibly eight stories tall, but did not stand out amongst the other buildings surrounding it. It was one of multiple condominium buildings in the area that had been converted from either old warehouses before the city grew up around them or from transitioned office buildings. A flat gray against a background of dark brown and red brick buildings along with the lights from nearby establishments added texture to the otherwise plain building. Those passing had no reason to wonder what lay within. Was the building a set of private offices? Perhaps just common private condominiums? No one paid attention. No one cared. Certainly no one would pick up on the fact it was a refuge for mixed races from another realm.

Approaching the front entrance door, Ella pretended to search for keys in her pockets but then discreetly put her thumb to the pad by the doorbell. A click sounded and the door unlatched offering them entrance. Finn looked behind him before walking in to ensure they were not followed.

"Is it spelled to keep mortals from knocking or watching too closely?" Finn inquired.

"Of course!" Ella declared, surprised he even had to ask. "We also have a private parking garage below the building so people are not truly sure how many are here at one time or are coming and going."

"Well done." Finn nodded.

Ella paused in what looked like a small entry. She turned to Finn who had also stopped, his mouth agape and his eyes fixed on a large cut metal sign.

Talaín Towers. Finn's last name was mounted on the wall before him for any who entered to see.

"I hope you do not mind, I named it after you. After all, you helped begin the program and birthed the ideas I am about to show you. I wanted you to have a piece of it," she explained quietly.

"Ella..." Finn's voice squeaked and he cleared his throat. "Ella, this means more than you know. Thank you." Finn pulled her in close for a sweet, romantic kiss.

Ella beamed with new energy in her step. "Now you are here I want you to be a part of it all. To start, I am not sure how you feel about this, but we have consulted on and off with a witch from the mortal realm on some of our enchantments to ensure the safety of mortals if they somehow get through them."

Finn thought about what she said, weighing the unknowns and risks. "That makes sense since we are unfamiliar with how our magic might interfere with them here. And why not have allies with the mortal witches if the need arises." Finn truly appreciated Ella's foresight and inclusion of his dreams and hope for the Twined's refuge. Talaín Tower. Finn smiled.

Ella smiled. "Come, I want to show you!" She tugged his arm through the dark entry, lit by two slits high above the large metal door. "The top levels still consist of several apartments and rooms for those with temporary accommodation needs. Now we also have a gym. Some actually prefer to use this training area because they are more comfortable here than within Tylínyth itself," Ella explained enthusiastically. The two walked further into the building. The entry opened up into what looked like a larger reception area manned by a tall, Nordic-looking man. He and his broad shoulders and large biceps leaned against the counter top. His face was roughened by time and weather, though his eyes were a bright, crystal blue. His long, blond hair was pulled back, tied at his back. When the man saw Ella, his smile revealed perfectly white teeth.

"Ella!" he bellowed in the cavernous lobby. Finn noted the lack of echo and felt all the more assured of the safe house. A missing echo in so large an area meant fantastic privacy insulation work.

"Luke," she replied with a smile of her own.

"It has been awhile since you have entered from this side of things. How is everything? Going well, I hope?" His brows pinched with concern as he came around the counter.

"So much has happened. But please, meet Finn. He originally started this program for the Twined with me long, long ago and has since returned from his mission. Please treat him just as if he were me."

Luke extended his hand in the customary American greeting and Finn shook his hand accordingly. "Pleased to meet you, Finn. Welcome to Talaín Tower. I'm assuming it is named after you then?" He snuck a glance with a sly smile on his face toward Ella.

Finn nodded. "Thank you. And likewise. As far as the building goes... I guess so." He gave an odd chuckle resembling the closest thing Finn might get to embarrassment.

"It is wonderful to see you again, but we are weary from our journey," Ella interrupted. "Let us update you and the others with the full story tomorrow. There is no easy way to explain—but the short of it is... that is, the portal inside Alandria has been disabled. For now. We are here to learn how all on this side have fared, to find out if everyone is all right inside as well." Ella exhaled, realizing how shaky her voice had become delivering the bad news.

"He needs to know the full extent if he decides to fight, Ella," Finn jumped in, "Maleina, one of our enemies, destroyed the portal as we were about to enter. Those inside had some warning, but we do not know how they fared."

Luke nodded with understanding and pointed at Finn. "I like him, straight to the point. Ella, you seem off your game a bit," Luke said with a wink.

"Yes, well... could you tell me the extent of the damage?" Ella brought it back around to the point at hand.

"We felt a big rumble even on this side. I didn't think that was even possible. To be honest, it fritzed out the doorway on our side, shutting access down for quite some time. Finally Sarah and some of the others were able to get it up just a couple days ago."

"A couple days ago?" Ella gasped. "They were trapped in there for days!?" Ella ran her fingers through her short hair, and the blood rushed from her face to her feet.

"It did a fair number on the electrical, affecting the door. Everything in the building was fine otherwise. We did what we could on this end and continued as normal as we could and waited," Luke continued and Finn leaned against the tall counter listening. "Like I said, once Sarah was able to get the system back up and running, we got in there as fast as we could. Took us down right forever to find anyone."

"In the caves?" Ella asked expectantly.

Luke nodded slowly, driving Ella crazy with the anticipation of what was to come. "Yes, all huddled in the caves. Most were just fine; a little shaken up and hungry, but otherwise just fine. They're tough, you've ensured they would be."

"Most?" Finn inquired. "Were some not all right?"

"The guards by the portal suffered some damage, but nothing that couldn't be fixed..." Luke turned away from them trying to hide a pained look as it flashed across his face.

"Tell me," Ella said with a hint of fear.

"Peter and Silas were trying to follow after you all had left apparently and were too close to the portal when it exploded. It was like a rocket of power and energy, carrying with it rocks and rubble... they were right in front of it when it happened. They didn't make it," he said sadly, hanging his head.

Ella inhaled and made a choking sound. Finn pulled her toward him and cradled her head tightly to his chest, holding her there, allowing her to have a moment of grief. Luke turned his head away, but not before noting the way Finn caressed her hair and smiled sadly. At least she now had someone to comfort her.

"They were the only ones?" Finn asked, his voice solemn and quiet. "Yes."

"What other damage?" Finn released Ella at her insistence and continued talking, which gave Ella a minute to regain her composure.

"The crops to the north were roughed up and obviously the rock damage where the portal was, but other than that not much else except some random boulders and scorch marks on the training field," Luke added. "The last of the damage really amounted to nothing in comparison with the loss of life."

"Thank you Luke," Ella reached for his hand and squeezed it. "I would like to show Finn the rest of the building tonight. We will retire and try to get some rest before heading into Tylínyth in the morning." She stopped and then looked full into Luke's face, searching for his undivided attention. "I need you to do something for me before I go, if you would?"

"Of course, Ella. Just name it."

"Send out a message to all registered. I am calling a gathering. I want those available to come, and those not available to come as well," she said thinking out loud.

"Everyone?" Luke asked surprised.

"Yes, everyone," Finn added. "It's urgent."

"I want them here in two days time," she added. Then looking up with gray depths of stillness in her eyes, she spoke, "Enact protocol Come Home."

Luke's eyes grew wide. "Done." He moved behind the counter and pulled open a laptop sitting behind it and began to type a series of keys.

"Thank you, Luke." Ella grabbed Finn's hand and pulled him passed Luke's desk and through a darkened hallway.

Finn looked back to say something to Luke, but the man was fast at work on his keyboard.

"I'm sorry for the loss of the two, Ella."

"So am I," she replied equally as quiet. She understood there would be casualties as they went to war for Alandria. This was part of what being a warrior and fighting for things you believed in meant, but it still hurt. She knew she needed to become stronger and that she would, but for the moment it was okay to grieve.

Stopping in front of a pair of doors, black metal doors found in any office building, Finn noted these were different.

"What are these inscriptions here?" Finn looked up and down either side of the doors and along the top. He realized as he studied the markings, these were no random symbols but others were words written in the language of the Elves, the language of the Shifters, and again the Faeries and even some Finn didn't recognize. Of those he did recognize, they were the same word.

"Welcome," Ella spoke the word just at the moment he recognized it.

Ella opened the doors to reveal a very large, seemingly wall-less room. Finn couldn't see the ceiling. He stood in awe—magic was everywhere.

"It's a mini Alandria?" he asked. "Like how we envisioned?"

Ella nodded with a big smile. "We call it Alandria2. It is an environment intended to simulate the different parts of Alandria in order to acclimate those who are not familiar with Alandria in small doses. Those with Shifter blood can experience the drier area and even feel what it would be like to live in their territory simply by being over there," Ella explained pointing to the pile of boulders and scattered sparse trees in one corner, then she pointed to the opposite corner. "Over there, is a small but life-like rendition of one of our forests. And over there is a green patch for those with Faerie magic to practice growing or just to be able to sit and feel what that magic feels like." Her face turned and her eyes lit with pride as they roamed through Alandria2 and what they had been able to accomplish inside a building not yet even part of the pocket realm of Tylínyth.

Finn, too, looked around with wonder. "It is everything we had wished it to be! You did it, Ella. You did this," he splayed his hands wide before him gesturing to it all. In one movement, he turned to her, lifted her and pulled her to him, their mouths met with intense contact and pulled apart with a smack. Ella giggled at the suddenness of his action.

"This was your idea, Finn. I was just able to make it happen." Her smile touched her eyes it was so wide. It had been one of her dreams to be able to show him this... their creation together.

"It's amazing, Ella, truly." Finn walked in to the center of the room and turned in a slow circle taking it all in, absorbing the moment with her and enjoying what he witnessed. He walked over to an area of lush greenery with vines trailing from tree to tree, creating a canopy over grass dotted with large fantastical mushrooms. "I cannot wait to see different people working in their spaces, feeling their intended magic and becoming one with Alandria though they may not even understand it all."

"It is wonderful Finn. You will love it."

"Tomorrow?" he asked his eyes lit with the excitement of a young boy, his fingers trailed along an overgrown mushroom and then over a large boulder next to it. Everything felt so alive with Alandria's magic. "I haven't felt it this strong even in parts of Alandria since I'd been back. We must make Alandria this strong again," he whispered.

"It will. And yes, tomorrow," she confirmed. "Let us go upstairs. I need some sleep before tomorrow." Stretching her hand toward him she awaited him to take it, the feeling of his skin against hers quickening her heartbeat.

Finn's eyes lit on hers heavy with question.

Ella saw the question in his eyes but dispelled it quickly. "We will sneak into the bunk rooms as I forgot to ask Luke what rooms were available to us." She blushed like a young girl to which she had not been in a very long time. "You to the boy's bunkroom and I to the girl's," she explained to his pouting lip. She chuckled. "When we get into the Tylínyth, you may share my cottage." She winked at him then sauntered toward the elevator that would take them upstairs. Finn trailed along behind her, appreciating her lovely curves as she went.

"I look forward to it," Finn said, his voice suddenly hoarse and quiet.

Chapter Thirty-Three

The Mortal Realm. Somewhere in Tennessee, USA.

After Daegan and Kaeleigh had taken some time to rest near the top of the mountain with the ruins, Daegan felt magic stirring, almost calling him, from deep within. He pulled Kaeleigh along with him, until they had traipsed through greenery and trees, dodging the occupied areas where neighborhoods had been built and up higher into the lands the tourist attraction owned but not yet developed. Both gasped once they got beyond the developed lands. The energy of the land was strong, allowing nature great dominion as it took over. Nature had its own energy, and its own hum of magic; nature breathed a refreshing breath of exuberance into each of them.

"It's so alive here, Daegan," Kaeleigh whispered, trailing her hand gently over tips of flowers, grasses, and newly sprouted trees bursting with the newness and hope life offered, untouched by human hands.

"It is, I felt my magic respond to it. It called me here." Daegan's gaze searched the area. "Here I can try to tune into the magic around us and see if I can get a location for our next destination."

"All right, tell me what I can do, if I can help," Kaeleigh offered, her smile large and genuine soaking in all the growth and magic of the area.

Daegan reached out his hand to hold hers. "Come with me, there is a tree over there to which we can have some shelter while we attempt to find the way." He pointed to a large tree against the cover of a small cliff face that loomed above them just high enough to create an umbrella of cover from any weather changes or hikers coming down from above them.

"Are there any people in the area we need to worry about?" she asked him, following behind.

"Close your eyes and use your senses. Do you feel anyone else nearby, Kaeleigh?"

Always the instructor, she sighed, but she did as he said. He paused to allow her a moment.

"No, I don't sense anyone nearby. Did you?" Kaeleigh bit her lip, checking her senses against his own more finely tuned set.

"Well done, I do not sense anyone in the nearby area. Still, we will be swift and not linger here longer than necessary." Daegan pulled her in close to the tree and they sat at its base, taking a moment to enjoy the beauty of the wild flowers, tall enough to hide them from initial sight. Daegan reached for her hand and laced his with her own.

Kaeleigh's eyes shot to their joined hands then up to meet his eyes. Wide and full of wonder, she turned and leaned her body in to his and with her free hand reached up and brought his head to hers. She kissed him, allowing him to feel her desire for him and he kissed her back.

A moment had passed and Daegan pulled back to see the pouting, reluctant face of Kaeleigh. He chuckled despite himself.

"I know, I know, we have other more important things to focus on." She sighed, but he tipped her chin up so her eyes met his.

"Not more important." He let his love for her shine through his eyes. "But more pressing. Once we have freed Alandria, we will have all the time for ourselves." Daegan smiled, thinking of the future—a rare thing for him to do.

"Do you think we really can free Alandria?" she asked, her voice full of uncertainty as she stared out at the beauty before them.

Daegan considered her question and turned to directly face her. She watched his face. Without doubt or hesitancy in his voice, he answered her. "Yes, I do. Not just because the timing of the prophecy and whether we together create the Sol-lumieth, or because everyone says we can. But because we must. The darkness believes we can and that is a sure sign. They would not be trying so hard to stop us. So I hold on to the small chance we can and so we will."

"If the darkness wasn't afraid that we would cause them any damage, they would be ignoring us not hunting us down trying to stop us." Kaeleigh smiled. "That makes perfect sense. They are afraid of what we might be able to do together." She paused and scrunched her face for a moment. "I do believe Alandria has gifted us with what we need to defeat them; she has called us to her side, to fight on her behalf and so we will."

"Yes, Alandria has equipped us with what we will need, it is up to us to use it wisely and protect it and her," Daegan added, nodding.

Kaeleigh nodded. "I have seen some astonishing things since I've come to Alandria and I want to share her magic with all who have yet to experience it."

"And we shall. But not until we find what we have come for."

"Right. Okay what do we do?" Straightening her back, she folded her legs preparing to be deep in thought.

"I will see if a wisp is nearby and call upon it. In the past, they have aided me in hearing from the Orchids or pulling the magical energy I sought out from the Earth, in turn, giving me a sort of trail to follow." His eyes took on a glaze of remembrance before he smiled then turned toward Kaeleigh with a smile. "That is how I found you."

Blushing, she smiled in return. "I'm glad they were able to help you."

He took her hand and held it comfortably within his. "Feel my magic, follow my lead, and include your own to learn how." Daegan trained his gaze ahead, focusing on a fixed point in front of them and relaxed his posture as much as could be called relaxed for him. His magic swelled from within, a tangible presence between them, before he released it with an exhale of air, blowing it and a call to magic Kaeleigh had not felt before.

Kaeleigh could feel what his magic and intent did and feel her own respond in kind, she the student to his teacher, and released hers in a similar fashion. Instead of repeating the message—the call to come—she added her own gratitude for the coming assistance. She watched through her eyes of magic as her own multi-colored thread joined with Daegan's blue one then both were swept into a current on the breeze, trailing out further and further until she could no longer see it.

"That was beautiful," her voice filled with awe. "Now what?"

"Now we wait, but hopefully not too much longer as dusk approaches." His gaze searched the surrounding area once more, seeking any human—or other—interference.

"Hmm, what could we do to pass the time?" Kaeleigh wondered sarcastically, tapping her finger on her cheek before she leaned forward to plant another kiss on Daegan's soft yet masculine lips. It was a short kiss, but full of sweetness.

Daegan smiled and even chuckled a bit. "That is one way, but I have something else in mind to pass the time."

"Oh really?" Kaeleigh interjected coyly.

Daegan jumped up, pulling her up with him. "I have never done this with another person before."

"You haven't? I have to say I'm surprised," Kaeleigh scrunched her brows together.

"But I think it is as basic in nature as it is in principle. So we should try, it will make things much easier for us."

"Um, okay, right now? Right here?" Kaeleigh looked around her at the ground, noting the soft mounds of dirt covered in moss and grasses. "That should be soft enough," she mused thoughtfully. "This isn't quite how I imagined it happening, but it's private enough."

"You have imagined doing this with me?" Daegan asked quizzically. "I was not aware you knew I could do this?"

"Well, yeah, I mean what girl wouldn't have. And like you said, it's something we all can do whether or not you've done it before or not." Her gaze found his and the confusion there only added to her own. "Wait, what are you talking about?"

"Transitioning or teleporting, it is known by many names." His head cocked, he watched her thoughtfully until the blood drained from his face with understanding. Then suddenly he burst into a deep belly laugh.

Kaeleigh couldn't help but laugh with him, the awkward moment passing quickly. Watching him laugh, seeing his smile, his utter enjoyment of the moment and knowing she caused that made her feel intoxicated. She wanted to be the one to put that smile on his face and cause his genuine laughter, always.

"That is not what you were suggesting we do with our time, was it Kaeleigh?" Daegan said a moment later, finally gaining his composure once again.

She shook her head and bit her lower lip nervously.

Daegan stalked forward, no hesitation, gripped her waist with one hand and behind her neck with his other. Pulling her in, he kissed her like he had wanted to for quite some time, since the first time he tasted her, leaving her breathless and dazed. "I want nothing more than to be with you in every way possible, but not like this, not here, you deserve so much more."

Finding her breath, but still a bit dazed, Kaeleigh giggled but then quickly brought herself to focus with a gulp of air. "Alrighty then... you said teleporting? Like traveling from point A to point B without physical transportation?" Still regaining her mental faculties, she tried to comprehend his words.

"Yes. In Alandria, I am certain you saw some doing it. It is easier to travel—as you say—there than here; it uses less energy but it is possible and we might need to use it to save time."

"I saw you disappear once... when you first met me back at my apartment... I thought it was my mind playing tricks on me, but you really did disappear didn't you?"

"Not disappear, relocate. But yes, I did. I have tried not to since then and when we were all together in Alandria, it did not make sense though I know Finn could have done such as well... but we had you and Chel and like I said, I have never tried to travel with another person before."

"I can learn this?" Kaeleigh's eyes flew open wide. "I could tele-port—transition—on my own someday?"

"Yes. At first I want to have you with me while you learn. It takes extreme focus and even time we do not have to learn the skill. But yes, someday, you should be able to do it on your own. Know that it takes considerable energy, and even in Alandria you will not see it often. We are taught young it is something to use sparingly, we have legs and means of travel so we should use those as well. If you attempt to transition before you are ready, you could end up somewhere you do not want to be—even in the middle of a lake or volcano—without meaning to. It can be dangerous."

Kaeleigh bounced on the balls of her feet with excitement. "Teach me! I want to learn." All thoughts of her misunderstanding and hor-monal overdrive quickly forgotten with the excitement of something new and magical to learn.

"We will start small, moving from this point over to that tree," Daegan pointed. "I will start by holding you close to me so not to get separated. Let me try first without you adding any energy to it. Simply feel what I do, feel the energies flowing through you. When it is your turn, you focus on where you want to go and direct your energy and magic to that very spot. Does that make sense?"

"I think so. Let's just try it. I learn better by doing and experiencing."

Daegan nodded and pulled her close to his chest, his heart pounded with a nervousness he was unaccustomed to, threatening to push through his defenses. Kaeleigh laid her head against him and placed her hand on top of his chest.

"I will be fine. I trust you and your magic, Daegan. Let's do this!"

Her confidence in him and his magic gave him the boost he needed to set aside his unfamiliarity and set his course for the tree. He breathed slowly in through his nose and out again methodically, almost meditative. He gripped her tightly to him, no room for error, for her to slip from his grasp. Focus set, he released his energy to travel from where they stood to the point right in front of the tree just ahead of them. The world around them grew gray and hazy, dematerializing into nothing then instantaneously materializing somewhere else, the color of the world swiftly returning along with their breath.

Kaeleigh panted, gripping Daegan for all she had within her, trusting him but fearful of the unknown and what should be otherwise impossible. "Did we do it?"

"Open your eyes, Kaeleighnna," he spoke softly.

She did and she looked around, they were now standing feet from the tree opposite where they had just been seconds before. Kaeleigh inhaled with wonder. "You did it!"

Daegan smiled slightly cockily, seemingly satisfied with himself. "Indeed."

"For a brief second, it felt like the ground dropped out from under me, but I wasn't falling. It was strange... but you really did it! That was exhilarating!" Standing to her tiptoes she offered him a chaste kiss on his cheek. "I'm so glad I get to experience these things with you. Thank you."

Stunned, Daegan gazed into her face unsure how to respond, but the expression in his face full of adoration and love, said enough for her.

"Let's do it again! We have to practice more," Kaeleigh said right away. "Was it harder or different for you taking me with you?"

"Actually, not really. I felt a little more energy deplete but not as much as I would have thought. This time I want you to add some of your energy to it as well so you can know the feeling, and we will travel a little further."

"Okay!" Kaeleigh's eyes lit with excitement.

Practicing several more times, the two traveled all over, venturing away from the area around them even throughout the state. Daegan felt confident they'd easily be able to teleport to any location.

"Can we go to another state?" Kaeleigh asked, wondering why she didn't feel more tired.

"Not right now. We need to allow nature to energize our magic once more. Plus I do not want to venture too far in case the wisp comes. They often come in the night rather than the daylight. Night is swiftly approaching."

"Right." Kaeleigh nodded and they went back to their place in the cleft of the rock that would provide them a bit of shelter should they need to stay the night. "Do you think one will come?"

"I hope so." Daegan surveyed their temporary shelter. "But if not, this will serve for tonight."

Waiting with the fading light proved to be exactly what they needed, soaking up the natural energy from the earth, the trees, what was left of the sunlight. Lying back against the rock, Kaeleigh sighed with contentment. "This is lovely."

Daegan smiled and reached over to hold her hand as they watched the sunset, and the natural darkness of night rise.

Kaeleigh stared at the sky, watching the first stars appear. "I think of my father often," Kaeleigh said, suddenly growing reflective. "I wonder if he is all right and if I will ever find him. He seems to get further and further away with all that is happening with Alandria and our missions right now." Kaeleigh sighed and turned her head toward Daegan.

He gave her a small smile. "I understand. We know he is alive. Alandria will help us find him when the time is right. I believe that."

She smiled at him and knew in her heart he was right. They did not have to wait long before a small glowing blue light fluttered slowly through the trees, bouncing from side to side on an unseen path toward them.

"Look!" Kaeleigh whispered, pointing toward the soft glow. "What is that?"

"That is our wisp. Be extremely quiet and slow. Sudden moves and noises can frighten them away," he whispered.

Kaeleigh watched with awe as the little glowing blue light made its way hesitantly toward them until it stopped right in front of them. Desperately she wanted to reach out and touch it, to hold it in her hand, but she refrained.

"Hello, little friend," Daegan said softly, with a voice Kaeleigh hadn't heard him use yet. "You know what I seek. Can you help us on our way?"

"Please," Kaeleigh felt compelled to add just as softly, "You are extremely important to our mission."

The little blue light moved in front of Kaeleigh and came so close she could feel its magic against her cheek. It tickled, but she held back except for a soft giggle. It moved back and something like a screen magically appeared in front of them. The wisp then revealed step by step what they should do by forming a type of map with pictures. The same blue glow as the wisp then highlighted where they needed to go. Within mere moments, just as cautiously as it had arrived, the wisp left them.

"Thank you," Kaeleigh smiled with a wave as it winked out once again hidden in the shelter of the trees.

Daegan watched her with amazement.

"What?" Kaeleigh asked uncertain at his gaze.

"You amaze me. I have never seen a wisp respond to someone like that one just did with you." He shook his head. "Entrancing you are, Kaeleighnna of the Orchids."

Blushing, Kaeleigh focused instead on what the map showed.

"That was a map to the Redwoods in California wasn't it?"

"It was. That is our destination, the Redwood forest. It did not indicate which part specifically though, so we will do our part and arrive then seek our next step."

Gathering themselves, their limited supplies, and backpacks, Daegan reached for Kaeleigh's hand. "Be aware once we arrive, there may be traps or trouble. I know not what might guard the book, we must be watchful."

Kaeleigh nodded in agreement.

As if on cue, a branch cracked in their distance. Both their heads snapped around toward it and cast out their senses. "Someone is there, Daegan," Kaeleigh whispered.

"Yes. It is an odd sense I get, but whoever is curious, watchful even, but there is an underlying malevolence, a danger. We must go."

Without further discussion, Daegan pulled Kaeleigh to his chest, held her tight and teleported them away from that area, away from Tennessee altogether.

Chapter Thirty-Four

The Mortal Realm. The Journey to California, USA.

After their third stop, Daegan bent over panting. "Daegan? Are you all right? Why do we keep stopping?" Kaeleigh asked, reaching for him in concern. They had stopped in flat fields full of corn, on the edge of a massive body of water, and were now surrounded by cascading mountainous peaks.

"We are being followed by that same energy we felt before we left Tennessee. I am trying to throw them off our trail," he answered, sucking in air. "But it is draining more of my energy than I had realized."

"I can help. Let me help add energy, use mine for traveling. We need to get there, I feel something coming and I'm not sure it's the person following us. It almost feels like they are playing a game with us, purposefully draining you."

Daegan watched as Kaeleigh looked out beyond them. She was using her *other* senses more than she had before and clearly they were becoming more and more a part of who she was. He nodded. "I agree."

"Where are we anyway? Those mountains make me think of Colorado, are we close?"

"Very. We are in the Colorado Rockies somewhere adjacent to our destination." Regaining his breath, Daegan stood and looked out with her, admiring the beauty of the craggy and snow covered peaks.

"It is beautiful, but we can't stay here," Kaeleigh said, her teeth chattering from the sudden cold of the higher altitudes. Winter was coming in this world, and it felt like it where they stood high above everything else around them.

"Time to go," Daegan concurred. "I need your help this time. Feed your energy through mine. I will direct the path, but your energy can sustain it longer than mine will at this point."

"You got it!" Kaeleigh's face beamed with pride, honored he would ask for her help, to be a part of it with him. "We do this together."

"Together." He nodded and pulled her in close once again just as the world around them faded from sight.

After a couple more stops, one in a desert and another in Yosemite National Park right in front of a geyser spewing forth its majesty, they arrived. Dawn met them as they stood right in front of a sign welcoming them to the Redwood forest. They weren't exactly where they had been shown in the vision from the wisp but close.

"Why did we stop here?" Kaeleigh asked, now panting a bit herself. She noticed Daegan seemed better off with her help and smiled.

"The magic of this forest blocks out teleporting even though it is a part of our natural magic, it is not one of Earth's. From here we walk," he explained.

And so they walked... for hours. The magic of the forest strengthened and energized them as much as it healed them of their depleted state.

"It's so magnificent," Kaeleigh breathed in wonder, her arms outstretched, staring up at the giant sequoias towering above them, the morning light shafting through the coniferous branches. "It is so much like the forest in Alandria, yet very different all at the same time."

"Yes, you are accurate. It is one of the few places I feel at home when I come to the mortal realm." Daegan breathed deep. The morning air revitalized him, refreshing him through to his soul.

After some time, finally arriving at a small clearing, they stopped to sit and enjoy the moment. "Do you have any idea which way we head now?"

Pausing thoughtfully, Daegan glanced around them but shook his head in denial. "I do not. I feel something, perhaps simply that we are close. What do you sense?"

Kaeleigh closed her eyes and extended her senses, her magic very close to the surface more alive than she had felt in some time. She was surprised she felt it so strongly in the mortal realm at all. Breathing calmly and centering her energy, she cast it out seeking what they sought—the

Book of Lenoria filled with the histories of Alandria and their former realm of Lenoria, rumored to hold untold secrets and ancient magic, along with the map and key they need to find and enter a portal into Exhile.

Daegan gasped. "Kaeleigh? Do you feel anything?" he asked with a strange inflection.

"I feel something, but I am not sure which direction yet," she replied, her eyes still closed, senses still extended.

"Your necklace is glowing, Kaeleigh," Daegan whispered as he scooted over on the log to where she sat.

"What?" Kaeleigh startled at his sudden appearance next to her, but looked down at the orchid necklace she had had for as long as she knew. She had meant to ask Hunter about it, but hadn't had the chance. Her mother had given it to her, she was fairly sure. It was indeed glowing; a soft purple light emanated from her necklace, pulsing faintly.

"Whoa!" Kaeleigh gasped herself. "It has never done that before. What do you think it means?"

"I would guess since it started when you were searching for the book, it has something to do with that."

"That's a logical deduction," she replied with a wink.

"Let us test it. Walk over there." Daegan pointed opposite from where they sat. She did so and the necklace faded fast. "Now walk that way." He pointed across in another direction. Kaeleigh did as he asked.

"It's glowing again!" She looked to him in surprise. "Did you know it would do that?"

He shook his head. "Just a hunch. Now one more time head a different direction."

She did and her necklace faded once more. "Well, I guess we head that way then." She pointed back to where it had flared brightest.

"I agree. We will take it step by step with our new book detector." He smiled at her and gestured she lead the way.

Luckily, there didn't seem to be any humans this deep into the forest as it took Kaeleigh a few tries and constant checking of her necklace before she learned she could feel when the light faded and when it surged in the right direction. "I bet if someone was watching from above, my staggering all over the place would be quite comical." She laughed even as Daegan took her hand and squeezed.

"You are doing magnificent and yes, luckily for you no one is watching." Daegan winked at her when she turned to him shocked he agreed. He shrugged. "You said it yourself."

"I did, it is true." Kaeleigh suddenly paused, stopping Daegan with her. Looking around, she caught his hand when he was about to say something but quieted him with the look on her face. Pointing to her ear, she asked him to listen, indicating she heard something.

"Yes, we are being followed. Have been for a little bit now, but they are keeping their distance though I cannot say why."

"You knew and didn't tell me?"

"We seemed safe enough for the moment, and you were occupied trying to understand something we need to know in order to find the book," he whispered in reply.

"Shouldn't we be concerned they will jump us when we are not paying attention?"

He nodded. "That is why I was paying attention."

"What if they are waiting until we find what we are looking for?" Her eyes flew wide. "That's it, they must be waiting for the right time once we find it. Can they hear us do you think?"

He shrugged. "I am not certain. There is something familiar about their presence though I can not be sure."

Kaeleigh's necklace began pulsing in frequent spurts, blinking as if making an announcement. "We're close to something." Turning in a wide circle, Kaeleigh stretched out her senses, Daegan did as well though he held his position.

"Do you feel it? It's strong."

"I do. I also feel something else, raw and dangerous, different from our pursuer."

Alarm fixed on her face she spun to face him. "What is it?"

"I am not sure. I have not encountered it before, but I do not like it. We must hurry."

"Search this area with me, we don't have much time," Kaeleigh instructed, heading in a circle around the area they stood. Surrounded by trees, both monstrous and young new-to-life trees accompanied by large ferns, Kaeleigh stepped around them. She dodged other ground covering, various greenery, and fallen giants no longer among the legends, their time spent among the living as they now fed the forest floor.

"Kaeleigh stop."

Stopping in her tracks, she turned to Daegan her eyebrow raised in question.

"Your necklace."

It pulsed fast and strong. Kaeleigh's eyes were frantic with the urgency of the moment, searching what was closest to her but finding nothing more than a very large sequoia tree; its base as wide as a car—if not wider. The root system emerged from the ground, large obstacles creating crevices and hollows all the way around it and up into sections of the tree. Kaeleigh gasped.

"This is it," she whispered. "My necklace is hot and solid purple. I was so distracted by all the energy surrounding it, I almost missed it." She looked to Daegan with wide eyes. "It's the tree, or under the tree, or in it? I'm not sure, but it is definitely the tree."

Daegan walked the circumference of the mammoth tree back to Kaeleigh. "I see nothing or sense anything outside of it, but the energy of the tree is very strong, powerful, and quite old, even older than methods the mortals have to date them. You have spoken with the trees before, try with this one, perhaps it is one of the Dryads or one of the Ancients—the trees brought either from the old realm of Lenoria or ones positioned since the beginning."

Kaeleigh nodded and stepped up to the tree then shot a glance back at Daegan. "Should we do this with the other one trailing us?"

"I will keep a watch, but we are running out of time so we will take the risk." Striding forward he leaned into her and whispered into her ear then kissed her on the cheek.

Kaeleigh nodded very slightly then quickly turned back to the tree slowly inhaling to steady her nerves.

"Okay. Here goes... everything." Kaeleigh pushed her magic out just enough to touch the tree and sense its energy, its life force. The tree was strong just as Daegan had said, just as strong as the trees she had encountered in Alandria. Placing the palms of her hands upon the smooth bark of the tree, she gently knocked with her magic.

Hello. If you can understand me, my name is Kaeleighnna and I am of the Orchids and of Alandria, feel my energy, feel my intention. I wish you no harm. Kaeleigh spoke through her mind, but knew if she spoke out loud she would once again speak in the language of the Dryads though she had never learned it.

I can understand you clear, young one. I know what you seek. I have been waiting for you. The Dark Elf knew of you, told me you would come, the tree replied.

"The tree understands me," she whispered to Daegan, feeling his presence close by her.

Are you of the Dryads?

In a sense. I am a NaNai, one of the Ancients from another world, transplanted here long ago.

You mentioned a dark Elf, I know not of him.

He said you would come for what I protect, that I should give it to you when you came.

You protect the Book of Lenoria? How do I retrieve it?

No, not a book, but a parchment. Your Ferrishyn will guard you, but to retrieve what I hold, I bid you to enter. You already hold the key.

I do?

The ornament you hold around your neck, it will allow you entrance.

Kaeleigh received a mental image of her walking into the trunk of the tree. Hesitantly, she took a step back and motioned for Daegan to come closer. "I have to enter the tree. It's inside. I will be safe, but you must protect the tree, it will be vulnerable when it opens to me."

Daegan turned her head toward him to see her eyes. He peered inside and nodded. "You will be safe. I am here. Get what we came for."

"I'm not sure it's exactly what we came for but she said it was left here for me by a dark Elf, do you know who that is?"

Daegan stiffened and frowned. "There is one known to have left Alandria long ago who was referred to by that title, one dangerous and self-serving, but one who could see into the future. I do not know how he would come to possess the book or provide any help to our cause, but perhaps I am wrong. Our time grows short here. Come out quickly, you will be safe enough unless the Dark Elf is inside the tree waiting for you, but I imagine he could not survive in there for very long. The air we need to breathe is too concentrated within the trunk so move swiftly."

"Well, that's reassuring," Kaeleigh mumbled under her breath. Daegan chuckled but took up guard. "Here I go."

Stepping back to the tree, Kaeleigh placed herself between root junctures, within a person-sized hollow. She wasn't sure exactly how to do it so she went with her gut and placed her necklace against the base of the tree while placing her free hand flat against the bark. As soon as her necklace connected with the tree, her magic involuntarily mixed with the energies of the tree, purple and green a twined mixture. Gasping, her hand went through the tree and she practically fell inside it, disappearing from Daegan's sight.

Welcome, young one. What you seek lies in the middle.

Kaeleigh caught her breath while looking around. Dimmed but lit by the trees inner life force, a green glow permeating the darkness. Fighting back a wave of claustrophobic panic, Kaeleigh noted the inside seemed much larger than she had thought it might. Settling the fluttering of her stomach, she examined the inside of the tree—how many people could say they have done that? Within the interior, a small room with smooth light tan, interior walls of bark stood before her. In the center a short stump and a blank piece of parchment sat. Kaeleigh moved forward to examine it but nothing was written on it. But when she picked it up, a soft glow illuminated then suddenly the parchment was no longer blank but filled with elegant scrolling handwriting, her name at the top.

Kaeleighnna,

I know what you seek, but it is not here. It was too dangerous to leave it here at the time so I moved it. I cannot speak of it but to you alone. This is a map to find me and ultimately the book. Proof from the book is included in case you or those with you are skeptical. Only you can read it, it is enchanted to your energy given to me by the one you called Hunter. His loss was a great wound as will many more be to Alandria. I bid you haste in finding me. Everything depends on it and I have done way too much to ensure its safety for it to be lost now.

Santori, the one they call the Dark Elf

"Well, isn't that convenient," Kaeleigh grumbled. "The search continues." She sighed and examined the letter along with the scrap piece attached to it. The parchment from the scrap was much older, and clearly held an enormous amount of magic. She had no doubt it came from the book itself. The only thing she could make out on the scrap from the book was a depiction of an orchid faded with time, but when she touched it, its ink grew darker and was the exact shape as the necklace she wore. "Well that seals it. We go to find the Dark Elf."

There is trouble outside, young one. You will not make it out of the forest alive.

"What? Who is out there?" she spoke out loud.

Dark creatures, known to many in this world as the Creepers—earth faeries gone evil from greed, they are neither alive nor dead bound as shadows of the night.

"It was daylight when I entered." Her face a mask of confusion while a sense of fear crept up her spine.

Time is different within an Ancient. Much time has passed. Darkness has fallen.

"Daegan," Kaeleigh breathed with worry. "I have to get to him. May he enter so we can leave from this place?"

It is my honor to serve Alandria and those who protect her, but you will not be able to leave from inside. It is doubtful you can even leave the forest from here. I will provide sanctuary to you and yours if you need to wait until the light comes again.

"Thank you and thank you for keeping this safe for me." Kaeleigh held up the letter. "If I do not return, I will always remember you. Be well."

As should you. Free Alandria, free all who reside in and are from.

Kaeleigh hurried to where she had entered the tree and tucked her letter into her backpack. She inhaled deeply, concentrated on what she had to do next if it was even possible, and blew the breath out with determined focus. Placing her necklace against the bark of the tree, she used her magic to open it. Stepping one foot out, pulling most of her body out with her hands, she spotted Daegan. The tree was correct, night had started to fall. Her stomach dropped at the thought of leaving him out there so long on his own. His back was to her, guarding the tree and her from what lie at the edge of the tree line. To anyone else, the creatures appeared as shadows moving in response to the trees and the wind, but to what her eyes revealed to her they were humanoid shaped shadows with evil intent. Kaeleigh had no idea how they would kill, but she definitely didn't want to find out. Daegan stood poised with his sword out, ready to fight though the shadows stayed hidden in the darkness of the trees until the last light had faded. Just as it did, they moved slowly forward. Not on Kaeleigh's watch.

Reaching forward, stepping out all the way, she grabbed Daegan's cloak from behind and tugged him toward her. "Come now!" she whispered so low only he could hear it. He didn't turn but allowed her to pull him towards her; Kaeleigh tugged hard, pulling him against her chest, closed her eyes tight and visualized where she wanted to go. Just as the first shadow had almost reached him, they vanished—teleported out of the forest.

Chapter Thirty-Five

Momentum caught up with them. Daegan fell back against Kaeleigh, taking her to the ground with him on top and expelling all the air from her lungs in a loud whoosh. He rolled off her quickly, jumping up with his sword extended in one fluid motion, but no foe was present. In fact, it was dark and very quiet wherever they had traveled to. His chest heaved and his breath came quick. "That was good timing. I have heard of those creatures but had never encountered any."

"They were waiting for nightfall apparently." Kaeleigh's chest heaved as well as she caught her breath. Daegan offered her his hand and assisted in pulling her up. As she stood, she straightened her shirt. "I'm sorry, Daegan I had no idea time worked differently inside the tree—never thought those words would come out of my mouth." Slightly dazed Kaeleigh took in Daegan to ensure he hadn't been fighting before she got out.

"I was not aware of that bit either, but no damage was done. You came out right at the precise time you were needed."

Daegan sucked in a breath as his guard dropped and realized where they were. "You did this on your own. You transported us across a long distance... out of the forest with wards against the very magic. Your power is growing again, Kaeleigh. Well done," he praised her as he strode through her little apartment she had left in Missoula, Montana checking to ensure they were safe for the time being.

"I did. I did it!" Kaeleigh beamed. "I didn't even think about it, I just knew we had to get out of there and this was the only place I could think of fast enough that I could visualize." Kaeleigh ran into her old bedroom and through herself onto her bed, just the way she had left it, made though slightly messy with purple pillows tossed haphazardly across the top.

"How much time has passed, Daegan? Since we originally left, I mean. Everything seems and feels the same. I thought for sure they might have tossed out all my things and rented my place out to someone else. Though I bet Chel's parents made sure that didn't happen while we were gone. I wonder what they know of all this," she pondered more to herself.

"Not much at all, time having passed that is. I would wager approximately a week has passed. It is hard to say. Time functions differently in Alandria than here and it isn't always an exact exchange," he replied from the kitchen.

"Yeah?" Kaeleigh jumped up and looked out the window at the trees in front of her window. Still the same fall colors though more of the leaves had fallen since the last time she saw it. "Whoa, that's kinda crazy." Moving away from the window she walked through her apartment herself and let herself feel nostalgic for the way her life used to be. Kaeleigh found Daegan sitting in the center of the larger couch, remembering he had sat there once before though it felt like lifetimes ago. She sighed. "It all feels different."

"What do you mean?"

"It feels like my place and all my stuff, but it doesn't feel like home, like I belong anymore. I guess it makes me a little sad."

Daegan's eyebrows pinched, creating that pesky crease down the center of his forehead she wanted to smooth out before it became permanent. "Why do you feel sad?"

"I loved living here, but it feels like it is time to say goodbye." She shrugged and instead of sitting on the small couch, Kaeleigh tucked her legs under her and flopped right next to him on the big one. "It's not a bad thing, it's just change and another transition. I should probably come back when all this is over and take care of all this and give up the apartment."

"You do not have to, Kaeleigh. You could keep it and visit if you wish," Daegan explained.

"That sounds nice, but not necessary. My life is in Alandria now... with you... and Chel—assuming she stays as well," Kaeleigh amended quickly with a slight frown, "and Hal and Finn and all those I have met and grown fond of." Wringing her hands, she suddenly felt nervous about her declaration to share her life with him in Alandria though it felt natural, still, she didn't want to assume anything.

Daegan cupped her cheek in the palm of his large hand. Kaeleigh practically melted into him. "Yes, with me, Kaeleigh. Always with me." He leaned in and kissed the tip of her nose.

Kaeleigh smiled and nuzzled into him slightly before she realized they were not there for a visit. "Oh! I have to show you what the tree had, but I'll warn you it's not the book," abruptly she changed the subject, jumped up and grabbed her backpack she had thrown onto the floor upon their crash landing. Kaeleigh gently pulled out the parchment from her bag and brought it over to him.

Daegan carefully examined the parchment she handed him, but frowned. "I do not see anything on it except for this older piece attached with what I think is an orchid on it."

"You don't? I guess it was just for me." Kaeleigh sat close to him again and her eyes lit with anticipation. "Let's try something. When I first saw it I didn't see anything either, but when I touched it the letter appeared." Kaeleigh reached back for the letter and sure enough the letters all became visible. She turned the letter and showed it to Daegan without him touching it.

"Fascinating." Reading it though, his brows began to furrow instead of raise in fascination. "The Dark Elf, indeed."

"What do you make of it? It's real isn't it?"

"I believe it is, yes. I can feel the power coming off the small scrap of paper supposedly from the book itself. The only thing to do is to follow the map and find the Dark Elf if he is indeed waiting somewhere for you." Daegan got up and paced in front of the slider door, in thought. "Yes, that is I believe our next step."

"I am not certain I understand this map though, it is not like any map I have seen." Kaeleigh twisted the map around, attempting to find a beginning point to it. "There are squiggly symbols and a circle with a smaller circle inside it almost like a bulls-eye."

"I noticed that. It appears to be some kind of cipher though it does not make sense to me. Perhaps it is keyed to you like the letter was."

Frowning and biting her lip, Kaeleigh stared at it hard as if something new might leap off the page at her. Huffing out her frustration, she put the paper on the coffee table, rose and went to the kitchen for water.

Not but a moment later she stormed back into the room carrying a glass of water for Daegan which she handed to him, but then strode quickly to the piece of paper.

"Ouch!"

"Kaeleigh what happened?" Daegan moved over to where she was.

"Oh nothing, the paper just bit me," she sucked her finger into her mouth.

Daegan cocked his head curiously and watched her closely. "I do not understand."

"It just means I got a paper cut, I picked up the paper funny and sliced my finger on the edge of it. It's fine though." Looking at her finger she squeezed it to see if it was done bleeding, but a drop bubbled to the surface. "I had an idea I wanted to try using magic on the paper."

But before she could, she touched the paper with her healing finger absentmindedly then gasped. "Daegan, look! When I touched the paper, the map... the real map leaped off the page at me, I can see it!"

He reached for the page, but then halted mid-reach to look over her shoulder and survey the map from there. He noticed where her finger had smeared a trace of blood right in the center of the circles. "It was your blood, Kaeleigh. Your blood released the map."

"Well, could it be any more cryptic? How was I supposed to figure that out if not by accident and my own clumsiness?" Kaeleigh shook her head. "Still, that's pretty cool, isn't it?"

"Yes, very *cool*," he smiled at her and even chuckled.

"So I still don't know where this is though." Tipping it at different angles, she studied the three dimensional map and the topography illuminated before her. "I know. Daegan in that top drawer of that little table by the entry I think I have an old atlas that should help us. Can you get it for us? I'm afraid if I let it go, I'll lose it."

Finding the book of maps, Daegan flipped through it searching for anything similar to what he was seeing.

"Check the midwest, it's pretty flat with not many hills from what I can tell," Kaeleigh guessed.

"Does this look right?" Daegan asked, holding up the map for her.

"Yes! It doesn't look entirely the same, but I can *feel* it if that makes sense. That's the right place, you found it!"

Kaeleigh collapsed the map by removing her hand and placing the magical parchment on the table once more. "I can't hold it up anymore," she breathed and let her arms flop as if she had been holding something heavy.

Daegan stiffened suddenly. "I can feel her... the one who has been following us," he explained at Kaeleigh's confusion.

"It's a her? How can you tell?"

"The energy feels feminine. There is a difference between male and female energy. You can tell the difference if you know to look for it."

"That makes sense." She nodded in thought. "Where is she?"

"Not too close, but close enough I can feel her when I tune into her energy. I wondered at first, if she had loosed those shadow creatures on us hoping they would eliminate us, or at least get us out of the way so she could step in and retrieve the book." He smiled with pride. "I bet she was not counting on you getting us out of there so quickly."

"That's right, take that!" Kaeleigh did a karate chop through the air. "I'm rocking the magic traveling now!"

Daegan's mouth dropped.

"Oh close that mouth," Kaeleigh laughed. "You'd better get used to it because I have some mad skills in the art of interpretive kung fu." She winked at him then grabbed her backpack and the letter, putting it in. Running into the kitchen she grabbed some water bottles then sprinted down the short hall. "I have to use the little girl's room, be right back!"

Kaeleigh came back into the living room to find Daegan staring out the back slider once more. She placed her hand on his back and whispered, "I'm ready when you are. No time like the present right?"

"She would not yet know it was the map we received and not the book, right?"

"I would think that, yes. What are you thinking?"

"I think it might be time to turn the tables and see who tracks us. Are you ready to play a game with me, Kaeleigh?"

"Oh, most definitely, my Ferrishyn warrior," Kaeleigh said slyly, rubbing her hands together conspiratorially. Holding on tight to him, she allowed him to teleport her out of her apartment—not even feeling the need to say goodbye. She would be back once to close this chapter on her life and then not again. Her heart and her home were now elsewhere.

Chapter Thirty-Six

Aidón took his time climbing the narrow, winding iron staircase. Though rickety at some steps, it was a silent climb up the narrow, dark channel—fortunately the next level was not far to ascend. Only a handful of Elves and possibly others knew of the hidden room, though many speculated the king would indeed have a secret room all to himself for his own seclusion, no one knew the full truth.

Upon reaching the top step, he moved onto a wooden plank floor covered in colorful rugs magically withstanding the test of time. Never did dust or dead critters accumulate in the secret room—he had often wondered about that, but assumed it was part of the original magic used to set up the room. Lanterns and candles burst into flame, light blazed at first then calmed to adjust for the atmosphere of the room, welcoming him to one of his favorite spaces. The ceiling height was magically taller than what a room in that location of the castle should have been.

Aidón sighed, allowing himself to relax. For the first time in many years, he was sitting in safety. He took a few minutes to revive himself, taking in all the room offered. He looked around and looked from map to map, and all he had left pinned on the walls. He had even detailed shifts of the staff in order to remember when everyone worked and where. Books and scrolls littered the shelves and the floor all around the room. One wide and tall shelf placed at the end of the room held more ancient tomes and scrolls—those he knew to be from special, private stock originally pulled through from Lenoria, and also the beginning documentation of Alandria, every race and all there was to know about each one. Many would kill for even the knowledge they still existed in

Alandria. For there was once a time when the other rulers had entrusted them to the King of Adettlyn for safe keeping all in one place. Many still knew some remained at Adettlyn, but knew not where they were kept. Aidón's fingers slid along the spines of several of them as he thought of the inhabitants of Alandria and his desire to see them united once again.

Aidón turned around, taking in more of the space around him but stopped. Certainly an ordinary eye wouldn't have noticed, but Aidón had a perfect memory of the secret room. One or two stacks of writings and documents had been disturbed, as if someone had thumbed through them, and other stacks were new. But who? Chills raced down his spine.

"Who else knows of this place?" Aidón asked quietly to himself. He moved in closer to examine the documents, noting they were of various locations of portals and the rituals needed to enact them. Frowning, Aidón touched them, moving them about gently so not to disturb their contents too greatly. Whoever was up here, was looking for a portal? To where, the mortal realm? Or somewhere else entirely?

A scuffing of a shoe on the wood floor at the opposite end where he stood, caught his attention. Aidón froze. Looking quickly for a place to hide, he squeezed himself between the bookshelf and the wall hoping to blend in with the shadows in that corner of the room. A short, portly shape of a woman materialized from not the stairs where he ascended but from what appeared to be another secret doorway he was not even aware of—how could he not know of another entryway? Yet he could not make out who it was.

The woman moved her arm swiftly near the walls. As she stepped into the light, her movement was recognized to be dusting as she held a stick full of feathers tied off at the end. Aidón held his breath, his eyes wide in surprise as he surmised it was the same woman he met in the hallway downstairs who he carried linens for. She looked at each of the lit holders and scowled; for the fist time noting the lights were already lit. Stopping her dusting, she peered into the room and squinted when she came close to where he hid, but passed right over him and continued her perusal of the rest of the room. Content that nothing seemed amiss she continued dusting, even turning her back to where Aidón stood, awaiting his discovery.

"You really should find better hiding places," she spoke without turning towards him.

Aidón gasped in shock but quickly went from surprise to confusion. "You saw me. Why are you not concerned I am here and who are you that you have access to this room?" He slipped out from his hiding spot and remained where he was not approaching the woman for fear of frightening her.

"Your brother gave me access many years ago—apparently he did not make you aware of it, however. He could be quite forgetful at times," she finished with a sad smile.

"You know who I am?" Aidón asked more shocked than anything else. "Did you know in the hallway?"

"I do. You are the rightful king of this castle, Aidón Sayaelíth. Yes, I did as soon as I saw the vines in the hall respond to you the way they did, coming back to life, recognizing you when no one else did." Her eyes were downcast, suddenly saddened.

"You do not recognize me, though?" she asked.

Aidón about to say no, halted his words and used his magic to look at her, really look at her as she apparently did him. He bit back a gasp.

"Atíllya? Sister, is it really you?" His eyes welled with unshed tears.

She nodded, appreciative he remembered her. "You have been gone so long. Ryek is no longer amidst Alandria," she added sadly in case he was not aware, "and I had heard rumors of allies forming in Tylínyth and sought to join them." Gesturing towards the documents on the table they explained why she searched for the portals out of Alandria. She was trying to find her way to the Twined.

"I thought you were also dead, but my heart said you were still alive. So I held out hope you would return," she admitted. "I have glamoured myself to remain at the castle."

"Maleina held me in her dungeons for all these long past years," he explained, "and now she comes to dine in my castle with my traitorous son." His fist clenched at his sides and his teeth grit tightly. "Does she come often?"

"Yes, I am afraid so. So many bad things have happened, Aidón." She inclined her head respectively, "Excuse me. King Aidón. I beg your pardon."

"Formalities are not necessary, Atíllya." He smiled. "I am glad to have someone in confidence here. I have met many new friends and have only a short time here. I cannot wait for you to meet Kaeleigh and Daegan and the rest of them," he rushed out excitedly.

She bristled at hearing the names. "Who are these to you, sir? And I have heard the name Daegan in this castle before."

"Yes, I believe he has been here before. I have much to tell you and catch you up. Are there more? More of you looking for alliances?"

She nodded with a great smile. "Yes. I have been quietly assembling a network of those who are sick of the current ways in Alandria and want to see her restored to her former glory. They want to fight, they are ready to fight, Aidón."

Aidón beamed at her. "Well done!" He moved closer, drawn in by the spark in her eyes. Anticipation struck deep in his gut. Perhaps his mission would not be as difficult as he had originally thought. His sister had done most of the legwork for him. "How many?" he asked.

"A great deal of the valley, and the surrounding towns and villages have a large number. The underlying feel from most was hope that change was coming. The people got wind of the prophecy coming to life and they have decided now is the time to rise up. Before they were complacent with the ways, living in denial Alandria was indeed in trouble of the darkness overwhelming them. But now," her eyes brightened and her smile grew, "now, they are alive with a passion for freedom of their people and for the land herself."

"How do you communicate? How does the network run?" Aidón asked excitedly.

"We use symbols posted in plain site in the markets, we use secret messages using the birds, and we have leaders for each area of the villages to organize those within their area since we cannot all meet at once. It can be challenging but it has worked so far just to get them assembled." Her eyes flew to her shoes then at the side wall before she looked back at Aidón. "I hope I did not overstep my bounds, but no one was here to take leadership that knew any of the old ways."

He moved to her and lifted her chin with his fingers, bringing her eyes in alignment with his. "You did perfect. Alandria will thank you. I thank you. You have done a great deed. And it saves me so much time trying to assemble them myself." Aidón smiled affectionately, then dropped his hand and retreated back to the table. "I still have some contacts here I was planning to contact in case they are not already a part of your network and to let them know I have returned." He looked around the room. "Actually, that is why I was up here. I need to find the keyhole," he said unconcerned whether or not she knew the secret since she was aware of more of the secret room than even he.

"Was I one of them?" she asked quietly.

"I included your name in the message centuries ago. I only did not know if you still lived. After the uprising, Ryek went into hiding as Hunter and at his instruction you did as well. I lost track of you," Aidón admitted. "I was not as proficient in the ancient magic as Ryek once was." He paused and refocused his purpose. "Once I send the message it would work like a message sent telepathically from me to everyone included. As it reached the receiver it would then ping back to me and let me know who received it. If any treachery slipped in since I had left within any of those individuals, the magic of the message would decipher if the being was a hospitable mind to receive the message and relay back to me with a warning if not. It sounds complex, but is indeed quite simple," he explained as he began to move about the room for the symbol he needed to locate the keyhole.

"Check the drawer within the cupboard of the bookshelf... the one on the bottom right," she instructed, pointing with her finger.

Aidón searched her face. "Most helpful, indeed."

"I found it once when I was looking for more information on the portals. I wanted to get into the Twined realm, I thought they could add to our numbers, they are from here whether they know it or want it. They can fight for Alandria," she added with a shrug and a sigh of frustration.

"You are absolutely right, but we have two emissaries who have been with them from the beginning and are continuing to train them to fight and use their magic. It is their hope they join us in the fight." Aidón looked out the window, thinking of Finnlan, Ella, Kaeleigh, and Daegan on their own journeys and hoped they were finding success and having safe passage. He would not hear from them again until it was time to meet for the final battle with darkness. Chills ran the gauntlet of his spine. It was possible his new friends would not make it through this alive; the thought saddened his heart for Alandria needed them.

"Aha!" Aidón exclaimed finding what he sought. Fumbling in his cloak pocket, he pulled out the key he had retrieved in the library earlier. The aged skeletal key glinted in the candle-light.

Atíllya moved in closer, her eyes curious with interest, to watch. "Is it all right if I watch?"

"You may," Aidón inclined his head in permission. He placed the key in the keyhole perfectly. With intense anticipation, he paused and sighed, the heaviness weighed upon him for what they were attempting to do. Releasing his breath, he steadied his shoulders and turned the key.

A green glowing light seeped from the keyhole accompanied with a subtle hum saturating the air. "It is I, Aidón Sayaelíth, appointed king of Adettlyn in King Ryek's absence. I have escaped my prison and have returned to free Adettlyn of its oppressor. Be with me or against me, but the time to fight is coming. Be prepared, look for the coming sign. With me reply 'aye', against me reply 'nay' and let your intentions be known." Aidón finished his speech, closed his eyes, and funneled some of his magic into the keyhole to send his message through to the pre-named channels.

Releasing the key, he backed up and sat on the chair his sister had pulled out for him, and he waited.

Hearing a gasp come from Atíllya not far from him, his head swiveled in her direction. Eyes narrowed, he watched as she closed her eyes and heard his message in her mind.

"*Aye,*" she responded in her mind, but it went straight to Aidón's mind like a small prick in his temple.

Aidón held his head suddenly hit with multiple responses at the same time, almost unanimous except for two "nays" which he recognized right away and stripped them from future messages. He acknowledged many he knew were in positions of leadership serving under or with Maleina but would bide their time until they could escape or provide a coup to rise against her in their arena. The two that had turned against him, he saw in her castle at Elnye once when he was being dragged around.

"Jethín of L'nalrinia has turned against us as well as Lonnât from the Mandü tre lan; they are both now in the service of darkness," Aidón said solemnly. "They will be missed."

"They now know you have returned," Atíllya spoke up nervously, "what if they inform Maleina?"

"She by now knows, I have escaped with her other prisoners. She may even be coming here to seek me out," he informed her. "Their lips will be sealed by the magic of the message, but it is not a stop all. If they deem to inform on me, then they shall." His eyes sought hers, suddenly saddened. "Which is why I will need to flee here and find a temporary hiding place until the time for battle. Is there any you trust in your network who would house me away from the castle?"

"Yes, I know just the place for you outside the city, in the small village of Anise; they will conceal you." She nodded her head as if the deed was already done. "I will be in contact with them." Breathing in through her nose, she bit her cheek. "I have to go before I am missed below. You must stay up here for the night. You will be safe, Syén is not aware of this room."

"That is a marvelous idea. How in fact, did you get here without going through the entrance in his room?" Aidón asked slyly, his eyes twinkled with curiosity.

"Through the passageway in the rafters," she replied matter of fact, confused he was not aware of it.

"I was not aware of that entrance," Aidón said suspiciously. "I wonder how it came about Ryek did not tell me."

"Perhaps because you had the bedroom. He explained I had a way to enter without approaching through your private suite," she added graciously with a hint of a blush.

"Right." Aidón nodded, moving right by the awkward moment.

"I will leave your presence and get into contact with my leader for the network, informing him of your presence so they know to look for you." She moved toward her exit and stopped, "Aidón do not leave this place until I come for you in the morning. Your safety depends upon it, promise me."

"I vow it," he said simply and inclined his head in a subtle bow.

She left the room and he sighed, a new weight suddenly sitting on his shoulders in the quiet and lonely place. "Well, I guess I shall get comfortable for the evening." He pulled blankets out of a trunk and immersed himself in scrolls and tomes he wanted to study.

Chapter Thirty-Seven

Aidón awoke just before dawn, a feeling of unease plaguing his mind. The birds chirped a lovely song welcoming the new day out the window in the nearby trees. He could feel the sun rising, hope on the horizon. But still he could not shake the feeling of impending doom weighing heavily upon him. Standing before the lone window, spelled to not be seen from the outside, he surveyed the lands before him, the lands that would once more be his when the time came—however, he felt connected to them even now since he was still king-in-fact and not deceased as many believed.

A knock at the door to the passageway alerted him to Atíllya's presence.

She slowly entered. "Are you awake my king?" she whispered.

"I am, Atíllya, please enter," Aidón said with a smile, her address of him giving him a spark of sunshine within his soul amidst the dreary morning.

Holding a tray out in front of her, he noticed two glasses. "Mmm, I smell something delicious," he murmured.

"I brought breakfast with some water and a coffee, I hope it is welcomed," she asked as she moved aside papers on the table and made a space for the tray.

"It is most welcomed, thank you," Aidón acknowledged and smiled. He sat down and began to eat. "Please tell me the goings on of the castle this morning. I have the most unpleasant feeling stirring in my gut."

Bending over to pick up the blankets off the floor and replace them in the trunks, she then placed the books back on their shelves, picking up after him.

"I think you have been playing the housekeeper too long," Aidón chuckled.

She blushed and went to the table and sat across from him. "Perhaps." She sighed then continued on. "The staff has been up early, preparing the food for the day. As you know Maleina will be arriving later today at some point, we are never sure when exactly. Mayhap that is what you are feeling?" she inquired.

"Yes, perhaps it is. I did not remember she was arriving," Aidón admitted.

"I also came to inform you Syén was headed to the throne room alone this morning. He does not usually move about the castle this early unless he has a meeting with Maleina. She has this way of contacting him through mirrors, there is one set aside in the observatory."

Aidón finished up his last few bites. "Can you get me through the castle using the catwalks in the rafters and any secret passageway you have discovered? I need to be unseen. I want to see how she does it." He stood up fully anticipating she would be able to guide him there.

"Yes, follow me. You have to watch your steps in some places as the rafters are not much more than beams. And be quiet as some places are thinner than others." She led him to the exit she used previously, and he followed her through the dark tunnels.

Coming down from the rafters, Atíllya led Aidón down a narrow spiral staircase behind the walls of the throne room. He had no idea so many passageways had been built into the castle. Aidón made note to fully explore them when he was in control of the castle once more, the very thought revived a spirit of enthusiasm he often felt as a youth. Oddly, it was not near as dark as he had first thought it would be within the walls. Some kind of a luminescent strip had been placed along several places on the ground to guide those who frequented the passageways to get around—mostly staff needing to get from one room quickly to the next.

Atíllya pointed to a place on the wall and mouthed "throne room." Aidón nodded and leaned his ear up against it, but all he heard were muffled sounds of two voices, one a man and the other a woman—Maleina.

"How can I get in there enough to hear?" Aidón whispered so quietly he was practically in her ear for her to hear him.

His sister beckoned him to follow her a little further and led him to a hole carved out of the throne room wall, but it was covered with a thick tapestry. How had he missed seeing this during all the time he had spent in that room? His brows pinched and he leaned his head close to the tapestry without touching it. He could hear much more clearly.

Their words seemed pretty general as she made plans for their arrival later that day. Aidón was in awe, he had never had the opportunity to see or use a talking glass to speak over distances. If the magic was safe, he would look into learning it for all the territories. It would make communicating so much easier over distances. Maleina had asked of their plans, but did not say more in detail. Aidón would assume it had been in the works for some time, but he needed to know what they had in store.

Her voice grew louder, and Aidón poked the tapestry out a fraction to see if he could see where they were. Syén was in the observatory, a partial level above the throne room where the ceiling was all glass and allowed them to have full sunlight and then again full moonlight during certain times of the days. Strong magic was practiced and enacted in the observatory. The room also held the most light in one concentrated place in the whole of the castle—a perfect place for working, and watching magic take place.

"You may not yet be aware, Syén, but my men lost several prisoners I had been holding. I have regained one of them in the hopes of another to soon follow," she sneered and cackled through the glass.

Aidón stiffened. Who could she be talking about? Kaeleigh or Finn? No they had gone different directions. Perhaps Chel or perhaps she bluffed.

"I believe one has reason to head your direction," she intoned, her voice smooth and seductive. "Keep your eye out for one who does not belong in your area, would you please do that for me?"

"Of course, my lady, but certainly there is none who could thwart your plans at this stage?" Syén added naively.

"Of course not, pet." She adjusted her cloak in the mirror and tossed a lone red hair away from her face. "I merely wanted to warn you to be on the lookout. I would like him returned to me or if not possible... killed on site."

Aidón was sure she was speaking of him and wished he could chuckle out loud, rubbing it in her face.

"We shall meet soon, love," Maleina signed off.

A growl erupted in his chest. He had no love for his son at this stage, but Maleina was using him and going against her own husband, Wren, whether in action or implication. He had tolerated her too long. They each signed off from the mirror conversation. Now was his chance. He attempted to step out from behind the tapestry, but Atíllya tugged on his arm, her eyes wide with fear. Shaking her head, she mouthed, "Do not go out there. He will kill you."

"He can try," Aidón mouthed back. He was determined. His son would not kill him while on his own; he had always feared his father's power—that was why he had someone else do the dirty work of trying to murder him once before though Syén stood by and watched.

She let go and ducked behind the wall so not to be seen. Aidón snuck out of the tapestry, sneaking up behind Syén when his back was to him so he would have no idea where he entered from. Once in place directly behind him he made his presence known.

"She will kill you, you know?" Aidón said matter of fact as an opener. He stared at his son's back wondering where they went wrong as parents or what happened that made his son turn from their ways.

Syén stiffened. Slowly he turned around, his eyes narrowed cautiously in disbelief. Cocking his head in confusion, he squinted attempting to recognize the man in front of him, but to no avail.

"I know your voice," he said cautiously as he tilted his head the other direction, seeking the man who belonged to the familiar voice. "I know not your face. Who are you?" he asked.

"Do you not see?" Aidón taunted, knowing his son was inept when it came to seeing through glamour.

Syén searched the man once more as he spun fully around to face the man in his throne room.

Aidón dropped his glamour, altering his appearance to his original one, the one his son would recognize. Syén's eyes widened, and he stumbled back a step.

"You are dead!" he spat nervously.

"No, in fact, I am not," Aidón replied his arms spread wide.

"I saw you and... I saw you die," he whispered back, his voice thick. At least he felt some remorse about what he had done to his mother.

"Guards!" Syén shouted but his words were lost in the air as Aidón flicked his hand encasing them in a dome of silence.

"What you saw, and what resulted after you left, were not the same thing. I am very much alive," Aidón continued, intent on having this conversation; possibly the only time he would ever again. "Your mistress was speaking of me among others. Did you know she held me prisoner for many years? She kept that knowledge from you, to what purpose I am uncertain, not that you would have concerned yourself with me, but I am sure it would have been to her advantage." Aidón let his words and appearance sink into Syén. Aidón could not help but relish in the satisfaction at rattling his son in such a manner; he had timed it perfectly. And yet after seeing his son, pity swelled in his chest at who his son had become, irresponsible and spineless.

"Yes, I am sure there was thought behind it, but it means nothing to me. To me, you are dead and will be once again," Syén declared as if citing something off about the weather. "What is your purpose here? Why have you come?"

"I thought it might be obvious," Aidón spoke nonchalantly as he moved in a wide arc before his son. "I have come to reclaim my throne and to ask you 'Why?'"

Syén moved forward, slowly and deliberately, unwilling to be caged where he stood. Mirroring Aidón's steps he, too, swept a wide arc from the observation level to the middle of the throne room with Aidón in front of what Syén deemed his throne and the main entrance doors to his right, keeping Aidón always in his sight.

"I think it is obvious you will not take *my* throne." Syén stepped back to where he could securely feel the chair designating the "throne" as if that was all it was against the back of his legs.

"Guards!" he attempted feebly one more time, but no action followed.

Aidón laughed. "Do I frighten you? Are you so daft you think my magic is not strong as it once was?" Aidón continued stepping forward, pushing into Syén's space. Anger rose suddenly in his chest and thundered out of him, "WHY?" His fists clenched at his sides, wishing he could pummel something.

"Why what?" Syén shouted back.

"Why did you kill her—your own mother? Why would you attempt to kill me?" Aidón returned through gritted teeth.

Syén's demeanor changed from charged one moment to uncaring and aloof the next. Aidón had to wonder if it was his original plan or if someone else had influenced his kill order. It mattered not, Syén still had carried it out and Aidón's wife was still dead.

"It was the only way to get access to my throne faster," he said casually with a flick of his hand as if it mattered not.

Aidón well versed in goading attempts, quieted his temper and took several steps to the side closer to the doors. He flicked his wrist once more and the dome of silence fell whether Syén noticed he was unsure. It did not matter. He would end their time together.

"Guards!" Aidón hollered and replaced his glamour with nothing more than a visual cue.

Syén cocked his head and narrowed his eyes in disgust that two of *his* guards came crashing through the throne room doors, throwing both large wooden doors to either side of the wall. Each guard rushed in and took a knee in front of Syén, standing in front of his throne, not even noticing Aidón's presence in the room.

"Your majesty?" one of the guards asked, his head bowed awaiting his king's need.

Aidón backed away, gritting his teeth seething at seeing who used to be h*is* guards on their knees before his son—worthless heir to the throne. Almost to the door, Aidón quickly realized more guards were entering from down the hall. His heart now beat much faster than it had before, he looked around the room for an alternative exit but found none. His only option: to retreat to his secret exit and hope he did not give away its location.

Unfortunately, one of the incoming guards spotted him. "You there, stop!" he shouted.

The other guards on their knees quickly jumped up, spears at the ready, and turned around, adjusting to the new threat and the incoming entourage as well.

"Remember, Syén, she means to kill you," Aidón reminded him though he was not sure why; his son deserved nothing less. However, he did not want Maleina to take his throne either.

"Ah pity," a female's voice tsked from behind several guards. Maleina strode through the doorway, a vision of beauty in a long purple gown with multiple layers of fabric piled one on top of the one beneath it except for the smooth bodice. A traveling cloak settled gracefully around her thin creamy column of a neck, shrouding her shoulders in an even deeper shade of purple. Her hair, the same mess of red curls cascading down her back Aidón had seen their last encounter. Maleina's eyes blazed with fury contrary to the pitiful smile she shared with Syén. "I do hate it when my plans get foiled." She spared a quick glance at the stranger in the room, but did not seem to notice who he was. "But I am afraid to say he is right, darling. I am here to take your throne from you."

Chapter Thirty-Eight

The insolent fool stood there in all regality as if he had earned his throne. Maleina sneered internally. She had set everything he had up for the sniveling little tool. He even believed they had a "relationship" in the wings, awaiting for the perfect time to bloom into a beautiful bud of ultimate power—the fool. Thanks to the stranger who announced her plan to Syén, she got to make the perfect entrance cutting all the initial pleasantries and could get right to the point. Seeing the shock on Syén's face when his fear was confirmed, was worth the wait unto itself. Maleina couldn't help it, she let out a cackle of glee, a release from the tense moment leading up to it. Even though it was *She* who ordered her to remove Syén from the plans, it played straight into her own to ultimately take Adettlyn—she just couldn't let her mistress know it worked to her advantage.

Syén remained where he stood, motionless, confused at the sudden onslaught into his throne room. "We just spoke," he stumbled over his words, looking from Maleina to her men, "how did you arrive so swiftly?"

Maleina laughed, "Oh dear pet, I was providing a distraction to surprise you." She looked at her nails already bored with the conversation. "I do like to make an entrance... you know that." Maleina removed her cloak, handing it to one of her men standing directly next to her. She sauntered slowly over to Syén, large eyes sizing him up from foot to head. Running a long finger, once again tipped in red, along his arm she savored in the way his body stiffened then relaxed at her attention. She leaned in close to him and whispered in his ear, "Your time has come to an end, Syén."

Syén inhaled sharply. "Father!" Syén shouted pathetically in panic, looking around the room not finding Aidón anywhere to be seen.

Maleina narrowed her eyes in confusion as she followed the path of his eyes. Anger surged through her. "He was here," she whispered. "The stranger." Understanding dawned on her at the stranger foiling her plan. Familiarity struck her at his presence, but she did not see through his glamour. She had been tricked.

"Search the castle. Find the man who was in here, now!" she demanded of three of her men, pointing them out the entrance. They left, spinning on their heels out into the hallway.

Back to his current plight, Syén returned her attention to him. "I do not understand. We had a plan... a deal!" his attempt at outrage quickly dissolved as her fingertips dug deeply into his arm.

"The deal changed," she stated matter of fact and removed herself from his arm. Taking steps away from him, she turned full circle admiring the throne room of Adettlyn. Her gaze lit with desire and hunger for the additional power this seat would provide her once she took control.

"Oh, yes, this will do nicely," she pondered to herself, "there is much untapped energy still in Adettlyn." Maleina licked her lips. Striding to the nearest wall, she trailed her fingers over the stones and the vines, fading and wilting to her visible eyes. Closing her eyes she could still feel the thrum of the energy, pulsing and desiring to thrive once more. Smiling, she opened her eyes. "The castle still has life in it... energy that can be harnessed for my purposes."

Maleina pivoted and moved back to face Syén who whispered to his man next to him, his second in command who nodded sharply. Syén spun to face her, his eyes narrowed and his hand at his side, fingers twitching to reach for his sword.

Her smile saddened dramatically. The visual of prey who had no hope to survive but still would try to fight was pathetic. She did not want this to be messier than it had to be. Moving forward step by step, her hips swayed confidently, and she looked directly into his eyes and paused. He did not fight, but returned her gaze and lifted his chin, the first true time he demonstrated his spine to her.

"There you are," she mumbled.

Finally, tragically, when she was about to strike him down, he showed potential to be more than he ever had been. Trailing her nail under his chin, almost affectionately, she gave him a genuine warm smile, leaned in and kissed him quickly and without emotion. Where her nail had trailed, she left a thin line of red in its wake, little beads of life swelled then slid down with the force of gravity against its will. Maleina turned away from Syén, her back to him, her features hardened, and her eyes flat and emotionless.

She turned to her man awaiting her command, tall at attention, watching her every move, willing to do whatever she told him. "Finish this," she directed and walked to the observatory shutting out the near silent sound of the first strike of a sword. Without seeing, she knew the swiftness of her men, Syén would not even have the chance to get his hand around the hilt of his sword, let alone pull it out to defend himself. Examining the light coming through the openings in the ceiling and how it dazzled through and onto the shiny white floors. Her hand flourished through the stream, allowing the light to play upon on her skin. Faeries did not absorb the energy from the sun light like the Elves did, but she could definitely use the energy the castle and others absorbed from the light.

"It is finished, my lady," her soldier interrupted her fascination with the light.

Turning, she saw two of her other warriors dragging Syén's body through the door to dispose of him. According to her earlier orders, they would stake his head out on the wall in front of the castle so all of Adettlyn and those passing through would see he was no longer in power. It was a crude but effective way to quickly change power.

Maleina nodded and returned to the throne, her men cleaning up the spilled blood left behind. Her men were quick and efficient, leaving hardly any mess to speak of. Making her way to the throne, she examined it with a critical eye. It was much smaller than her throne in Elnye, but for now it would do. Swiping her hand across the seat, wiping invisible remnants of Syén away, she turned and sat. Luxuriating in the soft cushion and the velvet fabric that covered it, Maleina ran her hands over the ornate woodwork and craftsmanship along the arms. Her last glance at the door revealed Syén's boots as they turned the corner then out of sight forever. She sighed.

"Now that the unpleasant part of our visit is over, let us take stock of the castle and those in service to it... us," she said, her lip lifting in disdain for the taxing part of overtaking a territory, but someone had to do it.

Syén's second in command came forward, kneeling down on one knee and bowed his head. "I pledge my servitude to you, my lady. I am at your service," he said humbly.

"Rise, gather the staff and see who else desires to keep their positions," she said giving him her first of many commands. He fled the throne room as if her needs were his primary desires.

Maleina sat in the throne admiring the room she now held sway over, awaiting her new subject who will further advance her plan to dominate and rule over Alandria, gaining more power as she did so.

~~~~~

At the edge of the passageway out of the castle through the back entrance he had first secreted through just the day before, Aidón gripped Atíllya's shoulders tightly. "Maleina has taken control of the castle and the kingdom of Adettlyn. You must get word to your network," he said quickly, his heart pounded and his breathing labored and short from the run through the passageways. Aidón had barely escaped the throne room. A perfect moment presented itself when all eyes were on the throne; he could not slip out the door as guards were too close, but he was able to slip into the hidden entryway cloaked in shadows. He had murmured a quick spell to cover the entrance from sight and he rushed with Atíllya as quickly as they could get away.

"I will get word to them," she agreed, nodding her head swiftly.

"You must leave the castle as well. You cannot be found out and used by the evil woman. I could not..." Aidón paused and swallowed thickly. He turned his head and growled in frustration. "I cannot lose you too Atíllya."

She placed her hands on either side of his arms and looked deeply into his eyes. "You will not lose me. Too many people are counting on me getting word to them," she said matter of fact, willing him to accept her decision.

He nodded sharply. "Gather those you need to get out of the castle. Be careful and get your message out. I have to leave now; if I do not she
~~~~~

will surely track me down. I am once more a wanted man," Aidón sighed. "I will alter my glamour and go into hiding. Wait for my signal, I will find you once you are able to get to your people and we will enact our plan."

Their eyes locked and gazed warmly at each other for a moment longer than the time allowed. "I... I am sorry you had the encounter you did with Syén. You deserve better."

Aidón gave a tight nod. "He made his choices. And now I make mine."

"Indeed. I will find you, brother," she assured him. Her palm affectionately rested against his cheek and she turned away suddenly. "Someone comes this way. You must leave now while the guards are busy being instructed of the regime change."

Aidón agreed and fled the rest of the way down the passageway, avoiding tools and buckets haphazardly left in the way. He cautioned one look back to see the edge of her cloak whipping around a corner headed back to a certain part of the castle.

Fleeing the castle was much easier than it should have been, but he took advantage of minor lapse in the guard coverage. Once in the cover of the forest he was able to pause, and catch his breath for only a moment. Aidón gazed back at the castle he had just reunited with and his heart broke, it dimmed further with the absence of his presence and perhaps the admittance of Maleina's. Seeing the front of the castle from the angle he was at, the flags waving the colors of their people, of the Elves, the symbols and pride of Adettlyn had changed. The blacks and reds swirled in a strange pattern resembling a coiled snake sent chills up his spine. His heart pinched at what she was going to do to his people and his home. Alandria was in more danger than ever before.

Hurrying deeper back into the shelter of the forest, he made his way to a clearing further away in order to make his way into Anise. Noting the many Ferrishyn who were now not only joining the guard outside the castle but also now patrolling among the townspeople and the market places outside the castle, he shrunk further into the shadows and readjusted his glamour to that of a much younger man now absorbing the look of a Ferrishyn warrior in order to blend in without hindrance.

With one last look at the castle, his heart shattered and his stomach heaved. There it was. His son's head pierced upon a javelin placed right outside the castle up on the wall front and center for all to see. His son had not been a good man, he had betrayed them in every way, he had hurt the place and the people he loved joining forces with darkness... and yet he was his son, had been a part of him, and now was no more. He took a brief moment to grieve the little boy he had nurtured long ago, mourning the loss of a child he would never know again.

Aidón ensured his sword was secured at his side, his boots were laced, and he looked the part. Then he began to run. He ran through the forest, he ran to Anise, he ran to find help for Alandria. He would send his messages and wait for Atíllya and those from her network to join him. Until he heard from Kaeleigh, Arileas, or anyone of their team, he would blend in and hide in plain site within Anise. And then they would fight.

Chapter Thirty-Nine

MANDÜ TRÉ LAN. TERRITORY OF THE SHIFTERS.

"Rise and shine, Princess," a voice mocked to the left of Chel as she slowly found consciousness. Danik.

"Oh my head," Chel groaned, gripping her head on the cold hard ground before she even attempted to move. "I think I'm going to be sick. What in tarnation hit me?" Chel slowly opened one eye and peered through blurry vision to find Samuel, Danik, and now Landon along with another Shifter named Lonnât sitting on large boulders inside some cavern lit with a handful of torches, the light bouncing frantically off the rock walls.

"That would be Landon," Danik's same irritating voice reached into the recesses of her brain and scratched its way down to her gut where the bile ignited, threatening to spew forth.

Chel lurched forward, dry heaving, tears leaking from her eyes. "Why? Why are you doing this?" she said between heaves attempting to calm her body. Embarrassed but grateful she didn't actually throw up in the small space they would be waiting in and have to smell it, she slowly rolled her body over and brought herself gently to a partial sitting position. Three pairs of eyes watched her with scrutiny. Chel glared back then wished she hadn't and gripped her head once more.

"She does have spirit," Landon chuckled and elbowed Lonnât in the side, looking to Samuel, "Too bad we have to give her over to Maleina, she'd make a great mate for someone in the tribe."

"Enough Landon," Samuel said, voice tired and strained. His eyes were bloodshot from the fire and held possibly even a hint of remorse. He sighed. "I just want to get this over with. If Maleina does indeed attack the territory we need to be there to defend it," he started to say with vigor then realized what he said and backpedaled, "I mean we have to keep up appearances with the tribe, right?"

"After all this, I am certain the tribe is going to find out who was behind it all," Danik griped. "We will not have a home to go back to, they will not accept us back." His voice took on a hint of fear and uncertainty, his choices catching up to him relatively quickly.

Chel just sat and listened, gaining whatever insights she could while she regained her strength. She could already feel her body starting to revive itself, thank goodness for Shifter healing.

"That is ridiculous," Landon guffawed. "I am their leader and they will deal with whatever we have to say. They will take us back and believe whatever we tell them." Simple as that. Lonnât nodded his agreement next to Landon.

Chel snorted but then quickly regretted it, her head pounding a rhythm she did not wish to hear again. She breathed slowly then chanced speaking. "Are you so sure, so arrogant to think no one will find out? And if that is the kind of leader you have been to the Shifters no wonder they are so weak and reluctant to fight for what should rightfully be theirs as participants of Alandria." She felt her strength returning and her ire striking a match getting ready to ignite a flame that would be hard to extinguish.

"You have no right, to come here and presume anything of the Shifters, you are not even a part of this territory." Landon stood and stalked closer to where Chel remained on the ground.

Her gaze glanced quickly to Samuel's, but she could tell he was conflicted. Good, he should feel some conflict of his actions. Chel took a page from Hal's book and remained impassive, pretending Landon's large stature didn't cause her any fear.

"You think you have access to them and can speak to them just because your father was the Chieftain once long ago? That time is gone and I am the leader now." Landon glared at her.

"I did not even learn my dad was any such thing until we got here," Chel spoke quietly in return. "I happen to care about this land and wanted to learn about who I was and hoped to love the Shifters whom I came from as well. But even if they do not fight, I will fight for them." Chel slowly tested her strength and the pain level of her head as she pushed herself up using the wall behind her for leverage. She was by no means anywhere close to his height or girth, but she had spirit and gusto in spades. Looking him up in the eye, Chel challenged the large man before her.

"I wouldn't do that, Chel," Samuel warned quietly from his boulder, still sitting.

Without taking her eyes away from Landon's she replied to Samuel, "Someone has to, and you don't appear to be the one going to do it."

Landon simply laughed, loud and boisterously in Chel's face. He was a big and intimidating man, but Chel was stubborn and she didn't like him. His reddish-orange hair, mustache and beard reminded her of an Irishman. *Would his animal be a disadvantage to her*? She wondered. *Probably*. He was quite bearish. *Yes, I bet it would be me on the bottom of the contest*. Since she couldn't take him on physically, she decided to find his weakness in something else so she could exploit it and hopefully stall for time. It would have to be good enough. She only hoped Hal, or her parents, or both would come before Maleina did.

"When is my captor to take me away?" Chel asked no one in particular, still keeping her eye on Landon and the other big guy. Though she did not officially win the challenge, as he looked to the side as he laughed at her, it was voided. Inside, she knew she could take him down in a battle of the wills. One day she would.

"Sundown," Samuel replied, picking at something intently on his boot.

Landon had taken several steps away from Chel, signaled for Lonnât to follow him, then walked around the curve in what appeared to be a tunnel. No signs of an exit came from that direction or the other, they seemed to be in the middle of either a tunnel or long narrow cave. Eyes growing wide, Chel remembered she did have ways to discover signs, she had her senses. She forced herself to keep her eyes open, not wanting to alert her temporary guards that she was thinking. She drew a deep, slow breath, facing the direction Samuel was sitting in front of; the air was thick and musty. *Hmmmmm.* She then did the same in the direction Landon had gone; there the air was musty but carried a lighter scent, a fresher one... *the exit!* If she got the chance, at least she knew which direction to head in. *Where would I end up if I went the wrong way?* Chel wondered. *Would it end or would it open up on the other side of whatever it was they were inside?*

Chel glanced at Samuel and examined him head to toe, his body shifted and readjusted multiple times—she could tell he was uncomfortable with what he was doing. "What about Callie?" Chel asked him quietly.

Samuel's eyes shot to hers quickly, stared at her and then shot back down to his shoe. "She is safe. I told you that."

"No she's not really. What happens to her when you get caught and end up in prison somewhere or worse?" Chel stared at him, taking in every nuance that he gave away when it came to his baby sister.

Samuel flinched and looked away. "The tribe will take care of her," he stated simply.

"She doesn't believe that. You taught her to fear the tribe. You taught her to believe that they would take her out if they felt she was a weakness or caused any trouble." Chel's hands found her hips. She knew immediately what he had told her was a lie based on the tick in Samuel's jaw. "But it isn't true is it?" She watched him turn to Danik.

"Check out the back end of the tunnel again, ensure it is still empty." Danik got up without question and did as Samuel ordered.

"You'd make a good leader if you used it right, Samuel," Chel admitted. "They listen to you."

"No, it's not true," he admitted. "Though she should know better. Yes, I drilled it into her when she was young. I couldn't risk her wandering around in case..." Samuel swallowed and looked away again, "in case, Maleina or her people found her. They would kill her. That woman wouldn't hesitate to use my baby sister against me. I don't know how she knew about her in the first place, but I have been in Maleina's service for far too long now. Fortunately, it was only the threat of me being available to her call when it came, and that didn't come until I went to the mortal realm to spy on you, well, your family. She sent me to see where your parents had gone and what they were up to. I wasn't prepared to meet you, but she used you as well and that destroyed any hope I might have had for a real future with you." Samuel turned back to face Chel. "I did hope for something real with you, Chel. I hope you believe me. I know there is no chance of that now."

"You think?" Chel snorted.

Samuel relaxed the tiniest fraction and even blushed. "For what it's worth, I'm sorry it is going down like this. I hope it can end better than it is supposed to."

Chel bit the inside of her cheek. "I want to yell and scream at you right now, but that's not going to help anything. I get it. What you are doing is wrong, but I know you're doing it because you think there is no other way to protect your sister and even the tribe—though I'm sure they can take care of themselves, or at least one time could." She paused and inhaled sharply. "I forgive you, Samuel."

"You do?" Samuel's eyes grew wide with surprise. Chel nodded. "Thank you. Though I can't just let you go, you know that right?"

"Yes, but perhaps you could turn a watchful eye while I sneak away?" she took the chance.

"Nice try," he laughed.

"Landon is bad for the tribe," Chel stated, changing the subject from something she couldn't do anything about.

"Yes, he is," Samuel whispered, darting his eyes to the direction Landon had gone. "He would take down the Shifters singlehandedly if it would prevent your dad from taking his position back. Watch out for him. He has dangerous connections and was already on Maleina's side before I got involved. I think she killed the previous Chieftain so he could take the position of the tribe."

"That makes sense," Chel mused, "She's got one hell of a long game in this."

Samuel nodded his head in the direction behind him. Chel recognized his signal. Danik was returning.

"Nope, nothing else back there, boss," Danik announced proudly and sat back down on his boulder, shoulder slumped. He couldn't have been more than sixteen, but his height and build suggested older when he tried to intimidate.

Samuel and Danik simultaneously stuck their noses in the air and stiffened on high alert. Samuel stood up and moved toward the direction Landon had gone but not yet returned. "Danik come with me," he beckoned with his arm.

"Don't leave me in here alone, Sam," Chel pleaded with wide eyes. Her senses were on overload and she could not make sense of what it was she was suddenly feeling. Though she was still unaccustomed to her senses, one she did recognize—danger. The little hairs on the back of her neck told her something was wrong, but what could she do?

"Stay here, Chel. We're just going to see what's out there." Samuel moved around the corner with Danik following him. Danik shrugged and gave her one last sloppy grin before he disappeared around the corner as well.

Samuel's voice shouted back to her from the entrance of the cavern, "I'm so sorry Chel." Then loudly and hastily, "Run!"

With nowhere left to go but through the tunnel, Chel hoped, rather counted on, an exit being at the other end. Chel ran as fast as her feet would take her. The blood rushing through her body shot adrenaline into her, pushing her forward, and she ignored her still healing head. Her heartbeat threatened to explode at the intensity of her panicked run. Looking back was her first mistake.

Red eyes peering out of a mass of darkness, sought her out.

Chel gasped in fearful outrage and shock at what she saw chasing her. The Droch-Shúil. She knew the servants of the Droch-Shúil—the creatures she had encountered before in the Caves of Vuldün—wouldn't be far behind. They were the last thing she wanted to face again.

Panic's grip clutched at her chest, and Chel began to physically feel her wolf stir inside her. *Let me out* her wolf coerced from the inside. *Protect. Love. Unite.* The wolf's feelings were quick and intense. For the first time, Chel felt what the wolf felt, heard it speak to her. She realized when she denied her wolf, she felt alone and rejected. The wolf just wanted to be a part of her, to be one as they were meant to be.

"I'm scared," Chel admitted to herself, to her wolf.

The inky black substance in the air caught up with her, surrounded her, and cut her off from moving any further through the tunnel. Chel stopped, not wanting to be caught in the tendrils of smoke, swirling now around her. It swirled faster and faster, stealing her breath away. No one was coming to her aid, no one was even in sight. Black and red was all she could see. Black swirled fast around her, trapping her where she stood. Red stationary, wide-set eyes stared into and through her, stripping her of any essential self. All she wanted to do was scream, but the spinning darkness was already so loud, she couldn't hear anything beyond it. Except her wolf begging to be let out, to be given a chance.

Falling to her knees, Chel felt her defeat. She saw no way out. Desperation had Chel lift her head, make one last attempt to see if anyone was running to her rescue, but they were not. She felt sick, lost in an overwhelming fear. Collapsing, she gave herself over to her wolf.

"Please help me, I don't know what to do," Chel begged, hiding her head underneath her arms.

I will take care of you, we are one the wolf promised. Chel surrendered her body and mind to the change she felt building for so long without outlet. Much faster than she thought it would be, and maybe less aware of all the shifts and changes she expected, Chel felt movement through her entire body but only a fractional amount of pain. The wind around her was still screeching and throwing a tantrum of force, but within her she felt a peace she had never known before. Complete and whole. Opening her eyes, she was startled to find the red eyes tilted, watching her at an odd angle.

"Do not think to hide or run from me in that form," the dark voice hissed at her, "I am ordered to keep you until the mistress comes."

I wouldn't think of it Chel tried to say but realized she hadn't spoken out loud. Looking down, she saw paws black and gold, and her orientation was much closer to the ground. Testing her balance, she moved a couple steps forward getting used to using four legs instead of two. *Wow. I had no idea it would be like this,* Chel was amazed.

We are two but we are one, I told you, the wolf also spoke in her mind.

Okay, I'm going to have to get used to that. Chel cocked her head, noticing all the details she had missed before looking through the eyes of her wolf. Her sense of smell was so much stronger, as was her sight and her hearing. She also found she could block some of it like she had learned to in human form when the animal thoughts and communications had become overwhelming.

The smoke moved in closer and closer, Chel perked her ears up and moved backwards tail tucked between her legs—which she didn't even realize she had control over.

This is surreal. I feel like I'm half driving and half in the passenger seat, Chel grumbled at her impatience, attempting to learn what she should do in a matter of seconds.

I have always been. Let me lead and you will learn, the wolf replied. *Together is what makes us strongest. That is how we should be.*

Okay. You're right, Chel mentally moved over and did the thing that scared her—second to the big scary Droch-Shúil in front of her—give up her control to the wolf.

The wolf howled, partly in a call to the wilds for assistance and partly a battle cry to warn the predator before them. Crouched to pounce, the wolf jumped into the darkness and tested the structure only to be thrown against the wall of boulders and crumble to the ground. Shaking her head in a slight daze, she jumped up and ran with everything she had to a side where she sensed it thinning. Once again, taking a pounding in her side off the boulders, she stayed crouched down realizing the Droch-Shúil itself was not the immediate threat but being contained, trapped for another purpose. Breathing hard, she rested her head on her front paws to regain her strength for what was to come next, eyes never leaving the swirling darkness and the unblinking eyes of thirst and blood.

Chapter Forty

Spotting Samuel and the imbecile Danik outside of a cave, Hal hid in the brush a short distance away and down wind. He was surprised Samuel had not yet noticed or scented his presence but he was going to be careful all the same not to help Samuel find him. His mother had not yet made an appearance, nor did he feel her presence anywhere; he knew he had little time. Samuel fidgeted, constantly looking back into the cave where Hal assumed Chel was being held, awaiting Maleina to come get her prize. Face ashen, Danik stared at the ground instead of taking his place, guarding the cave.

Just then, Hal heard a howl coming from inside the cave. Blood rushed through him as he instantly felt his heart in his throat, the pounding of it threatening to overtake his hearing. *Chel.* He took a deep breath, allowing years of practice as a warrior take over so he could regain his senses. He had to protect Chel, but he had to be smart about it or she could get hurt.

What options did he have? Chel must have shifted into her wolf, he decided. If so, she was trapped in the cave but alive. *Good.* He could get in and get her out, but what was happening inside the cave? Neither one would benefit if he ran up sword swinging without being sure what the conditions within the cave were, not to mention without knowing where his mother was or how she had this scenario planned. His heart wanted his feet to run straight into the cave, to dispatch the enemy quickly and rescue Chel, but sometimes stealth and wisdom outweighed the other.

Then again, he always trusted his heart and his gut. Halister casually strolled out of the bush line and caught Samuel's eyes. To his own surprise, Samuel's shoulders dropped, a subconscious reaction of relief.

His eyes shifted to Danik, but he just stood there pulling out his knife half-heartedly ready if Hal came at them with his.

"What is the meaning of this, Samuel?" Halister asked.

But it was Landon who saddled out from behind the side of the boulder, a smug and superior expression on his face.

"Ah an only slightly unexpected twist," Hal considered out loud. "Have you come to help me or impede me, leader of the Shifters?"

Landon smirked, a dark and evil smile on his face. "Either way, do you think I would assist you in anything, Faerie? Your fate here is of no consequence to me."

"What about Chel? She is one of your Shifters, the daughter of your previous Chieftain. Would you turn your back on her and leave her to whatever dark plans the twisted Maleina has?" Hal distanced himself from his mother by using her name, trying not to let out that surge of anger and regret bottled up within his chest.

"She again is of no consequence to me. For all I care, they could all go back to the mortal realm where they belong because they do not belong here," Landon spat. "Maleina promised us freedom from all of them if we helped her, and she has kept her promises to me for much longer than that. She will leave the Shifters in our territory alone if they are smart enough to stay in it." The threat of his words was there, ricocheting through the scattered trees and boulders.

"So let me get this straight... Maleina will leave you alone if the Shifters stay in their small little territory and do not venture into the rest of Alandria. Is that about right?" Hal pursed his lips. "Do you hear yourself? That is no way to live. You have condemned the Shifters to a partial existence. They deserve more, they deserve more than you." Halister moved forward slowly, his eyes never leaving Landon's, who was the greatest of the threats before him. Samuel wouldn't fight him back unless he had to, maybe not even then and likely only if Maleina prodded him.

"This is not your business, boy, go back to your castle and your pretty Faeries," Landon puffed his chest as if amused by his own words.

"I am pretty sure it is my business as this is a trap set for me, is it not? Are we not simply waiting for my mother to join us?" Hal watched Landon's eyes, taking in every slight variant; his pupils dilated at the mention of Maleina joining them—he too feared Maleina as he should.

Hal's shoulders straightened and his swagger stiffened, everything in his body altered from the casual Faerie intent on having a good time to the Ferrishyn warrior who needed the games to end. He took note of Landon's expression as he did so, an electric charge flickered in the atmosphere.

"Where is Chel?" Halister asked, all semblance of his casual air now gone and a deep simmering vat of vengeance in its place.

"You cannot get to her," Landon sneered in anger. "We will wait for mommy dearest to come for her wayward son."

"I will ask once more only. Where is Chel, Samuel?" Halister's words asked the one he was sure felt regret at his actions, though his eyes never left Landon.

"Do not answer him, boy, or you will not return to the place you call home again," Landon threatened.

"Is Chel in trouble? You called yourself her friend and more, Samuel. I cannot imagine you would want this for her or anyone," Hal coaxed.

Landon seethed, his anger now directed at Samuel palpable.

Samuel's eyes moved nervously back and forth between Landon and Halister. He gave up the pretense and nodded. "She's in the cave, Hal, but she's being guarded. And if that howl was any indication, she has shifted, maybe even given control to the animal."

"Samuel. Enough," Landon commanded, his voice fierce but his eyes held fear.

"Guarded by whom?" Hal pressed unconcerned with Landon, but the feeling of foreboding creeping up his spine leaving the fingers of fear were not a good sign.

Landon growled a deep, warning rumble in his chest.

Samuel's expression went slack. His throat moved slowly. "The Droch-Shúil. Sent by Maleina to guard her. Until she arrived." Samuel's choked thoughts sounded worse with each word he spoke. "It isn't supposed to hurt her, I made sure of that."

Halister froze. "So even though you know her past, her experience with the creature, you just threw her into a lion's den? You do not deserve her either." Springing into action he withdrew his sword and moved to the entrance of the cave.

"You will not be entering, boy," Landon moved to step in front of him, blocking his path, his arms folded across his chest.

"Yes, he will," Ray, Chel's father, declared stepping from behind a boulder, his arms folded across his chest, looking a formidable opponent. One by one, Shifter after Shifter stepped out from behind their hiding places surrounding the area. Some stood in animal form and some remained as people with swords drawn and bows trained directly on Landon.

Ray continued to move forward only a few steps. "I think you have just been voted out of position, Landon Wasel. Your reign for whatever it was has come to an end and will not be recorded in the book of Chieftains, but as a blight on our history." Ray snarled at Landon, his eyes fiercely upon him. He would not be escaping Mandü tré Lan.

Landon, who was not to so easily step aside answered with equal magnitude, "And who is going to lead, Rayalt? You who abandoned us so long ago to save your own family?" Landon swept his arms out wide, beseeching the masses. "Is that who you want as your leader? Someone who leaves right before things get tough, someone who will tuck tail and hide for years from his responsibilities?" A spark of satisfaction lit Landon's eyes as he saw several Shifters waver in their newfound conviction against him.

Ray nodded. "I did leave. You're right. I took my family and we went to the mortal realm. But that was *not* to hide and *not* to abandon you. I officially placed a Chieftain capable and sure to lead you and protect you while I was gone. I went not out of my own desires but to ensure the safety of Alandria's future. The heir—Kaeleigh—has come home and so has allowed us to as well."

"And we are to just take your word for it?" Landon laughed with derision.

"No, I do not expect you to," Ray admitted humbly. He looked each of the Shifters in the eye, considering his next words carefully as he picked up the emotion from each one. So many were afraid, but also so many were underutilized, ready for a challenge, ready to face that which opposed and oppressed them. "I do expect you to rise to Alandria's needs, rise to protect that which is yours," he spoke to the Shifters all around him, his voice escalating. "Alandria belongs to the Shifters as well. Be her protectors, be the Shifters you are meant to be, allow the spirits of your animals to come to the forefront and not be suppressed by the fear Landon and Maleina and others have put in you. It is time for this to end." Ray stared each and every one of them down not in oppression but in challenge for a better future, to challenge their animals within to fight for what was theirs, fight for what could be theirs and the future of their families. His wife, Lilane came up alongside her husband in show of support, but in her move, she saw Hal's subtle gesture to get into the cave and rescue Chel. The Cheiftain had truly returned and no one, not even Landon could deny it.

Hal slipped around Landon only to be met by Samuel. Arms crossed and feet spread apart in a solid stance, compared to his remorseful one moments before, he nodded to Halister and whispered, "Quick. Find her and take her away from here. I accept the consequences." Samuel's eyes softened more. "Please check in on Callie. She's a handful, but deserves a better life than the one I provided her."

"Why not stop me?" Hal slanted his eyes in question. Samuel shook his head and stepped aside.

"I vow to protect Callie if you are unable or not present." Hal placed his fist over his heart, a sign of his promise.

Another howl ricocheted down through the tunnel, lighting a fire in Hal as he flew past Samuel and into the cavern, running full out until he reached a sight that stopped him in his tracks. There was not a second more to spare.

Darkness was all he could see. Fast-moving darkness like a controlled tornado spinning in place, but this one was inside a cave. Looking up at the structure, Hal hoped it could hold up to the turbulent wind put off by the Droch-Shúil. And then a whine drew his gaze. Chel. There she was.

His breath hitched. Chel in wolf form was a magnificent sight. Her dark coat was spectacular, with gold and white marbled throughout her fur. As he searched through the dark haze, he realized she was lying upon the ground, struggling to get back up. Hurt.

Heat like fire blazed within his chest. Sword drawn, he sized up his prey. Stalking its every rotation; somehow it had multiple layers of differing rotations, some even opposite the others haphazard and chaotic. If he got too close, he would simply be swept in its motion. He knew his timing would need to be precise and calculated.

"Chel! Chel can you hear me?" Hal called.

Chel stirred and struggled to lift her head, her blue eyes blazing at him carried relief and desperation but also a warning. He heard her loud and clear with that one look: don't you dare die trying to save me.

Hal chuckled. "I will die saving you if I must, but I would much rather be the hero and have the damsel offer a kiss of gratitude. That sounds like much more fun to me."

She growled at him which only made him chuckle more. "Oh yes you will. I will have earned that kiss when you are free. Don't deny me my kiss or I might just leave you in there." Hal's expression fully trained on the Droch-Shúil once more, he searched for any signs of weakness. Frowning, he took steps to the side and watched how the dark wisps of its being changed and tracked with him, but he could not goad the creature to shift those murderous red eyes toward him instead of Chel.

Without a second thought, Hal followed his instincts and rushed the swirling mass, his sword extended. It pierced straight into the Droch-Shúil, but to no avail. He was simply thrown back several feet from where he started onto his backside.

Chel got up on all fours and yipped.

"I am all right. Stay where you are," Hal instructed with a twinge of frustration his initial attempt hadn't worked. He leaped back onto his feet sword ready for battle while he drew another, a short sword, from his boot. Targeting those eyes, he threw his short sword true. Had the creature been less transparent, he would have hit his mark, instead the sword clattered on the ground on the other side. Drawing his bow from his back, Hal cocked an arrow with the speed and experience as the warrior he was—aimed and released all in one smooth motion. Uttering a curse, he watched his arrow strike one of those large red eyes and soar straight through to the other side.

Chel looked back at those red eyes trained on her, the same that were ignoring Hal as if he were no threat. Her head swiveled back to Hal and growled, then moved toward the center of the Droch-Shúil.

"Don't you dare, Chel. I will think of something," Hal shouted, the frustration and fear apparent in his tone. "Stay where you are!"

Chel of course, didn't listen and lunged toward the creature once more and once more was thrown back as she had before, slamming once more into the stone behind her landing with a crash and a whimper.

"Chel!" Hal roared, running her direction as close as he could though he could not touch her. Hands on his head, he threw himself down on his knees. "What were you thinking?" he shouted. "Chel? Can you hear me? Are you alive?" His voice cracked. His eyes were wide with expectant fear as he anticipated the worst.

Chel moved slowly, raising her head to show those blue eyes. Her frustration and irritation were apparent in that short glance. Hal studied her carefully, reading what others might not have been able to see in those beautiful blues and her wolf's posture. Hands cradling his head, he realized what she was trying to tell him. "I missed it. I am so sorry, Chel. I did not understand."

She yapped at him once more, gesturing with her head toward the creature. Hal's eyes followed hers, but the only thing he saw were those eyes locked onto Chel, eyes of hatred and murderous rage, eyes not partial to its prey. But something else stuck out to him, he did not notice it before, traces of particles were pulling a part as if they had just been knitted together seconds before creating a solid force.

Halister's eyes widened with disbelief and awe at what Chel had been demonstrating to him at the expense of her own life—a way to kill or at the very least disturb the Droch-Shúil.

"There may be a way out of this after all," Hal whispered.

Chel stirred and struggled to get up, taking her time to get her feet solidly underneath her. At his notice, she seemed to have taken to her four-legged form quite easily.

"Give yourself a moment, Chel. This may cost us more than we want to give to be out of this." Hal gazed down at her longingly. "I sure wish I had gotten that kiss before we were in this mess. Oh wait, I did," Hal chuckled. "Well, I wanted to be your hero this time. Perhaps I still can be, but if something should happen to me, you should know your dad is taking back control of the Shifters, they will be strong again and they will fight for Alandria or join the enemy." Hal continued talking. "Samuel is remorseful, but it may be too late for him—you know, where my mother is involved. Oh and I vowed to protect Callie for him, though truthfully I did it for you, knowing she was your friend." Hal's head tilted and grumbled under his breath.

"I feel her. My mother will be here soon, if we have a chance to get out of this it will be now or we will be at her mercy. Are you able?" Hal's brow pinched in concern watching Chel get back on all fours, she licked a spot on her front leg that was bleeding and bent. Hal rubbed his chest, as a pain pierced right through his heart. "Chel you are not able. I will go home with my mother and plead for your Shifters. It will be all right," Hal said hearing the lie as soon as he said it.

Chel's head snapped in his direction, full of animal glare. "So maybe it won't. But I will deal with whatever comes."

Growling, Chel bared her teeth and took off hobbling toward the creature, leaving Hal helplessly watching, unable to stop her.

"NO!" Hal shouted, jumping to his feet, sword drawn chasing her from the outside of the spinning tornado of misty darkness. "Chel stop. I... I need you!" Hal shouted, his words stuck in his throat almost flummoxed they had come out of his mouth. Chel howled and moved faster, throwing herself into the wretched unseen face of the creature holding her hostage.

Thrown back, almost pushed as if she had bounced off something so hard and not only spun out from the force of the wind, Chel hit the ground hard.

All the air rushed out of Halister.

All he could see was Chel lying motionless on the ground, yet he remained helpless to get to her. Halister's gaze shifted to the creature's eyes, mocking her attempt at freedom. Rage built in his chest, anger unfurled from that place deep inside where he stored everything his mother had done to him and his people to Alandria, to Chel, to Daegan, to Kaeleigh and all the evil uprooting everything he loved.

The time was now. His desire for freedom from the darkness, his hope for Alandria, and his newly discovered love for a girl who could shift into a wolf exploded from his chest. With not only the skill of a warrior and the precise moment in time, but also a deep magic he had yet to realize was available to him, he drew his sword.

He saw it.

The moment when the darkness knitted together in a not-quite-solid state right where Chel had slammed into it. It was quickly vanishing as the seconds ticked by, unraveling back into the particles within the swirling darkness.

Hal charged forward, the cry of a warrior mixed with the howling rage of a man who might have nothing left to lose erupted from his inner core. Magic surged through his body from within straight into his sword. The sword grew hot to the touch and a soft blue light emanated from it, illuminating through the darkness as Hal held it stretched out gripped in both hands. He aimed his strike directly to the center of the mass where it was temporarily still fused together.

Hal felt his sword slice through the swirling darkness as he ran forward instead of bouncing off, taking him along for the ride. Like wading through mud, Hal trudged forward. No cutting or swinging his sword in this battle. His target was direct and he felt time slipping with every step he didn't get to the core. With one quick glance at Chel still lying on the ground, Hal pushed forward with all he had left within him.

"For Chel and Alandria!" Hal shouted plunging his sword into the core of the Droch-Shúil finally reaching his destination. The sword hit its mark, a reverberating shock moved up into his arm so fierce it knocked Halister back, leaving the sword stuck inside the darkness.

Hal leaned on his elbow, struggling to get up, but the desire to watch what would happen moved him. Eyes wide with surprise he saw the sword stuck inside the darkness, lighting up the entire cavern with its brilliance. The darkness of the Droch-Shúil spun faster and more erratically than before. The blazing red eyes now shifted from Chel toward him with something akin to surprise shining out of them, noticing Halister for the first time.

"You have not beaten us," a gravelly voice slithering out of darkness hissed at him. "We will return. *She* will come after *you* now."

The Droch-Shúil diminished its shape into the size and form of a common shadow then slinked out of the cave, leaving a deafening silence in its wake along with very little natural light for that part of the cave. Hal's sword, the only item giving off enough light to see Chel lying still, her chest slowly heaving, struggling for even shallow breaths. The light of the sword ebbed slowly as did the life that remained in Chel.

CHAPTER FORTY-ONE

"Chel," Hal called out but received no response.

Hal pushed himself the rest of the way up. Groaning at various pains he would rather ignore, he had to get to Chel. Closing the few feet between them, Hal ran his hands gently over her head though time was not on his side.

"Chel? Chel!" Hal shout-whispered, threading his fingers through the soft fur on top of her head. "You have to be all right. We made it. The Droch-Shúil is gone."

Tears he did not have time for filled his eyes, but swiping them away he examined her best he could with what little light was left from the sword. He quickly glanced behind him to realize many of the Shifters from outside the cave were now inside, staring at him and Chel, stunned by what had transpired. He had felt them come in moments before he vanquished the darkness, but he had not wanted to acknowledge them while Chel was slipping away. Shifters came closer, bringing torches of light and surrounded him, extending their lights so he could see.

"What can we do?" one asked quietly absorbed in the moment.

"Light. I need more light. Is any a healer among you?" Hal asked as he instructed.

Hal could feel her heart beat through the thick fur where his hand rested now on her back, the other gently holding under her wolf head, wanting... needing to feel her breath continuing to flow in and out, ensuring she lived.

"Our magic does not work that way, we have none you seek among us. I am sorry," a Shifter said, her head lowered with regret.

"Not good enough." Hal gritted his teeth. "I refuse to lose you now, Chel," he whispered for her ears alone.

Chel's mother ran up and fell to her knees on the other side of Hal, tears of blue streamed down her face as she buried her head in the wolf's neck. "No, no, no," she muttered over and over between sobs.

Her father squatted next to her as well and surveyed the unmoving body of his daughter in animal form. "She really is exquisite isn't she?" asked no one in particular.

Hal responded anyway, "She is."

Ray studied Halister's face intently. When he seemed satisfied with what he saw, he challenged Hal. "So are you. Do something about this. You have the magic inside you, you only have to seek it out. I know your heritage, boy, healing runs through your veins whether you knew it or not. I suspect that is why you've had success working with young Shifters in the past."

Hal looked at Ray, confusion written all over his face. "I know not what you speak."

"Try." Ray's eyes were big, pleading, holding back the torrent of emotion ready to break through the dam at any point. Her mother looked up, her eyes begging Halister. "Please try. I see you love her. If not for us, then for her... who she is to you, find your inner magic."

Halister stood in shock, perhaps from the revelation there was a healer somewhere in his lineage or perhaps from realizing he loved Chel—pointed out by her father no less. Hal nodded and closed his eyes.

His thoughts went to Chel, unsure where to start. He thought of when he first saw her, her spunk and her attitude immediately drew his eye toward her. But it was her eyes that had first captivated him, her eyes dragged him into her soul without his permission; after all, he had had no intentions of settling down. He was free and liked it that way. Chel had a way of attaching herself to people in a way others could not resist. She was the light that showed him the darkness he had been content to live with. She challenged him like no other had ever tried and he wanted to be the one she saw he could be.

Hal felt a stirring deep inside, similar to when he felt magic blossom to ignite his sword with the light they needed to push back the Droch-Shúil. He felt it and allowed it to grow inside him. He remembered all his lessons on magic as a younger man. He had always assumed he did not have much since he was never able to get it to work the way he thought he should be able to. Yet here the magic stirred, swarming within his inner core. It was as if the magic itself was excited to be used, to help, to create, to be unleashed.

Hal moved his hands gently over Chel's spine and up each of the wolf's legs ending up at the top of her head and neck. He gently pet her head and leaned down placing his head against hers. Whispering in her ear, he allowed his feelings to be known. "Chel, I need you to come back to this world, to me." He breathed in deeply and out slowly.

"I am going to try to use my magic, but I need you to do your part," he pleaded for her soul to acknowledge his words even if her ears didn't. "Choose to live, Chel."

Hal kissed her nose then stared intently, unflinchingly at her, releasing the magic ready inside him. He pushed it out from him directing it towards her. The wolf flinched, he knew by this that the magic had found its way to her body, but he did not know if it was enough to heal her. He pushed another surge of his magic outward until he exhausted himself and then pushed some more. Anticipation ran high not only in Hal but in those around him as well, so much so he could tangibly feel it in the air around them. With desperate hope, he called on the power left within Alandria from within his soul. He pulled on the source from which he came, pleading for enough magic for one life—a life he felt mattered to Alandria and her future.

Nothing happened. Sighs of sadness fell in unison.

Hal closed his eyes and bent his head, defeated his magic was not strong enough, expecting without experience it would be enough on its own was foolish hope.

"Chel!" her mother's voice cried, piercing his heart but it was not a cry of despair instead one of relief and hope.

Hal's eyes flew open. Chel's beautiful blue eyes were open, staring directly at him. Even in wolf form, he could read so much in her eyes. He laughed and buried his head in her neck with a grateful sigh to Alandria.

"She will be all right," Ray announced to the gathered Shifters. "My daughter—our future Chieftess—will be all right." He patted Halister's head as well as his daughter's.

"That is definitely good news," came a sultry voice echoing from the entrance of the cave.

Maleina, her timing impeccable as always.

Chapter Forty-Two

"Rayalt, do come out of the cavern, I have no desire to speak with you shouting from the entrance, nor do I have desire to snag my dress on a rock by going in there," Maleina intoned almost civilly.

"We have nothing to discuss, Maleina," Ray said flatly.

"Oh I do not think that is true. I smell smoke coming from your village and thought you should know," she replied innocently. "And I do not think the Ónarach joining you shortly from the opposite end of the cave feel as hospitable as I am at this moment."

Halister looked up at Ray, his eyes filled with apologetic despair. "I will go," Hal said quietly to Ray and Chel who was staring at him intently, willing him with her eyes alone not to go.

Ray cursed something in another language, significantly more guttural and harsher sounding than the language of the Faeries. "No. This needs to end. I will speak with her. Alas, we are in somewhat of a trap." Ray thought momentarily then called over two Shifters. "Colin. Danu."

They were large and muscled, each carrying a club type weapon. Each approached the now standing Ray, looking for all purposes the leader he had been years ago so easily stepping back into the role, and inclined their heads.

"In your service," each said individually having no issues submitting themselves to Ray.

"I am honored," Ray said placing his hand over his heart and nodding his head in response to their submission. "Take whoever you need and as soon as we step out of the cave head to the village. Do whatever necessary to get there and protect the village, send someone to ensure those who are too young or unable to fight have gone underground." He placed each hand, one on each of their shoulders and wished them well.

"Everyone else, if you so choose stand with me. Watch your backs, the abominable creatures the Ónarach approach from the other side. Let us go out to meet the darkness in that woman." He turned to Hal specifically. "Take her to safety. There will be no surrender or sacrificing yourself. We protect our own... that includes you now."

Hal looked into Ray's eyes and saw a man he admired in them, a man he respected, a man he would fight alongside, a man he knew his father used to be.

"I will heed your instructions," he conceded.

Ray nodded to Halister as he bent down and gently picked Chel up. She whimpered as he jostled her searching for the best place to hold her.

"Sorry Chel," he whispered into her ear. "I will keep you safe if my life depends on it." He could feel her chest rumble through her fur where his arm held her. "Deal with it," he growled back.

He followed Ray, Lil, and several other Shifters, blending into the group as they went out in a show of force, if they had a chance at all. Hal whispered under his breath a short warriors blessing upon the Shifters as they went out to meet his mother and possibly their fate. He had no idea what she had in store.

The Shifters watched warily, carefully observing everything in front of them as they moved. With ears listening, senses on overdrive, and taking in every little detail that might aid in their defense, they stalked out from the cave.

Maleina stood in the open a short ways outside the cave entrance, flanked only by a handful of Ónarach guards and her own Ferrishyn entourage; one set standing stoically set with weapons drawn at their sides, the other a dark presence of clones nervously waiting, daggers held out pointing at everything in front of them—the contrast staggering. The Ónarach licked their lips like a collective being ravenous for their next meal, hunger intent on devouring the life away from the Shifters. Flicking their scattered glances back to Maleina, they awaited her silent signal.

Ray gave his own silent signal and Colin and Danu handed their weapons to someone next to them, shifted into very large Black bears, and took off at full speed. Many others also shifted but some stayed in human form with weapons as they followed the bears off to one side with a group following them only to be cut off by another wave of

Ónarach and Ferrishyn hiding behind the bushes and boulders. Without hesitation, the Shifters began to fight their way through; the strategy appearing to be those in animal form getting through the enemy lines quicker in order to get to the village while the ones with weapons stayed to entertain the fight until they, too, could get through.

"Was that really necessary, Ray? Here I thought we could have a civilized meeting, you and I?" Maleina crooned though her eyes were fierce, zeroing instantly on her son and the wolf he carried.

"You said my village was on fire and we would like to keep as much of our home as possible, wouldn't you?" Ray in full control replied.

Her head snapped back to his attention, eyes blazing but the corner of her lip lifted in slight amusement. "Are you making threats, dear Ray? It will not do well for you to simply waltz back into Alandria after so much time away and start making enemies."

"You misunderstand, Maleina, I was merely stating you would do everything you could to protect your home and the people you love if there was a threat to it. Wouldn't you?"

Maleina flinched in the most imperceptible way. Ray had struck a chord, but she would be remiss to show it. "Of course," she intoned melodically. "Which is my purpose for being here... I have come for my son, it is time he returns home where he belongs." She sneered, taking in each of the Shifters derisively until she landed on Hal.

"Come Halister, let us be gone. You can bring your pet with you if you would like." Maleina smiled.

The Shifters behind Ray bristled and some turned animal stirred and made noises of discontent. Chel rustled in Hal's arms until he had to put her down.

"Do not do anything stupid, Chel, you know I would never call you my pet," he whispered into her ear as he ruffled the fur on her head, eliciting a shallow growl from her. Hal watched her as she got her balance and ensured she was able to stand on her own four paws before he turned back to his mother.

Hal ignored the jab at the Shifters—Chel specifically—purposed to get a rise out of him. "I have chosen to stay here for a time and learn of the Shifter's ways like the times before when we would learn from each other," Hal stated simply enough as if the plan had already been re-activated.

"That is absurd!" Maleina countered. "I will not have my son cavorting with these lower beings."

"There should be nothing to concern yourself over, Mother, as you have already disowned me," Hal said with a flat tone—business as usual—most would not hear the faint trace of pain within his words. Chel being as perceptive as always, perhaps even more so in wolf form, hobbled along his side and touched the tip of her snout against his lowered hand. Hal cupped her nose briefly acknowledging her, but did not shift his gaze.

"Fine so be it, Halister, you have brought this upon this territory. May whatever happens be on your shoulders," Maleina cursed.

"No. It will be on yours," the Chieftain declared. Stepping forward he threw his spear straight into the hearts of three of the Ónarach standing single file, skewering them upon it.

Maleina's eyes narrowed and gave her men the order, "Slay them."

It did not take long for the fight to be in full swing. Ray searched for the suddenly missing Maleina. Disgusted, she would not stay and fight that which she had started, he hollered to Hal.

"Get Chel out of here!"

"Right," Halister yelled back. He turned in a full circle seeking Chel. She was not where he had left her. He growled under his breath, berating himself—of course she wouldn't stay where he had asked her to. Moving quickly through the throngs of Shifters, fighting mindless Ónarach and skilled Ferrishyn warriors many of whom he had trained, he looked for her. The Shifters fought with more skill than he would have thought given their complacent responses to their call to fight. Not seeing Chel anywhere within their fighting vicinity, he prepared to head toward the village. A chill of unease ran down his spine. She wouldn't. He knew she would want to fight with them, to prove she had enough ability to hold her own. In a sudden panic, he called for her above the din of battle.

"Chel!"

He heard a faint whimper far behind him. Whipping his head around he saw a flash of black and gold fur out the corner of his eye. Carried by a large Ferrishyn warrior he knew from his days in training, Chel held still her eyes pleading with him to stay away from the trap. Next to the warrior was Samuel, Landon, Lonnât, Danik, and his mother; each holding hands connecting a chain with Maleina. She smiled a cruel and taunting smile at him, directly at him and waved her fingers in a teasing manner. Hal rushed them as fast as he could but when he got to the place they stood, they were gone. Vanished. All of them, his mother, the warrior carrying Chel, and all the Ferrishyn fighting the Shifters... simply gone. Hal had never seen so many transport out together; it took a lot of magic.

The Shifters did not miss a beat and continued to fight, simply adjusting who they fought from a suddenly invisible foe to the ones left behind—the unable to transport Ónarach. Power shifted, the mindless clones seemed to battle at only half the power and were quickly dispatched back to ash from whence they came.

"To the village!" Ray announced, sending all the remaining Shifters who stood with him back to their homes.

Hal fell to his knees, staring where Chel had just been. She slipped through his fingers. Ray came up behind him, placing his hand on Hal's shoulder. Hal sunk further to the ground. He had failed her.

"She took her." He paused, defeated but filling with a new sense of rage. "My mother took, Chel!" he roared.

A moment of silence echoed through the now eerie quiet.

"She will not harm her. Your mother is using my daughter," Ray paused, pained to speak his words but acting the leader he was once more, "she knows you will come, you have developed an attachment to Chel. Your mother is exploiting this."

Staring straight ahead, Hal's resolve returned with new vigor and passion. "Then it is me she shall have, though I dare say she may wish she did not." His chest heaving, Hal breathed in through his nose allowing the injustice to stir through his being. Something was coming alive in Halister and he planned on learning all he needed to know to be able to use it... against his own mother if necessary.

"I will bring your daughter back, Rayalt, Sir, I vow this to you," Hal promised, raising his fist over his heart. A single tear fell from his eye, making tracks through dirt down his cheek and landing on Ray's hand where he still clenched Hal's shoulder.

"I know you will," Ray acknowledged and didn't try to stop him. As a warrior he understood the fight, as a man he understood the need. "Come get strengthened and pack what you may need."

Hal stood and wiped his face. He began to walk back with Ray to the village. "I may need some help. I plan to meet up at Ehsmia, hoping Daegan and Kaeleigh will be there. They will want to help as well." Hal looked in Ray's face. "After this, the Shifters should be thrown off balance enough to listen. Get them on your side, ready to fight; the war for Alandria will be here soon enough. Word will come when it is time."

"Go with the heart of Alandria on your side," Rayalt said. He inclined his head and placed his own fist over his heart. "We will be ready."

Chapter Forty-Three

The Mortal Realm. Entrance to Tylínyth.

The next morning, Ella met Finn in the hall outside the bunk-rooms. There had been much activity that morning: greetings, pleasantries, and introductions after they had snuck in during the night before. Ella led Finn to the dining room area where they could sit and eat breakfast while they visited with those in residence at the Talaín Tower. After greeting several and introducing Finn to everyone, Ella sat gratefully holding a cup of steaming tea from the mortal realm. Twenty-five others had taken lodging in the tower—sometimes there had been double that number and sometimes half. It lifted her spirits to see the place in good use. Even more to her delight, were the stories she heard about many who had gone in to Tylínyth to help even if after some reluctance. As they learned about the plight of Alandria, the Twined people were rising to the occasion.

Ella smiled in reflection and knew what she needed to do. She then stood up on her chair to the consternation of Finn.

"Ella!? What are you doing?"

"Making an announcement." She smiled down at him where he sat. Her eyes glittered with anticipation.

"Good morning everyone!" Ella shouted above the morning din of conversation. All eyes turned toward her and voices hushed in anticipation. Ella smiled at them. "Thank you. It truly is lovely to see you all again. And for those of you who have not yet gotten to meet Finn..." she turned to Finn and beckoned him to stand up on his chair as well. "This is Finnlan Talaín of Alandria. He is one of the originators of the realm of Tylínyth and a visionary of this refuge along with myself and he has recently returned from a long mission. He has been anticipating meeting you all. He can be a bit prickly, but reassure yourselves he is vested in your well being and has been waiting for this moment." She winked at him and many chuckled at his surly response but then surprised even Ella with a quick turnabout and rolled her hand under his then kissed it like a prince. He then turned to the room and gave them a gentlemanly bow.

"Wow, where did my bristling Elf go?" Ella winked and enjoyed the playful banter with their people.

"Too much to live for now," Finn admitted honestly, directly into her eyes. "You did say *my*, do I belong to you now?" he asked unashamedly in front of everyone and got the satisfaction of seeing the slightest hint of a blush on Ella's face.

After a pause, her eyes still on his, she said, "You do." Then with a small smile leaned her forehead down to touch his, then gave him a swift peck on the lips to the cheers and shouts of all in the room.

It was hard not to bask in the excitement of being with Finn but the moments before them brought her to focus. "All right, settle down." Ella's face sobered as she scanned the group. "I am sorry I was not here." Everyone seemed to know exactly what she referred to. "I am sorry for Peter and Silas and what this loss means to us all." Then taking a breath she continued with courage. It wasn't everyday she made an announcement, let alone this one. "I have summoned all registered with us." The room released a collective gasp. "They should arrive within the next couple days." Ella rolled right over the growing titter, silencing it with her push forward. "We will discuss a plan and possible options for everyone when they all arrive. But until then, Finn and I will survey Tylínyth and take measure of what damage still exists, whether to structure or personnel. Today we begin to build again, today we restore what was lost." Some clapped and some said encouraging things out loud, and others nodded their head at the work to be done for the future. "Go about your plans for this day. Those of you who know of where we should look first, come with us."

Ella jumped down from the chair, Finn attempting to help her with the hand he still held. Some went back to whatever they had been doing, but several came up to them right away.

"Several were still in the caves because their cabins had collapsed last I was there," a young man said.

"Thank you, Jason, that was going to be my first stop," Ella stated.

"A large pile of boulders and debris has started to be cleared away from the crash site, but we believe the portal into Alandria is still not functioning," a lovely woman with fair skin and freckles said as she pushed glasses up on her nose.

"Yes, I am afraid re-opening the portal will take some extra time and magic we may not have accessible to us at this time. I am in communication with my grandfather about it," Ella added.

"Will I still get to witness the use of the Alandrian simulation room before we go? I could catch up with you or come back later, but I do want to see how they interact with it," Finn spoke quietly near Ella's ear.

"Of course!" Ella said, eyes wide with excitement for him. "That room has brought many Twined in touch with their inner magic and the belief there is somewhere they could belong if they chose," she offered softly. "Let us go now to Tylínyth and survey the people and the land then come back here before the evening meal."

"It's a date!" Finn smiled and offered her his arm to which she looped hers inside his and smiled in return.

"I have never been on what the humans call a date," Ella mused.

"Then it's done," Finn said with glee. "Some day when this is all over, I will take you on a mortal date."

"Then it is a date!" Ella agreed, nodding her head, and leading him to the portal entrance into Tylínyth.

~~~~~

Tylínyth was an extension of Alandria in the form of a pocket realm positioned between the mortal realm and Alandria. It was created with great magic pooled together from Arileas, Hunter, and many of the Elders and Orchids before they had been scattered throughout Alandria. An amazing feat of magic similar to the creation of Alandria, but not near as large and not near as much magic needed to enact it. In appearance it was a combination between elements of Alandria and elements of Earth to easily integrate as the next phase into preparing the Twined for the day when they could enter Alandria. It's many uses included a hidden training ground outside both Alandria and the mortal realm as
~~~~~

well as a home for those who had nowhere to go on Earth yet wanted to take that next step to discovering their magic and heritage from Alandria.

Ella breathed a sigh at the familiarity for which she saw upon entering. "It looks the same," she said relieved, looking around her with a smile.

"It does," Finn agreed. Where they entered, they were much closer to the mountain than where they had been the last time they entered on the opposite side where the collapsed portal into and out of Alandria used to be.

"Ella!" a man, roughly in his fifties with shocks of gray sideburns extending from a full head of salt and peppered hair, shouted from near the mountain, waving his hand and running toward her.

"Elder Tillin!" Ella responded with a smile.

He stopped several feet before her and stood at attention then bowed quickly before her. "We wondered when we would see you and hoped you weren't in trouble on your side of Alandria. We could not get through the portal; it had been destroyed," Tillin explained in case she was not aware.

"Yes, we had some trouble on our way back here," Ella said and gestured to Finn standing next to her. The man smiled and inclined his head to Finn as well, having met each other upon Finn's last visit.

"Are you well?" Concern colored Elder Tillin's eyes.

"Thank you, yes, but the portal is destroyed like you said. Finn and I had to enter through the mortal realm which is why it took us longer to arrive than we had intended." Ella looked around behind him, watching some of the various members begin to head their way. "Are you well?" she asked him.

"Indeed. We had a little trouble but most of us had been hidden in the caves and were kept safe. The land, as well as the guards, took a beating from the Alandrian portal exploding inward," he further explained, but his eyes grew dark and he paused. "I'm sure by now you have heard of the losses we did have: Peter and Silas." He raked a hand through his hair and looked away from Ella. "I told them not to go, but they felt strongly they should have gone with you all when you left; they wanted to be with Metrí." He brought his eyes back to hers and sighed. "No matter the reason why, the loss of their lives are on me."

Finn stepped forward uncharacteristically placing his hand on the man's shoulder. "No. This is on Maleina. She is the one who destroyed the portal causing all the collateral damage, the fault belongs to her."

"Finn is right, Tillin, this is her fault and she will be held responsible for it," Ella growled, her eyes fierce with anger, her fists tight at her side.

"What can we do?" Finn asked, looking around at the gathered. Finn saw that many had cuts and bruises, torn clothing, bandages and slings, evidence of having come through the hardship. Nonetheless, their spirits were high and any anger was overcome with hope.

"Most of those who live in the cabins and huts near the portals have moved into the caves within the mountain, following in case more explosions might be in the works," Elder Tillin explained, pointing toward a barely visible cave entrance. "I believe they would be reassured to move back into their homes if you think it is safe for them to, Ella."

"Let us go speak with them, but as for safety, I am not sure of that. Perhaps if they are comfortable they should stay in the mountain. However, I have enacted the Come Home protocol and the others will be arriving soon. We will need all the space available and most likely if many stay we will need to open more bunk houses here in Tylínyth and may need tents in addition. We still have room in the Talaín Tower but some may want to stay here within the realm itself," she informed him.

"How are the food supplies?" Finn asked. Ella smiled. It was wonderful to have him back at her side. She was grateful he was so focused on the right questions.

"We are low on some things, but overall not in bad shape. We have runners who do grocery shopping in the mortal realm on a regular rotation for the things we can't grow here ourselves. Some of the gardens got destroyed, but we have people gathering fruits and vegetables that might have survived," Tillin replied.

"Very good," Finn followed up.

Ella, Finn, Elder Tillin, and several of the others that had gathered around them walked together toward the mountain to take stock of the inhabitants and their wellbeing.

Several hours later, Finn and Ella had a good idea how everyone fared in Tylínyth. Overall, they were pleased with the responses of the people; angry and ready to fight to avenge the loss of their friends and their disillusioned safety. The fear she saw in many of their eyes, stirred anger deep in her core; for all they had worked hard for, for all they had fought for already, for all their futures she wanted for them to have... they would have their vengeance one way or another, she would see to it.

The afternoon was bright and a slight breeze blew through Tylínyth. Finn tipped his head to the sky, closing his eyes and breathing deep. Ella watched with fascination as he took a moment to feel the warmth of the sun, refreshing his soul with the energy of light. She slipped her hand inside one of his large roughened hands and caught the smile that spread across his face before he opened his eyes.

"They are well, Ella," Finn said quietly, relishing the fact the damage was not what it could have been.

"Yes, they are," she agreed. Looking around the open field, she took note of those working on the sidelines and those working in the gardens she could see. They were alive and well for now.

"Giving the people tasks and a focus has helped them shake off the stain of what happened," Finn also noted, following her gaze.

"Yes, it will not diminish their fears, but for now it will help put it aside." Ella sighed. "It broke my heart to see the fear in their eyes. They thought they were protected from anything within Alandria. I caused that. I should have better prepared them for anything... but even I did not anticipate something of this magnitude could happen to the portal let alone cause a reaction within our protected sanctuary."

"How could you?" Finn probed. "Maleina is off-grid and we are functioning a bit blind here. There is no way to anticipate her every move, but from now on we will do all we can to protect but also to train and prepare them. They deserve a fighting chance and they deserve to have all the facts to make their decision." Finn nodded, sure of what he said. He took her hand and pulled her close to his chest and then kissed the tip of her nose, holding her close.

"What do you think about training alongside them, Finn? You can add in magic they wouldn't expect and prepare them." She smiled up at him. "Then when you're finished, we will explore the interior Alandria experience you wanted to see so much."

Finn nodded. His eyes twinkled as he gently pulled away from her. "I would like that."

CHAPTER FORTY-FOUR

B ack in the mortal realm, inside Talaín Tower, Finn and Ella stood on the edge of the boundary that separated humanity from Alandria.

"It truly is unbelievable you have constructed this place within these walls inside the mortal realm," Finn mused, looking at a condensed version of the different types of climates, geographies, and landmarks of Alandria *inside* a building. The expanse of the room broke all laws of physics and the natural barriers of modern construction, housing a miniature replica of an entire world within a mere condo building.

"It is," Ella agreed with a large grin. She then pushed Finn to cross the barrier so he too could experience the interactive room for himself.

Though he stumbled into the room, he smiled, "All right, you do not have to ask me twice."

Ella watched Finn move slowly, almost unsure of himself or his surroundings, lightly trailing his fingers over a giant toadstool then running them down the bark of a large oak tree. He looked back at her with the mischievousness of a small boy glinting in his eyes. Finn jumped up into the tree, disappearing from sight. All Ella could hear was a playful hoot she could not even reconcile as being a sound Finn could make, but her smile from ear to ear said otherwise. The branches in the trees rustled as he leapt down and moved fast as an Elf could from section to section, stopping in each for mere seconds to glance at his surroundings. When he got to a place glowing with unnatural light, he paused and closed his eyes soaking the light into his skin; the illumination highlighted the subtle iridescent differences in his skin that signified him as Elf.

When Finn opened his eyes, they were bright with the essence of light absorbed into his being. He didn't know it was possible to recreate the energy he got from the sun or the moon from unnatural—or magical—means. "It feels like home," he breathed in awe. In the blink of an eye, Finn was back in front of Ella holding his hands out for her unnecessary inspection. "I can't believe it's possible," he began, "it feels authentic to how I feel under the Alandrian sun." He breathed fast, his excitement palpable. "Anyone unsure if they were Elf or unsure about Alandria would definitely feel an instant connection to it even here!" His eyes were still bright, but filled with wonder and anticipation.

"Yes, we have heard from others they experience similar things in each area that would resonate with their inner magic. Many we have identified and brought here were unaware of their magic but knew they were different from humans. We have used this simulation to help identify their origin magic, and it has never failed us," Ella explained, her eyes wide with excitement. It was a true joy to watch someone experience Alandrian magic for the first time and talking about it was nearly as exciting.

"It really is something amazing! I wish Kaeleigh and Chel could see this, they would flip out," he said. "Though I hope they're okay." Pondering their whereabouts brought his excitement level back down.

Ella peered at Finn, watching genuine concern shade his face. "I'm sure they will be. They have to be," she added in a much softer tone, hoping it was true. They needed all the allies the others could pull together. They certainly needed Kaeleigh.

"Come on, Finn," Ella changed the subject. "We need to head to the meeting hall. The others have been arriving for the last few hours while you have been playing." She winked at him.

"Hours?" Finn grabbed her arm gently as she turned away. "How long have I been in there?"

"Four hours, I think" she replied.

Finn stopped, his forehead scrunched in confusion. "It felt like only a short time, I do not understand how that much time could have passed."

"Similar to Alandria, time passes differently than in the mortal realm." She pointed to a sign next to the door with a clock and a digital box next to it. "Normally when someone goes in for a session inside mini-Alandria, they would put on one of these bracelets—similar to a watch in the mortal realm—and after a certain number of hours, it will vibrate to get their attention and inform them their time is up. For their safety, especially as they are first getting acclimated. We do not want them losing large chunks of time until they are ready to integrate into Tylínyth." She shrugged then added. "I did not think it was necessary to put one on you since I was close by and knew when to come get you. You did not even notice I had slipped away to conduct work and greet travelers," Ella smiled, "I am glad you enjoyed your time. It was partially your design. I am thrilled you got to fully experience it."

He pulled her close, feeling her heart beating where their chests came into contact with each other. Hers sped up just as his had. He gazed into her eyes and smiled. "Thank you, Ella. That was an incredible gift." His head slowly moved toward hers and just as their lips were touching, a door flung open startling them apart.

"Ella!" A young girl about ten ran into the room excitedly. "More have come!" She jumped up and down and waved her hands gesturing for them to follow, then ran out.

Finn and Ella both sighed heavily and laughed. Finn bent his head and rested it on Ella's tenderly.

"I guess it is time to go," he chuckled, pulling away. He didn't allow her to get too far and grabbed her hand, entwining his own with her much smaller one.

"Let us see how many have come," Ella said and led him out the doors.

~~~~~

After many greetings and introductions, Finn called for everyone's attention. "Welcome friends!" he shouted above the din of the room including an echo that amplified all the voices. Someone whistled and the group quieted down. "Welcome," he started once more, standing on a raised platform at the front of the very large auditorium-type room inside Talaín Tower. "Many of you have traveled far. We thank you for coming on such short notice. Please either take a seat or stand along the side so others' sight may not be obstructed."

Ella sidled up next to him and glanced out at those who had joined them. By now, those who were going to respond to the Come Home protocol would have arrived. The protocol was simple in name and
~~~~~

design. Simply it was an alert system sent out to all Twined registered with Ella's database. Those registered knew it was only enacted in dire emergencies and were required to make every effort to come, otherwise they were not required to come to the tower except for their yearly check-in. Some chose to live more as human and not seek out their gifts or Alandrian heritage, some chose to learn it then go back to their lives before they had been found with greater knowledge, but others chose to stay and integrate themselves into the program or simply live in Tylínyth.

More had come than she had thought, but still not quite as many as she had hoped. Still her heart soared to see those who did come.

"Thank you," Ella repeated. "For many of you, your connection to your heritage, to Alandria, is tenuous at best and yet still you came. I ask you to please listen to what we have to say then you will have the opportunity to make your decision to fully join or return to your homes."

"You are a part of this world, whether you have only known it for a few hours or for your entire life," Finn interjected seamlessly as if their speech had been rehearsed. He looked at Ella and gave her the floor with a wink.

"I am not going to waste your time or ours. I will be blunt, but have you known me to be anything but?" she asked rhetorically with a smirk then continued her speech.

"Alandria is dying," she said flatly. A heavy silence descended in the room, weighing upon each shoulder, some with greater connections it fell heavier but to all it fell and she let it. "She is dying but we have the chance to save her. Many of you have been ready for a fight for many years, and others of you have merely begun to think of training with our guard. Nevertheless, the time is coming to fight, a chance to save Alandria and what could be your future—whether she become your home or simply a place to learn your heritage for a season." Ella paused and her gaze consumed the crowd from one end to the other. Finn stood behind her, a sentry alert and stoic yet hopeful, his arms crossed across his chest watching the audience.

Ella began to tell the story of Alandria like they had not yet heard. She told them of Kaeleigh and Daegan, the Sol-lumieth, and the prophecy. Finn added in parts about the others they had met and worked with and the hunt for allies, bringing them up to date.

"Most recently—and those here can attest to this—Maleina found us in the forest within Alandria. We fought and we won, but not without casualties. Possessed by a greater darkness, she hurled a destructive spell into the portal from Alandria into Tylínyth and it imploded." Ella paused. "Not only did we lose our entrance into Alandria, but we lost two of our own. It has to end."

"Alandria is not the only realm to suffer if the darkness is allowed to continue," Finn began. "If Alandria dies, all the survivors will infiltrate Earth. Those of you who rely on the magic of Alandria will need to survive on the elemental energy of this realm to which there is a limit. We will become leeches to the mortal realm, siphoning off what little magic it has left, depleting it as Maleina is doing to Alandria. We will ultimately die off and take the magic of Earth with us. Could I be so selfish? Could you? There is time to stop it. There is hope to end it."

The silence was deafening. Finn moved closer to Ella, his feelings of uncertainty and unease made him agitated.

"What do we do now?" he leaned forward and whispered in her ear.

"We wait," she replied. Once more to the audience, she added in closure, "You have a choice. Stand with us and fight for Alandria, for the future of magic, for the future that could belong to not only you but your descendants if you so choose."

A shout came from the back of the room, disrupting the silence. "What makes you think once Alandria is saved, that we will be treated any differently? From what I understand any Twined within Alandria were ostracized and even cast out if not terminated."

Finn stepped forward. "In my mission over the last sixteen mortal realm years I served as guardian and friend to the Sol-lumieth—Kaeleigh—to whom Ella described to you. She is good and she has quickly already made friends with many of you, in fact, she came and trained with many of you already. It is her vow to make Alandria a better place including all of you if you so wish." He paused and his gaze became fierce passing over as many heads as he could. "I will not promise it will be easy. I will not promise it will be instantly different, but it will become the Alandria we all wish it to be. You can make it so. You will have to fight for it, for Alandria, for your freedom within it. But in it, you will be fighting for your future. You will be fighting for those who were unable to fight for themselves. The Twines in Alandria need us...you...to give them hope and strength. They need us to fight on their behalf, to show them all it can be different."

Indecipherable and murmured sounds rose from the audience, and with them another question. "When is this to take place? How long would we have to train and to be prepared?"

"We begin training right away," Finn clarified, "We do not know the exact time, but it approaches quickly. You will be trained as best as we can in whatever time we have, but you need know it may come swiftly indeed. I wish it were different, but this is our situation. We will arm everyone to their best strengths and come up with plans to use those who can fight in greater capacities. We have trainers and leaders magically and technically trained who are adept at just that. They will make you ready," Finn declared his fist clenched, raised like a gavel.

Ella nodded. "Not all will fight, those who cannot will be given other tasks to aid with healing if necessary, feeding and other tasks back at camp. We do not ask for children to fight, nor those women with children, but all are welcome to participate even back here in the realm of Tylínyth."

"How will we get into Alandria if the portal is destroyed?" another man asked. He was tall and slender with pale skin, most likely having Elf in his heritage.

"I have mentioned my grandfather to you, he is working on the other end to see if there is a way to repair and rebuild our portal. If there is not, then we have another portal from the mortal realm into Alandria, but it would be a little ways to travel there. Ideally rebuilding the portal would be our best-case scenario," Ella offered.

After another long pause followed. Ella held her breath as Finn wrapped up the speech. "Thank you for hearing us out. We truly hope you will join our fight to free Alandria and come home, but know that you will always have a place here even if you choose not to." Pausing he looked out with hope one last time. "We start training first thing in the morning inside Tylínyth at Training Field A near the mountain. If you have never been inside Tylínyth this is your chance, but take tonight and experience the mini-Alandrian simulation in the other room, feel Alandria, connect your heart to hers and see if she calls you home."

Finn took Ella's arm and ushered her off the raised platform pulling her away from the meeting hall. They needed a break before training started the next day and wanted to give their people the opportunity to choose without their presence interfering with that choice. If they chose to leave, then they would not feel bad about it in front of Ella.

"Let us give them time," Finn had whispered in her ear. "Take me to your cabin in Tylínyth and let's have our own time before all the fighting begins."

Ella had looked up at him, her eyes full of adoration and longing. Smiling she held on to him, stood up on her tiptoes and kissed him slowly on the mouth, transporting them to the entrance to Tylínyth in order to make good on his request.

Chapter Forty-Five

Morning had come quickly in Tylínyth after Finn and Ella had called all the Twined home for a meeting, delivering a clear call for them to fight. Finn arose early and exited Ella's little cabin among other cabins and bunkhouses scattered about the area. Tylínyth was set up similar to a large camp. Finn watched the sunrise, feeling the cool crisp morning like any other early fall morning in Montana, but there in Tylínyth the weather stayed pleasant all the time unless magically induced to simulate another kind for training purposes. Unsure if many would stay after their speech, Finn was anxious to get to the field first and wait. Then at the last moment, he decided that would be torture on his nerves to wait, and returned to ask Ella to come with him. He could think of a few other ways to release the pent up uncertainty, but they were both so distracted with the "what-if's" he thought visual distraction of the world around them a more productive use of their time. Plus he had all last night to reminisce on. The very thought made him smile. How he had gone so long without Ella was beyond him, his heart was so full around her; he felt all his possibilities at the forefront of his being once more when he was around her.

"What if no one else chooses to join us but our own warriors?" Ella had voiced her deepest fear.

"Some will choose to fight. But I have no speculation about how many," Finn admitted, also his greatest worry. His greatest desire was to free Alandria. Wanting to bring a show of force when the Twined joined up with the others, he truly hoped at least a quarter of them would be in that training field.

They rounded the corner from the village, and the training field came into view. They had both stopped in their tracks, mouths ajar. Not only had their warriors been there already waiting, but almost everyone had joined.

Ella, wide-eyed, gasped. "Can I trust what I see before me?"

"Truly," he shook his head, "It seems the heart of Alandria has called home her children, and they have responded."

Moving into the midst of them, passing through and by them, different ones clapped Finn on the back as a comrade would, squeezed Ella's shoulder and arm, shook hands, or simply called out they were ready to train. The amount of support they literally felt overwhelmed them.

Finn laughed out loud exuberantly then shouted, "Let the training begin!" Quickly swinging Ella up in his arms and around in a circle, he smiled. Love shone brightly in his eyes. He brought her down and kissed her fully and proudly on the lips in front of everyone. Cheers erupted, swords clapped raucously, and warriors cried out—sounds like music to Finn's ears in that moment. Putting Ella back on her feet, he swiped at a lone tear forming in his eye. Not missing anything, Ella wiped the pad of her thumb across his cheeks and then smiled in return.

"We did it. We brought them together for Alandria," she whispered her smile reaching her eyes.

"Now we have to train them!" another voice came from behind them, excited and loud. Elder Tillin, the guardian Ella had left in charge the first time they left, was holding a large weapon resembling a large two-handed Scottish Claymore sword. The excitement in his eyes declared he was ready to wield it as well.

"Yes, let us get to work," Ella nodded and gestured for Tillin to start it off.

Finn watched Ella as she pointed toward the weapons and gathered some of the women who had shown up as well. She would nurture them and teach them as only a woman could before integrating them with the rest of the warriors. He watched her walk away, a newfound purpose in the sway of her hips, and sent up a thought for a hopeful future they could enjoy together.

"Yes, let us get to work indeed." Finn walked around the training field, pairing up their experienced warrior with groups of the untrained. He adjusted weapon positions and instructed some to trade out weapons for something more useful to their height, stature, or strength. Many were raw but very eager to learn.

Drills filled the following days as members of all races—and mixes of more races than had been seen in Alandria; the few who were mixed Faerie and Elf had truly strong magic similar to Kaeleigh if they could find ways to harness it—came together to learn tricks and techniques which had been taught over the ages. His thoughts often went to Kaeleigh remembering how she processed some things or how she went about accessing or learning her magic; it helped him be able to work with the ones with similar, though different, magic. She would be proud, he'd decided. She'd love to see what was happening, to be a part of it, but he knew it was paramount she succeeded in her mission to find the Book of Lenoria.

With pride, Finn thought of Daegan, and all he had taught him. "Consider what you would do if you have a run in with Ónarach," Finn would cry alternating enemies and situations. "Use anything you can find especially fire, but do not let them touch you!"

Daegan had made an impression on Finn he now understood. He only hoped Daegan would be able to truly forgive him... and if not that, at least allow peace to grow between them.

The Twined were truly an amazing group of beings, immersing themselves into everything that could be thrown at them. Finn had even begun adding magic to random fighting groups, seeing how they handled the mix up, and they did splendid, beyond what he could have imagined for the limited time they had been training. He wasn't sure it would be enough, but the show in force he hoped made up for some of it. As he reflected on the Twined's progress, pride welled inside him. How much ground they had covered and gained in such a short time!

Suddenly Ella stopped in place, though Finn realized he knew it before he saw her. He'd felt her in his heart. He whipped his head around to where she had fallen to her knees. There were others around her, squatting close and waving their hands in front of her face to get her to respond to them, but though she was very much breathing and sitting on the ground, she seemed completely unaware of those around her. Finn dropped the weapon he held in his hand and ran to Ella.

He dropped to his knees directly in front of her. "Ella? What is it?" he asked, trying to stifle a panic that threatened his throat.

But Ella didn't answer. Finn looked to the women around her, his voice full of snap, "What happened?"

"We don't know, Finn. She was fine, in the middle of a sentence, in fact, then suddenly she stopped. Her face became blank like this. She just fell to her knees, and just this…" the girl, unfazed by his tone, trailed off.

"Did she say anything? Anything strange? Anything at all?" Finn searched.

They shook their heads, puzzled. Then one straightened up. "Oh, wait, yes! She said 'Grandfather' right before she fell."

Finn's eyes grew wide. "I did not think it was possible for him to reach her inside Tylínyth," he said relieved. To the others he explained, "She must be getting a vision from her grandfather. He has the ability, though I did not think he could broach the boundaries of the realms."

"What should we do?" another asked, her eyes large with worry.

"We wait. She will come out of it, hopefully with a message from Alandria," Finn replied, wiping a hand down his face. His stomach had fallen to his feet when he saw her go rigid and fall to her knees.

Moments passed when finally Ella gasped for air as if she had been deprived. Her eyes blinked spastically, and her hands reached for him instinctively knowing he was there.

"Ella!" Finn held her arms and did not let go even after she gained her bearings. "What is it? Your grandfather?"

She nodded swiftly. "It came as a shock, I have not heard from him since we left Alandria and it takes more magic to communicate across realm boundaries," Ella said, catching her breath.

"Ella, what did he say?" Finn's urged, full of impatience and excitement alike.

"Right." Her face sobered. "There is trouble. You and I are needed back in Ehsmia right away. It is not yet time to bring our forces, but we need to find out what the trouble is," she explained. She watched Finn's eyebrows pinch and unthinking, worried her own hands together. "He did say it was something about Chel, though he clearly said she was fine. For now. We do not have long though. Also, he wanted to know our progress and inform us he has been working with other elders on the portal from their side and though they could not repair the one that got destroyed, they were able to create a temporary one as needed, but he needs me to open it on this side as well. I told him we would be there soon."

Finn's face went ashen. Chel. "What could have happened to Chel? He didn't say anything else?" Finn jumped to his feet and pulled Ella up with him.

She shook her head. "No, he did not say anything else."

"Let us tie up our ends here and go," Finn rushed out, raking a hand through his hair.

Ella placed one hand on his bicep and the other on the side of his face, pulling him toward her gently. "Finn, look at me." When she had his full attention, she continued. "We will go quickly as we can, we will find the truth, and we will face it. Together."

He nodded, a peace falling within his soul. "You used magic on me," he acknowledged, but did not care as he kissed her forehead. "Thank you. I know you care."

"Come let us go speak with Elder Tillin and the other leaders to carry on in our absence. I do not know how long we will be gone, but the good news is traveling back into Alandria will now not be much of an issue and it will be faster." She smiled, excited to know a portal was available again. It would solve their main problem of how to transport hundreds of the Twined back into Alandria when the right time came.

Finn could feel that time approaching. More time to prepare, more time to train, they may even have a fighting chance to not only survive but to help push the battle in Alandria's favor. For now they had to get back to Alandria. He hated he had to withdraw from his role in training with the Twined, but what he hated more was the fear in his heart rapidly accelerating. What could have befallen his friend, Chel?

Chapter Forty-Six

The Mortal Realm.

"Are you ready, Kaeleigh?" Daegan whispered into her ear.

"Yes," came her reply just as he kissed her cheek close to her ear then he vanished, leaving her standing in an unfamiliar place inside the tree line.

Breathing deeply, struggling to catch her breath, Kaeleigh turned in a wide circle, eyes searching. "Daegan? Daegan where are you?" she called out. Nothing but an extreme line separating one large, tilled field from another. Shoots of green winter wheat were sprouting. Adjacent this field lie another filled with dry wheat which had already begun to be harvested and bailed. The only structure to be seen was an old, Victorian farmhouse far in the distance.

"Daegan?" she called again, with a hint of panic.

"He left you alone? How very un-warrior-like of him," a snide female voice said from further inside the small patch of forest. Jumping down from a high limb of one of the sturdy trees, a young woman not too much older in appearance than Kaeleigh landed with barely a thud. Her long black hair swooshed around her shoulders, some landing over her dark eyes as she braced her stance, a badass villain through and through. "He knew I was after him and left you to distract me, is that it?"

"You are after Daegan?" Kaeleigh asked, slightly taken aback. They thought she had been after the map. "Why?"

The woman shrugged her shoulders uncaring. "I am here to finish him off by stealing the rest of his soul."

"You gave that up a little easy." Kaeleigh frowned. She needed to keep her talking a bit longer.

"I see no reason not to tell you as this will be my last job then I will have my freedom." She shrugged.

"What's your job, what does it have to do with Daegan? And what do you mean by 'your freedom'?" *This was getting more confusing.* Kaeleigh tilted her head more curious.

Now annoyed, the other woman sighed and stalked forward several steps. "I am under contract—two technically I think—an assassin for hire. It's what I do, it's what I am. Daegan is my current target."

"You kill people as your job?"

"No. I kill people because of my *gift*," she spat out, "and others simply use it to their advantage."

Kaeleigh had to keep her talking. "What is your name? I'm Kaeleigh."

"Jinthíya. Jin." The woman clad in black leather from head to toe leaned casually against a tree. "I know who you are."

"What is your gift, Jin?" Keeping her talking, Kaeleigh looked around, searching for Daegan.

"I am a soul stealer. I steal people's souls." Eyes flat, tone flat, she betrayed nothing. However, she unknowingly betrayed more than she would have liked had she known what Kaeleigh saw in her.

"That must be a very challenging gift to guard," Kaeleigh genuine concern in her voice. She couldn't imagine an ability that could actually take someone's soul. However, she definitely could imagine how someone like Maleina or another seeking power would exploit such an ability. Kaeleigh saw the prison surrounding Jin, the one others put her in and the one she put herself in. Her heart reached out to Jin and suddenly wanted freedom for her as well.

"More of a curse," Jin huffed, crossing her arms.

"Why are you telling me all this?"

Jin shrugged once more. "You asked. Many don't ask. And as we are apparently waiting for Daegan to return, I figured why not."

Gripped by the hopeless desperation Kaeleigh saw in the woman's eyes, she couldn't help but take a step forward. Eyes widening on the other party, she cocked her head watching Kaeleigh.

"I'm so sorry, Jin. No one should be used the way you have been. Maybe I can help?"

"You would help *me*?" Jin practically spat as she pushed off and away from the tree. Not turning her back to Kaeleigh but clearly separating herself. "After all I told you I am capable of? You have no idea all I have done!"

"Yes," Kaeleigh said with all certainty. "I am not certain what I can do, but if you wanted my help, I would do what I could."

Jin considered Kaeleigh and her offer and called her bluff. "Kill Maleina and the one in the mountain who now holds my contract."

A small intake of breath gave Kaeleigh away. She had never killed an animal let alone a person; she knew in battle some would die, and to protect her friends and Alandria she would do whatever she had to, but she hoped for another way.

"I didn't think so," Jin replied hotly and began to stalk forward toward Kaeleigh.

"We would do what we could to give you your freedom, but you would not be allowed to take any more souls," Daegan's voice came from behind Jin, and she stiffened. A smirk rose on her face before she spun around to face him, leaving Kaeleigh at her back.

"There you are. I knew you were close. See, I have tasted your soul before when you were quite young, and I could have always found you had I had the desire to." She thought of the piece of his soul contained within the crystal amulet she now kept close. The *other* woman—the mistress of the mountain—who countered her contract with Maleina, promised her freedom if she handed over Daegan.

"Well, that's just disturbing," Kaeleigh commented from behind her, holding her place. Kaeleigh held a dagger Daegan had given her at her side, her hand at its hilt ready to draw if needed.

"It is, I agree," Jin added, "but convenient when someone needs me to find him."

"You have a choice, Jinthíya. You can leave here without trouble or we can make you leave, but I would advise you leave on your own. We have to meet with your new employer, and I intend to be there." Daegan stood solid in his stance, his eyes ever watchful in studying Jin's every move. A dangerous enemy to have indeed, especially when she could find him at will. He would have to see what could be done about that. He hoped Arileas would know more about how to accomplish that.

"I appreciate the opportunity truly," her voice full of sarcasm, "but unfortunately I am not able to simply leave empty handed." Jin pulled out a dagger in one hand and a small vial in the other and stepped toward Daegan. "I must have your soul young Daegan—though not so young anymore are you?" She gave him a sultry smile, Kaeleigh completely forgotten behind her. "I must have my freedom!" Jin growled, dagger pointed out. All she needed was to move within striking distance and slice an opening for his soul to come to her, like they all did.

"This is not the way to gain it," Daegan strongly countered.

"What would you know of it?" she spat, her rage evident in her eyes.

"I know more than you think I might. Maleina sought to use me, to bind me to her unwillingly and unknowingly in most cases. We can help you."

A slip, a dare to hope in her eyes, but there nonetheless, and Daegan gained the upper hand, moving so fast his sword was suddenly at her chest. Jin's eyes widened. "You never would have helped me would you?"

"We would and we will, but right now we do not have time to do all of that. We absolutely cannot have you stop our mission." Kaeleigh responded from behind her moving forward, trapping Jin between them her dagger drawn.

Something happened, the air around Jin wavered sending out intense vibrations like Kaeleigh and Daegan had never seen. Instead of vanishing like Alandrians do when teleporting, Jin's body seemed to slide to the side, trailing in her wake a ghostly essence of where she had just been allowing her to be free of their trap.

"Daegan! Watch out, she's moving!" Kaeleigh shouted with panic. A claw of fear shot up her spine—in one moment she could lose Daegan and there would have been nothing she could have done but watch his soul be ripped from his body.

Or was there...

Kaeleigh lunged forward and without thought, without hesitation, she threw her magic out between Daegan and Jin with a loud roar just as she saw Jin's form dart toward him at incredible speed. A burst of her magic shot out, creating an oval of shimmering energy. Jin ran right through it. She did not run into Daegan, but instead disappeared into the oval of magic.

Kaeleigh held her arms out in shock, afraid to let the magic go. "What happened? What did I do?" panic stuttered her tone.

"Let it go, Kaeleigh!" shouted Daegan.

As soon as she did, she collapsed onto her knees against a soft forest floor of lichen and mosses, mixed with dead fallen leaves, the fields still at their back. Her chest heaving, her eyes found Daegan's, her rock, her home then her breathing came easier.

"You're all right," her words barely a whisper. "I couldn't lose you. But what did I do?"

Daegan smiled, the corners reached his eyes. "You created a portal, Kaeleigh. Did you know you could do that?"

"No. I did what?"

"Like Arileas can, you created a portal. Though he can only open one inside Alandria as far as I understand. You opened one not only outside Alandria, but into it from the mortal realm. That is unheard of, Kaeleigh!"

"So I sent her back into Alandria?"

"Yes, that ought to give us some more time to complete our mission."

"Then let's get on with it." Kaeleigh took his hand and led him to the edge of the tree line, miles and miles of fields before them.

"You knew I had not left you alone back there, correct?" Daegan asked suddenly.

Looking up into his face, Kaeleigh placed her palm against his cheek. "I did. I know you would not leave me unless you had to. It was part of our plan to draw her out."

He nodded satisfied. "Then let us see where this map would have us be. This is the location it led us to?"

"Yes," she replied. "This is the place, though it is strange, isn't it? It feels peaceful and quiet on one side." She gestured toward the fields tended and the house in the distance. "But almost desolate and foreboding on the other." Kaeleigh pointed to the barren, dry ground in the opposite. "It's very strange."

Daegan frowned and examined each side, casting out his magic to either side. "It is strange. I can feel magic, good magic, near the house, but I feel a void of magic in the other. I have never felt such a thing before, especially in the mortal realm."

"What should we do? It's starting to get late," Kaeleigh noted as the sun was setting just behind the house.

"Well, we need to find shelter for the night. Your choice. We either stay in the forest or see what we find and take our chances at the house?"

Kaeleigh considered both options, looking back and forth between the forest and the house. Thinking of their last encounter in this forest, Kaeleigh shivered. The house was an unknown, but something about the house—or the magic of the house—called to her.

"The house. I don't know why, but something pulls me to it." Kaeleigh couldn't take her eyes off the lavender-painted beauty trimmed out with white accents amidst the windows and decking.

"The house it is then. We shall soon find out why," Daegan replied, trusting Kaeleigh's instincts.

After trudging through fields, they reached the large porch with a section enclosed by net to keep out bugs and critters. Paint chipped around the white trimmed windows, and areas of the deck was lifting or warping, yet the overall feel was enchanting. As they stepped up to the door to knock, the old-fashioned front door swung open.

Kaeleigh gasped and Daegan's eyes opened wide. Standing before them was a familiar face.

"Metrí? What are you... No, you're not are you?" Kaeleigh wondered, tilting her head confused. "I'm so sorry, you look like someone I know. Startled me is all."

A petite slip of a girl with a mop of white blonde hair half way down her back stood in front of her. Her eyes were a pale green, the color of the sea glass. Smiling bright without hesitation, the girl opened the door wider and allowed them in. "I'm Skye. Welcome to my home Kaeleigh and Daegan. I heard you might be coming. I have your rooms all ready for you. You must be tired. I can have food ready for you in just a bit, too, if you're hungry. Follow me." The girl prattled quickly as she walked through the entry into the main living area with multiple couches and places to sit. The decor was pleasant and traditional, putting both Daegan and Kaeleigh immediately at ease.

"You know us?" Kaeleigh's heart about stopped.

"Of course," Skye smiled as if it was a strange question.

"Did you say you heard we were coming?" Daegan asked suspiciously, causing Skye to stop and turn toward him.

"Yes. He told me you would be coming give or take a day or two, but otherwise you are on time." She smiled.

"I'm sorry, but who told you?" Kaeleigh asked now also suspicious though the girl gave them no feeling of malicious intent.

"Santori. He can see the future—well sometimes—but he saw you coming and told me I would need to be ready for you. He's a little strange, but means well," Skye answered matter of fact.

Kaeleigh shared a glance with Daegan, but they allowed Skye to continue showing them around the house and to their rooms upstairs. "My grandmother—she lives with me here—is in town for a couple days visiting family. She knew you were coming though, too, and won't mind you being here in case you were wondering."

Kaeleigh almost couldn't help her expression of joy that wanted to sneak out at the way this girl trusted them and talked so fast, it was endearing. Glancing at Daegan she noted he seemed to not relax, but lost whatever suspicion he originally had toward the girl.

"Skye?" Daegan asked as they ate some simple sandwiches she had made for them.

Her head shot up along with her eyebrows in response.

"Did Santori say, or do you know what we are supposed to do once we arrived here?"

"No. I expect he will be around soon enough, maybe tomorrow or the next day. He always knows when to show up." She shrugged finished the chip she had in her hand. "Until then, though, relax and enjoy the farm I guess. We have chickens so I will be up bright and early."

"Skye," Kaeleigh began hesitantly. "Do you know about us? I mean, where we are from perhaps?" she tiptoed around her real question.

"Are you asking if I know about Alandria and that you have magic and aren't human? Yes, I do." She smiled then winked.

"You see, I'm a witch—I come from a long line of elemental witches—living on the border of the mortal realm and another realm so I have to know about all kinds of things. And I've met people and have friends from other... places."

"That explains some things then," Daegan considered thoughtfully. Kaeleigh watched him, wanting to know what was going through his head. "I hope you will count us among your friends," he added.

"Of course I do. And I look forward to getting to know you both more. I hear a fight is coming to Alandria and there is much to be done. I am on your side and will do what I can if I can be of help. Tomorrow I can tell you about my magic and what I can do, if you'd like."

"I would like that very much," Kaeleigh said then a yawn slipped out.

Skye giggled. "But for tonight, I will say goodnight. You know your way now. Off to bed. Sleep well and dream peacefully." Skye inclined her head then shooed them out of the kitchen.

Chapter Forty-Seven

Kaeleigh woke up with a jolt, her heart hammering in her chest, her breaths coming in puffs. Looking around the room she was staying in, it took her a moment to recall where she was. Scattered paintings lined the window framing, a table with multiple instruments for charting stars mixed with neatly contained art supplies seemed to beckon. Seeing this office of sorts, Kaeleigh remembered where she was. At Skye's, in the old farmhouse. It was a lovely room surrounded with windows all around like a watchtower. Settling her mind and her spirit, she remembered her dream and leaped out of bed and quickly made herself presentable with what little she had brought with her. It was dawn.

Hurrying down several sets of stairs, she found Daegan already sitting at a barstool in the kitchen they had eaten in last night.

"You're up early," she commented, breathless from the quick descent.

Daegan turned to her and smiled. "Good morning." His brows pinched and he rose to meet her, placing a hand on her arm. "What is it? You look pale."

"A dream. I had a dream or not a dream... I'm not sure, it seemed so real."

"Kaeleigh sit down. Your hands are trembling. What is it?" Daegan guided her to the stool he had just vacated and placed his hands on either of her shoulders, sending waves of calm through her, helping her with her thoughts.

Nodding, she put one of her hands over his. "Thank you. That is better. I just am not sure how real it was and if it is to be heeded. But first, I smell coffee, is there any?" Looking around she spotted the source of the blessed scent she had not had the privilege of enjoying much on their journeys.

"I will get you a cup. You talk."

"In my dream, I was visiting with my mother and several others—the *Orchids*—and your mother as well, Daegan." Kaeleigh turned forward in her seat. "It was short, though it felt much longer as a dream, they warned me we needed to go back to Alandria. They said our mission to get to them could wait for now, but something else could not. We were needed in Elnye." Kaeleigh inhaled sharply and held her breath then blew it out slowly. "Do you think it was real? It felt real. We've come all this way, what should we do?"

Daegan slowly turned to her, watched her carefully. "What does your heart say?"

Kaeleigh stilled and sought inside herself, finding the peace she trusted. "It says to heed what they say. I feel something is wrong, but I don't know what. Can we contact Arileas from here?"

"I will attempt to. Perhaps the tree line would be sufficient as a contact point," Daegan wondered.

"Actually, I was wondering if the highest point in this house would work. There is power here, an energy I can feel. It might serve as an addition to our magic."

Daegan nodded. "Yes. I feel it too. We will ask Skye."

"Where is Skye?" Kaeleigh turned her head looking around the room and beyond for their host.

Daegan nodded to the window. "She is out in the field. Awoke at the beginning of dawn to feed the chickens as she said, but then she went to stand at the line between fields. She appears to be talking to someone—though I see no one—or simply out loud to herself. I find it strange." He frowned and gestured for Kaeleigh to look.

"I don't see anyone either." Pausing, Kaeleigh bit her lip. "Do you see the resemblance?" Kaeleigh hesitated, skirting around something.

"I do. Though I am not sure how to approach it yet."

"Neither do I. We should get to know her a bit more maybe." Kaeleigh turned back toward the window. "Oh! I do see someone, a man, he seems partially in a shadow though I'm not sure how, there is no tree or anything near there." Kaeleigh frowned. "I think we should go out there."

Grabbing the coffee mug Daegan brought over to her, she smiled and moved toward the back door leading outside. Daegan followed, held the door open above her head. Kaeleigh walked casually, admiring the beauty of all the flowers around the house. Winter's approach limited what could grow, but bright Mums, Marigolds, and other assortments of colorful beauty surrounded the area in pots or ground. Daegan, however, kept his gaze trained on where Skye stood, awkwardly speaking. Squinting in the bright morning sunlight, he still saw nothing. To gain clarity of what was before him, he fused his magic with his sight. To his dismay, Skye was indeed speaking with someone, a man, cloaked in wisps of shadow and darkness.

"Kaeleigh wait," Daegan reached for her arm, halting her. "We do not know who she speaks to, be cautious."

"I will," she said looking up into his eyes, upon his face. "I can see the shadows, but I also feel the light. Can't you? I think it's why he can hide or cloak himself in it, because he can use both the natural elements of both light and dark."

"That is what concerns me," he grumbled in return.

Tugging his arm, Kaeleigh pulled Daegan along with her, at her side, and approached close but not so close as to interrupt.

"Morning, Skye!" Kaeleigh called out to give her fair warning they were coming.

Skye turned with a bright smile on her face, waved. "Good morning to the both of you! Come meet my friend." She gestured to what appeared to be open space to the untrained eye. When she did, a man in his mid-thirties stepped out—his face was smooth of wrinkles but dark, piercing eyes held an ancient and mysterious energy, even danger to one not welcomed—from his rift between light and dark.

With slick black hair, those intimidating eyes instantly found Kaeleigh's, though slowly he inclined his head. Something within his gaze pierced her chest, she felt a fraction of his pain, his lot in life, and her heart went out to him. All within a brief second before Skye even got the introductions underway.

"This is my friend, Santori," she began. "He also has been waiting for you. He was the one who told me you would be coming, and you have." She beamed, excited of the fulfillment of prophecy.

"Santori, this is Kaeleigh and this is Daegan." Skye gestured to each of them in turn.

"I am aware, but thank you for that, Skye," he said slowly, his words drawn out, controlled.

Blushing, she angled a look at Santori and threw up her arms. "Well, of course you do, but it's always awkward if you don't finish the introductions. Then someone is left hanging and the conversations stills. I did my part. Now do yours."

Santori laughed deeply. "Forgive me. Indeed, I will do mine, thank you."

"You left me the map," Kaeleigh stated with sudden understanding.

"Yes, and the piece of the Book of Lenoria," Santori stated in turn, watching Kaeleigh closely.

"How did you come to possess and then remove a piece from an ancient and protected item?" Daegan asked with suspicion.

"You have every right to be cautious, Daegan of the Ferrishyn. It is a tale I will tell in part but first may I suggest we take this conversation to the patio for comfort. And perhaps if we are fortunate, Skye would offer her delightful tea and cookies she makes." His face took on a boyish expression, eyes alit from within, and a tug at the corners of his mouth.

Skye smirked, "Who can say no to that face? Come on and make yourselves comfortable. It's my grandma's recipe for the cookies, but mine for the tea. I use some lavender and mint from the garden and it is delicious if I do say so myself." She winked at them and led the way to the patio, got her guests seated and provided the offering she agreed to.

"I will only cover the basics of how I obtained the book then proceeded to offer it back to Alandria as it is a very long tale and causes me pain to recount it." Shadows passed over his eyes as he took a sip of his tea. "During what was supposed to be the peace agreements sixteen years ago, it was told to the elders it would all go wrong. King Ryek—I believe you have come to know him as Hunter then Grandfather," he eyed Kaeleigh and waited for her nod. "King Ryek pulled in a family of Shifters from the elusive line of the mystic snowy owls to protect and hide the tome in the mortal realm from the chaos that was about to ensue Alandria. He knew the darkness would be after it as it holds the secrets to Alandria and with those someone could rule over all the races to the destruction of all. I was among those Shifters, one of their family as I had not my own."

His expression grew dark with pain. "On our way into the mortal realm, we were ambushed and they were killed... all but one."

He paused at Kaeleigh's dramatic gasp of shock, feeling her underlying outrage gave him the encouragement needed to continue. "I took the Shifter child who survived and the book. Since then we have been moving it around constantly, keeping it out of the thoughts and minds of those who seek it—and they do, many do, they come regularly seeking what they cannot find nor possess. But they do torture any who stand in the way and I had had enough, sent my friend back to Alandria to hide where only the mystic owls knew to hide," his gaze took on a faraway look, "Truth be told, I'm hoping he will find others of his kind who survived their intended extinction. I took the book and hid it well. It will only be found by the one intended to find it; however, that does not mean it will stop others from pursuing it. Be warned."

"I am sorry for your loss," Kaeleigh said heartfelt, leaning forward toward him from her chair opposite him. "I know what it is to lose, that pain never truly leaves."

"I do appreciate your care, but I have a duty as well and I will continue to do my part. Then I can move on to pursue my own goals." He smiled mischievously.

"And what might those goals be?" Daegan pried unapologetically, his eyes narrowed, his face set.

Santori revealed the side to him others might see as the Dark Elf, the sneer that replaced the once softened expression as he spoke of his long lost friends. "That is my own to know, princeling. But do know I am on the side of Alandria. She was my home and my comfort when no one and nowhere else could be, for that I am in her debt."

"So you saw us come here, for the book. Does that mean you can predict the future?" Kaeleigh asked to change the subject.

Santori inclined his head, appreciating the change. "Foresight is what you would call it, and yes. Though not always predictable as events and wills change." His face hardened and his eyes grew dark, his hands fisted on the arms of his chair, yet careful to have put Skye's glass down before he shattered it within his hand. The moment passed and the storm in his eyes along with it. The others waited for the outcome with bated breath, but relaxed as he did. Daegan shifted a quick glance toward Kaeleigh though she seemed largely unaffected.

"What do we do next then?" Kaeleigh asked. "Do you know the way to Exhile?"

Santori swiveled his head, his gaze directed into Kaeleigh's. Approving of what he saw within her eyes, he sat back and crossed his feet at the ankles. "It is right outside Skye's field." He indicated where they had just come from. "The line between the barren and the growth."

"It is like a portal, but also like a rift between worlds. The science behind it is fascinating and incomprehensible, and would take too much time to get into," Skye said with a slight blush creeping up her smooth pale neck. "Sorry, I get carried away. But yes, it's there. In fact, I've gone through it before, though I don't like to stay long."

"I have told you to stay out of there, Skye. Why will you not listen?" Santori scolded. "Do you not care for your own protection?"

"Of course I do!" she retaliated. "But I have my own missions I need answers to and I feel pulled to it—one of them is in there. I can't deny it and you know I will keep searching until I find what I'm looking for."

Santori nodded with a soft sigh. "I do. But you may not like what you find when you find it," he said quietly. His concern for Skye apparent in the brotherly way he looked at her.

Turning to Kaeleigh and Daegan, she explained, "He's already seen me there finding something. I know even though he won't tell me any details." Skye huffed with frustration.

"That seems a strange place for a portal to have emerged—or have been created for that matter," Daegan mused.

"It was an unlikely one, indeed," Santori agreed. "You will meet one on your journey who can tell you more of its tale if you wish to hear it."

"Oooo cryptic!" Skye said hauntingly. "You'll get used to when he talks and when he gives bits of the future. Although, sometimes you can't tell the difference." She raised her shoulders unconcerned.

"You asked what you do next, Kaeleighnna of the Orchids," Santori began, his gaze trained on hers. "You return to Alandria. You have business in Exhile, but not this day. You are called back, you are needed." He paused. "The book is in Alandria, not far from where you will end up. To complete what you need to accomplish in Exhile, you must have the book. You will not return here for some time, there is another entrance from inside Alandria, within the dark craggy mountains near Elnye. For that is where you will go, but first to your hidden place for your mission."

Santori inhaled slowly through his nose, his gaze strayed from Kaeleigh to Daegan and back. "You both must return... soon."

"Now that was one of his foretelling tones," Skye pointed out, her eyes bright and excited. "I guess you have to leave. I will see you again. I know we will... in here." She placed her hand on her heart. "We are connected in some way and I have yet to learn of it."

Kaeleigh looked to Daegan. "I guess that confirms my dream then." Turning to the other two she explained her dream from the Orchids just the night before.

"You are more connected to them than I thought," Santori said thoughtfully. "Yes, they need you but also agree your place is for now in Alandria. I have the map you will need once your initial task is completed." He held out his hand, empty palm up. In a blink, an old textured parchment was there. He folded it and handed it to Kaeleigh. "Keep it safe, for it will guide you just as the last one guided you here to us. You will not need it until you are ready to leave Elnye."

Kaeleigh took the map gently and held it within her hands. "Whoa. I want to learn how to do what Santori just did." She smiled as she turned to Daegan. "I just need to run up and grab my backpack then we can go."

"All right. I have everything with me. I will wait here."

Skye and Santori sipped their tea between the small chat about the farm and how long it had been in Skye's family, a long line of elemental witches. Her mother had disappeared when she was but a toddler and her grandmother had come to raise her.

Kaeleigh slid into the seat next to Daegan and placed the map inside her pack, carefully with the other one she had. Unsure if she should ask or not, Kaeleigh looked at Skye and blurted, "Do you have a sister?"

Unflustered, Skye tilted her head. "You mistook me for someone when you first arrived, said I reminded you of someone. Is this why you are asking?"

"Yes. I'm sorry I meant that to be more gently delivered, not blurted without tact."

"I thought perhaps once maybe I did, but Grandmother won't speak much of the past or what happened with my mom. She truly doesn't know much, other than my mom experimented with magic she shouldn't have. She hid the journals my mom had been working on, all except the family grimoire—or book of spells—she deemed acceptable to learn from. She has taught me everything I know, and yet I feel like something is missing, a part of me I don't understand. Could I have a sister? Yes. But I truly don't know." She placed her hand on her heart again. "My heart says I have someone out there, some answers out there I need to find."

"I know the truth of that," Kaeleigh said, also placing her hand on her heart. "If I can I will help you once this task if finished. If you find your way into Alandria, I have someone I want you to meet, one who might be able to help you in your search."

Santori watched Kaeleigh, closed his eyes for a mere moment. Upon opening them, his mouth ticked and his eyes held a sparkle not there before. He nodded almost imperceptibly to Kaeleigh to which she returned. Indeed she had someone she wanted to introduce Skye to definitely, her heart sang with the truth of it. She vowed to herself she would bring Skye and Metrí together when the immediate needs were finished.

"I would invite you with us now, but I feel it is not yet the time," Kaeleigh said softly, sad it couldn't be, but felt the truth in it.

"I agree, Skye, it is not yet your time," Santori added. "But it is coming soon and more will be revealed when it does."

"Then it is settled," Skye said matter of fact.

Daegan stood and pulled Kaeleigh to her feet with him. "It is time for us to return to Alandria." He turned to Skye and bowed. "Thank you for your hospitality. We will meet again."

Kaeleigh lunged forward and wrapped her arms around the thin column of Skye's neck. "Thank you. I promise we will see each other soon. Practice up on your magic, for I feel you will need it."

Deagan inclined his head the slightest bit toward Santori. "Thank you for your assistance."

"Thank you, Santori. I know your story with ours is not yet finished. Until we meet again," Kaeleigh said and reached around his waist before he could stop her and hugged him. Unaccustomed to the action, he awkwardly patted her back until she pulled away.

He nodded, a strange expression of disarmed enchantment came over him. "Indeed we will meet again. Follow your heart, young princess then follow the map." He winked at her and returned to his tea and cookies, not yet ready to leave.

Daegan and Kaeleigh held hands down the steps of the front porch, then with a blink they were gone, back to their portal entrance that would lead them home back to Alandria.

EPILOGUE

"Metrí, my dear, you have progressed so much since you have arrived," Arileas encouraged the young girl left in his care. The two had been practicing and experimenting with the elemental magic Metrí seemed to have an affinity with. The darkness had been growing in Alandria since Daegan, Kaeleigh, Finn, and his own Ella had left in search of allies and the Book of Lenoria. For the time was coming, he knew, they would need all the allies and magic they could find.

"Thank you, Arileas!" She beamed, that shock of white-blonde curls bouncing and swooshing as she magically spun the air around them in a contained practice arena. Her eyes, the gray of a coming storm, lit with the energy of her magic. "I think I'm getting the hang of it!"

"Indeed." Arileas closed his eyes for a moment, felt the torrent of wind subside around him.

"What is it?" Metrí asked. "You seem distracted today."

"The time is coming." He opened his eyes, a far-off chasm dwelt within them. "The allies are gathering outside Adettlyn."

"Should they come here? Wouldn't it be safer for them all and less conspicuous?"

"Aidón indicated the time and place for the allies to merge. It is almost time to go." He inhaled slowly and smiled. "Finnlan and Ella have received my message. They will arrive soon." Then he frowned as he mentally sought out the others with his magical connection to Alandria. "Master Halister comes now with another, the wake of disaster and fear following him," Arileas sighed. "Maleina is up to something, though I cannot see what. I fear she will go too far." Arileas rose from where he sat and gestured for Metrí to walk at his side. "We will await them before meeting the allies."

"What about Daegan and Kaeleigh? Any word from them?" Metrí practically bounced on her toes in anticipation.

"Yes and from an unanticipated ally, it seems. They, too, will be arriving soon, though I think they will arrive just in time to leave again. They will find us."

"Do you think they found the Book of Lenoria?"

"Hmm. It seems not, for the Dark Elf I spoke with sent them back to Alandria with yet another piece to their journey. The timing is correct though, as we will need them here, I fear, for this next part before the battle begins," he replied thoughtfully.

"What part is that?" she asked hesitantly, fear crawling up her spine.

"Chel has been taken captive by Maleina, they mean to rescue her of that I am sure, although I am uncertain how much Kaeleigh knows. Chel's abduction weighs heavily upon Halister, he believes it is his fault."

"What?!" Metrí cried. "We will get her back, I know we will. Kaeleigh would not allow anything less."

Arileas nodded. His expression grew somber, but his tone sure and resolute. "The allies are gathering. All of Alandria's chosen are coming home. We will be ready for them as this next phase in the fight for Alandria has just begun."

"We will be ready."

✽✽✽✽✽

Thank you for reading *Fading Light*! I hope you enjoyed the fourth installment of Kaeleigh and Daegan's adventure! Things are getting intense!! Don't miss their continued journey as this unlikely group assembles the allies needed for the coming war. Discover who they will find and who they might lose to the darkness in the final installment: The Sol-lumieth!

Stay tuned for book 5 in The Age of Alandria series: The Sol-Lumieth coming June 26th, 2024!

Alandria is fading.
The veil between realms has thinned.
War is inevitable.

She, the mistress of the mountain in Exhile, has absorbed an intense amount of power and is poised to unleash the next phase of her evil plan. Meanwhile, the Droch-Shúil spreads fear and darkness across Alandria. If salvation does not come for the Orchids, their souls will be lost forever. Will *She* escape her sentence in Exhile and take over Alandria? Or will the one surprise she isn't expecting derail her?

Kaeleigh and Daegan rush back to Alandria after their tumultuous journey through the mortal realm, seeking the Book of Lenoria. Chel is in trouble. And the magical life force of the forests and territories of Alandria is being siphoned away, infiltrated by evil. The Dryads are doing all they can to keep the trees—and themselves—alive.

Unexpected friends have been found. The allies are ready to sacrifice it all to save their once beautiful realm, their home, but not everyone will survive.

Will the light of The Sol-lumieth be strong enough to stop the darkness or will this be the end of the magical realm of Alandria?

GLOSSARY OF TERMS~

PLACES

Alandria: A realm parallel to our mortal realm inhabited by several races of magical beings and creatures. Created by the Originators also known as The Orchids.

Exhile: Another realm—a pocket realm—where the condemned souls of the non-human go to spend eternity in unrest or until they are devoured and absorbed into the land, whichever comes first.

Lenoria: The original realm from which the creators of Alandria came. The darkness destroyed it. "Old magic" comes from this realm, but not much is remembered.

Feraánmar: The territory mainly inhabited by Faeries and the Ferrishyn.

Elnye: The capital city of Feraánmar.

Lumari: The territory mainly inhabited by the Elves.

Adettlyn: The capital city of Lumari.

Ehsmia: Home to the Ehsmian people (see below). A magical location hidden within the Kandrian Mountains, near Adettlyn, partially within the territory of Lumari.

Tylínyth: A pocket realm magically created via an overlay between the realms of Alandria and Earth (the mortal realm). It is home, sanctuary, and training ground to many of the Twined (see below).

PEOPLE/BEINGS/CREATURES:

Ferrishyn: (fair-i-shin) They are the warrior race of Faeries, mostly male, in the territory of Feraánmar. Physically more muscular and bigger builds than other faeries. Created to fight and protect. They serve as hunters, guides, and guardians. Elite members become a part of the royal guard or for the presiding Paladin.

Earth Faeries: The most common race of Faeries. They are cultivators and growers for the lands of Alandria, their magic strengthened from the earth itself even as they give back to it. A more peaceful people.

Ehsmia: (a.k.a. The Hidden People), An ancient race of faeries that have been in hiding to protect their race from extinction—though they are already believed to be of legend, if remembered at all. Their magic is stronger as they retain a fraction of the 'old magic' from their realm of origin—Lenoria—as opposed to the magic of Earth Faeries. Though they are blessed with long life, they are cursed with slow reproduction so there are not many remaining.

Elves: At one point were the majority race in Alandria. They have a base magic as most do in Alandria, but some are gifted with more abilities than others. Their magic is strengthened from the light of the sun, moon, and stars.

Shifters: A race of beings that have the ability to shift into an animal. Those of greater strength and magic, may have the ability to shift into more than one animal form rather than just one.

The Orchids: An illusive collective of heads from various races united together, originally to create Alandria, after they fled the darkness destroying their original realm of Lenoria. Considered the "Originators" and make up the group considered the Elders—though not all Elders are Orchids. Their goal: to unite Alandria against the darkness that stirs upheaval against the kingdoms.

The Droch-Shúil: Is an evil entity. It is an ancient host collecting souls that went bad—the unforgiven dead. It grows with the strength and magic of the souls it consumes. Also considered a kind of demon. It is subservient to whichever master controls it at the time, and ultimately will forgo its purpose to fulfill its master's wishes. Can be in physical form of a hooded dark creature or most often as a intelligent mass of darkness.

Ferriers: Not quite Faeries or Elves for that matter, an ancient creature nonetheless existing in Alandria but not of it. They are neither alive nor dead, but simply exist. They are not anchored to any particular realm as they are the ferriers. They escort souls to their beyond whether it be where they are transitioned into rest, reborn, or to Exhile. They are non-partial or so it is believed. They are not to be involved other than departures.

Ónarach: A faction of Elves—mostly—that chose to go against their nature and against their race by taking the lives of Elders in order to consume their magic for their own gain transforming them into something dark, creating the Ónarach. They are an unnatural abomination who take orders from a master. Usually, they function as multiples—clones—resembling something like the walking undead or a zombie.

Paladin: The governing rulers of a territory, specifically Feraánmar territory of the Faeries, that took reign when the King and Queen died.

Sol-lumieth: A new power, a new magic, that was foretold in an ancient prophecy to return the light and life—the hope—of Alandria.

NaNai: The ancient Oak trees that were originally used to contain and protect some of the ancient magic that was transported at the inception of Alandria. They were brought into Alandria and even scattered and deposited into the mortal realm by the original Elf lords of the forest, partners with the Dryads. As the ancient magic fails, so do the great oaks.

Dryads: Many came from the origin realm of Lenoria. Previously they had been a neutral party, refusing to get involved with the politics of magical beings. In Lenoria, they were threatened to be destroyed if they didn't side with darkness, but they did not. They are an ancient race driven close to extinction. Many escaped with the Originators and refuged in Alandria—some were taken into the mortal realm for safe keeping. They are majestic beings who protect and care for the forests of Alandria, guided and cared for by Andreinna, the priestess of the forests. Some can evolve into a human form, but others choose to become "grounded" and then are unable to move.

Twined: Half mortal and half Alandrian beings who were unaware of their magical heritage, and also mixed races within Alandria who fled recent persecutions.

* Several races that are present, or created, in The Age of Alandria series are inspired from various mythologies throughout history.

About the Author

Morgan Wylie is an award-winning and *USA Today* Bestselling author with several genres published from YA fantasy to adult paranormal romance and others in between. Morgan published her first novel, Silent Orchids, one year after moving across the country with her family on a journey of new discovery. After an amazing three years in Nashville, TN, and the release of two more books, Morgan and her family found their way back to the Northwest where they now reside. Still working everyday with great optimism, Morgan continues to embrace all things: "Mama", wife, teacher, host of The Lotus Bloom podcast for creatives, and mediator to the many voices and muses constantly chattering in her head... where it gets pretty loud!

You can find her and news on her books at the following:

MorganWylie.org

Morgan Wylie Books on Facebook

@MWylieBooks on IG and Twitter

The Lotus Bloom Podcast on most podcasting sites

Don't miss out! Join the Journey with Morgan today!

Newsletter of Enchanted Journeys

Or sign up at morganwylie.org

To show some love for this book, please consider leaving a review at the place of purchase or any of the locations it is sold. This means the world to an author!

THANK YOU!!